SOULFORGE

LEGENDS OF KOHR BOOK ONE

SOULFORGE

BRIAN ZEEFF

SOULFORGE
BRIAN ZEEFF

Print edition ISBN: 978-1-7354048-0-6
E-book edition ISBN: 978-1-7354048-1-3

First edition: 2020
10 9 8 7 6 5 4 3 2 1

WWW.BRIANZEEFF.COM

This book is dedicated to my wife who provides endless support and read my book despite it being Fantasy; to my son whose laughter inspires me every day; and my lifelong friend and fellow author who pushed me to finish what I started.

BETRAYAL

"The High Council would never condone the absence of not only their king but the lord protector as well. You know this, Alwyn." Borus Kalenthos stood defiantly against the cold of the night. Remnants of an ancient building lay sprawled out before them among fresh mounds of loose soil. The recently excavated site was a chilling reminder of a dark period in the history of the Ellandorians that witnessed a catastrophic loss of life across their entire world.

"Precisely - which is why they don't need to know. The queen is perfectly capable of handling my duties with the Council." Nemendes wore a grim face that was almost as dark as the seamless, black armor he wore. "I must see this threat with my own eyes."

Lord Protector Borus Kalenthos released a long sigh. "Are you certain there's no other way?"

"We must stop the corruption from the breach before it spreads any further." The king, Borus' oldest friend, glanced across the plaza at the company of men and women who awaited their return. "The Keepers of the Stone say there's precious little time to waste – especially in endless debates with the Council. The time for action is now. Are you prepared?"

"You already know the answer to that. Is there even a slight chance the Keepers are mistaken?"

Alwyn gave Borus a sidelong glance. "Are you truly willing to take that risk? Remember, they dedicate their lives to understanding the Abyssal Stone, studying every nuance of it, every flicker of the flame." He gave him a chiding smirk. "I also know you would have conducted your own research and drawn the same conclusion; otherwise, you wouldn't be here."

He already knew the king spoke the truth but still needed to hear it from Alwyn's lips. Borus shook his head lightly as he gazed upon the scholars milling about restlessly under the light of Ellandor's brilliant blue moon. "I realize there are no other viable options." He gestured toward the dig site. "I wanted to speak with you about High Councilor Sallus. I think he suspects our plan."

The king shrugged. "As he should. Wouldn't be particularly good at his job if he didn't. He'll get over it."

"I'm concerned he won't agree to let us pass through the portal."

Alwyn released a short burst of laughter, causing Borus to straighten indignantly as the king spoke. "That's your concern?" Alwyn appraised him with a sidelong glance. "There's not a single person I know who could stop you going where you want. Certainly, none here."

He could not help but grin at his friend's words. Borus often took for granted that his considerable size and legendary strength was unmatched in all Ellandor. "This is true."

"Of course, it is," the king replied with that mischievous Nemendes grin Borus had come to know. "You did the research. Are you confident in what you found? Are you certain this is the path we must take?"

He grimaced as he searched for the right words. "The old Keeper, the one with the birthmark on his face…"

"Elias," Alwyn offered.

"Yes, Elias. With my permission, he sifted through the ancient archives and confirmed the source." Borus withdrew a folded piece of paper from a pouch on his hip and held it before the King. "The master archivist found the glyph combination for us. This is where we must go."

Alwyn touched a glyph on his left bracer, causing a seamless helmet to fold upwards from the base of his neck and form around his entire head, covering his darkening visage. The covering also modulated his voice to one that could not be easily identified – even among family. "Seems the only option is to charge straight toward the heart and put an end to this. Let's not keep the others waiting any longer."

The two lifelong friends crossed the rocky plaza to rejoin the others. Borus spotted the impatient squint and long frown from Sallus as they strolled toward the new arrivals. High Councilor Onar appeared bored, most likely looking forward to breaking open some bottles of Braethian wine at the palace, Borus thought.

Sallus stepped forward, hands clasped behind his back. "Lord Protector? Are you going to explain why we've been summoned from our beds and brought out here in the middle of the night?"

Borus suppressed a smile as the short noble puffed out his chest indignantly. "This way, Councilors."

He led them up a nearby set of marble steps cut into a steep hill to a flat circle of stone. At the summit rested a curious table of black metal, smooth as glass. A pedestal had been erected on one side of the table to display a rough-hewn, egg-shaped stone. An unnatural blue flame engulfed it, radiating an icy chill to the surrounding air. Borus nodded to the Keeper standing nearby.

Sallus and the others studied the Abyssal Stone from the other side of the table. The attendants who accompanied them to the site, and two scholars, remained at the bottom of the stairs. Their apprehension was evident as they focused on their gazes on the dark artifact.

"Why has this dangerous relic been removed from the citadel?" Sallus demanded. Borus noticed the High Councilor had a bead of sweat forming on his brow as he glanced nervously between the burning stone and the lord protector.

Keeper Elias cleared his throat. "If I may." Borus nodded for him to continue. "Something has corrupted the energy of the stone. We must quickly find the source before it spreads to our lands." Borus noticed the man self-consciously hid a blackened hand beneath a sleeve of his thick, gray robe. It was not uncommon for Keepers who became complacent in their handling of it to lose fingers or more to the stone's icy flames. "The voices we've always heard whispering to us have become nearly indecipherable and will only continue to worsen."

Sallus frowned. "The voices?"

"Not in the sense that you or I have," the Keeper explained. "When we, as Keepers, connect to the power of the stone, it speaks to us in the form of visions. It is our strong belief that the One Power communicates its intentions through them. These visions are written down and kept in the sacred archives. We have made many advancements from the knowledge the stone has imparted to us."

Onar shook his head in disapproval. "Sounds like more superstitious nonsense to me," he spat. "What concern is it of ours? Many on the High Council would see us done with this last vestige of the old ways."

Elias paused before answering. "It matters because it upsets the balance of all the Realms. The Heart, known in the ancient tongue as Kohr, the confluence of all power, and the nexus of elemental energy, is being gravely afflicted by this corruption." He paused to allow his words time to reach them. "We are all connected to the One Power. This poisoned well of energy could affect it in ways we could scarcely imagine, eventually causing irreparable harm to the fabric of our world - ending everything we know and love."

"No," Sallus retorted firmly, "if you mean to access the ancient portals, then I must object. Our people survived in peace on Ellandor for centuries, only because our predecessors refused to delve into the affairs of other realms."

Borus already knew Sallus would oppose them. He was a strong opponent of the old ways - the time of the Travelers. "We must do something, regardless of risk. Whatever is causing the corruption is now threatening our world."

"The relic, you mean," Onar corrected him. "It threatens the stability of the Abyssal Stone. All else is conjecture. I would argue we no longer have any need for the stone. Centuries have passed since anything meaningful has come from it."

The lord protector straightened, giving a stern glare to each councilor in turn. "Any other objections?"

Sallus glanced at the Twilight Vanguard as his lip curled up in disapproval. "I assume it would do little good. It appears your mind is already set to the task."

"You still have the right to voice your concerns," Borus offered. "Although, as you have astutely deduced, by my right as Lord Protector, I have enacted the Twilight Contingency Protocol for the security and protection of Ellandor. It was not without deep thought and consideration of all arguments that I do this. I have consulted with the King, the Keepers, and learned sages to arrive at the singular conclusion that this is the only logical path for Ellandor. At my command, these four warriors and I will pass through the portal to where the Keepers believe the corruption originates and lead a scouting party to the source. If we can't close the breach on-site, we'll return with our findings and consult the Council for a solution..."

Stannis, the Vanguard leader, pounded a closed fist to his chest as he drew himself to attention before Borus, High Commander and Lord Protector. "We will not fail you."

Onar lifted a hand bearing ornate rings, then absently waved it through the air in resignation. "Very well. See it done."

The four warriors stood at the ready, prepared to carry out their quest. Borus noted that they had armed themselves with the best weapons and protections the architects of Ellandor had to offer. A powerful arsenal tuned to various Realms of Power, to be used only in the direst of times. He had hoped they would never be called upon in his lifetime.

King Nemendes, now included in their ranks, maintained his anonymity, clad in the same sleek armor as the others. It was forbidden to inquire about their true identities, which made it ideal for Alwyn to hide among them. The High Council tasked the Twilight Vanguard with protecting all of Ellandor and would never allow the king to travel to another world without support. Only the king and his lord protector were privy to the names of those soldiers who served them.

"This is absurd," Sallus growled. "What do these soldiers know of being Travelers? They shall do naught but put us at more risk. Real risk. And if this was your intent, why was it not brought before the Council?"

Lord Protector Kalenthos met his gaze with calm resolve. "That will be your responsibility now. I expect the two of you to let the Council know what takes place here."

"I will do no such thing. This duty falls to the king and the king alone." The councilor's face grew crimson with outrage.

"Why us?" Onar interrupted. His fat fingers tapped impatiently at his belt.

"Because I will be traveling with them, and someone must report everything that transpired. That duty falls to you."

The wind whispering through the trees was deafening in the silence. The high councilors were, at last, at a loss for words.

Borus raised his hand, holding the document from the Keepers to get confirmation from Alwyn to proceed. His friend gave the nod, and he turned his attention to the dark, metal table. Waving his hand over the black surface brought it to life with a surge of power that illuminated rows of symbols in a language older than Ellandor. Borus began touching them in the order given to him by the Star Scriber.

"I beg you to stop this madness. You must at least have the authorization of the king!"

Tapping the last symbol caused them all to pulse as if waiting for more. Borus saw Sallus step toward him from the corner of his eye, then turned in time to watch as one of the Twilight Vanguard moved between them.

"Do not open that portal."

"I understand your fear, Sallus, but we must boldly confront whatever is waiting on the other side of this portal - not cower from the phantoms of the mind. The decision has been made."

King Nemendes stepped up to the black slab and placed his hand on the end panel, opposite where the Lord Protector put his. The air shimmered, raising the hair on Borus' arms. A hole in the fabric of the world ripped open above the nearby circle of stone, revealing a dark scene full of rock and crimson skies beyond.

A metallic object struck the ground and rolled toward the portal. Borus recognized the glowing device as an attenuating orb. Crafted for the Twilight Vanguard, they were designed to release a surge of radiant energy drawn from the surrounding area to incapacitate large crowds. Borus knew the device was merely a non-lethal weapon, but there was no way to predict what it would do if mixed with the massive amount of power expended by the portal generator.

His head turned abruptly to the councilor. "What have you done?"

"What should have been done a long time ago. Destroy the portal."

Borus watched as the unstable blue orb rolled closer to the tear between worlds. Tendrils of energy reached out toward the humming portal, which in turn seemed to stretch with its own red light to meet it. One of the Twilight Vanguard attempted to intercept the orb, kicking it away from the portal. It landed amidst the others, with the hum escalating while sparking dangerously with blue and red energy.

"Everyone, run," the king shouted, preparing to dive for the screaming object that now lay at Onar's feet.

Borus felt the building energy pull at his core. Something was terribly wrong. The orb was designed to draw a limited amount of energy from the radiant realm. However, it appeared to be siphoning energy directly from the portal – an unknown dark power, enhancing it far beyond its intended design, as well as capacity. There was no time to think, only act. The king's safety was all that mattered.

Grabbing hold of Alwyn's arm, Borus jerked him away from the pulsating orb and flung the king headlong through the portal using his considerable strength. There was no opportunity to save anyone else. The others either stood in shock, ran for their lives, or hollered warnings as the orb reached its limit. Leaping with all his might, the lord protector dove through after the king. Before he breached the portal, he felt the searing heat of the explosion, and the impact of an energy wave launched him through the air. Rock and other debris tore at his legs and back as he tumbled violently into the alien world. And then, all went dark.

ARRIVAL

[FIVE YEARS LATER.]

"Take control of your destiny, lest destiny controls you." High Lord Draxian Kalenthos contemplated the words of his father as he found himself once again traveling on horseback through the woods of his boyhood. He grimaced slightly as he looked back at the scores of servants who traveled with him. It seemed destiny had already taken control, despite his desire to set his own path.

Resting a palm on the jewel-encrusted sword within its newly tanned scabbard, Draxian's eyes wandered to the dense foliage on either side of the hard-packed road. The land was alive with dancing speckles of sun that pierced the overhead canopy and gave off a deep sense of majesty. It had been over a year since he had last traveled to the capital city of Braethus, but unlike the previous trip, a contingent of honor guard and a small army of servants dressed in the deep blue and gray colors of his house followed closely at his flank. Like his gilded weapon, the parade accompanying the young lord was more a formal show than a practical necessity. Draxian would have preferred to travel alone. However, as the newly anointed Lord of Selvathas, solitude was a luxury rarely found. While the three-day journey had provided a much-needed reprieve, he would soon need to return to the tedious duties of the court.

Rounding a bend in the road, the trees parted to reveal a brilliant blue sky with scattered white clouds and, below, rolling fields with various red, purple, and orange wildflowers dotting the landscape. Draxian took a moment to take in the aroma of the flowers and budding forest, while a soft breeze lifted white petals from the blooms of a nearby orchard and scattered them beneath the hooves of his black mare. The beauty of it all made the thought of entering the confines of the city even more unappealing.

The sky-piercing towers of Braethus visible in the distance heralded the presence of the capital city, also known as the City of the Enlightened. It was a marvel to behold for the first time, and Draxian never grew tired of seeing it. Massive spires of smooth stone and perfectly molded glass stretched upward to dizzying heights above the capital, while gleaming roads of white stone wound their way into the city from nearly every direction, meeting at the epicenter of the sprawling metropolis. It was there that the royal palace sat atop a great hill – a symbol of strength and the pursuit of knowledge for all people in Ellandor. It was also home to his childhood friend, and heir to the throne, Crown Prince Arros Nemendes.

When Draxian reached the outer boundaries of the city, citizens began to line the streets to cheer or wave their greetings as he continued the ceremonial procession toward the palace. It was customary for visiting nobles and dignitaries to make a grand entrance, bearing standards of their houses and represented territories. Such regal pretensions had always made him feel a bit uncomfortable. As such, Draxian had insisted on a small entourage, considering what he could have brought. Next to the capital city, the territory of Selvathas, which his family presided over, was one of the largest settlements in Ellandor.

The road that led them into the city was wide and paved with white-washed brick. Storefronts appeared to either side, touting large windows for those passing by to browse their wares. All the merchants were taking full advantage of the lovely summer weather by setting up outdoor displays to lure more prospective customers. The vast amount of spices, exotic oils, and cooked meats for sale reminded him of his youth spent at the capital. Draxian and Arros had wasted a great deal of energy roaming the marketplace as children when not busy studying or training. They both enjoyed meeting artisans from far-away lands and listening to the bards singing songs of heroism, or watching performers acting out tales of Ellandor's past. It always made him long for an adventure of his own.

High Lord Kalenthos gave a friendly wave to a group of children who eagerly cheered at him, while palace workers scurried about the streets, using long poles to hang decorative lanterns above doors and on roof peaks. Volunteers from every family worked together to wrap strands of flowering vines around the corner lamp posts and stone bridges. They were preparing for the royal wedding. Draxian could scarcely believe his life-long friend was to be married the very next day. He always thought Arros would be the last of them to make such a commitment, but the Queen had different plans for her son. If he were to be king someday, and that day was fast approaching, she wanted him to have a suitable companion to stand beside him as first seat on the High Council of Lords. Apparently, one had been found and arranged from a neighboring land.

Ellandor had lived in harmony for centuries, working together to further their knowledge in all fields, including advancements in the architecture that made the city of Braethus and the massive royal palace a shining testament to their progress. The people had maintained the peace since that time by creating a system of government that joined all the kingdoms into a symbiotic relationship. Each territory contributed a different specialty to advance their culture. Arranged marriages between the ruling families had also helped to unite the kingdoms toward that end. Unfortunately for Draxian's friend that tradition still held strong.

Draxian was relieved when he had at last made it up the hill and arrived in the plaza that lay before the palace. A welcoming party waited for them on the marbled steps of the palace. The towering tree at the center of the plaza cast a long shadow on those steps. It was considered good fortune for arriving guests to be greeted by the king or queen within its shadow. It had been planted at the ceremony many hundreds of years earlier when the kingdoms had ceased aggressions and signed a doctrine to forever coexist in peace. Palace guards, the peacekeepers, in crisp yellow uniforms stood at attention along the path from the entry doors down to the plaza grounds. Rising before him, a massive triangular gate was lined with the colorful red and gold banners of the royal house. Draxian slowed his steed to a halt and dismounted, followed closely by his entourage of dignitaries and staff. Stable boys and girls appeared from seemingly nowhere and quickly took the reins to lead the horses away. After giving his servants a knowing smirk, he continued forward and watched as the great double doors swung wide. Behind them stood the Queen of Ellandor, wearing a brilliant white dress with gold trim, along with her attending servants adorned in brilliant red. She glided gracefully through the open doors and moved slowly down the stairs, stopping at the final step. Draxian searched expectantly for Arros who was surprisingly absent from the ceremonial greeting.

The young lord straightened his shoulders and took a deep breath, while his escort fell in behind him in loose formation. He waited until a young man dressed in the livery of the House of Kalenthos approached from the rear and held out a small box. The jewel encrusted chest was uniquely crafted and designed specifically as a gift to the royal family. Towering a full two heads above the boy, he nodded his thanks and lifted it from the servant's upturned hands.

High Lord Kalenthos' green traveling cloak billowed softly as he stepped forward and knelt before the queen. Upon reaching the ground, Draxian bowed his head and presented the small token. Rising once again to stand before her, the young lord turned his green eyes upon the monarch.

"Draxian, welcome back."

"A humble gift for your hospitality, my Queen."

A wide grin spread across her face as she studied his expression. "So formal, Draxian. I haven't seen you since last summer and this is how you greet me?"

"Um, well, with all these new duties..."

Queen Arillsa placed a comforting hand on his arm and looked intently into his eyes. "Relax, Draxian. You must know you've always been like a son to me. And now with your mother stepping down from the High Council, you'll be expected to take her place. Besides," she added, softening her voice so only he would hear, "Arros has been rather restless without your presence in the capital.

He's been spending a great deal of time hunting in the forest, yet never comes back with any game. I'm beginning to worry he's not taking his station to heart. This is one of the main reasons I thought it best to push the wedding sooner."

"Arros has always had an adventurous spirit. He seemed in good spirits when visiting my estate this spring. I wouldn't worry too much." He leaned forward, giving her a gentle one-armed embrace.

"Speaking of the Crown Prince – he awaits you in the private study," the queen informed him as she took the jeweled chest from his hands. "My son claims to have a surprise for you, and requested you meet him immediately upon your arrival."

"My gratitude." Draxian bowed his head in respect and awaited her response. "Your Majesty?"

"You're dismissed, my Lord."

"We'll see you at the banquet." Draxian turned and walked quickly up the steps to the gilded doors of the main structure.

"Just don't let him be late for his wedding tomorrow," she called from behind. "He's been searching for an excuse to delay it."

Draxian chuckled. "I make no promises, my Lady."

The grand entryway to the palace was lined with alcoves containing statues of past rulers and the heroes of Braethus. Most of them were portrayed in decorative armor wielding their weapon of choice. Weapons pointing to the sky indicated they had died in the service of Ellandor. It had been centuries since such an occurrence. He recognized two huge banners draped to either side at the center of the hall, displaying the usual red and gold crest of House Nemendes. Massive skylights of colored glass held together with strips of gold poured radiant beams over the narrow carpet leading toward the great hall from high above.

Another set of open double doors stood at the end of the long passage. They had glossy wooden panels, carved with intricate designs of trees and leaves, framed with highly polished steel along the borders. Draxian approached the sentries who stood near the opening to direct the petitioners and nobles that came to visit the palace.

"Balric, is that you?"

Turning his full attention to the approaching noble, the stocky peacekeeper reached out and clasped wrists with the young man. "Well met, my Lord. We've been wondering when you would arrive."

Visiting nobles and dignitaries filled the room beyond, waiting for their chance to speak with the royal family and other members of the High Council. They paused their conversations long enough to learn who was entering the hall. Everyone held recognition in their eyes, yet only a few gave quick nods of greeting before turning their attention elsewhere.

"Prince Arros commanded I send you directly to the library," Balric said, indicating the small door just to his left.

"My thanks," Draxian replied with a nod. "We'll have to catch up later."

"I pray you brought better wine with you this time. That Selvathian shite you gave me before was awful," Balric teased.

"Nothing but the best for the peacekeeper who saved my ass from a red bear," he retorted with a laugh. "We'll speak soon."

He started toward the door when a familiar voice called out to him. "Draxian!"

The young lord halted in place, then took a deep breath before spinning around with a forced smile. "Mother, I didn't see you there."

The High Councilor was in her element. She had styled her hair into a perfect mountain of curls and flaunted the most expensive blue silk gown she could find. Paired with a diamond necklace, rings, and ear studs, Draxian thought it to be a desperate cry for attention. "Be nice, Son."

"Forgive me, Mother. It's been a long journey and Arros is waiting for me."

"These gatherings are important to keep up appearances. Soon you'll replace me on the High Council and will need to speak for our house."

"I never wanted to be on the High Council. That's your dream, not mine." Appearance and station were all she cared about, Draxian thought.

Lady Yarra flushed red as she leaned in close. "Do not dishonor your father's memory by failing to uphold your duty." She straightened and inhaled deeply. "An appointment to the High Council is one of the most revered achievements on Ellandor. You should be honored by the chance to represent Selvathas before all of Ellandor." His silence prompted a resigned sigh. "Very well. We'll speak of this later. Will you at least sit with me at the banquet?"

"Of course." Draxian leaned forward and kissed her lightly on the cheek. "Until then."

Taking his leave, Draxian made long strides to the door leading to the western wing of the palace. A small metallic plate, painted a bright green, was mounted next to the unassuming wooden door. Pressing his hand to the plate caused it to warm to his touch. The lock hummed as it released its hold, allowing the door to swing wide, securing itself again once he was through. The passage was a stark contrast to the grand audience chamber he left behind. Random portraits hung in oiled frames and murals graced the walls, breaking the monotony of the drab stone.

Turning to his right at the first intersection nearly caused the young lord to collide with a group of cleaning staff holding brooms and fresh linens. Draxian quickly exchanged apologies, then continued down the corridor to the polished door leading into a private library belonging to the royal family – Arros' favorite place to study. Many of their daily lessons as children were taught in that room.

Pressing his hand to the red plate next to the heavy brass door revealed a long rectangular room lined with bookshelves that extended from floor to ceiling. There were hundreds, if not thousands, of volumes, copied from the main library at the request of the prince or his family. Draxian always liked the smell of the dusty, leather-bound tomes mixed with the burning oil of the lamps set about the room. Plush chairs formed a circle at the center to accommodate meetings, and a large desk of oak sat against the far wall.

Arros sat hunched over the desk, poring over some dusty book, as Draxian had expected. Books, some of them ancient in origins by their yellowed and delicate appearance, were scattered before him across its polished surface. He was so focused on his work, he failed to notice the arrival of his guest.

Draxian slipped his travel pack from his shoulder, dropping it to the floor. The sound caused Arros to startle. "I expected a grander welcome from the King of Ellandor."

Swiveling his head to see who entered, Arros smiled broadly and pushed his chair away from the desk.

"I'm not king yet, High Lord Draxian." Arros knew how much he hated using formal titles.

"After you marry Lady Imelda tomorrow, you will be." He saw the Prince's smile fade slightly. "It will be good, for you and Ellandor," he offered, to soften the blow.

"Now you sound like my mother." The arranged marriage visibly bothered Arros.

Arros raised his eyes to meet Draxian's. Despite his above-average height, the Prince still had to lift his chin to meet his gaze. "It's good to have you back at the capital, my friend. How was your journey?"

"We got off to a late start, and my horse threw a shoe on the first day. We rode hard to make it here in three days." Draxian nodded toward the pile of books lying open with yellowed pages on the dark wood surface. "So why in the Abyss did you want me to meet you here?"

"I've discovered something I thought you'd be interested in." A wave of realization swept over Draxian when he noticed Arros wearing his high black boots and riding pants. The Prince threw his crimson traveling cloak about his shoulders and snatched up his leather traveling pack that lay inconspicuously by the desk.

"Come on, Drax, we're losing daylight."

"But I just got here," the young Lord protested in vain. He knew once Arros set his mind to a task, it was nearly impossible to sway him. "I haven't even unpacked."

Arros pushed the door open and turned his gaze back to his friend. "Good, then you won't need to waste any time re-packing."

Draxian sighed heavily, then simply allowed his curious and adventuresome nature to take hold and followed his friend back down the corridor he had just left. "Are you going to tell me where we're headed?" he implored while rushing to keep up. "And don't just say, it's a surprise."

Arros gave him a sidelong glance. "You know the ancient ruins northwest of here?"

"Of course. I thought that area was off limits. Did the ban finally get lifted?"

"Not exactly."

"Then why are we going?"

"I hired a small team of archivists and scholars to help me secretly excavate the ruins," Arros explained in hushed tones. "They now have a theory on how to safely open that warded door to the vault below."

"Can't this wait until after the wedding?" Draxian pleaded.

Arros shook his head and made a dismissive gesture. "When that door opens, we'll be the ones who learn what was left inside by our ancestors."

"Or be first in line to get incinerated," Draxian grumbled to himself. The young Lord remembered being with Arros in combat training when news arrived of a tragic accident that took the lives of sixteen people, including their fathers, a member of the High Council, and several excavators and archivists who were working in the area. High Councilor Sallus was the only survivor, and he convinced the High Council to ban access to the vault below the ruins, ruling it was far too dangerous for anyone to attempt to breach its powerful wards. It had taken the past five years to come to terms with his father's death.

They took a detour down a well-lit hallway that bypassed the reception room and went beside the kitchens to avoid as many people as possible. Their path led them through the dining hall, which was being prepared for the banquet, then another larger library, and several closed doors to servants' quarters, to finally pass the peacekeeper barracks. The charismatic Prince smiled warmly and raised his hand in greeting to every sentry they happened upon to keep needless questions to a minimum. At last, they reached the end of the long hallway and the unassuming door where Arros led them to the stables.

"I'm certain your horse will be here by now," Arros announced, as he pushed open the door. Both men halted in place, nearly bumping straight into a nobleman who was attempting to gain entrance to the palace.

"Prince Arros," the surprised dignitary exclaimed, "where are you off to in such a hurry?"

It was High Councilor Sallus. "My apologies, Councilor. We're just going out for a short ride to view the progress of the new irrigation system and should be back in time for the festivities."

In addition to his ties to their fathers' accident, Councilor Sallus was also the older brother of Lady Imelda, Arros' betrothed. Sallus was now a senior member of the High Council.

"Not much has changed in the last couple of days since last you checked."

"Lord Kalenthos wanted to see the progress. It has been some time since he visited Braethus."

"I understand," Sallus replied with a smirk. "Perhaps when you return, we can discuss my latest ideas for building a new library wing honoring your late father over a tankard of Braethian ale. It could also be used as a museum to display the advances we made under his leadership."

The people of Ellandor valued knowledge and self-understanding above anything else – although Draxian knew the man well enough to realize there was something more to his proposal than Sallus was putting forth.

"A fine idea, High Councilor," Arros agreed with as much enthusiasm as he could feign. "Forgive me, but we really must get riding. The countryside tour will take time and we'd like to be back before we lose daylight." He then nodded to Sallus and continued onward.

"Of course, Your Highness."

Draxian gave Sallus a firm pat on the shoulder as he passed. "Good to see you again."

"And you as well, High Lord Kalenthos. Have a safe ride. I'll expect to meet you both after the banquet for a drink."

As Arros predicted, Draxian's horse was saddled and waiting for him. After greeting the stable hand who was brushing one of the horses from his entourage, he secured his saddle and climbed atop the large mare. The young Lord had to hurry to catch up, as his friend was already leading his own white and gray stallion past the kennels and toward the back gate.

THE STORM

The two young highborn men rode along the northern road where Draxian had only recently traveled. He was still too sore from spending all morning on horseback to enjoy the warm sun and afternoon breeze. After they reached the forest edge, Arros turned just inside the tree-line toward the site of the ancient ruins. The trail was mostly covered over by leaves and brush, yet the further they went, the more he noticed recent signs of travel.

"So," Draxian began, breaking the silence, "assuming we don't die horribly from an ancient elemental trap, what are you hoping to find?"

Arros turned his eyes downward in thought before answering. "I hope whatever lies beyond that door will give us some answers as to what happened to our fathers. Their bodies were not among those recovered."

"The scholars who studied the devastation believe they were standing too close to the detonation and their bodies were incinerated. I spent the last five years coming to terms with my father's loss." Draxian paused. "You should do the same."

Arros gave him a sidelong glance. "I've uncovered evidence to the contrary."

"Impossible. They were very thorough in their investigation, and the High Council had a unanimous vote confirming the findings. If someone has withheld information, it would be considered treason."

The Prince slowed his horse to keep pace alongside and raised an eyebrow as he spoke. "I met a witness who told me they were at the site during the explosion." Arros locked eyes with Draxian. "Our fathers may not have even been in our world."

"Councilor Sallus was the only survivor. There were no others present at the site. This was confirmed by the Council."

Arros made a dismissive gesture. "I don't trust Sallus. His story never sounded right to me. The door to the tomb is too far from where the blast occurred.

Draxian shifted in his saddle as he tried to make sense of the new information. Thoughts swirled before his mind's eye as he worked through all the angles.

"Do you remember the ancient tablet we found among my father's possessions?" Arros pressed.

"Don't tell me you've translated that, too?"

"My father left it behind for a reason," Arros explained, ignoring Draxian's sarcastic tone. "If I can decipher the symbols, then maybe it will tell us where they went."

Draxian rested his hands on the horn of his saddle as the memories ran through his mind. Both their fathers had gone to the site in search of a lost secret of their ancestors, just before the accident at the ruins. It had been nearly five summers since they had disappeared. The Prince and he desperately wanted answers. They always suspected there was more to the story, although no one could go near the site to investigate after the tragic death of his father Borus, the Lord Protector, and Arros' father, the King of Ellandor – along with all the archivists and excavators.

"Why now? And what do *I* have to do with this?"

"You'll see," was all he would say. Draxian knew it would be useless to pry further.

The damp, sweet air had a familiar smell and reminded him of their childhood running through these woods, hunting for rabbits. They soon crossed a small, shallow stream and arrived at a clearing before the ruins. Large piles of dirt were scattered about, some freshly made, while others had long-since settled into the ground from the previous expedition. For the first few years, the woods around the site had been heavily patrolled. Over time, the area lost its appeal for the curious citizens after believing it remained guarded. Draxian knew that Arros could easily access the peacekeeper rotations and assignments, and possibly be able to manipulate them himself.

The two young men dismounted without a word and tied their horses to a nearby tree, before taking a trail that meandered across the field toward the remnants of half-buried stone walls surrounding a large open plaza. The path led them past several short canvas tents hidden among the few broken walls that were covered with moss and dust. At last they came to the center of the dig site, where two sets of granite stairs were carved into the landscape. One set ascended about ten steps up a small mound to a large, stone platform with a rectangular pedestal at its edge. Three women and two men wearing dirt-covered traveling attire, were gathered around the table, studying it closely while talking amongst themselves. They all held up a hand in greeting upon spotting the new arrivals, then immediately went back to work.

The other stairway descended sharply into a tunnel in the ground.

The Prince motioned Draxian forward. "Let's check in with the Master Archivist," he suggested, indicating the stairs leading to the tunnel. "He's probably studying the vault door."

"Wait," Draxian halted the Prince with a hand on his shoulder. "Isn't that where the explosion occurred?"

"That's what everyone was told, but no. The bodies were found scattered above ground, right where you're standing."

Disquiet swept over Draxian as he glanced around him. "That's a bit unsettling."

Just as they prepared to make their descent, an old scholar with a long grey beard and dirty robes, stepped up behind them. "Your Highness." Both men jumped at the unexpected sound of his voice and turned. He bowed his head politely to Arros before also nodding to the young Lord. "And you must be Lord Kalenthos."

"Master Archivist." Arros placed a hand over his heart to calm it, then greeted the elderly scholar with a smirk. "We need to hang a bell around your neck."

The old archivist cackled softly to himself. "My Lords, welcome to the Aggaros dig site. Have you come to view our latest finds? We just finished cataloguing a few new artifacts found buried in a box near the control table."

"Indeed?" Arros turned to Draxian. "This is Master Archivist Garran, the witness I told you about who saw the explosion."

The young Lord nodded politely. "A pleasure, Master Archivist."

"The Prince has spoken quite highly of you."

"Truly?" Draxian furrowed his brow in disbelief. "Tell me, what did you witness that night so many years ago?"

The old man shrugged. "It has been several years, but I can assure you your fathers were not on Ellandor when the others perished. The One Power was watching over them that night. They traveled through the portal the instant before the explosion."

Arros stretched his neck to look past the old man and peer into the darkness. "Is the door still emitting that strange energy?"

Draxian's eyebrows arched high. "Energy?"

"The runes on the door are, yes," the archivist corrected. "Here. Let me show you both some items you may find interesting."

The elderly scholar led them over to a nearby tent that housed a worktable with various artifacts lying in neat rows next to an open book with fresh entries recorded within. Draxian edged in closer to get a better look at the artifacts. The most prominent of them appeared to be a polished black stone, rectangular in shape with no visible markings. Another that caught his attention, was a carved wooden amulet with a loop at the top to affix chain for a necklace. Draxian lifted it from the table and studied the strange patterns and designs. Arros picked up a brass stamp with a long handle that was likely used for sealing wax to documents.

The archivist leaned in closer and lowered his voice. "Per our arrangement, I haven't allowed anyone else access to my findings. Some of these artifacts will be of use in learning the truth about what happened to your fathers." The Master Archivist handed Arros the thin, black brick, then winked knowingly. "You both were meant for great things, I think. Remember – the One Power grants the tools to shape your own destiny, you only need to have the courage to use them."

When Draxian swiveled his head toward Arros, the Prince shrugged a single shoulder, indicating he did not know what he meant by that either. The two men turned away to look more closely at their prizes in the light of the sun. The young Lord admired the craftsmanship of the carved necklace, yet what intrigued him the most about it was the petrified wood. The grain was not from any known species found on Ellandor, and he had spent a good amount of time searching through wood samples for his new furniture at the capital.

"What do you suppose…" Draxian's voice trailed off as he looked up and found no sign of the elderly scholar who stood before them just a moment prior. "… this came from?"

Looking up from the black artifact in his own hand, Arros spun and then glanced around. "Yeah, the old goat does that a lot. Don't take it personally."

"Where did you say you met him?"

Arros cleared his throat. "He approached me in the city after I was meeting with… someone and had a theory on what happened to our fathers. It was shortly after visiting your estate at the Lakes of Elithia, and he asked if I would fund his research at the site."

"Ah," Draxian began, rubbing his chin as he scanned the clearing and the trees beyond for any sign of the mysterious scholar. "Still pining for Bellasa, huh? Don't blame you – she's a beauty."

Arros dropped his arms to his sides and stared absently into the dark tunnel. "I don't love Lady Imelda."

"No one expects you to. It may take time, but you'll come to care for her."

"If I ever have a son, I swear he'll be allowed to marry whomever he wishes."

"Same here." Draxian pressed his lips together in an attempt at showing sympathy.

The Prince took a deep breath, then handed Draxian the seal. "Here. You might find this interesting."

"Oh?" He took the tarnished brass handle and flipped it on end to view the crest showing a spiral-horned buck. His eyes widened in recognition. "This is an ancient seal from the house of Kalenthos. My house."

"Keep it as a token of my appreciation."

Draxian dropped his eyebrows and gave the Prince a sidelong glance. "For what, exactly?"

"Always standing by me." Arros' expression was unreadable.

He was up to something, yet Draxian was uncertain what it could be. "Perhaps we should go down and see this door before we begin to lose daylight. We have a lot to do back at the palace."

"Right," Arros agreed, slipping the stone and a few other items into his traveling pack before descending into the darkness. Arros snatched the lantern hanging from a hook on the wall as he passed. With only a wave of his hand, the cylinder in the middle ignited with a soft yellow radiance to light their way down the winding steps. The stairwell dropped steeply into the ground, spiraling dozens of steps down through thick rock. Draxian immediately noticed the texture of the walls changed as they reached the bottom, and a cool blue luminance created an ominous glow from somewhere ahead. After following a short hallway which curved around, they ended their journey at a door made from the same black stone as the artifact that Garran had given Arros. An eerie blue light emanated within the strange symbols carved into the face of the rock.

Placing his hand on the door, Arros frowned. "Feel this, Draxian. The door is hot, yet the rest of the walls are cold to the touch."

Cautiously, he approached and laid his own hand on the dark stone. Arros was correct, it was noticeably warm. Before he could draw another breath, a tingling surge of energy spread through his whole body. With a loud grinding that made them both retreat several steps, the heavy barrier moved inward, then slid into a recess in the wall. A gust of warm, dry air washed over the men from the chamber beyond. They both gave each other sidelong glances, then cautiously stepped forward.

Arros nudged Draxian playfully. "The old goat was right. It takes two hands from the correct bloodlines to open the door."

"Wait." Draxian halted in place and scowled at the Prince. "You tricked me into putting my hand on it?"

"Would you have done so otherwise? Touching the runes on a previous visit is what caused the door runes to start glowing. Just as with the black plates warding the treasury vault below the palace, we speculated that it took at least two specific people or bloodlines to open it. And since our families can be traced back to the first King and Protector of Ellandor, it only made sense that we would both be needed."

Draxian didn't answer, instead growling to himself to express his dislike of being used and proceeding into the chamber beyond. The room was perfectly round and lit by four large globes emitting bright blue light from their sconces set in the stone walls. At the center of the room was a circular column made from a solid black metal that appeared to swallow the light. The cylinder narrowed sharply at the center where the top and bottom were split. The two halves were joined only by a multi-faceted crystal the size of Draxian's fist. The bottom half of the column had some inscriptions carved on its face just below the crystal, beneath which was a rectangular indention.

Draxian whistled to himself in wonder. "What do you think this place was used for?"

"I don't know," Arros replied as he ran his hand over one of the glowing orbs. "I'm not sure how these have remained powered for so long. They aren't connected to an energy source I can see," he added, lifting it briefly from its sconce.

Draxian crossed his arms as he scanned the room. "Wasn't there supposed to be treasure in here, or at least some ancient books of wisdom? Now we have more questions instead of answers."

Arros stroked his chin in thought. "Maybe not," he countered, while lifting the rectangular stone Garron had given him from his pack. He then pointed to the indention on the column. "I think this might be a type of key, like the ones our ancestors used to open the gateways to other worlds."

"That's not a good idea, Arros. We have no idea what this thing does," he protested, shaking his head. "First, let the scholars do their work. See if it's safe."

"No," Arros protested, "I'm tired of waiting for others to research and deliberate for days without taking action. The longer we delay, the greater the chance we'll be discovered by the High Council." He clenched his jaw with determination as he raised his hand toward the opening in the column and inserted the dark artifact.

It fit perfectly into the indention, becoming flush with the stone. Somewhere beneath the floor, a steady rumble could be felt through Draxian's boots. Then, a brilliant white beam shot up the base of the column and struck the crystal. The light caused the gem to spin wildly, radiating a cascade of spiraling dots about the room.

Both men retreated several steps as the crystal burst to life. Arros was the first to relax his posture, looking over at his friend with a boyish grin. "You see, nothing bad happened. The world is still here."

"I guess so, but what's the purpose of this thing?"

"My best guess is it's supposed to power or focus something else. I doubt our ancestors created this place to make a pretty light display."

"Not all of our ancient ancestors' creations were benign. Maybe we should shut it down until we understand what it does."

Arros gave him a forlorn look. "But if we power it off, we won't be able to do exactly that." He sighed heavily and shook his head. "Always the cautious one, aren't you? Very well." The Prince reached out and tried to get his fingernails around the key – but was having great difficulty removing it. "It's stuck inside there."

"Of course, it is."

Arros drew a hunting knife from his belt and tried to pry into the seam yet could not slip the point between the key and the stone pillar. He was still scraping away when the sound of boots descending the stone steps echoed through the chamber. A female member of the excavation team appeared at the door and stood just inside the frame.

The woman stared wide-eyed at the swirling crystal, then shook her head to break the momentary trance. "Forgive the intrusion, Your Highness," she blurted.

"What is it, Yelarra?" Arros questioned.

Glancing once again at the spinning lights, the archivist drew her eyes back to the Prince. "The control table outside has just activated." She pointed toward the crystal. "How did you do that?"

Draxian stepped forward, blocking her view. "What control table are you talking about?"

"You must see this for yourself," she blurted before turning and bounding up the stairs.

"Let's go have a look," Arros called over, giving Draxian a slap on the arm. "The two objects must be related."

The tall, muscular man gave a long sigh of resignation. "Very well, but only because I know how important this could be to us. Although once we finish up there, we need to find a way to shut this down. Agreed?"

"Of course." The mischievous expression on Arros' face didn't inspire much confidence.

The woman led them up the winding stairs in a rush. They emerged back at the excavation site where Yelarra pointed toward the small hill at the center of the plaza, where the oblong table rested at the top of a short flight of stairs. The remaining four scholars, none of whom Draxian recognized, crowded around the table and scratched their heads in confusion.

Draxian followed the Prince up the hill to see the table, or control table as Yelarra called it, taking the steps two at a time. When they reached the platform, the archivists stepped aside to allow the men a better view. The table was as wide as the span of Draxian's arms, and about the length of his arm across. It was made of the same black metal as the column below. A circular platform lay on the ground before them. A secondary circle, three paces in diameter, had emerged from the center, lit with clusters of runes and writing that covered its surface – some of them changing from moment to moment. Like the door below, the symbols at the center of the control panel and on the surface of the platform glowed with a bluish-white fire from within. Even the presence of the sun did little to dim their radiance.

"Well, this is new," Draxian mused. "Looks like those puzzles mother used to do."

Arros scrunched his face at Draxian, then refocused on the runes within the strange pedestal. "I doubt our people wasted their time with puzzles linked to the realms of power. There was only one reference to an ancestor of ours who created a unique device to help him find this world. They called him a Star Scriber."

"A what?"

"In the original language, it also translates to mean 'navigator.' The writing here is partially in the ancient tongue, and something else completely."

Curious about what his friend was seeing, he moved closer and looked over Arros' shoulder at the strange carvings. As he examined them, he realized the runes were organized into several distinct groups. Some of them seemed familiar to Draxian. Then, the answer struck him.

"I recognize these other symbols. Do you still have your father's tablet?"

"Of course," Arros answered. He pulled his pack around from his shoulders and set it on the edge of the table. It did not take long for the young Prince to withdraw the artifact from within and hand it over to Draxian.

The small stone was thin, square and fit perfectly in the palm of his hand. Draxian scanned one side before flipping it over. "There they are!" He pointed to three ancient runes that stood out by themselves amidst all the others on the tablet.

"What of it?"

"Look here, the writing is the same," Draxian replied, tapping on one of the runes on the pedestal. To his surprise, the symbol changed to a deep red at his touch.

Arros' eyes went wide. "It's got to be the code sequence for the gateway! Draxian, you're brilliant!"

"If you say so," he said with a forced smile. "Now that we know, we should probably shut it down and notify the High Council."

"We can't. If we do that, we may never get any answers about where our fathers went, or why they never returned. The High Council will lock this place away and ban me from going near it." Arros crossed his arms in frustration and began pacing as he contemplated his next move.

"Whether a prince or king, you are not above the rule of the High Council. If we open a portal without their approval, it could cost us our titles – not to mention how dangerous it might be." He threw his hands up to emphasize his point. "You have no idea where it could lead, or if we could ever get back home. We could become lost like our fathers." When his friend did not budge, Draxian decided to try a different approach. "Your Highness. I'm supposed to be taking my mother's seat on the High Council within a month. I promise you, the reopening of this site will be first on my list of changes that need to be addressed."

The Prince stopped pacing and stood quietly, his crimson cloak undulating in the late afternoon breeze. They stood in silence for several moments. Draxian knew finding their fathers was of paramount importance to his friend. He too wanted to know, but they needed to go about it the right way – whatever that entailed. Although…

Shifting his weight to one side, Draxian hooked his thumbs over the top of his sword belt. "You went to a lot of trouble to get us here." Arros simply stared at the flickering console of glyphs. "The way I see it, without knowing how long this will remain powered or if we could ever get it started again, we might as well take a peek at where it leads. If nothing else, for the sake of your archivists who worked so hard on this project." Draxian glanced around at the men and women who nodded their agreement.

A grin formed on Arros' lips, a stark contrast to the focused determination in his eyes. "I knew you'd come around."

"But that's it." Draxian pointed a finger at him as though admonishing a child. "Once we open the portal and learn what lies beyond, we pull the key and shut it down."

"Agreed." Arros' attention was already focused on studying the tablet and comparing the writings with those on the table. He tapped the symbols when he found the ones that correctly matched. His finger hovered over the last rune as he tilted his head sidelong to Draxian. "Are you ready?" The young Lord straightened his tall frame before giving a nod. The final rune turned red at Arros' touch – yet nothing happened.

Yelarra pointed to the small plates on either side of the table. "It may still require both bloodlines to activate."

Draxian and Arros glanced at each other, then moved to opposite ends of the table. Arros immediately placed his hand on the stone plate, then looked up in anticipation. With a deep breath, Draxian reached down and pressed his palm to the cold surface. The runes pulsed several times, then the platform he was standing on began to shudder with the exchange of power. Not more than a dozen paces away, a ripple formed in the air. Draxian glanced around at the archivists, who were mesmerized with the opening portal.

"It's working!" Arros stepped away from the control panel and slowly approached the rift.

The blurred image from the portal soon began to clear, promising to give them a glimpse of what lay beyond. It looked to Draxian like rocky terrain with a dark sky in the background. There were occasional flashes of light, indicating a possible storm. They were viewing another world – one their fathers may have visited. As soon as the bridge between worlds was complete, a thundering crash erupted from just past the portal, and a bolt of red lightning struck the ground and arced directly to the table next to Draxian. The force of the blast knocked him from his feet causing him to roll more than a dozen paces away.

Arros had ducked low, then stared back in horror. Scattered about the area, the five archivists lay unmoving, yet that was not Draxian's greatest concern. The top of the circular console was split asunder, and radiant beams of white light were shooting wildly into the air. A dangerous force began to shake the ground beneath their feet, as the power which created the portal roared free of its confines. It was all Draxian could do to maintain his balance. He watched helplessly as fingers of lightning from the portal generator stabbed repeatedly at the sky, tearing holes high above – like fire burning through parchment. Beyond the breach in the tapestry of their world, he saw dark red clouds roiling in terrible fury. Hundreds of massive portals appeared high in the air as far as he could see, each showing the same scene.

Deadly bolts of red lightning lashed out from the other world with increasing frequency. Draxian pulled up the hood of his green cloak against the driving rain striking his face and momentarily blinding him.

Arros was checking on Yelarra when Draxian grabbed his arm, then jerked the Prince around to face him. The young Lord pointed back toward the way they had come. "We need to retrieve that key from the core, now!"

Arros quickly glanced back toward the unmoving men and women, seemingly in a daze, then nodded his agreement. They started toward the stairs when both men froze in place. A dark, winged form descended from the broken sky – a titan from childhood myths and legends. To Draxian's knowledge no one on Ellandor had ever seen an actual dragon. They were said to have existed in some fabled realm beyond the stars.

The mighty serpent flapped its wings in a wild effort to stay airborne then landed heavily at the top of the pit, crushing nearby tents and knocking over several ancient walls. It perched above the tunnel leading to the core and the key that powered the portal. The beast swiveled its massive head and watched the light spilling from the broken console with renewed interest. With wings spanning more than twenty men, the dragon was easily the largest creature Draxian had ever seen. Powerful muscles rippled beneath reddish-brown scales as it bellowed a roar into the air. The intensity of its cry gripped Draxian's soul and shook the loose stone at his feet as though Ellandor quivered before the beast. Fire streamed from its throat and pierced through the driving rain in warning to any who would offer a challenge.

Draxian pulled air into his lungs and felt the blood rush back to his face, as the sound of someone yelling for them to run snapped the young Lord back to reality. Taking a quick glance around to assess his options for hiding, Draxian spotted Master Archivist Garran beckoning for them to follow as he hobbled toward the trees.

"This way," Arros urged, as he spun about and darted across the platform past the raging column of fire.

The young Lord leapt into action without thought, taking the stairs three at a time toward the field beyond. Draxian followed the Prince as he ran toward the safety of the trees in the distance where the Master Archivist waited. Behind them, the great dragon leapt into the air with a strained flapping of its bat-like wings, then immediately fell back to the ground in confusion. Something kept it from taking to the air, eliciting a frustrated squawk from the creature. Draxian's heart pounded in his chest as he sprinted to keep up with his friend. His nose was filled with the putrid smell of burning sulfur, encouraging him to run ever faster.

The scaled serpent refocused its gaze toward the fleeing men, then began its pursuit. It took almost no time for the dragon to bound toward them. Just as they prepared to duck from its grasp, the two men were forced to jump back as a bolt of red lightning struck the ground before them. Draxian could feel his hair standing on end from the raw power emanating forth in a crushing wave. Their hesitation was all the dragon needed to close the distance. Like two field mice fleeing a hawk, Draxian and Arros started running once again – keeping low and praying the beast would miss with its clawed attack.

It was at that time a stray beam of light from the portal generator shot past them and struck a tree. Draxian felt a strange tingling throughout his body as the land shifted beneath them. The gaping tears in the sky were all around, revealing a mixed terrain from the collision of the two realms. Both men slid to a halt immediately upon realizing they had crossed beyond their own world. Turning his head, Draxian winced sharply as the mighty beast appeared above them. An intense feeling of hopelessness washed over him as he awaited his death – yet nothing happened. The great beast was disoriented and seemed to be searching for shelter from the crackling lightning and heavy winds.

An eerie warning cried out in the back of Draxian's mind. A moment later, his body was wracked by intense pain as the red lightning struck the dragon's wing and diffused, scattering tiny bolts of crimson energy that arced through both men. The ground rushed past Draxian's vision, as if abruptly hurled through the air – and yet Draxian did not feel any sensation of falling. Suddenly, his world went dark.

KOHR

A gentle hand on his shoulder startled Draxian awake. Through the haze that covered his vision he saw Arros leaning over him with a finger to his mouth, signaling the young Lord to silence. Draxian had no problem remaining quiet, as it hurt to even wiggle his toes.

"Are you well?" Arros asked in a hushed voice.

Draxian could barely hear Arros' whisper over the ringing in his head. "I think so," he managed to murmur back.

"That flying monstrosity is dead."

Struggling to see in the direction his friend was pointing, Draxian saw the lifeless form of the dragon behind him. Even in death it was a terrifying sight. Its reddish-brown scales were scorched along the wing and body where it must have been struck by the lightning, and dark blood oozed from around lifeless eyes and gaping jaws.

"Then why are we whispering?" It took great effort to push himself up to one elbow. His strength was slowly returning, but he still felt exhausted and dizzy.

"I heard voices nearby." Arros shifted the weight of the leather traveling pack looped over his shoulder.

"What happened?"

"We passed through to the other world." The Prince rubbed his chin in thought, as his eyes scanned the horizon. "Thankfully, that violent storm seems to have ended."

Following Arros' gaze to the sky, Draxian saw white clouds beneath a reddish haze as far as he could see. He no longer knew which way was north or south. They were obviously not in the ruins of Aggaros, or anywhere else on Ellandor for that matter. Large rocks littered the small, jagged hills around them; nothing but desolate and rocky wasteland covered with other-worldly plants filled the landscape.

Arros pointed to something beyond a nearby boulder. Leaning to one side, Draxian tried to peer around it to see what caught his friend's attention. His eyes widened in surprise when he spotted the small caravan that stretched along a dirt road in the distance. The caravan itself was not unusual, but the large, fat lizards that pulled the wagons were. They were rotund, grey creatures with stubby tails and powerful legs suited for pulling heavy loads. Twelve men wearing ragged clothing and holding spears stood near the caravan looking toward them.

"Are either of you injured?" A female voice came from behind them.

Spinning around, Draxian realized they were being confronted by two figures. The first, a woman who appeared to be close to their own age, was wrapped in a long, brown cloak. She pulled it tightly in front of her so that only the collar of her dirty white tunic could be seen peeking from beneath the material. A few strands of wavy blonde hair framed the soft features of her face, with the rest pulled back into a single braid.

The man next to her squinted at them suspiciously. He was middle-aged with a greying beard and stringy dark hair, wearing a blue linen robe. "The woman asked you a question, stranger."

Arros came to his feet and raised his open hands toward them in a gesture of peace. "Of course, friend. My name is Arros, and this is Draxian. We intend you no harm."

Looking from Draxian to Arros, then back to Draxian, the man shook his head. "The first appearance of the sun and blue skies in a thousand years, a freshly killed dragon, and now two nobles appear out of nowhere. We can't assume you're harmless."

The woman continued to stare. "Such strange attire. What empire are you from?"

Draxian forced himself to stand, then dusted off his trousers. "A city called Braethus."

"I have never heard of this place, Bray-thaas," she sounded out the word. The woman's piercing greenish blue eyes met Draxian's. "Where is it?"

"Uh, quite far, my lady." Draxian saw her tilt her head to one side, as though prompting him for more. "To the west, I think."

"The Western Kingdoms?" She continued to stare incredulously, causing Draxian to shift uncomfortably, as the young Lord wondered if he had said anything wrong. He had read stories from the ancient Travelers that it did not take much to offend people of other cultures. As with all politics, the best way to understand a new society was to watch how they interacted with others and listen carefully to what they said – or didn't say. "Cam, they must have been ported to our region through the storm. Although few people have ever survived such an aggressive magic."

Arros was quick to grasp her answer. "Yes, I believe that's exactly what happened to us."

"Sounds like as good an explanation as any." The man casually rubbed at a silver bracelet on his wrist. "Never met anyone from beyond the Serpent's Breath Mountains – always believed the Mist Valley was impassable."

"Is it true there are giants and lizard people roaming about the wilderness, devouring any humans they cross?"

Draxian saw Arros frown at the woman's question. Thankfully, her older partner interjected, giving him more time to think of an answer.

"Regardless of where you're from, you seem to have found yourselves in the middle of nowhere without enough supplies to last the night." The man chuckled and stroked his grey beard as he appraised their clean attire and total lack of travel gear. They must have looked very out of place, Draxian mused. "My name is Camoranthus. My friends call me Cam."

"And I'm T'mara." The woman continued to watch Draxian, giving him a tight-lipped smile. While she appeared friendly enough, he noticed her posture and stance were tense – as if expecting an attack at any moment. "We're on our way to Phondari. The Guardian's Keep is less than a day's ride if you care to join us. We can take you at least that far."

Smiling back at the two of them, Arros gave an accepting nod. "We would greatly appreciate any hospitality you could offer."

She let her cloak fall open, revealing the two wicked daggers she held in her hands. T'mara expertly whirled them between her fingers, then slid the blades into the scabbards on her belt. Draxian couldn't help but notice it held at least three other daggers that he could see. "Follow me, noble Lords."

Draxian and Arros exchanged wide-eyed looks, then cautiously started after her. They quickened their pace to catch up as T'mara led them around the mound of rock and through the boulders toward the caravan. Draxian continued to watch the distant thunder clouds moving away from them. "I've never seen so much red in a sky before. It stretches on forever in every direction."

T'mara gave him a curious look. "What do you mean? The Veil has always been that color."

"Always?"

"Except during the night when it's too dark to see much of anything. Everyone knows this," she giggled at him.

Draxian shook his head. "We usually just see this color when the sun is low on the horizon."

The woman stopped suddenly. "Did you say 'sun'?"

"Yes," he replied cautiously.

"Then, the blue skies we saw earlier are from your land?" T'mara raised an eyebrow at him.

"That's right."

She smiled again before continuing forward. "Wouldn't it be wondrous if the Thousand Years of Darkness were finally ending? There are those who believe that day is fast approaching."

"That would be… something," was all Draxian could answer. He realized they had to be careful not to say anything that would bring endless questions neither could answer. Knowledge was the most precious commodity in any world, and they needed to hold onto any advantages they might have from their own culture. And judging by their crude attire and quality of weapons, they had stumbled upon a primitive race of people.

"Is your friend a kind of Blade Master?"

"Uh, I don't believe so."

"The insignia on your tunic," she asked, pointing over to Arros. "It seems familiar to me."

Arros glanced down at the crest sewn into his cloak, the royal seal of his family showing a patterned shield within a ring of fire. "That's the symbol of my family, the House of Nemendes. Have you seen this before?"

"Nemendes," Cam shot back dubiously. "I wouldn't speak such a name openly – even in jest."

"Why? Have you met someone else by that name?" Draxian knew that Arros was reaching for any indication their fathers had traveled through the same portal. However, his enthusiasm was drawing unwanted attention. Even if their fathers were alive and well somewhere in this barren land, they might have made dangerous enemies. And neither of the men were trained to survive in such a hostile and unknown environment.

Draxian placed a hand on the young Prince's arm. "It's not that important right now. You mentioned a Blade Master?" he asked, attempting to redirect the conversation to something less personal.

"Correct," T'mara replied. "And I suppose you don't have those where you come from, either?" She huffed a laugh. "Not many true masters left, really, and they mostly remain hidden in the shadows. If you should ever encounter someone claiming to be one, they are likely not. A true master would never boast of their skills."

"Well said. And no, I've never met one." Draxian ran his eyes over T'mara, taking stock of all the knives and daggers hanging at her waist and on her thighs. He wondered what world they had fallen into, which required people to wield such an extensive arsenal.

T'mara gave him a warm smile before leading them the rest of the way to the waiting caravan. Twelve men with spears scurried about the small line of eight carts, their bulging contents held down with ropes and tarps. As they approached, the caravan guards stopped to stare at the newcomers.

"How long have you both been wandering the wastes alone?" Camoranthus pressed.

Arros shrugged. "We don't rightly know. Last thing I remember, we were running from that flying lizard, then awoke here."

The riders moved out of the way as they approached. Three reptilian mounts were roped together behind a cart full of wooden crafts. T'mara pulled saddles from within the small wagon and began strapping them over two of the beasts.

"Sounds like the dragon shielded you from the storm as you were carried here," she suggested, tossing one of the heavy seats onto the first lizard, earning an irritated hiss. "You are truly fortunate."

Cam shook his head. "I'm not sure *fortune* would describe being torn from a land of blue skies and a shining sun."

"Perhaps not," she allowed.

Dropping the subject with a dismissive wave, Cam climbed into the saddle atop his own mount and motioned for them to do the same. "Come, we've wasted enough time. We need to get to the keep before the Veil loses its light."

Draxian followed the man's gaze to the radiant mass of clouds above them. He assumed this was the Veil he spoke of. It seemed to give off a light of its own, and there was no way to tell exactly where their sun had positioned itself behind the impenetrable haze.

"He's right," T'mara agreed while walking over to retrieve her own mount. It was another scaled beast, yet hers was different. With longer, agile legs, and a tail with wicked spikes protruding from it, Draxian observed the overgrown lizard would be well suited for battle. Even the skull was shaped more like a shield, giving the rider cover from the front. "We all need rest, and some real food wouldn't hurt either. I know of a tavern that serves the best spiced tarlagon soup. You should try it."

Smiling, despite his ignorance of what a tarlagon was, Draxian politely nodded his agreement. "Sounds delicious."

"Uh oh, she's already found the way to your heart," Arros teased, punching his friend playfully in the side. "Feed him at your own risk, my Lady."

She winked back at Arros with a sly grin. "I'll take my chances."

The caravan rumbled into motion just as they settled into their saddles with Arros insisting on riding in the lead with Cam. Sitting in silence, Draxian took in the harsh gloomy world around him. The fat lizards with black stone collars encrusted in green swirls moved surprisingly smoothly and quickly for their size. Although it took some adjustment to the slight side to side waddle, they seemed to be making swift progress. Even so, the Veil's light made it hard for Draxian to judge the passage of time, and without the sun's orientation in the sky, the young Lord had little sense of direction. He knew not where they had traveled. And were it not for the strange, black obelisks lining the road, it would have been impossible to see the path in many places where rain appeared to have washed away the tracks of those passing on the hard-packed dirt.

Attempting to catch up with T'mara, Draxian kicked his mount in the ribs, which earned an angry hiss from the beast. As it snorted in contempt, he caught a whiff of the creature's foul breath which reminded him of rotten cabbage. Frustrated, he tried again, once more eliciting a hiss, followed by a deep guttural growl.

Observing his plight, T'mara fell back and pulled up beside him. "Have you never ridden a gek before?"

"A what?"

"Gekka."

"Can't say that I have," he admitted, his frustration growing. "How do you get these things to move faster?"

"They respond only to touch. We tap them with a stick or spear, like this." Smacking her own creature on the rump with a thin wooden rod, T'mara's mount leapt forward into a full run. Pulling back on the reins slowed it to a comfortable pace. "Now you try," she coaxed, while grinning back at him.

Reaching back, Draxian smacked the creature's hindquarters with his open palm, causing it to launch forward. The gekka's initial burst of speed was highly unexpected and nearly threw him from the saddle. The young Lord quickly pulled back on the rope attached to the gekka's collar to get it back under control. He managed to slow it down just a short distance ahead of her.

T'mara gave him an impish grin as she closed the distance. A playful glint in her blue-green eyes made him feel immediately self-conscious. "Not bad for your first time."

"I just need to find my balance. What type of creature is that?" he asked, indicating her mount.

T'mara gave it a friendly rub on the neck. "This is Grety. She's a taark."

"Ah," he acknowledged, trying to appear thoughtful.

Looking at him inquisitively, she slowly took her gaze away and focused on the road before them once again. "Was there something else you wished to ask me?"

Draxian stumbled through his mind trying to come up with a subject to keep her talking. "I was wondering what these obelisks were for. They seem to go on forever in either direction."

T'mara glanced to where he pointed then returned her gaze. "Do you not have storm wards in your empire?"

"As we've said before, we aren't from around here."

"Then surely that must be the reason you were taken by the storms. It's the only explanation."

"What do you mean, taken? The red storms have something to do with the portals?"

She gave him a sidelong glance. "I'm not certain what you mean by this. The lightning from the red storms is the reason so many shadow beasts walk the land. It is said that it all started when the sun was lost a thousand years ago, and Kohr was pushed to the cusp of the Void during the War of the Shadow Lords."

"Kohr?" Draxian's eyes widened in recognition. They hadn't simply entered a portal to another world, the two men had accidentally crossed into a Realm of Power. Kohr was said to be the Realm of Life-Essence and the nexus of all elemental energy. It was also the last place any sane Ellandorian would ever wish to find themselves. Arros would need to be warned.

T'mara wrinkled her forehead, then lifted her hand to indicate the world around them. "Yes, Kohr," she repeated. "What do you call it?"

Draxian searched the horizon with a long sigh. "Kohr."

"To answer your question, if the crimson lightning strikes people or creatures, they will cease to exist in one place and reappear somewhere else entirely. The obelisks along the road were designed to repel the lightning and shadow beasts, protecting those traveling between them. When a man or woman is taken by the red storms, it almost always kills them in the process. You are fortunate the chromatic dragon shielded you from this."

A knot tightened within his stomach. Draxian was beginning to get the feeling returning home would be far more difficult than he ever imagined. Traveling to another world was bad enough. Crossing into a Realm of Power was nothing shy of madness.

A cry from the rear of the procession caught his attention. A man nearby repeated the message, "The storm has returned."

Cam, at the head of the group with Arros, pointed into the distance where a high wall could be seen over the rocky hills around them. "The Keep is ahead! We'll take shelter there."

"Another storm," T'mara grumbled quietly to herself, as she urged her taark into a run. "Try to keep up, Draxian."

Crossing over the next rise of hills revealed their destination. To the right, a ledge sloped drastically toward the lowlands of endless boulders, rocks and sparse vegetation. On the left, stretches of yellow grass went on as far as he could see. Ahead rose a massive fortress with walls extending leagues in both directions. This appeared to Draxian as a frontier boundary, likely dividing two sovereign territories to limit or tax travelers.

Soon the entire group was riding for the towering walls of the Guardian's Keep. Looking over his shoulder, Draxian noticed a mass of darkness obscuring the land beyond. Flashes of red lightning within the rolling wall revealed a dust cloud rushing up fast. Soon, the storm's grumbling could be heard above the racket of the carts, and the groaning of the lizards as they pushed to their limits to stay beyond the reach of nature's wrath.

Draxian stared in awe as the sides of the structure came into full view. The granite wall stood as tall as twenty men and surrounded a keep. Tiny men atop the great barrier rushed around as others, spotting the group's approach, held the gates open for them to seek shelter.

The thunder of the storm was deafening as it bore down on them. Draxian nearly jumped from his saddle when the lightning began striking with deafening intensity. Even worse, the strong, trailing winds continued to push them forward. Debris lifted into the air, quickly obscuring their vision.

Pulling their cloaks about their faces to keep the sand and dust out of their lungs, Arros and Draxian held on as they finally passed through the gate. The last of the caravan rushed through just as the storm reached the open portal, striking the wall like a sledgehammer, nearly knocking the last two carts on their sides.

As the gates groaned under their own weight with the stress of closing, the caravan took shelter in a passageway twenty paces wide, just behind the great wall. It was likely used for inspecting caravans before being allowed further into the city.

The gate mechanism squealed as it struggled against the wind to close the heavy doors, as the gale struck. The abrupt force slammed its massive weight against the stone frame. Wooden timbers shuddered and bounced before finally coming to a rest. Two guardsmen quickly pulled a lever that slid a heavy metal rod into place, locking them tight.

Both men dismounted and rejoined the caravan as they settled within the shelter of the wall. Draxian surveyed the immediate area, including the townsfolk who shambled past. There was a distinctly oppressive feel to the town. It also smelled like piss, and not all of it from the animals, he suspected. Among the many caravans taking shelter within the walls were residents shuffling through the crowd or huddled out of the way in various places. Many extended their hands, pleading for help, but all kept their heads low in acquiescence when the watchmen of the Guardian's Keep walked by.

He watched as six warriors of the watch made their way toward Cam and T'mara. The men all wore violet tunics with a black skull boldly displayed on the front, and carried swords forged of a dark metal with jagged edges in their grips, as if expecting to use them. Cam and T'mara both stepped forward and pulled their right sleeves back to show the leader something on their wrists, while keeping their heads bowed in respect. The man in the lead, a pale-skinned brute with a heavy scar on the side of his head, began speaking quietly to the caravan master. Cam nodded and began gesturing toward several of the gekka who pulled covered wagons of merchandise. The guards moved to inspect the goods, extracting their tax as they went. By the way everyone avoided their gaze, these guardsmen were feared.

"About time you got here," an old woman spoke from nearby. Her hair was damp, and her clothing was in tattered ruins. With milky eyes, she squinted at Draxian, as if trying to see him better, while leaning on a walking stick.

"Pardon me?" Draxian looked at Arros in confusion before turning his attention back to the blind woman.

"There be no pardons in this place, traveler. You best keep that in mind."

Draxian forced a smile. "My gratitude for the advice."

The old woman grumbled something unintelligible to herself, then continued on her way.

Draxian motioned for the Prince to follow him further from the caravan to keep anyone from overhearing their conversation. "Arros," he began cautiously. "I know where we are."

"Kohr," he answered, without even a hint of concern.

"Wait... You already knew?"

"I suspected it was where our fathers had gone, and Cam confirmed this. Garran told me our fathers believed whatever was happening here was somehow connected to Ellandor."

He stood there in confusion, blinking at the Prince. "You mean to say, you intended on coming here?"

"Correct. Only you were supposed to remain behind and reopen the portal for me after a few days."

"But it takes both our hands to use it."

He shrugged a single shoulder. "I didn't know that until today."

"What about the wedding? How could you possibly hope to get back in time for...?" Draxian cut himself off, his eyebrows dropping with a new understanding. "You never intended to go back to Ellandor."

"Does it matter?"

"In this instance – not really." The young Lord sighed heavily, then looked around. "Well, Your Highness, tell me you at least had some semblance of a plan if you managed to get here?"

"First, let's drop the titles and ranks. We're just two ordinary men from the Western Kingdoms."

Draxian folded his arms and gave his old friend a stern glare. "We're nothing like these people, and this world is already making me uneasy. There's a taint, a sickness in the land that's almost perceptible."

"I know. I felt it as soon as the portal opened."

"And yet you had already resolved to go through, without regard for the danger and potential destruction it might cause."

Arros leaned his back against a large stone pillar. "I deeply regret that you were forced to come here with me, although I won't apologize for doing whatever was necessary to find our King. This is the Realm of Kohr, not the Abyss. We just need to be smart and adapt."

"Are you certain? This is exactly what I imagined the Abyss must be like – only colder." Draxian shook his head in resignation. If he ever expected them to get back home, they would have to adapt to their new world. "You're right, we should join T'mara for supper and see what we can learn, starting with this Guardian's Keep. We need to start somewhere."

"Good thinking. She's taken an interest in you – for whatever reason."

"Maybe it's…" Draxian narrowed his eyes and smirked. "Nice one," he shot dryly. "Let's just hope we don't meet anyone who has actually been to the Western Kingdoms."

"From what little these people know about the place I don't think that's going to be an issue. But we probably should not mention our blue skies and warm sun to anyone. We do not want to attract attention from the local authorities. If our fathers came through the portal somewhere nearby, they may have stopped here as well. We should ask around."

"Assuming that's true, what happens if you speak with a person high in power that they somehow wronged? Have you seen how unfriendly these people are?"

Arros glanced around to make certain no one was watching, then rolled back the sleeve of his right arm to reveal a black metal bracer of exquisite design. A devious grin spread across his face. "Don't worry – I came prepared."

GUARDIAN'S KEEP

They have the best stew here," T'mara announced happily. "And you'll love the honey bread."

The small tavern she had taken them to was not far from where the caravan had entered the walled town. After the storm passed, Draxian and Arros helped their new friends secure the carts and mounts at a nearby trading depot, then T'mara offered to lead both men to her favorite tavern. It was a modest place nestled among a row of crudely built mud brick and stone buildings.

Draxian felt a little uncomfortable with everyone staring at them, although he understood why. He imagined their clothing looked quite out of place. Even the common material of his green cloak was spun with a tightly woven fabric that was impervious to being soaked by rain. Despite it not being properly laundered in several days, it was still nearly spotless compared to the ratty grey and brown garments he saw covering many of the locals.

Arros seemed oblivious to the prying looks and curious gazes. He sipped his honey wine with a calm demeanor and a regal presence. The Prince allowed little to bother him, as he had grown to adulthood with all the citizens of Ellandor gossiping about his every action. Draxian was often subjected to this intrusion in his own territories yet had never quite grown comfortable with it.

"Tell me, how did you get involved with the caravan?" Arros queried. "You don't look much like a merchant."

T'mara glanced around before she spoke. "That's because I'm not. Cam offered me a position to help guard his wares while traveling back and forth from Annis to Phondari. I also like to sing at a few of the taverns for a few extra coins."

Arros tilted his head to one side. "You carry yourself well-enough. With all those weapons, are you certain you're not a Blade Master?"

She snorted a laugh. "The ones I've met are nothing more than glorified guardsmen. Hunters, however, are true warriors, able to kill with a single strike."

"You say that as if the mere title makes an expert." Arros leaned back in his chair and narrowed his eyes. "Even the best huntsmen will rarely take down large game with a single shot."

"Ah," she asserted thoughtfully, "I forget you are new here." T'mara pulled back her left sleeve to show Arros her wrist. Draxian leaned over to have a better look and immediately noticed a rune burned into her flesh. "This is the mark of the Chosen Hunters."

Arros gave her a playful grin. "As opposed to those who elected not to get branded?"

"Feel it," T'mara encouraged. "It's not what you think."

Seeing that Arros did not make any move to do so, Draxian reached over and lightly ran his fingertips over the mark. It immediately lit with a red glow, indicating it was far more than a simple scarring – possibly a way to officially identify a Hunter as genuine. "Amazing. Does it hurt?"

She shot her eyes to Draxian with a look of surprise. "Why did that happen?"

"What, is it not supposed to be red?"

T'mara leaned back in her chair to scrutinize Draxian further. "It is an enchanted mark that allows us to cross borders without being taxed or harassed by the patrols. Also, it helps warn us of those who might hold dangerous magic."

Arros quickly pulled her attention back to him with a dubious expression. "Did you say magic?"

"Yes, magic. Don't tell me you have no idea what that is either."

The Prince continued to watch her with a cool gaze. "It's a word some cultures use for a concept they don't understand."

Draxian bit his lip. That had done it – T'mara quickly abandoned her query for a chance to grapple with Arros. He certainly knew how to stir the woman's pot. "I know what magic is. *You* are the one who appears to be lost here, not me."

It was at that time a skinny boy appeared next to the table with a tray of steaming bowls. Draxian mimicked Arros' example and once again refocused on the subject. "Excellent, the food is here," he proclaimed. The young Lord gave it a long sniff as a ceramic bowl was placed in front of him. "Smells wonderful." Yet in truth, Draxian found the smell of the muddy substance reminded him of rotting cabbage, masked with heavy spices.

T'mara continued to scowl at Arros until he gave her a warm smile and winked to let her know it was only a jest. Slowly, the Huntress relaxed her posture and pointed a sharp finger at him. "You, I will be watching," T'mara teased, then focused back on Draxian and his soup. "Try it."

The young Lord forced a smile and then lifted the wooden

spoon to his mouth. As he slurped up a chunk of dark meat, he could not help but notice that Arros was observing him even more intensely than T'mara. The flavor was unlike anything he expected. Some of it was familiar, although masked with a strong spice that lightly burned his tongue.

"Do you love it?"

Draxian finished chewing and swallowed. "Actually, it's quite good."

T'mara grinned like a little girl and gently touched his arm. "Told you so."

"Give it a try, Arros," Draxian prodded.

Pausing briefly, Arros finally scooped a mouthful and then swallowed hard. He gave Draxian a covert glare before faking a smile. "Indeed, most excellent. What did you call it again?"

"Spiced tarlagon soup." T'mara hunched over her bowl and began eating hungrily.

"What's a tarlagon?"

She offhandedly waved toward the door. "You've seen the taark I ride?"

Arros' eyes widened slightly, mirroring Draxian's. "What about it?"

"They look a little like that, only they come to about knee-high and run on two legs. Why? What do you call them?"

The Prince blinked several times. "Lizard runners," he offered.

The Huntress snorted a laugh. "Yes, that describes them well enough."

"T'mara, you mentioned that you like to sing," Draxian interjected. "I've always enjoyed a good tune."

She brightened at his words. "I'd love to sing for you. Have you any coins?"

Draxian was about to reach into his belt pouch, when a deep roar sounded far in the distance that echoed across the land. Panicked cries erupted from outside the tavern as the citizens scattered. Before he had the chance to puzzle over what had caused it, Arros and T'mara were already on their feet and moving toward the door. Following close behind, Draxian reached the exit and watched the streets from the side.

All along the road, people scattered, many dragging children with them or pushing carts of goods to clear a path down the middle. Those who could not make it to the safety of the buildings began dropping to their knees and bowing their heads. This act of obeisance continued in a wave that swept all the way down to the keep itself.

Draxian waited in anticipation until finally spotting a lone man strutting regally down the center of the road. He was tall with dark hair and handsome features. His shirt was made from finely spun blue silk and his black pants matched his boots. The townsfolk kept their heads down to avoid his gaze. Tugging at their sleeves, T'mara motioned frantically for Draxian and Arros to keep out of sight. Both men gave each other sidelong glances, then did as she requested.

As the mysterious figure neared them amid the eerie silence, a familiar elderly woman broke from the line of observers and stepped into his path. Her frail form and disheveled hair framed a face that held many years of hardship. She leveled her walking stick at the man's chest bringing him to a halt.

"Your reign of darkness is near its end, vile one!" Something about the woman's voice sent chills up Draxian's spine. "The Undying will soon be a faded memory." She emphasized her statement by spitting on him.

The entire city appeared to hold its breath as the mysterious man continued forward with an evil grin spreading beneath cold eyes. "Not today, witch." With a casual swipe of his hand, the old crone's throat was ripped asunder. The woman's hands went up to stop the fountaining blood, and she burst into a violent fit of coughing. As if he had done nothing more than brush away a buzzing fly, the degenerate nobleman moved on as the woman sank to her knees. No one made a single move to assist her.

Unable to watch such an atrocity, Draxian started for the doorway when Arros caught his shoulder and pulled him back inside. "Don't."

"We can't just stand here and do nothing," he whispered angrily.

T'mara reached over and placed a comforting hand on his arm. "Please, remain here. The Undying Emperor Thartalagor won't hesitate to kill every soul within this town if it amused him to do so."

Draxian gritted his teeth in rage, feeling helpless to assist the old woman. Whoever the dark figure was, there was something about his cold gaze that was less than human. And what Emperor walked, unescorted, through a crowded city?

Emperor Thartalagor had not gone more than a dozen steps beyond the tavern when he stopped in place, then started to turn. "Are there any others who wish their blood spilt in defiance of their ruler?"

T'mara urgently rubbed Draxian's back. "What rage you hold, please let it go," she whispered. "He can sense your defiance."

Gritting his teeth, Draxian took a deep breath and thought of his home near the lakes. At night, he would watch from his balcony as the shimmer-fish jumped from the water, leaving trails of radiant sparkles in their wake. The melodic cooing of the night gulls would often harmonize and sing him to sleep. He believed it was the most beautiful region of Ellandor. His breathing and pulse both calmed as he changed his focus.

The Emperor finally continued on his way. "Remove that filth before I return from speaking with Lord Trimenius," he commanded, pointing a crooked finger toward a small detachment of four guardsmen with short spears. They bowed and immediately responded to his demand. Lifting the old woman by her arms, two of them dragged her limp form down the cobbled road. The people waited until the despicable man was far from sight before once again rising.

Arros scowled at Draxian, then pulled him back toward a private corner. T'mara was content to remain by the door and keep watch. "Have you lost your mind? You don't know what kind of enemies we face."

"I apologize," Draxian replied with all sincerity. "I don't know what came over me."

The Prince shook his head. "I understand, but you need to remember we're in a new land with different cultures and laws. We have a unique opportunity to learn what happened to our fathers. If they came out of the portal in the same area, then perhaps they met up with the Lord of this keep." He placed a reassuring hand on Draxian's shoulder. "We'll wait for the Emperor to leave, then see if we can get an audience with Lord Trimenius for ourselves."

"Those people did nothing to help her."

"Because there wasn't anything to be done. Do you honestly believe you could have saved her? The woman knew she would die – and probably with purpose."

He furrowed his brow. "She sacrificed herself merely in a show of defiance? To what end?"

"To illicit this very reaction from you, or anyone else who is tired of living under a yoke of oppression." Arros clapped his shoulder. "If you want to honor that brave woman, then never forget this moment. She gave her life for a single opportunity to speak something important and make damn certain you listened."

"I would have settled for her buying me a drink." Draxian looked back to see T'mara glancing toward them from further away. "You're sure about meeting with this Lord Trimenius?"

"Did you have something better to do?"

He finally huffed a laugh at the Prince's steadfast resilience. "I suppose not."

"Then its settled. Let's go make a friend."

Gazing back toward T'mara, Draxian gave her a reassuring grin, then turned his attention out a window to the black, marbled walls of the keep looming in the distance. And the trail of blood marking the way down the cobbled road.

73

74

INVITATION

"My Lord," the guardsman breathed heavily, "Emperor Thartalagor Deathskull has arrived and is demanding an audience."

Trimenius felt as though an anvil had dropped on his chest. Straightening his white robes as he arose from the padded seat, the Lord began walking slowly toward the door of the audience chamber.

"Is there anything else, Cyrran?" he asked when he saw the man still standing there.

"Yes, my Lord. Old Lorsa approached the Undying Emperor and told him his time was at an end."

The tired Lord of the Guardian's Keep looked at him curiously. "And?"

"She's dead, of course."

"I see," Lord Trimenius mumbled, staring at the floor in deep thought. After a moment, he looked back into Cyrran's eyes.

"Have any new travelers come into town since the sky tore open?"

"Just Cam and his caravan passing through to Phondari. Nothing unusual about that."

"Ah."

His servant was just beginning to turn to announce his unexpected guest when he stopped. "This might be nothing, but two wealthy merchants, or noblemen, were seen traveling with the caravan – possibly to do business in Phondari."

"How do you know this?"

"Their extravagant garments were not something you would see on mere guards."

Trimenius stroked his chin nervously. "Extend an invitation for them to join me for drinks." He placed a hand on Cyrran's shoulder and leaned in close. "Do not accept their rejection of this offer. Enlist the Chromatic Guard to escort them directly here if you must."

Bowing quickly, the man rushed from the room to carry out his orders. Once again alone with his thoughts, Lord Trimenius lifted a silver chalice to his lips. His hand trembled in fear of his first appointment, making it difficult to sip the sweet wine. "One Power watch over me," he beseeched.

Draxian sat in silence at the table while T'mara and Arros took turns ripping at the loaf of honey-bread sitting between them. He had lost his appetite and was content to ponder his situation.

"You called him an Undying Emperor?"

T'mara finished chewing and leaned over the table toward Arros. "They are said to be thousands of years old – born long before the War of the Shadow Lords which took the sun from the sky."

"How is it possible to steal a sun?"

"I wasn't there. However, my distant ancestors fought in that war and passed down the stories from that time. They said it was the act of a single, evil god who cursed this land. Many great heroes arose to fight him. Eventually he was defeated, although not without great cost to the world."

Draxian's curiosity overtook his melancholy. "Did this self-proclaimed god have a name?"

T'mara's eyes widened, as if he had asked the woman to give up her soul. "The Fallen One – he who cannot be named."

Arros squinted in thought. "Just to understand correctly – you aren't permitted to say his name aloud, or you don't know it?"

"If enough people were to speak his true name, it could break the seal to his prison, and the Fallen One would rise again to give the people another thousand years of darkness."

"Uh, huh," the Prince retorted dryly. "Yeah, wouldn't want to risk that happening."

T'mara pursed her lips at him. "You are not a nice person." She scooted her chair closer to Draxian, then slipped her arm around his. "I like your companion better."

"Am I supposed to be insulted?"

Draxian watched their exchange with a curious expression. Nothing Arros did was without purpose and being rude was not in his nature. He patted T'mara's arm. "Don't worry, I'll protect you, my Lady."

She stared at Arros with a victorious smirk. "You see, Lord Prince? That is how you make friends."

Both men shot each other a glance at the realization she had heard more than they intended, then Arros leaned back in his seat. "That's some excellent hearing you have, Master Hunter."

"I pride myself in knowing the nature of the people around me." She released Draxian's arm, then lowered her voice. "Why are you truly here? And do not tell me it was an accident." When neither of the men answered, she tapped her first finger lightly on the table. "This way station is not just a boundary between empires. The Guardian's Keep was built to study those with magic. There are Hunters whose sole purpose is to find these magi and bring them here for testing."

Draxian had to ask. "What kind of testing?"

"Few know the truth of what the Undying are searching for, but they have been much more active in the last few years than in all of the history of the keep." She leaned and folded her arms. "Do not go searching for answers here, or you may get your wish."

The Prince tilted his head. "What does it matter if anything happens to us? We're just mean, wealthy nobles who can't survive a single night in the wasteland without assistance."

She met Arros' gaze for an uncomfortably long time. "There's nothing weak about either of you. I see you watching the people. How they move, how they react. The first time my eyes caught the gaze of an Undying, it was my seventeenth winter. I wet myself and couldn't stop shaking for days." She looked back and forth between them. "You are dangerous."

Draxian cleared his throat. "Then why..."

"Because," T'mara interrupted, "you are not evil. I also know this to be true."

Arros gave her a soft smile. "I've clearly underestimated you, my Lady. Apologies." The Lord Prince started to say something else, when he closed his mouth and slowly reached over to touch the bracer hidden beneath his sleeve. Draxian heard someone approaching from behind while spotting T'mara also carefully reaching into her cloak, looking like a serpent coiled to strike.

"Greetings, my Lords," came a voice from behind him.

Draxian turned his head to see a man standing in the livery of a manservant, being escorted by three women wearing full plate armor. The highly polished metal was unlike any he had seen thus far. It glistened with colors of red, blue, and green that appeared to shift of their own accord. Such metallurgy should have been beyond their ability to create. He wondered what realms of power they had connected the armor with, and what power it bestowed on the ones who wore it. Draxian had too quickly judged the inhabitants of Kohr by the impoverished few he had met.

The man continued. "His most distinguished Excellency, Lord Trimenius, requests your presence at the Guardian's Keep."

Draxian glanced to T'mara, who was ever-so-slightly shaking her head that it would not be an intelligent decision to accept. "Did he, now?" The young Lord came to his feet, towering a head taller than the warriors. "And what did we do to deserve such a grand honor?"

"His Excellency heard there were nobles gracing us within the city and insisted that you come meet with him at once."

"Is he not otherwise engaged with his most recent arrival?"

"Emperor Thartalagor Deathskull will not remain long. He never does."

Arros finally stood and flashed his usual charming smile. "We would be delighted."

"Splendid. If you will follow me." The manservant bowed politely and stepped to one side.

The heavily armored guard to his right held up a hand to halt the Prince. "Wait." The red sash over her left shoulder distinguished her as the leader of the three.

Arros lifted his eyebrows. "Is there a problem?"

"That cloak. Take it off."

"I have no weapons."

She stepped forward and pointed at the embroidery of his house crest. "This symbol is not something you will want to wear in public – whatever your allegiance."

The Prince studied the woman's posture for a time, then reached up and unclasped the cloak. After pulling it from his shoulders, the Prince handed it over to the woman's waiting arms. She quickly rolled it up, then stuffed it under her arm and stepped to one side. "After you, my Lord."

Arros left his pack beneath the table and passed T'mara, lightly dragging his fingers across her shoulder. "Watch our possessions, please."

"Of course," she responded quickly. T'mara then reached over to Draxian and took his hand in hers, giving a reassuring squeeze.

He returned the gesture. His eyes softened as he looked at her. T'mara's eyes were filled with worry. "We shall return soon," Draxian assured her.

The Huntress nodded and let go of his hand as he walked off after his escort.

Arros and Draxian approached the towering walls of the black stone keep along with their heavily armed escorts. The young Lord marveled at the seamless rock walls that made up the structure. It was obviously erected with the aid of a powerful form of elemental energy. Ellandor had used such methods for hundreds of years, yet not to the magnitude he observed before him. Through advanced architectural manipulation, they found that towers could reach much higher without the need for wider bases or buttress supports. While not as large and resplendent as the palace of Ellandor, the Guardian's Keep had a deeply foreboding presence that was meant to demonstrate the strength of the Undying Emperor who built it.

They arrived shortly after the red haze began to yield to the curtain of night. Blue orbs slowly lit with enough intensity to keep the streets well-illuminated. It gave a contrasting and cheerless ambiance directly opposed to the angry crimson sky of the daytime. Draxian wondered if this was done purposefully, or if they merely got tired of refueling lanterns. Either way, it only reminded him of the warning T'mara had relayed. The Undying were searching for those who could manipulate the Elemental Realms of Power. Magi they called them. Draxian's ancient ancestors had chosen Ellandor for the express purpose of limiting those dangerous abilities. Their world had an exceedingly weak link to the realms of power so magic, as it was called by many, was greatly diminished.

Greed and the lust for power were difficult natures to overcome. And yet his people had done it through self-understanding and the active pursuit of knowledge. They had learned long before that lack of education and self-discipline was the foundation of all troubles within their society. Once that was accepted, all other problems began to quickly dissipate. Poverty, over-population, sickness, and the desire to accumulate possessions were all but eliminated. If one wished to feel wealthy, they only needed more knowledge and to surround themselves with the love of family and friends. Draxian felt nothing of this equilibrium on Kohr. The land was tainted with dark energies and an unidentifiable foulness that partially obscured his senses.

As the party approached the main gate, four burly sentries caught hold of the thick bars and began pulling as one. The massive door swung outward, groaning under the stress of its own weight. Draxian noted the entryway guards wore the same grey and black uniforms as those in the surrounding town. In contrast, the three guards with them wore plate armor of extremely high quality. He wondered if they represented the elite guard for the keep, or a completely different faction. It was obvious how the people tended to keep from drawing the eyes of the local patrols. However, his new escorts caused many to turn away in alarm or simply leave the immediate area. Whoever they were, they commanded genuine fear.

Once inside the entry bailey, Draxian spotted to his right, a winding path leading up to a heavy iron door. Nearby, rested six carts with steel cages, each nearly tall enough for an average man to stand. Each had archaic runes, likely used to contain people with extraordinary gifts. He could not help but wonder how many men and women had been dragged through that door, never to be seen again. It was disgustingly barbaric.

They passed through the keep's main double doors with barely a glance from the sentries, who stood in crisp militant fashion with long decorative pikes. Each locked their gaze forward like regal statues. Just beyond, the large corridor ended at an intersection with a door to a receiving chamber, then split to the right and left toward separate wings of the fortress.

Their small procession halted as the loud shouts of the Emperor echoed through the halls from just ahead. At the direction of their leader, the other two warriors ushered Arros and Draxian to an antechamber nearby until the tirade was finished.

"I don't care if we have to drag every citizen in here one at a time! You will find all those who use magic and keep them here until I can view them for myself."

"A thousand pardons, my Lord. But we don't have the resources or space to accommodate so many. Perhaps if you would tell me what you are seeking, my Hunters can narrow down the search for you."

There was a long pause before Emperor Deathskull answered. "Mages with specialty power are of the most interest."

"Also, the most difficult to capture. We will not fail you, my Lord."

"See that you don't. For the moment, you are irreplaceable. Pray that never changes."

Draxian watched the vile man exit the receiving chamber

and stomp toward the exit. When he noticed the female warrior standing in the hall, his head lifted slightly, and the Emperor slowed his pace. Coming to stand nearly toe-to-toe with the woman, he scrutinized her with a dark intensity. Draxian expected him to strike her as he had done with the woman in the street, but instead, the warrior casually lifted her helm. The commander's soft features felt incongruous with her hardened demeanor. Short, dark hair, pulled back into a small braid, framed a face that seemed too young and perfect for a warrior of her position.

The warrior met the Emperor's gaze without fear. "Thartalagor. What is it that has your scales bristling on this fine evening?"

"Commander Rellan. What an unpleasant surprise. You've found yourself quite far from home."

"As have you. What brings you from your hole?"

He took a slight step back to better observe the brazen woman. "Why are you here? Is the Empress searching for anything in particular?"

"Same as you, I imagine."

"And what would that be?"

She gave him a smile that failed to touch her eyes. "Information. It's what the Chromatic Guard live for."

Emperor Thartalagor pointed a sharp finger at her nose. "Stay out of my way, or your Mistress will be promoting a new commander."

"That would be unwise, Thartalagor. Nothing escapes the eyes of Dellahara." She tilted her head slightly. "Or have you already forgotten what happened the last time you irritated the Empress of Dragons?"

The Undying clenched his hand into a fist and narrowed his eyes dangerously. "You've been warned." Without another word, the angry tyrant pushed past the commander and exited the fortress.

Commander Rellan waited until the Emperor was gone, then turned and motioned for Arros and Draxian to follow. The other Chromatic Guards lightly urged them forward with the manservant jogging ahead to announce their arrival. Draxian could imagine what mood their host would be in after such an unpleasant encounter. Glancing toward Arros revealed him searching all around while his hand casually touched the bracer beneath his sleeve for reassurance.

The interior of the receiving hall was a stark contrast to the gloomy exterior. Inside, the walls held beautifully decorated tapestries depicting battle scenes and landscapes amid striking reliefs carved into the walls. At its center and surrounded by white marble, a remarkably detailed statue of a dragon peered down at them. It was eerily similar to the one that had come through the portal on Ellandor.

Their escort led them across the room to a private chamber and urged them inside. At its center, a long table ran the length of the room, surrounded by bookshelves lining the walls. A solitary, white-robed man turned as they entered. His pale features bore the lines of age, and his head was nearly bald, save for the grey tufts of hair behind his ears.

The manservant bowed. "My Lord. Your guests have arrived."

Trimenius held a silver chalice in one hand while motioning the group forward with the other. "Welcome to the Guardian's Keep," he proclaimed warmly. "I'm Lord Elrenar Trimenius. And who might you be?"

The Prince stepped forward and gave a cordial bow. "You may call me Arros, and this is Draxian," he stated plainly while extending a hand toward the Lord. "Forgive me for being so forthright, but we were surprised by your invitation."

"We so rarely get noble guests from other lands. Most brought here have little to offer in the way of conversation." He stepped forward. "Your accent. It's not of the Northern Empires."

Draxian clenched his jaw muscles as he waited for Arros to answer. "We were raised in the Western Kingdoms until recently traveling here."

"Then you are quite far from home. Come, sit," Trimenius invited, pointing to the soft chairs positioned before a blazing hearth.

Commander Rellan bowed her head politely. "We will speak later, my Lord. Enjoy your evening."

"Of course, Commander. And my gratitude for the gifts of fresh fruit and spiced tea from Dellahara. They were well-received."

Draxian casually watched the manservant escort the three warriors in their shimmering plate armor from the room. The second warrior had the Prince's red cloak tucked beneath her arm. As for the leader, Commander Rellan, she glanced one last time at Arros with an unreadable expression before disappearing beyond the threshold.

Trimenius pointed toward a nearby table. "Would you like some Annarian wine? This particular stock was aged for more than thirty summers."

"That would be perfect," Arros returned.

"Yes, please." Draxian knew they must accept the offer or risk insulting their host. He just hoped it was better than the tarlagon soup he tried earlier.

As their host began pouring two goblets of wine, he gave them a curious glance. "Tell me, how are matters in the Western Kingdoms? We rarely get news from that region."

Arros accepted his cup of wine with a nod of gratitude. "When last we were there, the capital city was preparing for a big wedding between two houses."

"Yes," Draxian added. "Between the Prince and the daughter of a rival Lord. I'm certain you know the type: irresponsible, impetuous, with little regard for the opinions and safety of those closest to him."

The Prince glanced over to his friend and gave him a slow blink of condemnation, causing Draxian to smirk in victory. Trimenius had fortunately missed the covert exchange. "Yes, I know the type. My own nephew would fall into this category. He tends to favor the far more barbaric means of assessing magi brought to the Guardian's Keep. Old practices I have worked hard to eradicate"

Arros nodded thoughtfully. "And what is the purpose of this grand inquisition? We overheard a bit of your conversation with the Undying."

"Ah." The old Lord set his chalice off to the side and then laced his fingers together in front of him. "When I was first assigned to this post, the Guardian's Keep was a stronghold used mainly for inspecting goods coming back and forth between the cities of Phondari and Annis. Only in the last ten years has it been used primarily for testing rogue magi."

"And magic is forbidden here."

"As it always has been. Annis still tolerates some practices, as the Undying Emperor Zantharnakan Bonewing has never felt threatened by its use – so long as it doesn't harm other citizens. Emperor Thartalagor, however…"

"He was looking for something specific."

Trimenius gave Arros an amused grin. "Which he will never find, be assured."

Draxian watched as the two men continued to stare at each other until it became uncomfortable for the young Lord. Arros finally ended it by leaning forward. "Nemendes. Have you heard that name before?"

"For certain." Lord Trimenius retrieved his cup once again and took a long draw from its contents. "You have his same piercing eyes."

Draxian sat up straighter at the acknowledgement. "You mean he was here? Was there another with him?"

"And you must be Lord Kalenthos' son." The older man nodded his respect to Draxian. "Your father was a person of great integrity and deep convictions."

He could hardly believe his ears. Arros had been right about their fathers entering the portal to Kohr. "Do you happen to know where they are now?"

"Draxian…" Arros warned. The Prince slowly turned his head toward Trimenius. "Forgive him. We've not seen our fathers in a long while. They were presumed dead."

"I can't speak to that, my Lord. However, I do know where they went from here." The Lord of the Guardian's Keep arose from his chair and walked over to a bookshelf. He withdrew a thick leather volume and removed a folded piece of paper from within its binding. Trimenius returned the tome to its place, then shuffled back to his seat and handed the paper over to Arros. "Inside you'll find a map of the Northern Empires. You'll need it to help you navigate our lands." The Prince opened the yellowed drawing to study it. Draxian quickly leaned over to view it while Trimenius continued. "Far to the southwest of here is a place called the Ebon Waste. Within the center is the lost city of Orakh. None that I know have reached this place and returned. Your fathers went to study a dangerous magic they believed threatened both of our lands. The answers you seek are there."

Arros handed the map to Draxian for his inspection, then turned to the Lord. "And they never came back from that region?"

"No one ever ventures into the Ebon Waste and returns." He leaned closer and lowered his voice. "Your fathers were the first to do so."

"How do you know? You said that was the last time you saw them."

"Others have spoken to them since, and I was instructed to bid you follow in their path."

Draxian's head snapped up from studying the map. "You were expecting us?"

"For many years now, Lord Kalenthos." He gestured absently toward the nearest window. "From the towers, we witnessed the clouds split apart. And for the briefest moment, a blue sky and warm sun." Trimenius sniffed loudly. "I'd never seen the sun before today. That was the omen prophesied to mark your arrival."

The two Ellandorians glanced at each other then back to the Lord. Arros cleared his throat. "Forgive me. I'm not certain what you want us to say."

"Then say nothing. It would be best that way. You've barely stepped foot in these lands and already your enemies are beyond count." He lowered his chin and his eyes burned with intensity. "On the chance this fact has eluded your notice, all seven of the Undying Emperors are searching desperately for the two of you, Lord Prince, and they will not be the only ones to seek you out."

THE ORDER

The soft glow of an otherworldly light emanated from above the corridor where Lord Elrenar Trimenius walked. Unlike a torch that cast haunting shadows, this was steady and filled every corner with its illumination. As was always the case, his mind failed to recall how he got there. It felt as if he was in a dream. Almost.

Trimenius passed many doors in the hallway, but not all of them were accessible. However, they did not matter. There was only one he desperately sought – one that he needed. He continued onward until arriving at the correct spot, yet something was clearly wrong. The door was no longer there. A rising sense of panic began to take hold, and his chest tightened, making it feel as though his next breath would not come.

"No," he bellowed to the wall. "It can't be gone!"

The Lord stepped back and began glancing around him and further down the hallway. Perhaps he had made a mistake, and it was simply not where he believed. Or better yet, the doorway had moved, and he only needed to continue searching. Such a thing was not unheard of when it came to the Order.

Pressing forward, Trimenius came upon a door with the correct markings at last. His hand went to his chest and he breathed a long sigh of relief. "One Power be thanked – there you are."

With his resolve restored, Trimenius reached out and touched the symbol for infinity that was boldly displayed before him. The door instantly disappeared, and he found himself in a dimly lit room with smooth white walls, decorated with intricate paintings of fantastical landscapes. Wooden blocks with strange writings upon them were scattered about the floor with various dolls. A small bed with rails rested on one side and a rocking chair on the other. In it, sat a young woman with long, blonde hair that cascaded down to her lower back. She wore a soft pink robe and held a little girl comfortingly in her arms. The girl couldn't have been more than two summers in age, yet Trimenius recognized her mother's dazzling blue eyes.

The woman was quietly reading something to her daughter when she ceased her rocking and turned her eyes toward the intruder. She held the Lord's gaze for a time, then called out to the side. "Gretla?"

Another younger lady with dark hair quickly entered from a side door. "Did you need something, my Lady?"

"Would you take Pharaura out for a quick walk? I have a matter to attend to that will require all my focus."

"Of course, my Lady." She gently stepped forward and took the child from her arms. The girl went willingly. Yet just before they departed the room, Pharaura appeared to turn her tiny eyes toward Trimenius and watch him with curious intent.

After a few more moments, the woman rose from her chair

and turned toward Trimenius. "I was beginning to think you wouldn't come."

The Lord bowed deeply to her. "Forgive me, my Lady. I sought you out as soon as it happened." He licked his lips nervously. It was only the second time he had stood before her. "The path to your door has changed."

"Think nothing of it. Now, Elrenar, what do you have to report?"

He took another step forward. "Events are unfolding quickly. The sky tore open just as the Order predicted."

"Was that ever in doubt?"

"No, my Lady." Trimenius nearly fumbled over the words. "I only meant…"

"Be at ease, Elrenar." Her eyes seemed to pierce right through him. "I now have another task for you. One that is vital to the next stage of the Great Awakening."

"I serve at the pleasure of the Order. Always."

"Excellent." The woman folded her arms. "We have kept something hidden deep within the Guardian's Keep for many hundreds of years. It was meant for you alone to find. This is your most important task yet."

"How will I know it?"

She gave him a chiding smirk. "Seek the mark, of course."

"Seek the mark," he repeated unnecessarily. "Then what?"

"The next part will not be so easy, as we have placed wards against anyone who does not speak the proper phrase, nor complete the necessary ritual. As such, I would advise you listen with the utmost care. There will not be a second chance."

He puffed out his chest and gave her a single quick nod. "I'm ready, my Lady."

"Then let it begin."

It didn't take long for Draxian and Arros to return to the tavern. Both men had walked in silence, contemplating everything they had heard from Trimenius – but more than that, they could feel unseen eyes upon them the entire way. With a simple glance, the two lifelong friends decided it was best not to speak of certain things in public.

T'mara was waiting impatiently at the entrance to the tavern with Arros' pack over a shoulder, biting her thumbnail nervously. An expression of great relief swept over her face as they emerged from the crowded streets and walked casually up to her.

"Bloody Abyss! You had me worried."

Arros gave T'mara an amused grin. "I didn't realize you cared."

"Not you," the Huntress shot back. "I meant Draxian." She reached out and touched his arm. "What happened? You weren't gone as long as I would have expected."

The young Prince snatched his pack from T'mara, then began digging through the contents while Draxian answered. "He just wanted to meet the new nobles visiting the city."

"That's it?"

He shrugged at her. "Were we to expect a parade in our honor?"

"What's a parade?"

"It's…"

"Not important," Arros finished for him. "Did you go through my pack?"

T'mara appeared genuinely surprised by the accusation. "No. Why would I care about your dirty laundry?"

"Clever." He narrowed his eyes. "Well?"

T'mara watched him for a time, then finally rolled her eyes. "What did you expect? I didn't want to get caught with contraband in the Guardian's Keep." She pursed her lips. "Besides, I have no idea what any of those… things, are used for."

Draxian's eyes narrowed suspiciously. "Wait. What did you bring with you?" He grabbed for the pack, but Arros jerked it back from his reach.

"Nothing important. Just a few comforts from home."

"That better include some coins to trade with."

The Prince gave him a wry smirk. "Of course." He began reaching inside the leather flap.

"Near the bottom, in a black purse on the right," T'mara coached from his side.

Arros stopped momentarily, then gave her an exasperated sigh. "I suppose we should just be grateful you didn't help yourself to anything." He withdrew a bulging fist-sized pouch and tested the weight. After a couple shakes of the purse, his head swiveled toward T'mara in accusation.

"What?" she said defensively. "I only took a couple silver pieces. Someone had to pay for the meal. Besides..." The Huntress leaned in closer to Arros and dropped her voice to a whisper. "You have enough gold and silver in there to purchase your own caravan ten times over."

Draxian drew his neck back in surprise. "How much did you bring?"

"Fifty crowns."

"Oh. That's not much."

T'mara's eyebrows arched high. "Not much?" She circled her arms around both of theirs, then began leading the men back into the tavern. "I've only held a single gold piece like those once in my lifetime. It was ancient and worn but considered priceless."

Draxian was immediately confused. "You don't have gold here?"

"Of course we do. It's just not that pure, or common." They continued back toward the table. "Now, are you going to tell me why those soldiers from Dellahara wanted to speak with you?"

They reached the worn wooden table and Draxian pulled out a rickety chair for T'mara, allowing her to sit. "They didn't ask us any questions. Just escorted me and Arros to visit with Lord Trimenius."

T'mara waited until both men were seated, then leaned over the table and lowered her voice. "They wore the insignia of Empress Dellahara's elite guard."

"And?"

"And? They were the Empress' *elite guard*." Draxian and Arros exchanged puzzled looks, then turned back to T'mara. She huffed a laugh at them. "I swear by the Lord of Destruction, you two will be dead by night's end without me to keep you from doing something foolhardy."

Arros frowned. "Who's the Lord of Destruction?"

She shot him a dark glare. "Now you're just being insulting."

THE CHROMATIC GUARD

"This grain looks to be tainted."

Camoranthus stepped up to the cart to peek at the grain spilling from the torn burlap sack. "Tainted my arse! This is prime quality barley."

"Then why is it dark?"

He waved the inspector off. "A few of the bags just got damp in the red storm. It's nothing to be concerned with."

"Wet grain is the main cause of the white taint. Any *damp* bags will need to be confiscated." The burly older man in the black leather jerkin waved several guards forward. They immediately went to work sorting through the sacks.

"Wait!" Cam said. "Allow me to sell them locally. If they are used right away, any possible taint should never appear."

Chief Inspector Gronrig reached up and rubbed at the scruff of his chin. "We'll let you donate the bags to the local taverns or inns, if you warn them to use it right away, or allow the grain to dry properly in the open air. You'll need to provide a dry sack to us as well, for quality assurance."

Cam already knew from past encounters that Gronrig had a twisted sense of moral virtue that would not allow him to take a bribe but taking goods under the guise of protecting society was another matter. The Chief Inspector's only job was to hold the quality of goods traded between Phondari and Annis to the highest standards. Should any spoiled food get through and accidentally poison the city stock, his neck would be the first to stretch in a public execution.

"Aye," the caravan master concurred. "I agree to your terms." At the very least, Cam believed his perceived generosity would earn him a hot meal and a free place to stay for the night. He knew all of the tavern owners well.

Gronrig pointed toward the end cart which carried several small crates. "What's in there?"

"It's just my own private reserve of honey wine."

He reached over and placed a meaty hand on Cam's shoulder, then gave him a sinister grin. "Well, we should probably check to make sure the seals on those bottles are tight. What do you say, Cam?"

The caravan master forced a smile, while trying to ignore the Inspector's rank breath. "I assure you they've been sealed properly with cork and wax."

"Just like you assured me the barley was passable?" He pointed toward the crates. "Let's just open a few bottles to be certain."

"That won't be necessary," a woman's voice commanded.

Cam and the Chief Inspector turned to see three Chromatic Warriors approaching. Each wore the standard of Dellahara's elite. Furthermore, the leader had a red sash over her left shoulder to indicate her rank as the Empress' second.

The inspector bowed clumsily to her. "Commander Rellan. It's an honor to once again have you visit our humble way station."

"Did I hear correctly? Were you trying to force this merchant into handing over sealed goods?"

"Well... I..." he sputtered.

She strode up regally and stopped within a pace of him, all while resting a hand lightly over the jeweled pommel of the razor-sharp sword at her side. "Because the Dellaharan Accords for the Northern Empires clearly state that no merchant goods shall be seized or destroyed without warrant, or just cause, unless properly compensated per standard guild rates."

Cam carefully stifled a grin as Chief Inspector Gronrig licked his lips nervously. "We were just looking, is all. Of course, I would never exceed my authority."

The commander nodded to one of the other women in full armor, who immediately walked over and then knelt to examine the sacks of grain thrown to the dirt by the city guard. "Everything looks in order to me, Commander."

She turned back to Gronrig. "It appears you've just purchased eleven bags of barley, Chief Inspector. Enjoy."

He narrowed his eyes at Cam, then reluctantly bowed his head to the commander. "As you wish. My mistake."

As the Inspector turned to leave, Commander Rellan called to his back. "If you're thinking about any further harassment of this merchant, I will inform Lord Trimenius that any future compensations must come directly from your personal wages. And should you not possess enough, your blood will suffice."

That last proclamation was enough to cause him to stumble slightly. The five city guards quickly abandoned their posts and exited with him, as none wished to be left behind with the Chromatic Guard.

Cam turned and bowed to the commander. "Mistress. I'm profoundly grateful for your intervention."

"We always remember our close friends, Camoranthus." She reached behind her toward one of the other Chromatic Guards. The small leather pouch placed in the commander's awaiting palm clinked with the tell-tale sound of coins. He couldn't help but notice that the same warrior had Arros' cloak tucked beneath her arm. "Your information was quite valuable." Commander Rellan passed the purse over to him. "The Empress is most pleased with you."

He bowed graciously. "I'm ever at the service of Dellahara, Mistress."

"It warms me to hear you say this. We have another task for you – one that will reward you far greater than what you just received."

Arros stared deeply into the flagon of dark liquid. "What did you call this again?"

"Fire root ale."

He sniffed deeply. "Smells a bit spicy."

T'mara shrugged. "It's what the men around here drink. But if you believe it's too strong for your palette…"

The young Prince glanced around at the other patrons. "No one else ordered it."

"I'll drink it," Draxian finally interrupted. Snatching the wooden mug from Arros, he quaffed several gulps of the black substance. After slamming it down to the table, he grinned back toward Arros. "Smooth," he choked out, then broke into a stifled fit of coughing. It wasn't so much the strong taste of alcohol that gripped him, but the burning spice that was used in creating the toxic concoction. Furthermore, the tongue-searing effects continued to worsen by the moment.

"Smooth, huh?" Arros taunted. "I'll take your word for it."

By that point in time, Draxian could only lift a hand and nod his submission.

T'mara nudged the muscular man playfully. "It's an acquired taste." She then turned back toward Arros. "Did Lord Trimenius have anything to say about ever meeting your fathers?"

Arros looked at her with one eyebrow arched. "Heard that part of our conversation, too?"

"Yes," she replied with a smile. "In truth, I can see other's words by watching their lips. I only got part of the conversation. But you two really should be more careful if you don't want others listening in."

The Prince sighed with resignation. "No one has seen them for many years. Although we may have a place to start."

"You're welcome to come with the caravan to Phondari, if it helps."

Arros shook his head while withdrawing a folded piece of paper from his pocket. T'mara lifted the candle from the center of the table and set it to one side. This allowed him to spread the map between the three of them. "We plan on traveling to a place called Orakh."

"What?" She nearly shouted the word as her eyes widened, then quickly dropped her voice to speak in hushed tones. "Are you mad? No one can survive through the Ebon Wastes to reach it." T'mara gave Arros a serious glare. "The only thing you will find there is your imminent death – and that's assuming you survive the distant journey."

Draxian cleared his throat, finally able to speak. "What's in the Ebon Waste?"

It was right at that moment when Cam stepped up to the table to join their group. "The Ebon Waste?" He glanced at their map, then turned toward Draxian. "I'm surprised you haven't heard of it in your travels. The Ebon Waste is a cursed region surrounding Orakh for many leagues. Everything in that place is dead. The ground has turned to ash, and any living creature foolish enough to venture within will slowly wither and rot. No one has ever returned."

"Sounds wonderful," Draxian quipped. "Surely much of what you heard has been exaggerated."

"I don't believe so," T'mara quickly disagreed. "My father once saw the black waste in his travels. He told me that it felt as if death itself had claimed the land."

"There has to be a way through," Arros argued. He then turned to his lifelong friend. "Remember the haunted tales we heard of the Caldonian Marshes back home?"

"Of course."

"Well, they said similar things about it. Yet our fathers crossed it not once, but twice."

"These are not idle rumors." Cam moved around the table to sit in the last remaining chair. "If you try to venture beyond it, you *will* die."

Draxian noticed the slight smirk that touched Arros' lips. Cam's statement was an insult to his ability. The young Prince disliked being told of his limitations and would do everything in his power to prove the caravan master wrong.

"Don't worry about us," the Prince grinned, accepting the unspoken challenge. "We'll find a way through."

Giving him a short chuckle of disbelief, Cam shrugged his shoulders and leaned back in his chair, his greying beard resting on his chest. "Very well. Each man has the right to die as he chooses. As for me and T'mara, we have our own business to attend to."

Arros pressed his lips together and nodded politely. "We appreciate you bringing us this far."

"Wait," T'mara interrupted. "We can't just send them into the badlands without a guide. If they would have me, I would like to join them on this journey. At least as far as Breck," she added, looking to Cam for his blessing.

His jaws clenched at her request, yet he maintained his composure. "You already have a contract with me. What lost treasures do you believe can be found in Orakh that's worth risking your life for?"

Arros laced his fingers together and leaned over the map. "We were told of a library within that contains a wealth of knowledge. We believe our fathers went in search of this as well."

Cam looked at them in disbelief. "What moron filled your head with such nonsense? The Infinite Library of Orakh is a myth."

Arros tapped his finger on the map. "Then why would Lord Trimenius mention it?"

"Perhaps he said it in jest or didn't believe you would truly undertake an impossible quest." Chuckling to himself, the caravan master rose from the table. "Go chase your fables if you wish, but T'mara and I will not be going. Of course, if you are willing to give up this foolish quest, you're both welcome to join our caravan headed to Phondari tomorrow."

Draxian sighed heavily. "The offer is appreciated, but Arros is right, this is something we *must* do."

"That's your choice." He nodded to T'mara. "We should get back to the caravan and check over the wagons. They took quite a beating from the storm."

"No, Cam, I'm not going with you," the Huntress returned with steadfast resolve. "If they have any chance at making it through the badlands, they'll need a scout. It's the right thing to do."

"You don't owe these men anything. We already saved their lives once, is that not enough?" He pointed in the general direction of the caravan. "I need someone I trust to lead my caravan to Phondari while I take care of some business here at the keep. These fools can hire another guide if they wish."

T'mara rubbed at the mark on her forearm as she listened to her friend and mentor lay out his ultimatum. "My mind is set,

Cam. I will find you when I'm done. I promise."

Cam glared at T'mara for a long time before speaking. "I've learned long ago not to waste my efforts on reversing your path once it's set," he spoke quietly. "If you wish to travel toward your doom, who am I to prevent it?"

"Are you sure about this?" Draxian asked her, ignoring the merchant's comment.

"For certain," she assured him. "I can lead you safely to the border of the Ebon Waste." T'mara gave him a forced smile. "After that, I can't promise anything."

"Excellent," Draxian exclaimed with genuine delight. "We'd love to have you along as a guide."

"We still need to discuss your pay for not finishing the journey to Phondari," Cam promised. "Meet me in the morning." He nodded politely to Draxian and Arros. "Please watch out for her. T'mara is like family to me."

Draxian dipped his head slightly. "You have my vow."

The caravan master turned on his heels and crossed over to speak quietly with a man behind the counter, which Draxian assumed was the owner. After Cam was safely out of hearing range, T'mara watched the both of them curiously. "You truly believe your fathers went to Orakh?"

Taking an uneasy breath, Draxian stared into her emerald blue eyes. "There's no way to be certain of anything, and yet we still need to try. It's all we have."

Giving him an encouraging smile, T'mara reached across the table and placed a hand over his. "If anyone can do it, I believe you will find a way."

"You have my eternal gratitude."

Arros watched the two with a slight grin of amusement, then started to rise. "I'll secure three beds for the night and grab another bottle of mead." He halted in place, then leaned back toward Draxian. "Unless two beds would suffice?"

"Well," T'mara mocked playfully, "I know how precious few coins you brought along. Would be a shame to waste what little you have on such a trivial matter."

Draxian's face flushed from her teasing. "Three beds are fine."

THE AWAKENING

Lord Trimenius stepped over several small puddles and had to stop occasionally to inspect the different passages. Water dripping from the ceiling hissed in the flames of his torch and splashed in the dark pools at his feet as he continued forward.

A few times he was forced to backtrack to another tunnel. It had been a long time since he had visited the labyrinth of corridors that once held vast amounts of goods confiscated from inspections or taken from those found with the gift of magic. It was likely to be filled again, based on the Emperor's increased interest in the gifted.

He followed the twisting maze of tunnels far beneath the keep, moving with haste until finding the correct passage. Just as the Lady of the Order had promised, a circle was carved on the right support column next to the wall. Farther down, on the opposite side, another larger circle could be seen. Closing one eye, Trimenius repositioned himself so the two circles appeared to join in the middle. "Infinity," he breathed.

The tiny space between the symbols appeared to point farther down the hallway on the left. With his heart pounding in his chest, Trimenius stepped over to the wall and held his torch up to inspect the stone. He saw nothing other than thick rock. Closing his eyes, the old mage reached within himself and called forth the magic from the Elemental Realm of Fire. Opening his eyes, he lifted his open palm. A small blue flame born of magic flickered, illuminating the wall. Another circle was revealed, this one containing an inverted triangle within.

He took a deep breath. "Blades of fury guide my path to vengeance. For only through the cleansing fires of destruction, shall healing come to the land."

With a shimmer, a square section of stone no more than a pace's width disappeared. It revealed a cavity containing a round medallion with an ancient symbol of unknown origin. Behind it was a clear, palm-sized gemstone. Carefully setting the torch to one side, he lifted the tokens from their tomb with trembling hands. The moment the flame within his hand was released, the small vault disappeared.

Trimenius had no real understanding of what the medallion represented, yet it had been hidden by the Order around the time the Guardian's Keep was first built – nearly one-thousand years ago. Such careful planning had been set into motion and passed down for millennia – and the Lord of the Guardian's Keep was not about to fail the trust instilled within him.

He placed the crystal in his side pocket, then continued down the corridor where it abruptly ended. As he lifted the medallion towards the wall, a mirrored impression of it instantly appeared within the stone. Trimenius pressed the medallion to the glyph.

The sound of grating stone on stone was heard as the wall pulled backwards, revealing a small chamber behind it.

Torches on either side sparked to life as he entered the confined room. The focal point of the far wall was a small, white marble dais holding a black marble pedestal at its center. Carved into the white marble was the figure of a gold dragon twisted about a large triangle. A ring of fire encircled the image and flames poured from the beast's mouth. Upon the small shelf, atop the black pedestal, rested an exquisite knife.

Trimenius kneeled before the stone image. Reaching out, he carefully swapped the medallion for the knife, resting it gently on the pedestal. He dug into his pocket withdrawing the large gemstone. As expected, it fit perfectly into an impression within the carved triangle. The door behind him slid closed, sealing the chamber. Everything was prepared. Trimenius held his arms out wide and tilted his head back as he began to speak the words that had been burned into his memory.

"Ancient powers of the forgotten age, your servant compels you to heed my call." The crystal lit up with a silvery light, casting a warm radiance upon him. "Lord of Shadows, the gathering storm approaches. The sky has been torn and the Travelers walk among us. May their deaths mark a new age for the Realm of Kohr. Whether through darkness or light, let their blood spill true."

Grasping the decorative knife tight, Trimenius cut a small incision into the fleshy part of his palm. He reached out and drizzled blood from the seeping wound over the medallion. To his eyes, the metal seemed to drink the blood insatiably. When it appeared as if it could no longer take any more, Trimenius reached out and lifted the medallion. Something was different. The metal felt brittle and light.

There was only one more step to complete the rite. He placed both hands around the medallion and focused his will on the

Spirit Realm. "What was lost, be found. What was forgotten, be remembered. I bid you awaken."

With little effort, Lord Trimenius snapped the medallion in half. A silver mist glittered around the broken remnants for a single moment, then quickly dissipated. And just as the magic in the air faded, so too did the torches.

Kyreena gasped as a wave of energy surged through her. Her flesh felt warm and tingled from the unexpected assault. Glancing around at her surroundings, it felt as though she had just awakened from a bad dream, leaving her with a pounding headache. Kyreena's mind was clouded, leaving little memory of how she had got here. Only the cold iron bars of the large, covered wagon felt familiar. Kyreena thought it was odd that all the other dozen or so captives were women of similar age and build. Only the color of their hair and eyes varied slightly. It was evident their captors were quite particular.

"Kyreena." The soft voice from her side captured her attention. A woman of maybe twenty-seven to twenty-eight summers touched her arm lightly while whispering to her, "Are you well?"

Through the haze that was her memory, a name came forth. "Lorisa?"

The woman positioned herself before Kyreena and clutched her shoulders tightly, staring into her eyes with a concerned look. "Do you know where you are?"

Her gaze drifted to the tarp that blocked her view beyond the bars. "No." Shadowy images were slowly beginning to take form in her mind. "Do you?"

"We're somewhere in the middle of the badlands. We left the main road several days back."

Kyreena nodded carefully as she tried to make sense of her surroundings. "How long have I been here?"

"You truly must have hit your head when you were captured." Lorisa shook her head. "It's been at least twenty days since I was purchased, and you were already here when they placed me in this cage."

She forced a smile. "Thank you for looking out for me."

"If we don't help each other, then who will?"

Kyreena took in the faces that watched her from around the cage. They each shared the same vacant expression of acceptance. Whatever fate awaited them, Kyreena knew she had to find a way to escape her captors. Something important needed to be done, and she cursed her own memory for not understanding what that was.

It was later that day when the cart stopped bouncing and shaking over the rough road and the journey began to feel much smoother. Peeking through cracks in the tarp, Kyreena spotted several broken pillars dotting the landscape. They were rolling through ruins of some sort. Perhaps it was an abandoned military fortress or temple to an old god, she mused.

The sound of chisels on rock and rolling carts could be heard nearby. Rock dust hung thick in the air, filtering into the cage. It smelled like what she imagined a quarry would smell like.

The wagon finally came to a halt. The rear tarp was pulled back, spilling in the light of the day and a cloud of dust. Slaves, both men and women, swung pickaxes or pushed hand carts full of rock and ore. Armed guards kept the captives moving and punished those who stopped to rest with brutal beatings.

Four guards in dirty tunics appeared before them. She observed no crests or insignias upon the men. Several of the women cowered toward the back, or held each other tightly, fear evident on their faces. Lorisa slipped her hand into Kyreena's and laced her fingers.

"Final stop, slaves." The man in the lead lifted a key and placed it into the iron padlock. He twisted it until the loop pulled free from the chains circling the door. "Everyone out." When no one moved, he became more forceful. "Now!" The caravan guard reached inside and grabbed the ankle of the nearest woman and jerked her out of the cage. Frightened, the captive shrieked as she fell to the ground, hitting the hard-packed dirt flat on her back to the sadistic laughter of the three other men. "And that's what will happen…"

He never finished his threat. From nowhere, a blade sliced through the air and took the man's head from his body. The three men jumped back, then bowed low as a large man stepped into view. "Anyone else feel an urgent need to damage my property?" The men shook their heads vigorously. "Wise decision." The man looked impossibly strong with a chest like an ox and twisted muscles over a tall frame. He wore a sword on each hip and a loose black uniform with no insignia, like his men. "Clean up this shite," he commanded to the others. They quickly rushed forward to remove the head and body of their fallen companion, while the muscular leader held out a hand to Kyreena. "This way, please."

Not wishing to offend the large brute, Kyreena placed her fingers in his to be assisted gently from the cage. The moment she touched his cold skin, a feeling of dread swept over her. There was something about his essence that felt less than human and creeped her flesh to the bone. Despite his polite and calm exterior, the man was anything but chivalrous or kind.

Lorisa was next to exit, followed quickly by the others. Kyreena took in her surroundings. The caravan was surrounded by high plateaus of orange and grey rock, granting only two paths for an escape. A small fortress was carved into the side of the nearby cliff face, and the doorway appeared to have been hacked open with an axe. Ruins of a large, black-ore structure were scattered in a wide circle, as if a titanic blacksmith's hammer had fallen from the sky and smashed it to pieces. It appeared a new, smaller tower had been constructed within it by salvaging some of the remains.

The muscular man led them toward the opening in the cliff face, where another soldier of equal girth and height awaited them. He looked over Kyreena and the women as if studying cattle ready for auction. Finally, he nodded his approval and motioned for the slaves to follow.

Inside, they were led down a dark stairway. Kyreena glanced at the smooth wall beside her, then slowly reached out to feel it. A memory of a young man flashed to the surface for an instant, then was gone. He was someone she once deeply cared for, yet she could not remember his name. The gentle touch of a hand on her back reminded Kyreena to keep moving. She knew without looking that her friend, Lorisa, had brought her attention back to the present. The thirteen women shuffled down the stairs and into a large hall. At one end was a great archway made from the same black ore she had seen above. Beneath it, four more large, heavily muscled men were sliding a stone sarcophagus toward the center of the chamber. It was made of polished black marble with gold inlaid around the circumference of the lid.

Kyreena and the other women were forced to kneel in a line before the dark stone box. The large brute who helped her from the wagon stepped before the women and glowered down at them. "No matter what happens, don't move. Fail to do exactly as told and your head will be parted from your bodies. Understood?"

Several of the captives broke down in tears, but Kyreena was too frightened to do anything more than nod. As she fought against the fear that gripped her tightly, it became difficult to breathe. The powerful figure turned and reached over to the sarcophagus. He took hold of an embossed golden standard of two swords crossed behind a sun, then twisted it to the right. He stepped back, then waited.

Kyreena trembled from the strange feeling sweeping throughout her body. Some form of dark, ancient magic was awakening. There was a moment of silence before the scream from one of the captive women shattered the quiet. The shadows around the marble box had begun to move, sprouting dark tendrils from a rising black mist. The first reached out for the screaming woman, then more appeared and began lightly caressing Lorisa and a woman next to her. Each of the captives whimpered in terror. Kyreena waited for her turn, yet it never came. It was as if she held no interest to the dark abomination – a blessing for which she quietly thanked whatever divine hand had intervened on her behalf. Finally, all the tendrils withdrew except for one. The woman to the left of Kyreena was abruptly enveloped by the dark tendril. Her scream was so chilling, it was as though it had breached the barrier between the Abyss and Kohr.

The large men stood to the side, unmoved by the horrific display. As the young woman wailed in agony and thrashed about, her skin quickly withered, darkened, and decayed, as muscles shrunk to the bone. Only moments after her screams ended, the withered body of the unfortunate slave crashed to the stone floor in a spray of dust. Kyreena felt the woman's life energy being absorbed into the mist, then sucked back toward the sarcophagus. The dark rite was over as quickly as it had begun, leaving nothing but a dried-out husk of shattered bones with untouched blonde hair. Kyreena gasped at the shocking scene, clenching her teeth to stifle a whimper of despair.

As the last of the life-draining tendrils vanished within the stone box, the leader of the large men motioned toward the captives. "Take them to be fitted with irons and put to work on the tower. We have no more use for them here."

"Understood." The massive soldier turned to the women, then gestured toward the stairs. As expected, the remaining slaves were all too eager to distance themselves from the chamber where they had witnessed the dark ritual.

Kyreena was the last of the women to be herded toward the stairs. She glanced back just as the men removed the lid to the sarcophagus and peered within. A feminine hand reached up and took the leader's hand, allowing him to pull her into view. To Kyreena's horror, she wore the face of the captive who had perished.

"Welcome back, my Lady. You've been asleep for quite some time."

THE JOURNEY BEGINS

Dark shapes darted silently through the swirling smoke amid giant pillars that rose into the night. Armed only with his hands, Draxian stepped cautiously through the marbled hall, searching carefully between the columns. His footsteps echoed hollowly through the empty chamber. The young lord had no memory of how he got there – only that a foreboding sensation of dread occupied his thoughts.

Something drew him forward, calling from the darkness in a melodic voice that was too irresistible to ignore. The young lord approached a marble altar made of stone so dark it appeared to be a relic torn from the Abyss. From its depths, writhing tendrils of shadow shot forth. Draxian's heart quickened as the cold tentacles enveloped his entire body, cutting off all light. In an instant, the breath was ripped from his lungs and his vision spun in dizzying circles. In the next, it was over.

Draxian sharply sucked in a gasp of fresh air as he found himself standing on a mountainside trail, peering down a steep slope that ended in a sheer cliff ten paces from his boots. The cold, crenellated walls of an ancient temple could be seen in the distance. Its squat form was built into the side of the mountain. The foreboding entrance reminded Draxian of the gaping maw of a dragon, like the one that chased them here, beckoning him to be devoured whole.

Draxian noticed a shadowy fog swirling about his legs, as though it were alive. Not wishing to remain any longer than necessary, he waded through the crawling mist, following the path up the mountain.

The faint sounds of a furious sword fight could be heard nearby. Approaching slowly, the echoing of pounding blades became more intense as the distance narrowed. Upon rounding a large boulder, Draxian finally located the two combatants.

A sense of awe swept over him as he watched the dueling swordsmen. Never before had he seen such speed and grace demonstrated. One stood with his back to him, dressed in gleaming chainmail with a scarlet cloak about his shoulders. He fought with a curved blade in each hand. However, it was the other warrior who caught his interest. His stature was surreal, with thick shadows clinging to him, creating an almost wraith-like appearance. Draxian couldn't make out any details, but the figure's tall, powerful form radiated a dark energy.

Without warning, a blade pierced through the silvery chainmail of the smaller man. Blood gushed forth from the wound as the sword was pulled free. The man's choking cries chilled him to the bone as the warrior fell to the ground.

Draxian was certain he knew the man from somewhere, yet his memory was still fragmented. Kneeling to inspect the familiar face before him, the fog of his mind began to clear with a startling revelation. It was Arros. His friend choked on pink froth spewing from his mouth, bloodied fingers extending toward the young lord.

Draxian gripped his hand tightly. "I'm here, my friend,"

The prince's jaw worked, as if trying desperately to warn him of something – yet the words wouldn't form. Moments later, Arros released his grip when his body relaxed, and his stare grew vacant. Anger and despair coursed through Draxian's veins as he searched around him for the degenerate who had murdered the Crown Prince of Ellandor. Reaching over, he quickly snatched the two swords that once belonged to his fallen companion. Draxian bounded to his feet to search desperately for the fiend. Thunder echoed through the mountains, carrying a warning that repeated over and over within his mind.

"You're next."

Draxian startled awake to an incessant pounding at his door. He recognized Arros' voice calling out his name. For once, hearing the prince's harassing bellow was a genuine relief. Draxian pulled himself groggily to his feet, the nightmare still haunting him as he shook the images from his head. It had felt so real.

"Drax!"

"Just a moment," the young lord called back, as he began collecting his newly purchased supplies about the tiny room. Draxian had washed up and packed the night before to allow them to leave at first light. As such, it only took the large man a moment to slip on his boots and gather his traveling pack. The new brown leather satchel had the smell of freshly tanned and oiled hide.

Lifting the heavy iron latch securing the door, Arros greeted him with an expression of concern. "Is everything well? You're normally a light sleeper."

"Fine," Draxian lied, putting the nightmare to the back of his mind. "I didn't sleep well is all."

Arros furrowed his eyebrows, indicating he knew there was more to the story – yet graciously refrained from pressing the issue. Following close behind the prince, Draxian was led through the common room and outside the inn. They crossed the road toward the stables to retrieve the two fat mounts Arros had purchased for them. The older stableman had already secured the saddles on their reptilian steeds, and the bags on the gek were laden with provisions and water. T'mara was just finishing preparing her own mount, a sleek and powerful taark with a distinguishing red spot under each eye. Arros had been disappointed to learn that taark were a rare breed, and none were available for purchase throughout the entire town.

"It's about time you got around," T'mara admonished with a chiding grin. "We'd best head out before it gets too late in the morning. Night travel in the badlands is extremely risky."

"Did you settle your affairs with the caravan master?" Draxian asked.

"Cam and I spoke just a few moments ago," she answered with a hint of regret. "I hate that I was forced to break an agreement. But more than that, Cam was always there for me – especially when my mood was at its lowest."

Draxian glanced at the solidly packed dirt floor, then back to her. "It's not too late to rejoin him if you're having doubts."

Her eyes immediately shot to his. "Not at all. I will make it up to him when next we meet." T'mara took her taark by the reigns, then began leading it from the stables. "I truly am looking forward to this journey. It's my first escort contract where I get to take the lead."

"Contract?" He turned his gaze toward Arros.

"And she doesn't come cheap, either."

T'mara nudged the prince playfully while passing. "In afterthought, I probably should not have discussed the true value of those forty gold coins."

"Forty-nine after purchasing everything we needed," Arros corrected.

T'mara halted her mount and gave a playful smirk. "Are you certain? I was sure there were only forty by my count." Arros scowled then started to reach inside his pack when she called over to him. "Just teasing."

"Hilarious." The prince paused for an indecisive moment, then continued searching for his coin purse anyhow. After a quick inventory, he nodded to himself and glanced up to meet Draxian's gaze. "What?"

"Nothing," he responded with a grin.

Arros narrowed his eyes at the large man, then began leading his gek after T'mara. They continued down the main road toward the massive gate. It was still quite early, and as a result, most of the merchant stands were empty and small shops were shuttered. However, a few wagons could be seen making their daily stops at the taverns. In principle, the ancient town was like any other city back on Ellandor – the people did whatever was necessary to thrive.

The new morning air filled his nose with the scents of frying salted meats and poached eggs. Nearby, glistening dew covered the tiny shoots of weeds that grew along the walls of the buildings. A small girl in dirty rags watched Draxian pass with silent curiosity while clutching a crudely stitched doll. Despite giving her a warm smile with a friendly nod, the child continued to stare, unblinking. The lord sighed heavily at the appalling living conditions and widespread poverty he observed with every corner they passed. He hoped that other towns fared better. If not, it meant that Kohr was truly a miserable world with little hope of recovery.

A line of citizens had already formed at the tall gates where they had entered the previous night. Numerous farmers and their workers walked before them, preparing to tend the fields outside the walls. Their large gek pulled the carts containing their tools to plow and work the harsh soil.

"Does no one remain near their fields?"

Glancing over at Draxian, T'mara shook her head. "The people are forced to live inside where they have protection from the storms. It would be too dangerous for them to stay outside the walls at night."

"Are the red storms common?"

T'mara nodded vehemently. "I have seen many that have lasted for days. Most dwellings caught in a storm like that would be destroyed without a black obelisk nearby. Furthermore, the storm ward ore used to make them is rare, and mostly needed to protect the roads and cities. The large risk is not worth the small reward. As such, all take up residence within the city."

Draxian found it difficult to imagine how it would have been growing up in constant fear of the fierce red clouds and the terrible storms they brought. It was difficult enough to accept he and Arros were stranded on another world, with no obvious way to return home. No doubt the Queen and High Council were scouring the land for any evidence to solve the mystery of their disappearance. He truly hoped someone had survived to tell their story. The prince's original plan had entailed leaving Draxian behind to tell of Arros' quest and to reopen the portal home. Nothing had gone as expected.

As they slowly exited the Guardian's Keep, Draxian urged his mount to move alongside T'mara's. "Has your land always been so harsh?"

"For as long as anyone can remember."

The young lord tilted his head. "No. I mean, was there ever a time when your people lived in peace, or without fear of storms and the Undying?"

"Did you not have scholars back home to discuss such matters?"

"Indulge me."

T'mara shrugged a single shoulder. "It was said that before the time of the Thousand Years of Darkness, the land was beautiful and filled with endless game to hunt. There was peace between the people, and those who possessed magic within their blood were considered commonplace."

"What happened?"

"The Fallen One happened." She said it so matter-of-factly that Draxian decided not to press her further. If their storms back home became as terrible as the ones on Kohr, countless lives would be lost. The people of Ellandor would not have access to the storm ward ore that she described. More specifically, he worried about his family and the lands they governed. His people would depend on the young lord's protection and guidance through such adversity. It was his duty to find a way back to them. If Orakh truly contained the forgotten knowledge of previous ages, there was a remote chance it would also have information on hidden gateways to escape Kohr. Draxian knew for certain that his ancestors had visited it many times before – and even lived among its people. It was also possible that their fathers had been looking for this same knowledge. Although, if they truly had found it, the young lord surmised his father should have returned home long before now.

He wasn't certain if his sense of foreboding was his own apprehension over Lord Trimenius' warning, or the sickness within the land itself. Yet, he could not shed the feeling that something sinister was waiting for them. They needed to remain vigilant.

Camoranthus drew his hood low as he watched T'mara ride from the city alongside the two men. His disguise had helped him get close to their small group without being noticed. T'mara's fascination with Draxian bothered him greatly. Cam trusted no one, especially nobles, around the woman he loved. He had eliminated many of the lustful men who had tried to take advantage of her in the past. Draxian would be no different. She was oblivious to his aid, of course, never knowing the many favors he performed for her from the shadows.

Drawing his ratty cloak tighter about himself, he watched them move off the main road toward the southern badlands. His mercenaries had agreed to escort the caravan on its way to Phondari in his place to sell their wares. Cam had promised them all T'mara's and his share of the profits for completing the last leg of their journey without the two Hunters to protect the caravan. The coins Commander Rellan had given him for reporting the whereabouts of the noblemen were more than enough to make up for the loss, and then some.

The two strangers were somehow important to the Empress of Dragons, and Cam was an opportunist. Commander Rellan's request did not, however, include keeping the two nobles alive. If one of them happened to die it was no concern of his. If just one continued to breathe, he could continue to report their whereabouts and get paid handsomely.

Strolling casually among the farmers and their carts, Cam waited until they had descended to the lower badlands and were nothing more than dots on the horizon. Losing sight of his quarry was of no consequence to a Chosen Hunter, such as he. The distance between them was to make certain T'mara did not spot his approach. Cam was considered one of the best, and yet T'mara was born to the wastes, and lived among the savages known as the Shadiere. They claimed to be the True Hunters of the land, and their deep connection to it was no wild boast. However, they were clannish and wary of outsiders – only hunting the shadow creatures that followed the storms.

His attention was suddenly drawn to the sound of heavy boots approaching from behind. Cam smelled a familiar scent as the man neared. He would recognize the foul breath of Chief Inspector Gronrig anywhere.

"Stop there, citizen. I don't recall seeing you pass through the check point."

The Hunter had tolerated the inspector's abuse for years. Each time the man took things from him it chipped away at his patience. Cam tolerated it so he would have the freedom to trade between the three kingdoms. It would ruin his business if he were to kill an inspector at the keep.

"By the authority of Lord Trimenius, we need to inspect your belongings before you leave the Guardian's Keep to ensure there is no contraband," Gronrig pressed. When Cam continued to ignore him, the inspector grabbed him by his bicep to stop him.

The Hunter's patience had finally expired. Palming a thin blade that had been hidden in the silver bracelet on his wrist, its point not much broader than a needle, he drove it into Gronrig's opposing arm as he was spun about and gripped tight. The black poison on the blade worked quickly, preventing the man from calling out for aid.

Cam stared hard into Gronrig's pained eyes. "You shall steal from me no more." It gave him deep satisfaction when the inspector finally appeared to recognize him through the pain. Gronrig stood frozen long enough for the Hunter to walk into the crowd before collapsing face first into the dirt. Cam knew the poison brought about a painful, but quick, death.

Cries for help brought a quick response from the city guard. The distraction allowed him to retrieve his mount from just inside the gates without notice. The Hunter leapt into the saddle and exited the city once more to continue his mission. Because T'mara was not expecting pursuit, their tracks were simple enough to follow. With his quarry set in his mind, Cam urged his eager taark forward.

129

THE BLOOD PLAINS

They had left the main road and the protection of the obelisks in the morning, and by early evening there was no sign of the Guardian's Keep. T'mara had led them confidently into the barren lands and rarely spoke for much of the day. On more than one occasion, Draxian caught Arros, wrapped in his new red-brown cloak, looking back the way they had come. He seemed suspicious of the locals and expressed his apprehension from the moment the group left the road. Draxian, on the other hand, had long since shrugged off the feeling of unease, and decided to focus on what lay ahead, rather than behind.

The Blood Plains, as T'mara called it, were essentially rocky badlands with oases scattered throughout. She explained that few people traveled through this area because of the difficult terrain and the dangerous creatures that roamed the region. Vegetation was sparse, consisting mostly of low-lying shrubbery, and the occasional needle trees that had evolved from centuries of harsh conditions, making them short and twisted to withstand the strong winds of the storms. However, it was the abundance of red clay in the soil that likely gave the area its name.

Draxian's gekka seemed at home in their bleak surroundings, following T'mara's taark with tireless determination. Every few hours they would make a short stop to allow everyone to rest from the incessant bouncing caused by the uneven landscape. T'mara explained she had learned from a young age, the longer one stayed in the same location, the easier it was for something to catch you unaware.

His throat parched from the dry air, Draxian took a long drink from his water skin before closing the gap between himself and T'mara. She appeared to be contemplating something as she scanned the horizon.

"Everything well?"

"So far," she replied, still sweeping the plains with her eyes. "This region is not as familiar to me. I've only been this way a few times before."

He huffed a laugh. "I'm just amazed you know where you're going without any points of reference."

She cast a curious glance over her shoulder. "What do you mean by this?"

"Without any landmarks and the constant cloud cover, it would be easy to become disoriented."

"It is a feeling more than anything," T'mara answered. "For the moment, we head south to connect with the road toward Breck. After renewing our supplies in the great city, we can take the forgotten path to reach Orakh."

"I take it that not many would ever wish to travel there?"

T'mara lifted her eyebrows. "You would be the first."

"Second, actually."

The huntress grinned. "Yes, it appears insanity runs in both your families."

"We don't have a choice. This is something we need to do if we're ever to learn what happened to our fathers."

"I am not doubting your word," she returned carefully.

"Just our sense of self-preservation?"

The Huntress chuckled to herself. "Something akin to this, yes." T'mara glanced back toward Arros to see his reaction to her jest, then immediately drew her neck back in confusion. "What is he doing?"

Draxian swiveled his head, then quickly lost his grin. "Arros!"

The prince turned back in his saddle to face him. Strapped to his head, was a thin, polished white plate of metal that wrapped around to completely cover his eyes. "What's wrong?"

"Why do you have that?"

He glanced behind him once again. "I'm certain something is following us. It's just not radiating enough heat to be distinguishable."

T'mara giggled at him. "And hiding your eyes will help you find it better?"

Arros looked back at her in confusion. "Huh?"

Draxian tapped his own temple in annoyance.

The prince immediately understood. "Oh." He quickly removed the vision enhancer from his head and gave Draxian an apologetic shrug.

"A luxury from home?" The two of them were too focused on each other to answer her.

"Dare I ask what else you have?" Draxian knew bringing advanced metallurgy devices from Ellandor to other worlds would never be condoned by the High Council. Granting unnatural leaps in knowledge to a younger civilization could sow corruption and chaos. This was one of many reasons his people had broken away from their distant ancestors.

Arros was just returning it to his pack when T'mara urged her taark around and rode up next to him. "May I?"

Draxian gritted his teeth and widened his eyes in warning, but the prince simply ignored him. "If you wish." He handed the device over to her for inspection.

T'mara studied it for a time, then strapped it over her head, just as he had. "What is its purpose? You certainly cannot fight with this over your eyes."

A mischievous grin spread across Arros' face. "Apologies, Drax, I just can't pass on this." He leaned over and touched the activation symbol on the side.

The Huntress immediately tensed, sitting up much straighter. She slowly looked around the horizon, then lifted her hand up to study it. "What in the blood-soaked Abyss?"

"Fun, huh?"

She huffed a laugh. "That was not the word I was going to use." T'mara lifted the visor for a moment, then returned it over her eyes. "Why does the land show in different colors?"

"It helps me distinguish between living creatures and rocks. Although it works better at night." He reached over and took her hand, then gently guided her first finger toward another symbol on the side. "Press and hold this for a moment."

"Why? What does it…" T'mara's mouth dropped open in shock. "This brings everything closer to my eyes." She laughed in delight while scanning the distant landscape.

Draxian shook his head at Arros in admonition. "Aside from your ill-advised showing of it, best not to forget there's nothing here that can recharge the energy once its expended."

"It's not like anyone of this land could ever learn how to reverse-engineer it."

"Are you sure about that? Those women working for Dellahara certainly had some interesting armor."

"And," Arros shot back, "most of the required metals can only be found on…" Arros caught himself. "Our island in the Western Kingdoms."

T'mara lifted the vision enhancer from her head and handed it back to Arros. "You do realize I do not believe you are truly from there, correct?" When he refused to answer, she turned her taark back to face south, then used her spear to start it trotting. "Where you are from is not as important as what I believe you will do while here."

Draxian reached back with his slender rod and tapped the gekka on the rump to get it moving as well. "And just what are you expecting from us?"

"Great things," she replied enigmatically.

He turned back in his saddle to give Arros a quick glare. "See what you've started," Draxian grumbled as he continued onward. "I have yet to take my place on the High Council, and already I envision them stripping us of our titles the moment we return."

"That's not true," Arros called to his back. "First, how would they even find out about it unless you told them? And second, they don't have the authority to take my title – only yours."

For the remainder of the day, T'mara continued guiding the men on a winding trek over treacherously steep hills and through canyons of dangerously sharp rocks. She had demonstrated an uncanny knack for finding hidden pools of water and edible plants for their mounts. The Blood Plains were sparse with wildlife, yet Draxian did spot some life, such as a herd of giant porcupines, and a strange walking tree that T'mara identified as a morthra. He also learned the hard way what a tarlagon was, after leaving his rations unattended on a nearby rock while he took a drink of water. The lizard runner was so fast, the young lord only saw a blur out of the corner of his eye, then the dried fruit was simply gone. He recalled similar encounters with a few of the larger birds around his estates back on Ellandor. Some of them were bold enough to snatch the food from his hands when dining outside on the terrace. Overall, the young lord found the Blood Plains to be the most inhospitable region he had ever visited, and they still had at least another day before reaching the main road to Breck.

The small group had settled beneath a rocky knoll to keep their fire from being seen by anything that stalked the night. Arros was in high spirits and offered to take first watch. This suited T'mara well, since she believed the most active time for the predators was late into the night and toward early dawn. When she asked him if he would like to borrow a spear, the prince politely declined. Draxian knew that he had brought along a mollifier bracer to protect himself. The black metal bracer on the wrist of Arros' right hand was like those worn by the peacekeepers back home. He wondered if Arros truly grasped what types of terrors roamed about. If the dragon they had encountered served as any measure, the prince would be laughably outmatched using a weapon that was only meant to temporarily incapacitate Ellandorians who tried to fight or cause disturbances.

Draxian found it difficult to sleep on the hard-packed soil, and it felt like he had only just closed his eyes when Arros woke him for his shift.

"Draxian," the prince gently called to him.

"Already?"

Arros frowned. "It's been several hours by my estimate, but the nights here seem longer."

"Very well." Draxian crawled to his feet, then stretched to soothe the aching from his back.

"Here." Arros held up the vision enhancer. "You'll want this."

He shook his head. "Conserve the energy. I'll be fine."

"Suit yourself." The prince gathered his blanket, then placed it over Draxian's to double the thickness. "What?" he whispered. "Not like you're using it."

"I will later."

Arros chuckled to himself, then scooted the mat next to T'mara's. At first, the Huntress lifted her head questioningly as the prince laid down and pressed his back to hers to share warmth. She simply smirked to herself, then went back to sleep.

The light of the campfire did not extend far by design, yet Draxian wondered if that would work against them. He stepped out into the night, taking care not to make any noise. Even the insects chirped with strange tones that made him feel uneasy. He continued to listen for large movements and tried to allow his vision to adjust to the night – yet it was as if the light had been swallow by the Void, and no amount of time would allow his sight to get any better.

Somewhere in the distance, a vicious growl erupted from a large beast and echoed as it attacked its prey. Immediately afterwards, a high-pitched squeal was heard, followed by tormented screams. It was abruptly cut short, as the beast's life was violently ended.

"Shite," Draxian cursed to himself, while drawing his sword. He tested the weight of the cold, etherium steel blade nervously, wondering if he would even catch sight of his opponent before his own cries echoed in the night to be silenced by a hungry predator.

Gritting his teeth, the young lord stalked back over to where Arros lay, then knelt to find his pack. The prince was using it as a pillow. When Draxian started to wake him, Arros' hand slipped from his cloak and held out the enhancer. "Say it," he taunted without opening his eyes.

Draxian grunted in frustration. "You were right, I was wrong," he whispered in annoyance. "Satisfied?"

Arros chuckled at the large man when he snatched the device from the prince's grip. Draxian then shambled back to his previous post while strapping the enhancer over his head. There was no telling how long the device could remain active without needing to be charged with energy, yet he was certain it would last days if Arros had done so just before they had been displaced from Ellandor.

Immediately upon touching the activation symbol, the world came alive to his sight. The land appeared in various shades of green and blue, with the occasional glimpses of yellow and red dots in the distance. *Small animals most likely*, he thought to himself. T'mara's taark snorted restlessly behind him. Something was wrong. The nagging splinter in the back of the young lord's mind had escalated to a feeling of dread.

Draxian spotted something moving in the distance, not more than a quarter league away. Reaching up, he touched the symbol to focus in on his target. Whatever it was, the beast's body had nearly the same temperature as the rocks around it. Upon exponentially increasing the power of the enhancer, a familiar form began to take shape. It was a taark, like T'mara's, with a saddle and bridle – but no rider.

Draxian scanned the plains to one side for other signs of life. As he swiveled his head back in the other direction, he was just in time to see a large red blotch descend upon him.

It was deep within the cradle of night that the Empress of Dragons walked through the serene gardens behind the palace in Dellahara. Resting atop a massive, inverted mountain, the ancient city had been ruled by her bloodline for over three-thousand years. Long before the rise of the Undying abominations, Dellahara had always been the true seat of power throughout all of Kohr. Her Chromatic Warriors were masters of information gathering, always keeping the eyes of the Empress of Dragons upon her enemies. Nothing escaped her attention. Adreana Dellahara was present at the time when the radiant sun was lost to the madness of the Fallen One and had trudged her way through the Eternal Night. The long years had not touched her face, yet inside, she felt the weight of her age and all the misery she had endured to finally reach the edge of the Thousand Years of Darkness.

The Empress paced near an old fountain shaped like a fish, attempting to keep her impatience from pushing to the surface. At last, footsteps of the approaching contingent of guards reached her ears. With her back still turned away from them, the Elite Guard halted in place.

"What kept you?"

The commander knelt low and bowed her head. "Forgive me, Mistress. We had to set certain safeguards in place, should our agent fail in his mission."

Adreana Dellahara turned around to face the kneeling woman. "Rise, Commander."

Rellan came to her feet, then nodded to the six women in armor behind her. "Dismissed." She waited until they had vanished through the back entry to the palace before turning to the Dragon Empress. "I have something for you, Mistress." She pulled her satchel around and lifted the flap. "We recovered this from one of the men." A bundle of red cloth was produced and held out to her. Rellan waited. "Mistress?"

It took the Empress a moment to realize she was holding her breath. Carefully reaching out, Adreana lifted the intricately woven cloak from her commander's fingers. She ran her thumbs over the soft fabric, then turned it around until finding the crest of the House of Nemendes. "It's true. The Travelers have finally arrived."

"Yes, Mistress. Just as you foretold."

The Dragon Empress slowly brought the cloak up to her nose and smelled deeply. "I recognize this scent." Her eyes turned to Commander Rellan's. "The one you took this from – what was he like?"

The commander dropped her gaze to the ground in thought. "I only met Arros and his companion, Draxian, briefly. It was obvious they were out of place at the Guardian's Keep. Even so, there was a subtle confidence in Arros' demeanor that is so rarely found these days. He had that same look in his eyes that I often catch in yours."

"Oh?"

Rellan slowly nodded. "The one that makes me feel like you know something I don't."

"Perhaps, for him, the opposite is true?"

"Mistress?"

Adreana hugged the fabric to her chest. "It could be that ignorance of what he faces has created the illusion of courage."

"That could also be an explanation – yet I felt something deeper from both men."

"And that is?"

Commander Rellan lifted her chin. "The outsiders are far more dangerous than they are willing to show others."

The Empress of Dragons gave her a soft smile. "They had better be, or their time here will be short indeed." She reached out and placed her hand on Rellan's shoulder. "You've done well. If you'll excuse me, we have an unexpected guest."

The Commander glanced uncertainly around the area, then bowed to the Empress. "Of course, Mistress."

Adreana watched Rellan exit the gardens and return to the palace. It was unsettling that the magical wards had not detected the intruder's approach. "You must have received the same message as I."

A dark form materialized from the shadows and stepped forward. His black cloak hid the man's features, and his footsteps produced no sound. "I have." It had been many years since she had laid eyes upon him, and his ominous presence was no less alarming.

"All our preparations have been for this moment."

"Are you certain this time? We've been wrong before, and many have died for it."

The Dragon Empress held out the cloak. "The sky has torn, and the dawn approaches."

The dark figure stepped into the light of a nearby orb which glowed with a soft blue radiance. He reached out and touched the crimson fabric, tracing the crest with his fingers. "Where are they now?"

"Lord Trimenius sent them to the city of Orakh to find the Infinite Library."

"A fool's errand."

Adreana drew herself up and narrowed her eyes. "You don't believe they will reach the Oracle?"

He turned his head slightly to one side. "They will, with my assistance."

A flash of anger crossed her face. "You will do no such thing, Shadow Lord. They must find their own way, without any interference."

"Too much is at risk. Tell me you don't have eyes upon them at this very moment." It was an accusation, not a question.

She pulled the red cloak to her chest, then began pacing back and forth. "Do you truly believe I don't wish to fly to them right this instant and make certain they follow the correct path?" Adreana spun to face the tall man. "You will do nothing to disrupt the balance. The Order has foretold that the Travelers must die before a new age can arise. If this were somehow prevented, we would stand to lose everything."

"I will do whatever I feel is right. You don't command me or my men, Adreana. There are old debts that must be repaid."

The Dragon Empress took a dangerous step forward. "And neither do you have the authority to act of your own volition, Lord General. You know this well. Return to your post and guard the Twelve Gateways. The Travelers must never be allowed to leave Kohr."

144

12

AMBUSH

With the visor covering his eyes and adjusted to peer into the distance, Draxian was taken completely by surprise. Something hard struck him on a single nerve cluster in the bend of his shoulder, causing the large warrior to grunt in pain and drop his sword. Another stout strike to his legs and Draxian found himself lying flat on his back. His shoulder felt on fire as he reached out for his fallen weapon. A mighty swing toward where he thought his opponent was, sent shattered stone flying into the darkness. T'mara had been correct in her original assessment. The vision enhancer made it extremely difficult to fight. He had no idea where his attacker was.

T'mara rushed to his side to check on him. Draxian's failed strike must have alerted her. The Huntress' silent assessment consisted of a glance, which quickly turned to the darkness around them. Leaping over him, spear in hand, she ran off to grapple with his attacker.

Draxian jerked the visor free with his left hand, then tossed it aside. T'mara and their new opponent had disappeared beyond the radius of the light and could be heard battling in the night.

Arros appeared next to him with his arm held up and sleeve rolled back to reveal the black bracer. "Are you well?" he asked quickly.

"Not so much." Draxian rubbed at his shoulder as he tried to lift his right arm. It was stunned from the precise blow to the nerves and would take some time to recover feeling. Moving his hand away from the wound, he saw a small amount of blood glistening on his palm in the glow of the nearby fire. The small amount did not alarm him.

"I can't see them. Where's the enhancer?"

He nodded off to the side. "Somewhere over there."

Arros darted toward the area he indicated, then began searching around the dark rocks. "Are you certain?"

"Maybe," Draxian confessed, irritation clear in his voice.

The sound of wood striking wood continued for some time until a figure fell to the ground nearby. He was dressed in dark clothing with a scarf wrapped tightly around his face. Before Draxian could reach for him, T'mara pounced into view with her feet landing to either side of the groaning man.

She pointed a spearhead at his throat. "Do you yield?"

He reached up and tapped her shaft in an act of submission. "I yield."

"Good," T'mara scolded. "Because I do not believe your heart would last much longer."

Arros had just recovered the enhancer as Draxian stepped closer. "T'mara?"

She reached down and held out a hand to the man on the ground. He took it and pulled himself back to his feet. "You remember Cam, do you not?"

The caravan master pulled off his scarf and stared at Draxian for a moment, as though he were surprised to see him standing there. A wry grin soon pulled at the corner of the merchant's mouth. "Next time you're on sentry duty, it might be a good idea not to cover your eyes."

Draxian took a dangerous step forward, when Arros caught his arm. "Let it go." The prince turned back to Cam as he rolled down his sleeve to cover the bracer. "Your advice is well received, Master Hunter. However, I would not test our defenses again without fair warning."

"It was not meant to offend. This is a game T'mara and I have been playing for many years now."

She shook her spear at him. "And you have yet to catch me unaware."

"It's that damn taark of yours." He shook his head, then walked over to retrieve his own spear. "Always smells danger."

"Perhaps if you were nicer to yours, it would protect you as well."

He rested the spear over his shoulder. "It's just a beast."

Draxian also retrieved his weapon, then returned it to his scabbard. The feeling was slowly beginning to come back to his arm, leaving only a dull aching. "Not that we don't appreciate your company…"

"Aye," Cam acknowledged. "After a good deal of consideration, I decided that T'mara was right. It would be rude to not help you find your way around our land." While he appeared genuine with his words, Draxian could not dismiss the sensation that he was not revealing everything.

Although T'mara was of a different opinion. "That was brave of you to travel alone through the badlands just to assist us."

He waved off her compliment. "Think nothing of it. You've saved my skin on more than one occasion. It's time I return the favor."

Draxian glanced over and exchanged a covert look with Arros. He was not convinced either, but kept his suspicions carefully guarded. "Since my heart is no longer at risk of pounding out of my chest," the prince began, "perhaps we might get some rest?"

T'mara turned to both men. "Good idea. Now that Cam is here to assist, we'll watch for the remainder of the night."

"Are you certain?" Draxian stepped closer. "My shift had barely started."

"You are paying for my services. That includes allowing you both to rest knowing that nothing will take you unaware."

Arros pushed out his lower lip. "Well argued." He promptly spun around and walked back over to the mats to rest.

Kyreena awoke to the sound of movement nearby. She was being held with the surviving women in a guarded holding pen, just outside the ruins. There were dozens of other such cages within the temporary wooden stockade her captors had erected. The others held men of varying ages and diminishing levels of health. Most were dirty and grizzled after days spent in hard labor, while other slaves appeared fresh, their wide eyes glancing around fearfully. Her captors were building a strange tower-like object of black storm ward ore – like the kind used for the road obelisks. However, this larger version with an ornately designed crown turret, was topped by a metal ring in which a large crystal hung suspended. Its primary function was still unknown to Kyreena, yet everything about its nature made her believe the tower was not beneficial to the people of Kohr.

When Kyreena lifted her head to peer around the area, nothing caught her eye. She could have sworn the sound of footsteps were near, yet only a single guard was pacing on the far end of the slave pens. Lorisa snuggled into Kyreena's side to share warmth and stirred restlessly throughout the night. The poor woman had experienced something terrible within the probing tentacles of the dark cloud beneath the ancient ruins and trembled uncontrollably for the rest of the evening. Kyreena counted herself lucky not to have been touched by it or she would likely have the same reaction.

Through the dim torchlight at the perimeter, Kyreena watched a large man emerge from the shadows, and begin walking toward the black tower. She recognized the brute as the same one who had helped her from the cage when she arrived. Following his path with her eyes, Kyreena spotted another figure already standing at the base of the tower. It was a woman in a white hooded robe with stitching of an orange sun rising. Her arm was stretched out, allowing her fingers to lightly brush the strange patterns etched into the surface.

"I thought I'd find you here."

The large man's voice was soft and distant, yet the more Kyreena strained to hear them, the clearer the voices became to her ears.

"It's even more beautiful than I imagined." The woman didn't turn as he approached. "I'm impressed with your progress. Everything is just as we hoped."

"Have I ever made you a promise I couldn't keep?"

"No, Father. You were always masterful in finding creative ways to solve a difficult task. How did you construct this without anyone knowing?"

As the two figures continued the conversation, Kyreena tilted her head slightly with interest.

"We purchased slaves to assist in the hard labor. Bringing in workers from the distant towns would have led to needless questions. No one will miss these people."

"Slavery is acceptable in the Northern Kingdoms?"

"Northern Empires," the man corrected. "The Undying have

slowly taken away the liberties of the people, bit by bit. It is now permitted for a deeply indebted person to be sold into slavery for years at a time."

"And the Resistance simply accepts this?"

"The Resistance you knew failed long ago. It's true, there are scattered remnants of those who claim to follow in their spirit, yet these minor cells are a distant candle to the might and power they wielded when you were among them."

The woman gestured toward the sky. "Much has changed during my long slumber – and much hasn't. There is a deep sickness within the magic of the land."

"The Verge. It's spread far beyond Orakh and continues to grow. The closer we get to the breach, the more unstable magic becomes."

"Is there nothing to be done? The distortion in the Spirit Realm is making it difficult to focus my power."

"I fear my knowledge of such things is limited. Although we may have larger concerns. Something happened yesterday that we did not expect. I'm not certain what it means."

"Oh?"

There was a long pause. "The sky tore open near the Guardian's Keep."

"The what?"

"It's a fortress waystation between Annis and Phondari, used to inspect goods before passage. More recently, the Undying, Thartalagor Deathskull, has been using it to interrogate rogue magi."

The woman gave him an exasperated grunt. "No, Father. The other part."

"I wasn't there. We've only just received the accounts from those who were nearby."

"And?" she prompted.

"Many witnesses saw the sun and a blue sky for only a moment."

There was a long pause from the woman. "I've always wanted

to see the sun. I was born after it was lost to the Shadow Realm. That must be the omen we were to watch for to mark the ending of the Thousand Years of Darkness."

"In my experience, nothing is random." The large man turned his back to the woman. "I've had strange visions when I attempt to rest and meditate."

"Tell me."

"They are difficult to describe. In the most recent of them, there were two men, not of this land, fighting atop a mountain. I could not make out their faces, but somehow knew them – or they knew me. It was confusing. Every time I close my eyes, the visions come. Sometimes they are battling others, sometimes they fought against me – but always, they fail. Yet no matter what the circumstances of their defeat, everyone in my dream dies shortly after they do."

The woman gasped. "The Travelers. A text from the Prophets of Avarron once described the arrival of the Travelers at the end of the Thousand Years of Darkness. They would come just as you said, in a flash of blue skies and a shining sun – a promise for the return of the dawn." She reached out and touched his arm. "You said they died in your dreams?"

"Correct."

"Perhaps it was a message sent to you by the Great Master – a warning. If the Travelers were to die here on Kohr, we will all soon follow."

"How can we stop it? My dreams never showed their likeness, or where they could be found."

"We don't need to know their faces. Even if these men should dress like the local inhabitants, they will not be like the people of Kohr. You above all others should know this."

The tall man rubbed his chin in thought. "Indeed. I have encountered very few Travelers in all my years. They always present themselves as soft-spoken and weak to keep their opponents off balance. Many of my brethren fell victim to such tactics. I will not."

"When our forces arrive, they will aid us in finding these men."

"We won't be the only ones searching for them. If the Empress of Dragons should locate the Travelers first, or worse, the Undying…"

The woman drew back her hood, allowing the blonde locks to spill down her shoulders. Kyreena immediately recognized the young woman who arose from the sarcophagus. The lady in white reached up and touched the man's cheek. "I realize, in the past, I haven't been the best daughter, or grateful for all you sacrificed to keep me alive beyond my natural lifespan – but trust in me now. This is *our* time, Father. The dawn is fast approaching."

153

DEMONS

Draxian stared at the backs of the two Hunters from atop his gek as they both regaled them with stories of their travels. T'mara's laugh was warm and heartfelt. The two companions had shared many adventures and faced down creatures that sounded worse than any of the young lord's most terrifying nightmares. Arros had been riding most of the day in silence. His eyes were constantly searching the wasteland for an invisible enemy, yet none appeared. Twice, the small group had changed directions when a distant red storm was seen on the horizon. With no protective obelisk in sight, the Hunters were greatly fearful of being caught within the maelstrom of deadly lightning. Draxian knew from his own experience that it was far more dangerous than the worst naturally occurring weather he had encountered on Ellandor.

It had been more than three-hundred years since any Travelers had left Ellandor to visit and trade with other worlds. Their gateway had been sealed in a vault deep beneath the palace, after a deadly plague had inadvertently been brought back from another land and decimated the population. Those who were not strong enough to combat the sickness while a cure was researched, faced a painful and gruesome death. Nearly a tenth of the total population had perished within five days, and upon the twelfth morning, when the cure was finally discovered in Braethus, a little more than a third of the people of Ellandor were lost. The old family rivalries were all but forgotten, as the rulers of every region came together to form a World Council. It was unanimously agreed upon, the Gateway of the First Ones must be sealed away, and all the territories would unite under a single representative Ellandorian government.

Arros must have also discovered what King Nemendes had learned – the gateway beneath the palace would never allow them to cross over to Kohr. Not without a portal generator which had allowed their ancient ancestors to settle upon Ellandor.

"There," T'mara called out with excitement. "I can see an obelisk!"

Draxian stretched up in his saddle to look where she had indicated. Sure enough, a black spire could be seen to the southwest of their position. They had finally reached the road to Breck. It would be three more days to reach the city, but T'mara had assured the two men that they would pass several small outposts on the road where they could trade for fresh food and water.

The Huntress started her taark into a run. "Race you to the road!"

"T'mara," Cam called out, as the huntress charged forward with reckless abandon. He glanced back at the young men and shook his head. "That girl has too much spirit for her own good."

Arros lifted his chin to peer across the boulder strewn plain toward T'mara. "Something isn't right."

Draxian followed Arros' gaze and spotted the Huntress quickly slowing her taark to a halt. The giant lizard stomped the ground nervously and thrashed its head from side to side.

"Wait here." Cam readied his spear and smacked his own taark into a run.

They watched the Hunter charge toward T'mara with all haste. Just as he neared her position, a hulking form launched from behind a boulder and knocked him from his mount. Cam ducked and rolled at the last instant, narrowly escaping the thing's grasp. The moment his legs touched the ground, Cam was already repositioning his body to ready for the next attack. It gave the Hunter a valuable moment to ascertain the identity of his opponent.

Thin, leathery wings helped the man-sized insect glide over Cam and spin about to face its prey. The creature had six long, skinny legs built for jumping on its armored lower body, and two pincers on its upper torso, like the much smaller mantis of Draxian's homeland. It had no head or eyes that could be easily discerned, only a long finger-like protrusion coming from the neck which uncurled into the form of a deadly pike, with teeth.

T'mara watched the Hunter and beast face off, yet to Draxian's surprise, she did not move to intercept. Instead, the Huntress pulled her taark around in a circle to search for more of the creatures. She turned her attention to something beyond one of the nearby rock outcroppings, then struck her taark in the rear and charged.

Draxian could no longer stand idly by. Fear for T'mara's safety, and an inexplicable urge to protect her, caused him to draw his blade and set his own mount into a run when Arros called out to him, "Drax! Stay there!"

He hesitated, then turned toward the prince. "I need to help them!"

"We can't!" Arros pulled back his sleeve to reveal the black bracer. He touched a symbol embossed in the dark steel, and a small, notched cylinder rose from the top to aid his aim. "Don't you understand what's happening? We're being separated to make us easier prey."

Draxian quickly glanced around the immediate area. "Where?"

"There's one." Arros pointed toward several large rocks nearly fifty paces from his position.

At first, Draxian could not make out anything. A moment later, a slight movement caught his eye. It looked like a long stick, at first, until he discerned the remainder of the body which was cleverly camouflaged into the stone around it. The creature appeared to be waiting for him to draw near.

"I'll try to hit it with the mollifier."

"Don't show off any more technology from home unless it's absolutely necessary. I've got this." Draxian dismounted and began making his way to the creature, whose mass was not much greater than his own. He just needed to stay clear of the sharp appendage and claws. As he crept closer, the creature began lowering slowly as if preparing to lunge. With a firm grip on his blade, the young lord abruptly charged forward. In response, the creature leapt at him with astounding speed, feeding tube extended to spear him in the chest. Draxian dodged to one side while slashing with his sword. The edge cut into a raised claw, severing it in half. The instant the young lord's weapon made contact, a jolt of energy surged through Draxian's body in a shocking wave of pain. It ended as quickly as it had begun yet left his muscles trembling and slightly drained of strength. "What in the Abyss?"

"Finish it," Arros urgently called over to him.

Draxian spun around just as the creature recovered enough to make a second attack. The monstrosity scurried forward, then darted its long mouth back and forth like a scorpion's tail. With each strike, a small amount of acrid liquid was secreted from the end. Poison, he mused. The smell reminded him of rotting cabbage.

Timing the creature's stabbing motions allowed him to jump in close. Cutting downward with all his might, his blade severed the mouth near the base, then continued its path to sink deep into the thick shell of scales. A wave of pain struck him, forcing him to his knees. His heart threatened to explode from his chest. Draxian cried out and released his grip on the sword, its blade still buried in the creature's back. Unfortunately, his valiant efforts had only managed to enrage the beast. The creature thrashed about and pulled the blade free with its last remaining claw. The sword clattering to the ground as the shadow creature turned its attention back to the young lord.

"Drax! Get up!"

His friend's words were faint above the pounding in his head. "I'm trying," he hollered back through gritted teeth.

Just as the predator of the Blood Plains started forward, a long spear shaft sprouted from the space between its neck and the severed feeding tube. With little more than a flinch, the beast dropped to the ground and went still. Draxian turned to see T'mara standing on a boulder nearby with her arm extended.

"Thank you," Draxian marveled.

T'mara placed her hands on her hips. "You shouldn't strike a shadow beast with such a weapon. Their connection to the Shadow Realm will drain your strength unless attacked from afar."

"Now, you warn me."

She grinned and started to retort when something caught her eye. "Watch out," T'mara screamed at Arros.

The prince spun around, just as another mantis creature leapt toward him from behind. Without thinking, Arros lifted his arm and aimed it toward the beast. A deep *thud* resounded in the air, just as a sphere of blazing light shot forth from his bracer. It hit the monstrosity straight on, disintegrating its mouth, and searing a hole the width of two fists down the length of the body, before cutting a hole into the earth. The creature flopped ungracefully to the ground in front of Arros, still sizzling from the scorched flesh.

None of the three companions moved for several moments while they attempted to understand what they had witnessed. Cam finally appeared next to Draxian and glanced over toward the corpse. "What happened to that one?"

Arros turned his head and forced a smile. "Must have eaten something that didn't agree with it."

The caravan master stepped closer to inspect the wound. "Perhaps, if it was feeding on molten rock." He turned back to T'mara. "Did you see what happened?"

It took the Huntress a moment to realize he was speaking to her. "Huh? Oh… no, I didn't."

Draxian could feel his strength finally returning. He crawled back to his feet, then walked over to retrieve his sword. "What are those things?" he asked in an effort to divert the Hunter's questioning. There was something about the man he distrusted.

"Skraglars," she replied quickly. "They always hunt in groups of three to five. If you manage to spot one, then at least two others are already flanking your position."

Arros nodded thoughtfully. "Clever animals."

"They are not animals. These creatures are demons from the Shadow Realm, brought here through the red storms."

"And the storms originate from the Shadow Realm?"

"Correct." She pointed to the dark, woven-steel bracelet on her arm. "My distant ancestors once lived in that place as well. It changed them. I must wear this to siphon the dangerous energy away to keep from harming anyone who touches my skin. The gek and taark are also from that place. They have special collars to make them safe." T'mara pointed toward Draxian's blade. "Even without skin to skin contact, using a weapon such as that will not protect you from the deadly touch of the Void."

The young lord sheathed his sword. "Is there a way to protect myself from that happening again?"

Cam directed his eyes from the charred skraglar back to Draxian. "The Chosen Hunters use handles and grips made from voridium, or storm ward ore, as most people call it. This keeps the life-draining effects from reaching us when using close-quarter weapons. After they're dead, the creatures lose that connection." He frowned at the severed appendages from the skraglar Draxian had fought. "How did you cut through this? Is your weapon enchanted?"

The large man folded his arms and squinted curiously at the Hunter. "No, just good steel and a sharp blade. Surely you have swords sharp enough to do the same?"

T'mara jumped down from her rock and stepped forward. She gripped her spear, then jerked it free of the creature's body. "Nothing that sharp." Using her spear tip, the Huntress pointed toward the wound. "We must pierce the softest part of the skraglar's body where the neck meets the mouth. The brain is located just beneath." To demonstrate this, she stabbed repeatedly at the scales on the back and sides with no evidence of damage. "You see? Very tough."

Draxian drew his blade and motioned for her to stand aside. Once she was clear, he flipped his sword around and thrust downward into the thickest portion of the hide. The tip pierced through and sank halfway into the body. "Perhaps you need to rethink your sharpening methods."

T'mara's jaw dropped. "How in the Abyss?" She quickly dropped her spear and gently shoved Draxian out of the way. "Let me try."

"By all means." He stepped aside and watched her with amusement.

The Huntress gripped the blade with both hands and tried to pull it free, but to no avail. "It's stuck." She then stood on the corpse, directly over the handle, and lifted with all her might. Every muscle in her body strained as the sword slowly worked its way from the hide. When the tip nearly emerged, T'mara jerked the blade free. The force caused her to stumble backwards into Draxian's arms.

"Careful," he chided. "I already had my hair trimmed a few days ago."

She returned his smile, although this gesture caused Cam's face to darken slightly. T'mara stepped away from the young lord to inspect the blade, turning it in the light. "This is a strange metal. It has a slight green tint."

"It's called etherium. The raw ore is difficult to separate from other impurities. Although if done properly, it creates a metal that holds its edge well."

T'mara whistled to herself in astonishment. "There are no imperfections or nicks. It looks as if you only just purchased it from the smithy. How much do you think it is worth?"

Draxian reached over and took the weapon from her grip. "In your land, it is likely priceless. So don't get any ideas."

"I would never." T'mara appeared genuinely wounded by his jest.

Cam quickly came to her defense. "As far as I know, T'mara hasn't stolen a single item in her life. It's not in her nature."

"My apologies," Draxian said. "It was a failed attempt at humor." He bowed to her.

The Huntress stepped forward and placed her hands on his upper arms. "You are forgiven." When the young lord drew in his eyebrows at the gesture, T'mara chuckled to herself. "In my tribe, to touch another on the arms as such shows great respect and trust."

"How so?"

"My hands do not grip a weapon, and from this distance, you are free to easily attack."

A soft grin creased his lips, and Draxian reached up to place his hands on her arms as well. "You have my gratitude for killing that creature."

She moved in closer until their feet nearly touched. "Skraglar are some of the weaker demons of the Shadow Realm that walk this land. Promise me you will not attack any of them without me nearby to be your hunt sister."

Draxian raised an eyebrow. "My sister?"

T'mara broke away, laughing at his jest. "You are not a fool. You know what I truly mean by this." She snatched up her spear. "We need to continue our journey. The smell of death will bring many predators."

The young lord turned back to speak with Arros but found his attention elsewhere. Cam was studying the burnt hole in the creature, while the prince watched him from the side with a glare of deep mistrust. "Arros?"

He slowly shifted his gaze back to Draxian. "Yes?"

"What happened to my mount?"

The prince glanced around, then shrugged. "If I was being forced to carry your heavy arse all day, I'd run too."

After T'mara recovered their mounts, the group continued down the road toward the city of Breck. The Huntress had ridden her taark further ahead of the two men, while Cam trailed behind to ensure nothing approached from the rear. Draxian waited until they had traveled for several more hours before finally speaking quietly with the crown prince.

"Arros?"

He glanced over, then shook his head. "I have no idea."

"Do you even know what I was going to ask?"

"The mollifier. You wanted to know why it behaved like that."

Draxian frowned. "Maybe you pressed the wrong glyph?"

"What?" Arros scrunched his face at the absurdity of the question. "The bracer only has three settings – on, off, and discharge."

"But that mollifier isn't standard issue – they're supposed to be silver like those the palace guards carry. Where did you get it?"

Arros shifted uncomfortably, then glanced over. "The Twilight Protocol."

Draxian's face drained of color. "How in the icy Abyss did you get access to that?"

"I'm the Crown Prince of Ellandor. If anything were to happen to my mother, someone else would need to have access to the Vanguard armory in case of an emergency."

"And you didn't think to test it before bringing it here?"

Arros gritted his teeth and spoke testily. "Of course, I did. It worked just like a mollifier."

"Then what changed?"

"How should I know?"

Draxian took a deep breath and tried again. "If they gave you access to the Vanguard armory, you must know a little about how the technology works. How are those different from what the guards use to stun an unruly citizen?"

"Well," he began, "the standard mollifier must be recharged regularly. I needed equipment that drew energy directly from me or the surrounding environment. Only the Twilight Vanguard has that kind of technology."

"For good reason." Draxian shook his head and sighed with exasperation. "Are you saying that being on Kohr is overcharging your mollifier?"

Arros glanced over to him. "No. This model draws its power directly from me. That's all I know."

"From you? Does it hurt?"

"No."

"But was it designed to channel bursts of energy at that level?"

"Probably not."

Draxian drew his neck back in concern. "What do you think that means?"

"The bracer is likely to burn out with continuous use… or worse."

"I'm almost afraid to ask."

Arros turned and lifted his eyebrows. "It might detonate."

"Pardon me?"

He waved Draxian off. "It's an unlikely scenario."

"Kind of like a portal generator getting hit by red lightning?"

"That wasn't my fault. You were never supposed to come to Kohr with me."

"Well, I did. And now, instead of lounging around in luxury at the palace, drinking celebratory wine and eating little cakes at your wedding, I'm riding this disgusting, overgrown lizard, and wandering a desert wasteland full of demons – all while being hunted by powerful enemies who want nothing more than to see us dead."

Arros smirked back at him. "In other words, you're having the greatest adventure of your life?"

The corners of Draxian's lips curled up into half a grin. "Precisely."

BRECK

It had been nearly three days of travel before Draxian spotted the walled city of Breck looming in the distance. As expected, the small group had passed a good number of caravans trading between the city-states. Arros had purchased bows and arrows for both men at the first opportunity that presented itself. Despite assurances from T'mara that the creatures tended to shy away from obelisks along the road, neither of them wished to be caught without some form of ranged weapon. Furthermore, Arros had promised Draxian to avoid using the over-powered mollifier unless it was an absolute emergency. T'mara discreetly told them magic was outlawed within most of the lands, and it would be difficult to explain to the local government that Arros' bracer was not intended to be lethal.

Resting on a plateau that towered two hundred and fifty to three hundred paces high, the city was well fortified against invaders from all sides. To the west, a large port could be seen next to the river, allowing for frigates to trade from the northern towns.

"There's the city of Breck," T'mara called excitedly over to Draxian. "It has been a few years since I came through here. Our contracts have mostly been between Annis and Phondari."

Draxian nodded thoughtfully. "Was this where you grew up?"

"No. But it was the first city I ever visited. Does your home also have amazing places such as this?"

His eyebrows shot high, as the young lord tried to come up with an answer. While the engineering of Breck rivaled that of the Guardian's Keep, in contrast with the cities on Ellandor it seemed crude and basic. "We have our share of beauty."

She nodded her understanding. "It is impressive to see the steep walls, and try to imagine how they were built, but I find it difficult to understand how so many can live in such a close space."

"We have cities as well, though not so densely populated. We've never had the necessity for high walls or fortified cliffs."

T'mara frowned at him. "Are you not afraid of invading armies or shadow beasts?"

"Never."

"Never?"

"We live… far enough from people that it's not worth their time to invade our lands."

She appeared content with Draxian's answer, yet still wanted more. "Is there a woman you left behind?"

"No, unlike Arros no arranged marriage for me, and I have made no pledge to any woman." He turned to her and smiled warmly. "Just haven't found the right one, yet."

"Or perhaps she is closer than you think." T'mara's cheeks flushed slightly upon meeting his gaze. "And what do you mean by 'pledge'? Is this like a marriage proposal?"

"Not exactly." Draxian had forgotten he was in a different land whose traditions could be completely different than what he experienced. "Tell me about courtship among your people, and I'll answer you as best I can about mine."

"Well," T'mara began carefully, "growing up with my tribe was different from that of the big cities."

"You and Cam lived outside the walls?"

"Not Cam. Just me." She glanced back to see the older Hunter still trailing behind their procession with Arros, comfortably out of earshot. "I was born a Shadiere, a True Hunter."

"And that's different from the Chosen Hunters?"

T'mara nodded to him. "Indeed. The True Hunters are born to the land, not sheltered behind great walls. We learn to hold a weapon as a child, even before speaking. Hunting is our life. We are taught to find the weakness in all creatures of magic and keep them from destroying the land. That was the price of our freedom."

"I don't understand."

She took a deep breath. "I told you before that my people came from the Realm of Shadows, where we received our connection to the Void."

"Yes."

"That was also the home of the Fallen One. He had enslaved many of my ancestors and left the rest to die upon the Land of Eternal Night. They wandered the rocky wastes for hundreds of years before a great mage appeared. He summoned forth the Lord of Destruction and asked that he open a doorway back to our home on Kohr."

"Lord of Destruction?" He smirked to himself. "I like it."

"He was a powerful being who saved and protected my people – and one of the great heroes of the War of the Shadow Lords who defeated the Fallen One. In return for this blessing, my people swore to always defend the world against the dark beasts of the Realm of Shadows."

"And every generation afterwards was indebted to this man?"

T'mara shrugged. "I would not be alive if not for him."

"While that might be true, it's a lot to place on a people."

"Some have argued this."

Draxian gave her a somber look. "I imagine they would."

She glanced behind her toward Cam. "The Chosen Hunters have a different view."

"Oh?"

"Indeed. You see, the Shadiere can never have children with anyone not touched by the Void. It is just the nature of the magic. However, long ago, two mated Hunters of the Shadiere embarked on a great quest with the daughter of the Dragon King. As a reward for their devoted service, the princess broke the curse upon the two Hunters – allowing them and their descendants to have children with anyone they chose."

"Thus, the Chosen Hunters," Draxian finished.

"Yes. But after a time, they realized they could no longer remain with the Shadiere, yet still wanted to keep the teachings and skills of the Hunter."

"And Cam is a descendant of these two people who left the Shadiere?"

"It's possible. Others have been brought into the Chosen Hunters over the last few hundred years that weren't related at all. They have a citadel in Breck where many will meet to train."

Draxian studied the distant city. "And their primary purpose is to guard merchants?"

"No." T'mara urged her taark closer to him, lowering her voice. "They are used to find and kill those with dangerous magic."

He narrowed his eyes. "That mark on your arm."

"It helps to warn us if one is near and will identify us as Hunters for border guards."

"You've said that before. How does it work?"

"It will signal us with a strange tingling and glow with bright shades of blue, depending on how close we are to the mage."

"Why do you think it turned red when I touched it?" The young lord needed information, and T'mara had proven herself to be trustworthy.

The Huntress dropped her voice to a whisper. "I have no idea. It did not warn me that you were a mage, and yet it might be, with it glowing red, that you are the most dangerous of them all."

"And what do you believe?"

"After seeing what your companion did to that skraglar, it appears to be in my best interest to not speak of such things." She glanced back once more. "Cam's loyalties are to coin. He does not understand that holding the trust of another is greater than any amount of wealth."

He leaned over and took T'mara's hand. "It's just as Arros said; we've greatly underestimated you."

"This is true." She squeezed his hand back, then released it. "Now, I have told you about my people, and you've still not answered my question."

Draxian shifted in his saddle. "Ah, yes. Relationships. My people value knowledge, and the sharing of such, above most everything. With that comes honesty. So, when we care for someone, it's expected we are honest about our feelings."

"Will that not just cause heartache if they do not feel the same?"

"For a time. However, would you rather tell the other person of your affections and risk them not feeling the same, or live with the regret of finding out you missed the opportunity to be together?"

T'mara dropped her gaze and smiled to herself. "Your beliefs are much like the Shadiere."

"My people rarely marry. For us that level of commitment can be problematic when one or both change their feelings over time – and it almost always happens." Draxian pressed his lips tightly together. "For me and Arros, life is more about duty to our people, than finding fulfillment in the arms of another."

"Then you never…"

"Never what?" Draxian tilted his head. "Couple with another?"

T'mara bit her lower lip. "If we are discussing the same thing."

"Finding a partner to share affections with is easy enough. Finding someone to commit yourself to, who complements you in every way… that's tough."

"I understand." T'mara grinned back at him. "Then you must have many children at home?"

Draxian shook his head. "None. There's no unauthorized breeding in our land."

"How is this prevented?"

"We have ways of keeping females from getting pregnant until the appropriate time. If a couple wishes to produce a child, they must first demonstrate their willingness to remain together and raise the child in a nurturing home. They must make a pledge to one another and file a petition. Once their petition is approved, the woman can conceive. Once the child is of age, since they are not married, they can go their separate ways if they wish."

"That sounds like a lot of work to have a child."

"As it should be." The young lord gestured toward the city. "In our land, food and resources are abundant, and we still practice restraint. Yet I recall the retched living conditions of all those poor children back at the Guardian's Keep. If your people worked more on creating a better life for future generations, instead of filling it with too many mouths to feed, perhaps this world… er, land," Draxian corrected, "would be much more pleasant for those who live in it."

T'mara considered his words carefully. "Your people must be very wise." She huffed a laugh. "I do not believe I have ever met anyone like you."

"You've met Arros."

"He is not the same."

The Huntress had Draxian's attention. It was not often that he had the chance to get such a unique outside perspective. "What do you see with Arros?"

"It is not difficult to understand his motivations. He has a mission to find his father, and nothing will keep the Lord Prince from achieving victory." T'mara scowled to herself. "But while his actions appear to be random and without strategy, the exact opposite is true. That makes him dangerously unpredictable."

"And I'm not?"

"No. You defend those in need with little regard for your own safety. This will be your downfall if not tempered. You obviously come from a rich culture with beautiful ideals. However, Arros has already accepted that he is in a merciless land that will require him to be equally so. You have not."

"That doesn't mean I'm weak."

"Of course, not. It makes you righteous. But here good people don't live long."

Draxian leaned in closer to her. "You didn't have to help us get to Orakh. From where I sit, that means you're a good person as well."

"Or, it just makes me a foolish little girl who wants to impress a handsome outsider." Now it was Draxian's turn to blush. "And did you say Arros was to be married?"

Nerris Vesslen sat in his balcony chair overlooking the main gateway. He had reserved the room in the inn for the last two days because of the perfect view it gave of the caravans and travelers entering the city of Breck. His back was aching from remaining stationary for so long, and Nerris was frequently forced to stand and stretch his muscles. Yet despite his soreness, it felt wonderful for him to be back among civilization. It had been over ten long years of elite training and isolation since his recruitment and, at times, Nerris truly believed he would go mad without the occasional visit to the tavern or whorehouse. For this reason, the middle-aged soldier was relieved to be assigned a secret mission that would allow him to walk among the populace.

It was getting toward evening before Nerris finally spotted a small group of four emerge from the great archway to the city. A man and woman were in the lead, riding a gek and taark. Not far behind, two more followed.

Nerris could feel his heart pounding while he withdrew a palm-sized crystal from his hidden trouser pocket. Peering within, he concentrated. "Lord of Shadows, hear me."

An image of a cloaked man appeared within and spoke. *"Report."*

"I believe I've found the ones you seek. It's a small group of four, not traveling with a merchant caravan."

"Tell me what you see."

Nerris knew this was a test of his skills of observation, and one for which he excelled. "This is the first time two of the men have been here."

"Explain."

"They're looking around at every detail of the city and its people, as if trying to get their bearings."

The man nodded beneath the hood. *"Excellent – continue."*

"It appears as if the woman is a Hunter – possibly Shadiere."

"How do you know this?"

Nerris rubbed his chin as the group passed beneath the balcony. "She's wearing a storm ward bracelet. Combine that with the blonde hair and obvious arsenal of weapons, and there you have it – Shadiere." The soldier waited for a reply. When none came, he glanced down at the vision stone to find that his master was no longer staring back at him. "My Lord?"

"Behind you."

Nerris nearly jumped out of his boots at the appearance of a cloaked figure from the balcony door. Clutching his chest and taking a deep breath, the soldier shook his head at the frighteningly stealthy nature of the one standing next to him. He pointed toward the group that was just passing beneath them.

The tall man stepped forward to get a better view. In all the time Nerris had known him, the Lord of Shadows wore an emotionless mask of calculating tranquility. However, the gaze from beneath the hooded cloak shifted to one of concern, and his body tensed upon recognition. "The Travelers," the dark figure whispered to himself. His eyes wandered over to meet with Nerris'. "You've done well, Lieutenant."

"My gratitude, Lord General." The soldier folded his arms as he watched the small group halt at one of the larger stables to board their steeds for the night. "What's next?"

"Ingratiate yourself with the Travelers and find a way to join their group. You were chosen because of your previous life's experience. More than any of the others, you have the best chance of success. Just remember that one or both of their companions may be an agent for the Dragon Empress."

"Understood. Can you give me any insight to help know their minds?"

It took only a moment for the imposing man to formulate a strategy. "The Travelers are momentarily off-balance in our land. They will be untrusting and guarded – yet take care not to underestimate their intelligence or ability to adapt. Reveal only what is necessary of your past and avoid subjects that could lead back to your true loyalties." He stepped closer and watched Nerris with an intense expression. "And I say this with the utmost sincerity… don't ever lie to them."

Nerris swallowed hard, then bowed his head slightly in respect. "Understood. I should take my leave and greet our new friends."

Just as Nerris started for the balcony door, the hooded figure caught his arm. "I'm placing a great deal of trust in you. If you are discovered or captured, you know what to do."

Nerris reached over to grab a long, leather satchel leaning against the nearby wall. The pack contained provisions and his two swords. He quickly slung it over his shoulder, then bowed. "I won't let you down, Lord General."

Draxian wrinkled his nose at the pungent odors of the city market. Various animals of every size were being housed in cages or pens. The young lord even recognized a few species that could also be found on Ellandor. It was reasonable to assume that his ancestors had long ago brought them to or from Kohr. Chickens were certainly common enough. However, only a few horses could be seen, and of a slightly different breed than those they had back home. Draxian reasoned that the harsh conditions of the wasteland made them unsuitable for long treks.

When the group arrived at a stable large enough to house all of their mounts, the young lord dismounted and waited while T'mara and Cam set off to find the stable master. Arros handed the reigns of his gek to a grimy boy who smelled of animal dung. He removed his pack from the beast and then flipped a silver crown to the lad. "Take good care of it."

The stable boy caught the shiny coin baring the Ellandorian sigil and inspected it in the light. "Whoa!" His grin went as wide as his face could handle. "Thank you, milord!"

"Of course. Now you can purchase some better clothing and a toothbrush."

The boy's expression turned to confusion. "Huh?"

"Never mind," the prince chided. "Just keep that safe. Now, off with you."

Nodding to Arros, the youngster led the gek through the gate and into an area with a high fence.

Draxian chuckled to himself as he strode up to Arros. "I'd wager that's the most wealth he's ever possessed."

"Agreed." The lord prince glanced around uneasily. "We need all the friends we can get, though."

"Something bothering you?"

He lifted his chin slightly to gesture toward the main gate. "We're being watched."

"I'm sure it's nothing. People are naturally curious of outsiders."

"No." Arros stepped closer and lowered his voice. "This is different. I can't help but wonder if we were expected to come here."

"Nobody else knows our route."

"True," the prince allowed, "but there's only one place we can resupply before making our way toward the Orakh."

Draxian took and deep breath, then folded his arms. "Do you suspect Cam may have betrayed us?"

"Possibly. Although there were a few others who could have also known our intentions. Our fathers appeared to have made a few powerful enemies on Kohr."

"It just doesn't make sense. What did they hope to accomplish by rampaging through such a volatile world? Your father was regarded as one of the most diplomatic and just leaders in the history of Ellandor."

"That's because they weren't forced to live with him." Arros smirked to himself as he recalled his childhood. "By the time he was finished each day deliberating with the High Council, his *legendary* patience had run its course."

"I remember." Draxian lifted an eyebrow. "Although you were quite skilled at observing his temperament, and deliberately tested your father with absurd notions which even *you* didn't believe."

"He always knew I was just checking his resolve."

"No," Draxian began, "you were trying to manipulate him – just as you're doing with me and T'mara. I'm not a fool."

"Are you certain? Because a lovely indigenous female is blatantly offering her affections, yet you scoff, as if such musing is beneath consideration. I know you well, Drax."

"Then you should also realize that I plan to leave this place as soon as a way can be found." He shot an accusing finger at the prince. "Don't shake your head at me. The last thing I need is to be distracted from my purpose by a love-sick girl. There's no future in it." In response to Draxian's tirade, Arros simply pressed his lips tightly together and narrowed his eyes. The young lord's shoulders dropped in dismay upon finally understanding. "She's right behind me, isn't she?"

"Do not fear, my Lord," T'mara snidely retorted from over his shoulder. "This 'love-sick' girl will still honor her agreement and protect you until reaching the Ebon Waste." She angrily spun away from them, then abruptly stopped after a few paces and turned once again. "And you were correct about people being honest with their feelings. As such, you should know that I no longer wish to be close to you." T'mara stormed off to join Cam as he strolled toward a nearby inn to get the group some rooms.

Arros patted Draxian on the shoulder. "Oh, yes. My dastardly scheme to pair you with T'mara is advancing perfectly."

The muscular lord slapped a hand to his forehead. "Forget what I said the other day about having the time of my life – I'm truly starting to hate this place."

NERRIS

The remainder of the day was spent in awkward silence. Arros refused to give any useful advice to Draxian on his misstep with T'mara, citing that the young lord needed to take some time to reflect on his situation and come up with his own solution. This was a typical Ellandorian stance of self-understanding. Draxian already knew that he had spoken out of frustration and did not intend to hurt T'mara. However, it was the making amends part which confounded him. Arros was much better at such matters, since his entire life was spent avoiding the scrutiny of his every action, or inaction by the people. None of the citizens meant the prince any personal harm through their gossip. It was more that he was often used for teaching examples. If Arros did something thoughtful and kind, the citizens would say to their children, "If this situation is presented to you, be more like Arros." If he made a mistake, the reverse was done and they would ask, "How could

Arros have handled this problem differently?" It was little wonder the Crown Prince wanted nothing more than to be away from it all.

The curtain of night had been dropped for nearly a turn of the hourglass before Draxian decided to make his way back to the inn. He had spent much of the afternoon learning as much as possible about the culture from speaking with the chatty merchants along the crowded streets. Being a head taller than the average man in Breck made his attempt to blend into the populace exceedingly difficult. Also, personal cleanliness was nearly considered a religion on Ellandor, and he generally found the opposite to be true with the locals. He had yet to speak with a food vendor that did not have greasy skin and dirt-laden fingernails. It made him thankful to have an iron stomach when it came to such things.

Like those of the Guardian's Keep, the citizens of Breck generally kept to themselves and only walked the streets when necessary. The regular patrols, consisting of five guards in blue and green gambesons, walked in grim unison. Each carried a single sword at their hip, with an ever-present crossbow in hand ready to use. Draxian was uncertain if they truly expected an assailant to leap at them from the shadows at any moment, or if it was simply a display of power to intimidate the masses. It put him on edge each time the guards glanced his way, regardless of the reason why, as if simply being an outsider was a crime.

Draxian pushed open the heavy wooden door to the inn's common room and spotted T'mara sitting with Cam and Arros off to one side. She never made eye-contact with him, yet the young lord knew she was aware of his presence. Normally, the Huntress would scan the area for any threats as new people approached her space. Now her focus appeared to be locked on something Arros was discussing, as if desperately trying to avoid noticing him.

Arros turned and smiled as the tall noble approached. "Drax! Just in time."

"In time for what?" Draxian casually sat on the bench next to T'mara.

"To get us another pitcher of honey wine." The prince slid the empty container across the table.

T'mara quickly snatched it away, then stood. "I will get it." It took only a moment for her to disappear amongst the growing crowd of patrons.

"Is she still angry with me?"

Cam huffed a laugh. "If she were angry, you wouldn't be alive. T'mara is obviously upset by something you did – although I would not worry too much. I have been at the sharp end of her spear on more than one occasion. Just tell her you are sorry for whatever great offense she believes you committed, then all will be forgotten by morning."

By the look on Arros' face, Draxian had the distinct impression that even a heart-felt apology might not be sufficient. "I'll speak with her when we get a moment."

Arros withdrew the map from his pack and unfolded only the bottom right portion to conserve room on the table. "Cam and T'mara believe it will take another four days to reach the edge of the Ebon Wastes, then another two on foot."

"Why on foot?"

Cam shook his head. "You don't understand – nothing living can survive in that place for long. Even the shadow beasts stay clear of the region."

"Does anyone know why?"

"It's called the Verge – a forbidden place teetering between the world of the living and the dead."

Arros scratched at his unshaven chin. "Perhaps it's a breach to the Spirit Realm. The laws of nature would become more twisted the closer we venture to the event horizon."

The Hunter shook his head in confusion. "I'm not certain what that means, but it sounds like a few more reasons to abandon your mad quest."

"We're not expecting either of you to follow us into the wastes."

"At least I know you're half-sane. That's something."

The Lord Prince leaned back in his chair. "You can just set camp and wait for our return."

"If you do manage to return, don't be surprised to find nothing but scattered supplies and bones."

"You just told us the beasts don't go near the ash. The two of you should be fine."

Cam narrowed his eyes at Arros. "If this foolishness of yours brings harm to T'mara, I'll make sure you pay dearly for it."

Draxian glanced around. "Not to change the subject, but where is T'mara…?"

The three men stood as one and searched the crowded room, until they spotted her at the counter. She was speaking with a middle-aged man, a mercenary judging by the sword on his hip. They laughed at some private joke. Cam pursed his lips and let out a quick whistle, catching her attention. Without even glancing their way to acknowledge the call, T'mara lifted the pitcher from the counter and motioned for the stranger to follow her. Draxian could not help but notice the dark expression on the caravan master's face. It would be natural for him to be concerned for her well-being, yet there appeared to be something deeper brewing behind his gaze. Arros held an unreadable expression – which generally meant there was something bothering him which he did not want others to know.

T'mara set the pitcher in the middle of the table, then stepped aside to allow everyone to view the newcomer. "This is Nerris. He used to be a mercenary with the Free Companies."

"Nerris Vesslen, at your service," he introduced himself with a genuine smile.

Arros reached over and clasped wrists with him. "Well met, Nerris." Draxian could not help but notice the prince held on to the man's arm for much longer than what could be considered a casual greeting. "What brings you to Breck?"

"What makes you think I don't live here?"

"The long traveling pack you're carrying." Arros flashed him a smile that failed to touch his eyes. "Also, I noticed you're staying at the Bone and Twine Inn."

Everyone watched Arros with bemusement, then turned their eyes to Nerris to learn if Arros was correct. The mercenary laughed and nodded. "You're quite observant – an excellent quality. I was watching the people passing from my balcony when the four of you arrived earlier." He leaned in closer and lowered his voice. "You didn't act like someone who has ever been to Breck."

"What gave it away? The fact that I still have all my teeth?"

This caused the man to laugh even harder, somehow placing Draxian at ease. "You forgot to mention the smell," Nerris quipped in return.

"I was trying to be polite." Arros gestured toward the table. "Join us."

"Delighted."

Both he and the prince were the first to sit, followed by T'mara and Draxian. Cam repositioned himself to sit next to Arros, and likely to be within striking range of the newcomer. T'mara quickly swiped the cup that was obviously meant for Draxian, then filled it with honey wine. She set it in front of Nerris, then grinned. "Here. Tell Arros what you said about the old road."

Nerris lifted his mug in salute. "Much gratitude, lovely lady." He took a sip, then turned to Arros. "The latest reports have placed Grazlak's Brigade camping a few leagues to the south. If you're planning on taking the path to Arlinshire, I would be especially cautious."

Arros looked down at the table. "Arlinshire? It's not on the map."

Nerris reached over and pointed. "It's a walled town near the river." He looked up and frowned. "Why else would you be heading south?"

T'mara snickered to herself. "They wish to traverse the Ebon Wastes."

"For what purpose?" The look of concern was evident.

Arros narrowed his eyes at T'mara, then turned back to Nerris. "We're not on holiday. This is an expedition to find the lost city of Orakh."

"Interesting." The mercenary stroked his cheek. "You're searching for the Library of Infinite Knowledge?"

Cam smirked. "A fool's errand, I'm certain you'll agree. It's just an old legend to draw in travelers to their doom."

"Nay," Nerris retorted. "That place is not a myth. I know of two men who went there and back."

Draxian was the first to speak. "How long ago?"

"It was some years back that I heard this."

Cam folded his arms defiantly. "So, you didn't speak with them directly? Nor did this person show you proof?"

Nerris' gaze darkened. "The man who told me this was not an idle gossiper. I trust his information as fact, not rumor."

"And was he with the Free Companies as well?"

"No." The mercenary refocused his gaze back on Arros. "You know I speak the truth, yes?"

The Lord Prince watched him with an amused smirk. "So far." Arros lifted the pitcher of wine and filled his own cup. "I sense a proposition forthcoming."

"I'd like to join your team of scouts."

Draxian shook his head. "I don't think that's a good idea. We're already risking the lives of our two new friends."

Before Arros could speak, T'mara reached over and placed a hand over Nerris'. "I believe it would be safer to have another with us who has wandered through that region." At that moment, Draxian realized he could have spoken any opinion, and T'mara would have argued the exact opposite.

"Just as the lady said," Nerris mocked.

Arros tilted his head slightly. "And what are your fees for assisting us?"

"I only ask that you bring me back something of that place."

"Why?"

Nerris chuckled at the prince. "Do you jest? Even a rusty butter knife that has been recovered from the lost city of Orakh would be considered priceless."

"Well-argued."

T'mara gasped, then grinned like a little girl. "Could you bring me back an ancient spear?"

"I wouldn't mind a few trinkets myself," Cam added.

Arros held up a restraining hand. "Assuming we make it back alive, I'll look around for anything useful that could have survived all those years."

Nerris slapped the table, causing everyone to jump in their seat. "Then, what are we waiting for?"

"Morning would be nice," the prince growled in annoyance. "We couldn't help but notice how dangerous it gets after dark."

The mercenary folded his arms. "This is true. But it also means we won't be spotted by raiders."

"And you're telling me that you can see in the dark?"

"It's a simple skill that's more common than you think." Nerris turned toward T'mara. "Correct?"

The Huntress gave him a wisp of a smile. "Correct."

From the vantage of her cage, Kyreena watched the large men roaming about the camp. It had been many days since she had awakened from her dream-like state, to find herself living a nightmare. She still struggled to understand how fate had led her to this place. All the other women had been sold into slavery to pay off personal or family debts. Kyreena, on the other hand, had no recollection of family, or debt owed. Illara believed she was not purchased but captured by the slavers while traveling. According to her new friend, Kyreena was tossed into the cage, wounded and unconscious. That was likely the reason she did not have a slavery brand upon her forearm like the others. In fact, Kyreena did not have a single identifying scar upon her body. Lorisa surmised that she was taken from a noble family and was likely to be used as a ransom. Unfortunately, Kyreena could not remember anything helpful to solve the mystery of her origins.

Kyreena spent her time learning as much as possible about her captors and her surroundings. The slave camp was filled with laborers who were pushed to their limits under the heat of the day, swinging heavy pickaxes and splitting stones with hammers and chisels. Unlike the men, who worked at cutting and hauling the strange black stone, the women of the slave camp continually brought water and supplies to the laborers. The large guards who carried two blades were ever vigilant of runners and those who failed to work. Kyreena never saw them exact cruel punishments, yet their presence created an ominous tone that caused the slaves to tremble under their harsh tongues. As much as they threatened a painful death, she had yet to witness any of their overlords truly carry out such a vile sentence.

The strange woman she had seen take her friend's form rarely made an appearance during daylight. It was usually at night when she would survey the progress of the tower. However, the lady in white had spent the last day of construction watching and guiding the final stages. When the last ornamental block was finally placed, a cheer went up from all the workers. In celebration, the woman ordered that everyone be given the remainder of the day to rest. Wagons containing large barrels of wine were rolled into the stockade, and libations were distributed generously. It was the first time Kyreena had seen any of the slaves laugh and smile. Lorisa and the other women were quick to drink their fill. Kyreena had other plans. She had noted the patterns of guards and considered many different methods of escape. There were certainly numerous opportunities to get away – although she had yet to learn exactly where the camp was located. Every slave she asked had the same answer. They had been brought in by a covered wagon far from the main roads, and none knew which way to find the closest city or town. Kyreena was unafraid to set out on her own – it was Lorisa that she was fearful for. The young woman had little stamina and would quickly wither out in the wastes without having ample food and water available. Unfortunately, stealing and carrying that much would give their captors plenty of opportunities to find them.

"What are you looking at?"

Lorisa's query pulled Kyreena from her thoughts. "Something is happening at the tower."

Her companion scooted closer to peer in the same direction. "It's difficult to see anything beyond our cage."

"They are gathering in a great circle about the tower. The lady in white is at the base, touching the stone. Her head is down, and she's whispering to herself."

"You can see all that?"

"And hear it."

Lorisa giggled at her. "You're teasing me."

"No." Kyreena gave her a sidelong glance. "My vision has been getting better with each day."

"How? Magic?"

"I don't believe so. Does that not require training?"

Lorisa shrugged at her. "Maybe. Because it has been outlawed, nobody would dare try." She dropped her tone to a whisper. "Well, perhaps those in the Resistance might."

"What do you mean?"

"You've never heard of the Resistance against the Undying?"

Kyreena lightly shook her head. "No. Who are they?"

"Nobody truly knows. It's said they've been around since the beginning of the Thousand Years of Darkness."

"Then they have spent a thousand years wasting their time."

The young woman tilted her head. "Before my father died and left my family with many debts, he used to speak to us about such things." Lorisa laced her fingers with Kyreena's. "They have been gathering their numbers and waiting for the right moment to strike."

"How will they know?"

"They await a sign from the old gods – a promise from them to descend from Ictharia and smite our enemies and heal the land."

Kyreena squeezed her hand. "Then what do they need an army for? Will the gods not bring their own?"

"I can't answer that."

It was at that moment when a memory flashed in the back of her mind. "Someone once told me that the old gods were banished to the Radiant Realm for crimes of hubris."

"That doesn't make sense. Who would be powerful enough to imprison the gods?"

"The Fallen One, perhaps."

Lorisa released her hand and then shook her head. "Do not

invoke that name – it brings bad fortune."

"And how could our situation get much worse?"

No sooner had Kyreena spoken, than the tower began to emit a deep hum. The tone pulsed with a steady rhythm, and purple glyphs began to ignite all over the tower. At the pinnacle, the large gemstone spun slowly at first, then quickly gained momentum until it brightened with a reddish hue. The entire valley surrounding the tower was illuminated with the crimson light. Any slaves not too drunk to awaken, climbed to their feet and stared in wonder.

"What do you think that does?"

Kyreena did not have an answer. A strange sensation filled her mind, as she firmly clutched the iron bars of their cage. Shortly after, the great doors to the mesa temple split down the center and pulled wide. The sound of boots marching in step met her ears. Closer and more numerous they became, until the first of the soldiers emerged. Garbed in black hide with metal plates and spikes covering their chests and legs, the army slowly made their way down the valley path – as if already knowing where they marched. For the next turn of the glass, Kyreena watched with morbid curiosity as a steady procession of armored men, five rows deep, poured forth. She was beginning to think there was no end to the number of soldiers the woman in white was summoning. Finally, the last of the men emerged, and Kyreena rested her head against the bars. "Nineteen-thousand, six-hundred and forty-five."

Lorisa whistled softly to herself. "How do you suppose they plan to feed all those people?"

"Seriously?" Kyreena turned her head and raised an eyebrow. "An army of nearly twenty-thousand men just appeared from nowhere, then marched off to who knows where, to do who knows what – and that was your first concern?"

THE CHILDREN OF DAWN

With Nerris and Arros in the lead, the group of five companions set out from Breck at the first hint of dawn. Draxian's efforts the previous day had procured two more taark for their caravan. Without T'mara to guide him on the purchases, the young lord was forced to take the merchants at their word. The golden crown Arros had given him went further than anticipated. It had not only bought the new mounts but allowed him to load both gekka with supplies and tents to last them for thirty days if managed properly. Nerris had his own taark and gear, yet Draxian noticed he was having the same difficulties he and Arros were in getting used to a new mount.

The expedition first had to secure passage with a large ferry to cross the Deep Water River. This nearly cost Arros his new taark when it became unruly and slipped partly off the edge into the water. T'mara and Cam were quick to assist the beast, and for the remainder of the short voyage, the Huntress remained close by to continually soothe it. She seemed to have a natural affinity for working with the large lizards.

After leaving the ferry behind, it was almost midday before they finally stopped to rest the mounts and stretch their legs. Sliding off his taark, Draxian knelt to pick a blade of blue grass with sharp thistles to study it closer. It was unlike anything he had seen back on Ellandor. The entire ecosystem of Kohr had evolved toward survival in harsh conditions. He wondered if it were even possible for the land to recover, should the red veil finally lift, and the sun return in its full glory.

"Do not allow your taark to eat those plants," T'mara's voice came from behind. "It will make them sick."

Draxian stood and then turned to face her. "I'll remember that." She nodded while starting to walk away. He caught her arm before she could leave. "Wait."

T'mara halted in place yet did not face him.

"Would you walk with me for a moment? Please?"

"We should not wander far. The journey is long."

The young lord gestured ahead of him. When T'mara began moving, Draxian quickly caught up to her side. "I've been trying to come up with the best way to apologize to you, and no words appear to be enough." When she failed respond, he continued. "I know how much you value honesty, so I won't insult you further with worthless platitudes."

T'mara halted, forcing Draxian to do the same. "I am listening."

"It's no secret that Arros and I have been displaced from our home and are sorely ill-equipped to deal with the daily problems you face. It takes true courage to survive in the badlands, and I wanted to acknowledge the strength we have found in you. Not many would have come to our aid, and Cam is most likely here to protect you, and nothing else. I spoke out of line yesterday, but in that moment, I was being truthful in saying that I want to find a way back to my home."

"I am not a child," T'mara protested. "If you do not find me attractive, that is just the way of things. It is plain that Cam has deep affections for me that cannot be given in return. He has been like a father and teacher, yet I feel nothing more."

Draxian folded his arms. "Understandable. However, it's important that you know why I said what I did. It took me some searching to find the answer, and I'd like you to hear it."

"Very well."

"Something is terribly wrong with your land. The closer we get to this lost city of Orakh, the stronger the sickness feels. It is starting to erode at my emotions, and I find myself lashing out without understanding the reasons why. Arros seems to be managing it much better, yet even he is seeing conspiracies all around us, where there may be none."

T'mara drew in her eyebrows. "He does not trust me?"

"It's not you. He doesn't trust Cam or Nerris. Arros believes they're hiding something from us."

"We all have our own reasons for being here." The Huntress dropped her eyes to the ground. "I, too, miss my home and family. When I told my father that I wished to travel with the caravans and see all the big cities, he did not understand. My brother was away on a hunt, and I was certain he would have spoken for me – but I did not want to miss the opportunity to join with Cam."

"Did he forbid you from going?"

"It is not like that with my people. We believe that giving your children the freedom of choice is the greatest love." T'mara lifted her chin to gaze into Draxian's eyes. "He was offended that I wished to travel with one who claims to be a Hunter. The Shadiere have no equal in this skill."

The young lord gave her a wry grin. "That's a bold statement."

Instead of responding, T'mara bent over and retrieved a clod of dirt that fit into her palm. She handed it over to Draxian, then pointed. "Throw this far into the air."

Intrigued, he tested the weight as T'mara watched him with passive indifference. "I can throw this a good distance. Are you certain?"

"I am ready." To his surprise, T'mara closed her eyes.

"Here goes."

Twisting to one side, Draxian hurled the densely packed soil as hard as possible. Before it had gone more than a dozen paces, the Huntress drew a throwing knife and sent it flying. With far more speed than his eyes could follow, T'mara's blade hit the clod, shattering it into a cloud of dust. She reopened her eyes. "Now you can retrieve my knife."

"Whoa," Arros called over from next to their mounts. "Nice throw!"

It took Draxian a moment to realize his mouth was hanging open. "How is that possible?" He took a step back. "And with your eyes closed, no less."

"I told you that the Shadiere have a deep connection to the Realm of Shadows. With it, a True Hunter can sense the target and guide their spear or knife to it every time."

"And this is a common skill?"

"*Banth sen shar*," she spoke in the ancient tongue.

"Shadow magic."

A small grin touched her lips. "You understand."

"A little of the language, not the concept." Draxian started walking through the scattered patches of grass to locate the lost throwing knife.

T'mara was not far behind. "Do you not have those who can use this magic in your land?"

"Not if it's what I think you're describing. It is difficult to harness the negative energy of the Void without understanding its basic principles and properties. Most of it is theoretical, although we do use radiant energy in abundance. It's the foundation of much of our technology."

"Are you speaking with words from the language of your home?"

Draxian chuckled to himself. "Perhaps. My apologies." He immediately spotted the metallic sheen of the blade, then bent over to recover it. "Here it is."

T'mara gently took it from his hand. "You still think me a silly little girl?"

"I never did." The young lord moved in closer and placed his hands on her upper arms in a show of respect. "My fear is that I could easily grow to care for you... far more than I wanted to admit." He shook his head. "You told me before that the people of the Shadiere cannot have children with those not of your kind."

She thumbed at the bracelet. "Which is why I wear this – so that my magic does not keep me from at least being with another who is not of my tribe. I will not be able to carry a child, although it does not keep me from trying anyhow."

"Great," he shot dryly. "Now you're using Arros' logic."

T'mara giggled. "He is a wise leader."

Draxian barked a laugh. "That's a bit of a reach. We'll just stick with him being a 'resolute leader' for now." His hands slid down T'mara's arms to grip her fingers. "As for us... let us just wait and see where this journey leads. I would hate for us to get attached, only to never return from the Ebon Wastes. Fair enough?"

She squeezed his fingers. "It is."

It had been a long night for Kyreena. She hadn't slept, due to the deep, relentless hum of the tower pulsating in her head. None of the others appeared to notice it or were not bothered if they did. At times, the young woman wondered if eventually she would go mad. Even covering her ears did nothing to stop the cacophony. Kyreena wondered if she was truly hearing the sound, or if it was simply in her mind.

"Kyreena? Are you well?"

She hadn't realized it until Lorisa touched her shoulder, but Kyreena was rocking herself back and forth in synchronization with the rhythm of the tower. "I need to be away from this place."

"Don't we all."

"Can you not hear the sound of the tower?"

Lorisa tilted her head to the side. "Yes. I think I can hear the big gemstone spinning at the top."

"Nothing else?"

"What is it that I'm listening for?"

Kyreena stood, then shook her head. "It's nothing."

"She hears the resonance of the magic." Both women turned to see the lady in white standing nearby. "The incessant droning becomes rather annoying after a time, does it not?"

Lorisa dropped her eyes to the ground in a show of humility, but Kyreena watched the woman without fear. "I can't make it stop."

"You must have elemental magic in your blood. I can't sense anything of significance from you, but the breach to the Spirit Realm distorts much of my inner sight." Dark circles had formed around her eyes from lack of sleep, yet she still managed to smile. "My name is Aressa."

"Kyreena."

"It's my pleasure to meet you, Kyreena." The lady stepped forward and waved her hand toward the chains holding the door to the cage. Without her touching it, the lock fell away, and the chains unraveled. "Will you join me for a walk?"

Uncertain what would happen if she declined, Kyreena nodded, then stepped outside the stockade. None of the others moved or made eye contact with the woman. "Where are we going?"

"I'll show you."

Without another word, Kyreena followed the woman out of the cluster of slave pens. They continued toward the open doors of the ancient temple built into the side of the mesa. The large men bowed their heads as the lady in white passed, yet never spoke even a casual greeting. It was just as Kyreena's foot crossed the threshold to the temple that the humming of the tower ceased.

She placed a hand to her head and sighed with relief. "It stopped."

"Indeed." The woman gestured toward the floor. Fresh glyphs were scratched into the surface. "I created a barrier against the noise of the tower. It took most of the night for me to figure out that it wasn't an actual sound that I was shielding myself against. The Abyssal ruckus was making it difficult to catch up on my studies." Aressa gestured toward a table stacked high with leather-bound books and scattered paper.

"What is the purpose of the tower, if I might ask?"

"It provides a magical sustenance for my army. For those with magic who are not attuned to draw from its nourishing energy, the emissions can be irritating when nearby." Aressa pointed toward a bowl of fruit on the table. "Would you care for something to eat?"

"Please." Kyreena crossed over and quickly selected a ripe peach. She took a large bite, causing a dribble of juice to spill down her chin and drip to the floor. She moaned quietly at the sweet taste, a stark contrast to the gruel the slavers fed them.

"We will begin carting the male slaves to mining quarries today. From what I understand, it's no place for women of any station."

Kyreena swallowed, then looked back. "What will you do with us?"

"I've no need for slaves or attendants." Aressa lifted her hand, causing an apple to rise from the bowl and fly straight to her fingers. "You and the other women will be sent to Breck for resale. I'm hopeful that your next master will treat you with kindness."

"I'm not a slave." She lifted her forearm to show the woman in white. "Those men took me prisoner against my will." Kyreena decided it did not serve her to tell Aressa that she didn't remember any of it.

"That's truly disturbing to hear." She turned her head to the side. "Graalar?!"

A large man appeared from a dark corner of the temple, as if he were once a part of the shadows. "Yes, my Lady?"

"Come here this instant."

The muscular brute came forward and bowed his head. "Is there a problem with this slave?"

"Indeed." Aressa folded her arms and scowled. "You were present when she arrived. Did you ask the slavers where they procured the women?"

"Their papers indicated some had been purchased in Phondari, and others in Breck."

"Did you verify the accuracy of these claims?"

He shrugged in confusion. "That would require extensive questions and travel. Rhaulin requested highly specific females – Ullag's men located and purchased them for us."

Aressa reached over and caught Kyreena's arm and lifted it toward the man she called Graalar. "They captured at least one of the women. Her family may be searching for her even now."

The large man's face darkened in rage. "Forgive me, my Lady. I was not aware of this treachery. What would you have me do?"

"When Ullag's men arrive this morning with the carts, tell them to refund your coins and return this poor woman where they found her."

Graalar slightly lifted his chin. "Is there to be no retribution? I could find Ullag and…"

"You will do nothing beyond my commands," she interrupted. "Now go." He bowed his head in respect, then strolled back toward the shadows. Aressa turned to Kyreena. "You have my sincere apologies for the misunderstanding." She lifted her palm and held out three silver coins. "This should help compensate for the work you provided."

Kyreena graciously accepted the coins and closed her fingers around them. "You have my eternal gratitude, my Lady."

"There's no need. We must all work together if we are to rid this world of the vile Undying Emperors."

"That's what the army is for?"

"There is no army that can defeat creatures born of such a powerful magic. It will take the combined efforts of many formidable factions to restore the light to Kohr."

A slight grin touched her lips. "Are you the Resistance?"

Aressa stepped forward and placed her hand on Kyreena's shoulder. "Even better. We are the Children of Dawn."

17

GUARDSMAN, THIRD CLASS

"Guardsman Merrick!"

The young soldier looked over his shoulder to see the sergeant at arms crossing over to his position. Merrick was pacing his usual route along the lower gatehouse wall, protecting the path to the castle of Phondari. It was a tedious job, yet it provided him food in his belly and a roof over his head.

"Here, Sergeant."

The gruff man with heavy whiskers placed his hands on his hips. "Captain Tollas wishes to speak with you. Head over now."

Merrick frowned in confusion. "You mean Captain Brazenwood?"

"No. Captain Tollas at the palace. Get moving."

"Yes, Sergeant," the young soldier answered quickly. He saluted with his fist to his heart, then crisply turned and marched toward the stairs. Merrick was uncertain what he had done to be called to the palace. It had only been a couple of seasons since he had finished his training and was assigned to sentry duty at the lower gatehouse. He spent most of his time greeting visiting nobles, screening other sentries, and opening and closing the gate. Merrick was ready for a more demanding position.

After descending several levels and moving past the barracks, Merrick emerged from the lower gatehouse onto the brick road. Taking the winding route up the hill would be easier yet cost him valuable time. Experience had taught him it was best to not keep an officer waiting. Instead, he took the narrow stairs of stone that ascended directly to the top gatehouse. It was a steep climb up hundreds of narrow steps that quickly caused his legs to burn and his breathing to labor, despite the exhaustive training he endured as the King's guard.

Reaching the upper gatehouse, the sentries barely glanced his way as he passed beneath the massive stone archway. When he emerged, the tall spires of white stone became visible and the road circled around to the main doors. The four palace guards waited patiently as he approached, then held up a hand.

"State your business."

"Guardsman, Third Class, Merrick Whiteforge, here to see Captain Tollas."

The sentry waved him through. "Third door on the right, then down the hallway to the end. Someone can direct you from there."

"Gratitude." Merrick saluted, then proceeded through the heavy palace doors and entered the great hall. Fluted columns of white marble had been placed every ten paces in perfect rows. Large tapestries depicting battle scenes and landscapes covered much of the walls, and the banner of Emperor Thartalagor Deathskull hung from the ceiling as a constant reminder of his ever-watchful gaze.

After turning down the correct corridor, he made his way past the barracks of the elite guard to the officers' quarters. It took Merrick a short time to locate the correct study. His father had taught him how to read for trading in the cities. The door was partially opened, so the young guardsman peeked his head inside while knocking softly.

"Captain Tollas?"

A middle-aged man of over forty summers sat at a heavy wooden desk with piles of papers in neat stacks. His light brown hair showed signs of greying and his face was clean-shaven. Without looking up, the officer motioned for Merrick to enter.

"Close the door behind you."

The guardsman did as ordered, then stood at attention. "Guardsman Third Class, Merrick Whiteforge, reporting as commanded."

"Merrick... Merrick," the man whispered to himself while sorting through the papers until finding the correct sheet. "Ah, here it is." He glanced over the contents, then finally looked toward the guardsman. "We're doing a simple review of all the guards assigned to posts near the castle. Anything that looks out of the ordinary is sent to me."

Merrick shifted uneasily. "Captain?"

"It says you're from Turan's Run?"

"Yes, Captain."

"And that's located near Breck?"

He nodded once. "Correct."

"I see." The officer stood, towering nearly a head taller than the young guardsman. "What makes a man wish to join the army of a neighboring empire? As I understand it that town was all but destroyed by bandits nearly two years ago."

Merrick swallowed hard. "As I told the admissions officer; I was in Breck with a friend at the time the raiders attacked."

"At ease," the captain soothed. "I wasn't accusing you of participating in the incident. We just want you to explain your reasons for coming to Phondari. It's not in the report."

"Apologies, Captain." Merrick dropped his eyes to the ground. "We had been petitioning Breck to station more than four soldiers in our village. My family had a forge that made bridles and collars for all the gekka and taark in the region. Turan's Run was a league south of the main road to Phondari, and was often overlooked by the larger caravans, so it wasn't considered a priority."

The Captain reseated himself. "Continue."

"Over the last ten years, or so, more and more soldiers were sent out to search for those using magic. As a result, it allowed bandits to organize and frequent the towns with little fear of soldiers interfering with their schemes. They caused trouble for a lot of folks and, at first, the few guards we had did their best to keep the peace – but after the ruffians started showing up in larger groups, even the soldiers were afraid to interfere."

"What happened?"

He took a deep breath. "A few days before I left with a family friend to sell bridles to the stables in Breck, three mercenaries appeared in our village. I believe at least one of them was a Hunter. They didn't purchase anything, just wandered around, looking at the people."

"Just studying the villagers, not merchandise?"

"Yes, Captain. It was a bit odd, which is why I remembered them." Merrick clenched his jaw. "I knew something wasn't right, but we needed to get the shipment into Breck, or lose our contract to another forge."

Captain Tollas laced his fingers on the desk in front of him. "We heard the town was destroyed, and all property of value stolen."

"It's true." Merrick choked on his words. "But that's not all."

"Oh?"

"There were no survivors left in the village, including my parents and younger brother. To add to it, we could find none of the older children among the dead. At least fifteen people were missing – most of them younger men and women."

Tollas leaned forward. "You believe they were captured and taken back to the raider camp?"

"No, Captain." Merrick glanced behind him, then lowered his voice. "I believe they were taken by slavers, then sold in Phondari."

"Truly?" The captain leaned back in his chair and folded his arms. "All indentured servants are here to pay off debts – nothing more. They will have proper paperwork with the magistrate's seal. Without it, any servant can seek assistance from the government and the slavers risk execution."

The young guardsman lifted his chin. "With respect, Captain – documents can be forged, and who would believe the word of someone with a slave mark burned into their forearm? Even if the officials took a moment to investigate a claim, there's no one left in Turan's Run to verify the truth."

The officer nodded in thought. "That makes sense. However, it still doesn't explain why you're here."

"I wanted nothing to do with an empire that won't protect its own people from being slaughtered or sold. If my being here can keep others from the same fate, then at least my life will mean something."

"You can't protect the border towns by walking the walls in Phondari." He narrowed his eyes suspiciously.

Merrick considered his answer before speaking. "No one has seen or heard from my people in the city of Breck, Annis, or any of the larger towns. I heard rumors of someone purchasing large numbers of slaves. In most cases, the slavers headed in the direction of Phondari."

"And based on that, you believe the slavers came here?"

The guardsman knew his story was weak. He was unsure who he could trust but felt this was not the time to be silent. It could be his chance to get the help he needed. "No, Captain. I finally found a reliable witness who saw at least one of the captives sold in Phondari."

"To whom?"

He took a deep breath. "The palace."

Captain Tollas tilted his head slightly. "Only the most trusted staff work here. We wouldn't have use for an indentured servant – they have no loyalties."

Merrick's shoulders slumped, his hope fleeting. "I'm certain you're right. Forgive me for bothering you with this, Captain."

"Not at all." The officer stared off to the side, as if considering something important. Finally, he turned back to Merrick and sat up straight. "Can I assume you would recognize this person if you saw them?"

"Without a doubt – she grew up with me."

"After everything you've gone through to get yourself stationed here, I would hate to think it was all a waste." Tollas retrieved a pen and bottle of ink, then began scribbling on a piece of paper. "I want you to deliver this to some friends of mine in the residential district. They might be able to assist you with finding out what happened to your people." When the captain finished, he rolled up the flax paper and dropped it into a decorative tube. He then drizzled hot wax over the top and stamped it with his seal. "Take this to a boarding house called the Dragon's Chambers located in the fourth district. Ask for Veklass and tell him that Tollas says he still owes him a bottle of honey wine."

Merrick took the cylinder from him and saluted. "My gratitude, Captain... truly."

"He'll give you something before you leave. Bring it back here and hand it only to me. Understood?"

"Understood."

Merrick decided not to wait until his shift was over to deliver the message. Having the seal of a captain for the palace guard tucked beneath his arm made him feel important for the first time in a long while. He was uncertain how the man could help, but if the captain believed it was a possibility, Merrick had hope of saving his friends.

It took more than an hour to walk down to the outer edges of the residential district and find the boarding house. The building consisted of two floors made of ancient stone, similar to the rest of Phondari. Even so, it did nothing to dim the magnificence of living in a city that floated high above the Aldrinn River. Not even the wisest of scholars understood how the magic worked, only that the city had floated in place for well over two-thousand years. It provided a natural defense for the capitol city, forcing invading armies to attack from the long bridge to the gatehouse.

When Merrick reached the building, he pushed open the front door and glanced around. The small common room was lit by a single lantern that illuminated the empty chairs and tables scattered about unused. In one corner an older woman sat in a squeaky wooden chair as she worked on a blanket at her loom. She glanced up to the young guardsman, then motioned with her head to indicate a nearby door. Merrick stepped toward it and knocked twice.

"Go away," came a gruff voice from behind it.

"I'm looking for Veklass – I have a message for him."

Merrick heard chairs scooting across the floor, and several footsteps darting about from beyond the door. When it finally opened a crack, an older man with heavy whiskers stared back from the slit. "What message?"

The young guardsman held up the tube. "Tollas wanted me to tell you that you still owe him a bottle of honey wine."

"Did he...?" The grizzled man narrowed his eyes. "As I recall, it was the other way around."

"I can't speak to that, friend."

The door pulled further back and the man reached out a soiled hand. He quickly snatched the cylinder. "Wait here." Veklass slammed the door closed, leaving Merrick to stare at the heavily nicked wood, as if it had been frequently used for knife practice.

It didn't take long before the old man returned, then motioned for the guardsman to enter. "Well, don't just stand there and let the flies in."

Merrick huffed to himself and stepped inside. Instead of finding the expected living chambers, the room was stacked with wooden crates, many of them displaying the imperial seal burned into the side. There were no other people present, which made the guardsman wonder if he had imagined the sound of numerous footsteps.

Veklass stopped just a few steps into the room and reached into a box on a nearby table. "Would you like a couple smoked sausages to bring back to your special lady?" He withdrew several tubes of meat that had been stuffed into dried intestines and wrapped in wax paper, then held them out to Merrick.

"I appreciate the gesture, but there's no lady waiting for me," Merrick replied, refusing to take the gift.

"For a friend then. Surely you have those," the old man said, pushing the package into his hands until he had no choice but to comply.

"My gratitude."

Veklass placed his hands on his hips. "Now, what is it you need?"

"Captain Tollas thought you might be able to help me find some missing people."

"On the chance it has eluded your notice, it's a big city. You'll have to be more specific."

Merrick took a deep breath, then began recounting the same tale he had spoken to the captain. The older man was content to listen and nod occasionally. When the guardsman finished, Veklass stroked at his beard. "And you believe some of your villagers were sold as slaves in Phondari?"

"I only know about one. I'm not certain about the others."

"Ullag is the largest slaver in these parts. He would have the resources to bribe the inspectors and forge documents. Nasty fellow, he is. Shouldn't go poking your head into his business, if it could be helped."

"Then how can I find out if he's behind the massacre of my family and friends?"

Veklass motioned him closer, then placed an arm around Merrick's shoulders. "I may know someone... who knows someone... who might have had dealings with him," he began cryptically. "Give me a few days to ask around."

Merrick exhaled in relief. "You have no idea how grateful I would be. Is there any payment you would like in return?"

The old man patted his back. "That is not how this works, my boy. We do a favor for you, and you do a favor for someone else."

"That's all?" He was immediately confused. "How will I know what that is?"

"It's up to you." Veklass gave him a friendly wink. "If we won't help folks out when they need it, then what's our purpose for being here?" He gestured toward a boarded-up window. "The land is dying and people wonder why it's happening. It's because most folks are the kind to spend their entire lives taking, and there are far more of those than the ones who are giving."

Merrick nodded in understanding. "Sounds like something my father would say."

"He sounds like a smart and decent man. Was your father with the Resistance?"

At the mention of the Resistance, Merrick's stomach rolled. To even speak of the ancient insurgency in Phondari was considered a crime. "He... I don't..." the guardsman stammered.

Veklass held up a hand to indicate that he needed no answer, then reached into a nearby crate and produced a small pouch. "Give this to our mutual friend and tell him the honey wine was in the kitchen, exactly where he said it would be. Remember to say that."

A little confused, Merrick took the leather sack and nodded his appreciation. Without another word, the young guardsman exited the building with the small leather pouch and a package of sausage. He waited until his feet touched the street before testing the weight of the mysterious purse. It had been securely tied so that only by cutting the leather strings would someone be able to view the contents. Placing it within the larger pouch on his sword belt, Merrick began making his way back toward the palace. The sausage still in his hand made his stomach rumble. Knowing that he would likely get punished for bringing back an item that may have been stolen from the royal provisions, the guardsman unwrapped a portion and bit into the end. The sausage was tough and chewy, yet even without it being reheated, it was one of the best he had ever eaten. This revelation only served to solidify his suspicions.

Merrick glanced over and noticed four children nearby halt their game of 'grab the rock' to watch him eat. Viewing their skinny, pitiful frames caused him a twinge of guilt. "Would you like some?" The children nodded vigorously yet stayed seated in the dirt. Remembering that he still wore his uniform, Merrick smiled warmly. "It's fine – I won't hurt you." As they cautiously stepped forward, the guardsman began breaking the sausages into four pieces. They held out their hands in anticipation, the youngest of them, a little girl of no more than four summers.

"One for each." Without a single word of gratitude, the children darted away as if they feared he would demand the sausages be returned. Merrick chuckled in amusement, then started back for the palace. *The old man was right*, he thought to himself. *It feels good to give something away with no expectations of payment.*

By the time he arrived back at the palace, the red sky was darkening to a dull grey. None of the other guards challenged him, and Merrick suspected it was mostly due to being recognized from earlier. Captain Tollas was still in his study, sifting through pages while referencing an old book.

Before Merrick's knuckles could rap on the wood, the captain called over to him. "Come in, Guardsman."

Moving inside, Merrick closed the door and stepped up to the desk. "Reporting as ordered, Captain."

Tollas watched him with an unreadable expression. "Do you have something for me?"

"Yes, Captain." The young guardsman reached into his pouch and withdrew the leather purse. He placed it on the desk. "The man who gave this wanted me to tell you that he found the honey wine in the kitchen, just where you said."

Captain Tollas made no move to reach for the pouch. "Did you look inside?"

Merrick could feel his face flushing. "Of course, not, Captain. I'd never!"

"I believe you." The captain stood and moved around the desk to face him. "What did you learn?"

"Nothing yet."

"That, I don't believe."

He glanced around to give him a moment to think. "I swear, Captain. He said he needed a few days before consulting some of his contacts."

"That's not what I meant, Guardsman." For whatever reason, Merrick found himself sweating under the intimidating gaze of the officer. "What did you learn?"

He swallowed hard. "Nothing for certain. Although I think that place might be a haven for the Resistance."

"And what are you going to do about that?"

Merrick was uncertain of the correct answer, so he simply didn't speak.

"Well? I asked you a question!"

"Apologies, Captain. I can't, in good conscience, report about something without proof of a crime."

Tollas sat back on the edge of the desk and folded his arms. "So then, if you hear a scream coming from a back alley, you would ignore it simply because there was no immediate evidence of foul play?"

Merrick could feel the trap closing in upon him. As such he decided to try a different approach. "Captain, I've seen neighbors accusing neighbors of being in the Resistance, simply because they didn't like that person. Their homes were upended and possessions seized. Those who do not immediately confess as sympathizers are beaten in front of their children. Even if found innocent, which rarely happens, their lives are never the same. I joined the Phondari Guard to help keep folks safe, not to be a part of some kind of mass inquisition."

Captain Tollas allowed a slight grin to escape his lips. "You're a good man, Merrick." He reached over and lifted the leather pouch. A small knife seemed to appear in his hand from nowhere and Tollas cut the leather string holding it tight. Once free, a large black disk fell into his hand. Made of storm ward ore, the palm-sized item had golden writing on it that Merrick identified as magical glyphs. "You brought contraband into the palace – a crime that holds a severe penalty."

The guardsman's stomach flipped on end. The Captain had been testing his loyalty to the Emperor, and he had failed. "I swear I didn't know."

Tollas placed the disk back into the leather pouch and handed it to Merrick. "Of course you knew. You saw that boarding house was filled with crates of supplies from the palace – even sampled it yourself. I can smell the rare spices on your breath that are cooked into the Regent's personal sausages." He tilted his head. "Do you deny it?"

Merrick lifted his chin and stood at attention. "No, Captain."

"Finally, he speaks the truth." Tollas moved back around behind his desk and then reseated himself. "You're dismissed."

The young guardsman remained where he stood, trembling in fear. "I don't understand."

"What's not to understand? You were sent to a house in the fourth district and found a haven that you believed was being used by the Resistance. When they gave you an unknown package to deliver to me, you felt duty-bound to open it. After discovering an item that appeared to be magical in nature, you immediately reported the incident to the Watch Commander." His eyes narrowed. "Understood?"

Merrick exhaled, not realizing he'd been holding his breath. "Yes, Captain. I'll head there immediately to report you as a traitor, and a Resistance sympathizer."

He pressed his lips together. "As I said before, you're a good man."

SLAVERS

It was around midday when the slavers arrived in the camp with their covered wagons. Kyreena had been allowed to retreat to the quiet sanctum of the temple whenever the droning pulsations of magic from the tower became too much for her. Otherwise, she was free to move about the camp as she saw fit. Much of that time was spent talking with her friends and fellow slaves Lorisa and Illara. Both expressed curiosity as to why Kyreena was allowed to roam without supervision. That was something she wondered, as well.

Kyreena was studying the murals on the walls of the inner temple when Aressa stepped up next to her and spoke. "Beautiful, aren't they?"

"Yes," she answered without moving her gaze. "The details of the carvings are amazingly well-preserved."

The lady in white nodded her agreement. "It's written in the ancient tongue."

"It's a prayer to honor the God King and Queen."

"Impressive." Aressa's smile was genuine. "So very few people are still around who can even read this text. Where did you learn it?"

Kyreena shrugged a single shoulder. "I'm not certain."

"Perhaps in Annis. From what I understand, magical studies are still allowed within Emperor Bonewing's territories."

"Possibly. I have no memory beyond my capture."

The woman stared at Kyreena with more than a passing interest. "There is something different about you that I have never before encountered. I don't quite understand it, yet my instincts tell me you're more than what can be seen on the surface."

"If it was truly so, I would like to believe I wouldn't have been so easy to capture."

Aressa released a small laugh of amusement. "Well-argued." She reached over and took Kyreena's hand. "Perhaps you just need someone to guide you on your path to a better understanding of magic. You could travel with me if you'd like?"

A wave of nausea set into the pit of Kyreena's stomach, and a cold shiver shot up her spine from the woman's touch. Something hidden about her was the source of Kyreena's unease. She politely pulled her hand free. "It's kind of you to offer, but I need to find my home and family. I'm certain there must be people worried for my safety."

"Do I unsettle you?"

She didn't wish to lie to the woman yet felt it prudent to not offend her either. "The noise of the tower was giving me a headache."

"Is that all?" Aressa was searching her face for a reaction. "You seem troubled."

"Perhaps it's the face you wear. I knew her for a short time."

The woman in white lifted her chin in understanding. "Ah. You must have been present when a host was chosen as my vessel."

"She died next to me." Kyreena swallowed hard at the memory as it replayed itself in her mind.

"I was born a very long time ago. My father believed I would be imperative to ending the Thousand Years of Darkness and bringing light back to Kohr." Aressa walked around Kyreena in a long and slow circle as she continued. "He tried everything to extend my life, as I imagine any father would. Some of his efforts were more brutal than others. As the search continued, I inadvertently became deathly sick from a failed experiment. There was no choice. My life essence was torn from my body and placed in a magical container. Only through the valiant sacrifice of that lovely woman, could I be here today to free the land from the curse of the Undying Emperors." She halted in front of Kyreena. "This woman was a true hero of Kohr. How many people can you name, slaves or otherwise, that have been remembered in history with an abundance of worth?"

"I can't speak to that – although it would have held more value if she was given that choice."

"Very well. Having that option, what would you have said?"

Kyreena considered the question carefully. "I imagine anyone would want to be remembered as such. However, you speak as if success is your inevitable outcome."

A gentle smile appeared on Aressa's lips. "In time, you'll come to understand the true power behind the Children of Dawn. When that day comes, I hope you'll join us. For now, the caravan awaits to take you home."

The slave caravan continued rolling throughout the remainder of the day. The thick canvas was pulled down so Kyreena could not be certain, yet it felt as if they were going in a different direction from the path they took to get there. Ogrod, brother to Ullag, the slaver who owned Lorisa and the eleven other women, forced Kyreena to ride with the slaves in the cramped cage. The men were being sent to a quarry to finish off their debts, but the women were to be taken elsewhere. As such, the small caravan split off from the group after nearly a turn of the glass.

"Did they say where we're being taken?" Illara whispered to Kyreena.

"Possibly Phondari – I truly don't know anything for certain." She looked around at the concerned faces of the other women. "They promised to take me back to where I was captured – but not where that was, nor when they would do so."

Lorisa laced her fingers with Kyreena's. "I have less than two years left of my debt. Promise me you'll come to Breck when its finished and find me?"

"If I could, I would pay off every debt of those here to free you."

The women all nodded their gratitude and Illara reached over to hug her. "I wish we could go with you."

"That would make me happy." Kyreena released the young woman. "How much to pay off your debt?"

"I was accused of stealing coins and a valuable ring from a merchant. The magistrate sentenced me to five years of servitude." Tears began to well in her eyes. "I didn't do as he claimed. He was angry that I refused to wed to his son."

Kyreena drew her neck back in shock. "Would he not need proof of such a crime?"

"They found a purse of silver and the ring under my bed. I'm certain he placed them there for the guards to find."

Lorisa spat on the ground. "I hope you go back there someday and make him suffer for it."

"I've dreamed of that every night."

Kyreena lifted her chin. "What was his name?"

"Jhonrig. A silversmith in Breck."

"I'll remember that." She glanced around at their faces. "What would happen if you were to escape?"

Lorisa shook her head. "We can't – even if it were possible. If we do, our debt is doubled and another from the family must repay it. My little sister would be next, and she's only ten summers. I could never do that to her."

"I see." She placed her hand over Lorisa's. "They say that the end of the Thousand Years of Darkness is upon us. Perhaps slavery will be as well."

"I pray you're right."

A short time later, the caravan came to a halt. In the distance, a low rumble of a storm could be heard. The fifteen soldiers assigned to escort the caravan were calling out orders to set up the wards and secure the cargo. The door to the cage was unlocked and the canvas pulled aside. Ogrod stood at the exit and placed his hands on his hips. "Red storm on the horizon. There are some nearby rocks that you can go behind for a privy break. If the storm heads this way, the cart will protect you from the lightning and possibly some of the beasts that have been known to appear. If you try to run away, my archers will shoot you in the leg and leave you for fodder." He swept his arm around in a grand gesture. "We're leagues from the closest town, even if you knew which way to head. I can promise you won't survive on your own for more than an hour past dusk with the smell of blood in the air." Ogrod stepped to one side. "On your feet, slaves! Let's go!"

The women quickly exited the cage, one at a time. When Kyreena's feet touched the rocky soil, Ogrod caught her arm and began roughly pulling her away from the group.

"Let me go," she protested.

The portly brute smelled of stale wine and sour sweat. He ignored her until they had moved a good distance away. Finally,

Ogrod released her with a shove, causing Kyreena to fall on her rear. "Now that we're alone, what's this I hear about you accusing us of wrongful enslavement? You cost me thirty silver today."

She climbed back to her feet and held out her arm. "Do you see a slave brand?"

"What?" Ogrod snatched her wrist and studied it. "I don't understand. You should have one."

"Then where was I purchased from?"

It took him a moment to answer. "Breck."

"That's not what the others say." She tilted her head. "What was my debt?"

"Know your place. I don't have to answer to a mouthy runt like you."

Kyreena folded her arms. "You promised Aressa to take me home."

"Who?"

"The lady in the white robe."

Ogrod narrowed his eyes menacingly. "You think I give an Abyssal shite what that mad priestess wants? The moment she forced me to hand over that silver, whatever freedom you think was owed vanished."

"People will be looking for me."

"Lies. We found you traveling alone, and in the middle of nowhere."

Kyreena poked him sharply in the chest with her first finger. "Hah! You *did* capture me – I knew it."

Ogrod's face contorted with rage. "Makes no difference. No one even knows you exist."

"The others do."

He stepped in close, causing Kyreena to lean backwards to keep his rank breath from reaching her nose. "Tell me, little girl, do you even know your own name?"

"Kyreena."

"Kyreena what?" When she didn't answer, it was his turn to bark a laugh. "Hah! You don't know it, because I gave that to you. Kyreena Davaros was the name of a girl who killed herself during transport last season. Her drunkard father sold her into slavery when his debts grew too large. I still have her contract."

"That's not true." Despite her saying it, deep down she knew the vile man wasn't lying. "My name *is* Kyreena."

Ogrod grinned at her through yellow, stained teeth. "Good – keep with that thought. Her contract was for three years. My own brother docked my share for allowing that little rat to die."

"You're a degenerate."

"I don't know what that means, but I suggest you make nice, darling. You even think about causing trouble, I'll make certain the others are sold to some particularly nasty lords." He grabbed Kyreena behind the neck, then pulled her in close to whisper in her ear. "The kind that have been banned from purchasing slaves, due to an unusual amount of accidental deaths or disappearances – if you know what I mean."

"You wouldn't."

"We'll be passing near the land of one of those very men in a few days. I'll be certain to introduce you." He gently released her, then gave Kyreena a smile that made her skin crawl. "He'll just love you. Truly."

PRINCE ARROS

It had been an uneventful trek through the southern plains. Arros had alternated back and forth between Cam and Nerris to probe deeper into their shady backgrounds. Three days had passed since exiting the gates of Breck and making their way toward Orakh. The taark Drax had purchased for him was quite unfriendly at first, yet with Cam and T'mara's coaching, he managed to drastically upgrade its temperament from deep loathing to more of a passive indifference. The only reason Arros managed to avoid losing a limb to the beast's jagged teeth was due to the taark's shield-shaped skull preventing its neck from turning back that far. To his dismay, it still tried at every opportunity.

Arros gave as much distance as possible to Draxian and T'mara without looking as if he was doing so. It was obvious his old friend was having a difficult time accepting there was no way to get home. If such a path existed, the prince was certain his father would have found it long before Arros and Draxian arrived. The young lord had quickly ascertained Arros' intentions, and nearly ruined the prince's scheme with his brash words.

Nerris was easily the most interesting of the two other men. His stories of travels and conquests with the Free Company helped to alleviate the boredom due to the lack of scenery. However, it was interesting to the Lord Prince how every story appeared to take place in his youth. Nothing of the last ten winters was mentioned. When Arros questioned him about it, he simply replied that he had decided to remain in one place and work on bettering his swordplay – that and Nerris needed to keep low from a contract on his life.

As for Cam, Arros was particularly curious about his shift in priorities. He had made his opinion known about how important it was to finish his caravan contract to the city of Phondari, yet when T'mara refused to go, he followed from a distance for over a day. Cam disapproved of the Huntress' romantic intentions toward Draxian. In fact, the only person he disapproved of more was Nerris.

"And that's how I met my third wife," Nerris finished.

Cam shook his head. "Did it ever occur to you that in all your boasting, your stories never end with you being content with any woman you found?"

"I thought my happiness was simply an unspoken truth."

The Hunter gave him a deep scowl of disbelief. "You're happy?"

"Of course – I've had a full and rich life."

Arros gave him a sidelong glance. "Until about ten years ago."

"And what about you, my mysterious friend?" Nerris deflected, choosing to ignore Arros' statement. "You've barely spoken a word about your own travels. A pretty face like that must have beheld many beauties in your land. Come now, Arros – tell us a rousing tale to get our blood surging."

Draxian glanced back at him, reminding the prince to keep their origins carefully guarded. Although, if he were to reveal something from their homeland, how much worse could this world get. "Very well. Would you like me to tell you about the woman I left behind to come to this land?"

Nerris grinned back. "Please, do."

"I wouldn't mind hearing about her," Cam agreed.

Arros took a deep breath. "Her name was Bellasa. We met after I saw her perform in a play at the grand theatre."

"What's a play?" Nerris interrupted.

"Do you not have performers who act out stories before an audience?"

"Like a bard or minstrel?"

Cam shook his head. "I think he's referring to a dramatic troupe."

"Ah, yes – known a few of those sirens in my day as well. Please, continue."

Arros lightly shook his head. "Anyhow. I was so moved by her performance, I begged Drax to invite her to meet with me for a private dinner."

T'mara turned to Draxian. "What did you say to make her agree?"

"Say?" The young lord looked back at Arros, then shrugged. "I walked backstage to where she was changing out of her costume, then told Bellasa that Arros wanted to meet her."

"That's it?"

"What else should I have said?"

T'mara grunted in exasperation, then looked back at Arros. "Describe how she looked on the day you met."

The prince drew in his eyebrows as he thought of an answer. "I remember lovely features and a cute dimple in her right cheek when she laughed. Her thick mane of black hair had been loosely braided down her back, set with jeweled hairpins. Those eyes sparkled like blue diamonds, dancing in a chamber of a thousand candles, and her lips were painted pink with glistening flecks of pearl dust. She was wearing a long dress spun from silver thread, accenting her soft, milky white skin. The gown was cut sharply down the front to her navel and laced together with a pink ribbon to perfectly form to her breasts." Arros smiled to himself. "Bellasa tripped on the rug just as she approached the table to greet me. I barely caught her before she fell to the ground. To this day, I could swear she did it on purpose."

"You see," T'mara called over to Draxian. "That is how you describe your mate to another." She turned her attention back to Arros. "And you plan to marry when you return?"

It was Arros' turn to give Draxian a chiding glance. "No, that's a story for another time."

Cam gave Arros a sidelong glance. "Are you certain this was a real woman?"

"She sounds a bit like how I've heard the Empress of Dragons described," Nerris proclaimed. "It's said that Adreana's legendary beauty is only matched by the swiftness of her wrath."

T'mara turned in her saddle. "Do not even mention her name. It is said the Dragon Empress has eyes everywhere."

Arros was amused with their banter. "Why do they call her that?"

"You should know – you came close to being dinner for one of her pets."

"Wait..." The prince leaned in closer. "You believe she may have intentionally sent the dragon after us? Can she do that?" All three of them nodded in unison to Arros. He exchanged a look of concern with Draxian, then reached over to his pack hanging from the saddle. After recovering the map that he had received from Trimenius at the Guardian's Keep, the prince studied it closer. "You said Dellahara is her family name, correct?"

"Yes," T'mara confirmed. "Her personal guard were the ones who took your cloak."

"Fortunately for us, Dellahara is located on the far side of this map. Let's just hope she stays there."

Nerris stroked his chin. "Do you think she would have an interest in us?"

"Probably not, but my father has a way of attracting unwanted attention. One of the Empress' soldiers recognized the crest of my house."

"Oh? What house is that?"

"Nemendes. Ever heard of it?" Arros watched his face for a reaction.

Nerris did not respond. Instead, he pointed ahead of the group. "Just over this rise we should be able to see the Ebon Waste in the distance. This is as close as I have ever come to entering it. You'll soon understand why."

T'mara urged her taark ahead of the group. When she reached the top of the low hill, she jerked her mount to an abrupt halt. The rest of the group exchanged worried looks, then rode forward to join her. As soon as Arros maneuvered his taark next to Draxian's, he sat up higher to get a better view. Nearly a league ahead of them, an ashen desert of scorched land stretched as far as the eye could see. The dismal and forlorn region was only overshadowed by an eerie, green fog-like mist that only thickened the further in it went. Despite the horrific scenery, the cheerless region was not what held the Huntress' attention. Just before them, hundreds of chest-high mounds were scattered about at random. Obviously not naturally occurring, they reminded Arros of large anthills.

Cam leaned toward T'mara. "Have the True Shadiere ever seen something like this?"

"I don't know." The Huntress nervously fingered her spear. "I left them before fully completing my training."

Nerris shook his head. "These dirt mounds weren't here before."

Arros glanced over to him. "How long ago?"

"Perhaps eleven or twelve winters."

"We should circle around them," T'mara warned.

Cam nodded. "I agree."

Without further discussion, the Huntress pulled at the reins to lead her taark away. Arros started to follow her example when a section of the ground moved nearby. Releasing a deep, throaty wail of fright, the prince's taark launched toward the field of mounds at a run.

"Arros!" Drax cried in warning.

The Lord Prince jerked hard on the reins in an attempt to regain control. With a loud 'snap,' one of the leather straps broke free of the bridle. Within moments, Arros found himself darting toward the middle of the field with no way to control his mount.

"Jump," T'mara shouted from far behind.

Not requiring further encouragement, the prince snatched his pack from the saddle and leapt to one side. He hit the hard-packed dirt and rolled several times before sliding to a stop. Only a scant moment later, the ground collapsed beneath his fleeing taark, sending it tumbling into a sinkhole. His mount scratched and clawed at the sides in an attempt to escape yet couldn't get a firm grip on the loose soil. The panic was evident within its eyes. Arros raced over to the edge to get closer to the taark in a futile attempt to catch the bridle, knowing that his added strength would not be enough to help pull the heavy beast to safety.

T'mara called out to him from nearby. "Leave it!"

The prince turned to see her twenty paces away, beckoning him to jump on the back of her taark. With a growl of frustration, Arros started toward her when his trapped mount squealed in anguish. He glanced back and stiffened at the horrific sight. Two worm-like creatures had burst from the sides of the sinkhole and set upon the taark, tearing at its flesh with three sets of mandibles, each of vastly different sizes working in unison to shred the poor beast apart. They had sleek brown skin and dozens of tiny, clawed arms protruding from their bellies to assist in digging and traveling underground. Each creature was nearly the thickness of the prince's chest, and twice his height in length.

"Hurry!"

T'mara's urgent cry forced Arros to tear his eyes away from the screeching taark. It was then he spotted six more of the worm creatures emerging from nearby mounds and skittering straight for the Huntress. He could never reach her in time to flee. As such, he drew back his sleeve and activated the enhanced mollifier. Summoning his will forth, the bracer discharged a brilliant sphere of light to strike the nearest attacker. The power of the blast tore the creature in two, sending both halves spinning away amidst the sound of charring flesh. Again, and again he fired, each ball of raw energy searing through a swarming worm with terrifying precision.

As Arros rushed toward her, the Huntress lifted her arm to cast a spear. In the same instant, one of the creatures burst from beneath her taark. The frightened animal reared back, sending T'mara rolling down its back and to the ground. Arros waited until her mount bolted toward Draxian and the other men back on the hill before firing another sphere. The shadow creature's head exploded into a shower of flaming char.

"Arros!"

The prince waved his old friend off. "Go! I'll get us to safety!" Not waiting to see if Draxian obeyed, Arros ran forward to help the Huntress recover to her feet. She held the back of her head and moaned in pain. "T'mara?"

"Leave me," she muttered.

"Not a mouse's chance in the Abyss." Arros reached into his pack and withdrew a black rod about a pace in length with a flat, circular headpiece. All about him, hundreds of nightmare worms began to emerge from their mounds and converge on them. Their mandibles clacked with intent. Using both hands, Arros twisted the split shaft in opposite directions, causing it to abruptly extend to eight paces long. He slammed the staff into the ground. Red glyphs blazed to life along its length, and a translucent dome of force descended over top of them in a shield of energy.

Arros exhaled a sigh of relief when the first of the creatures retreated from the touch of the dome. It took only moments before they were surrounded by a raging sea of living creatures, all trying to push their way into the shelter. The prince was uncertain how long it would hold, yet there were no other options. Sitting T'mara up, he checked her for any serious wounds. A large lump was forming on the back of her head where it was sleek with blood. With eyes still closed, the Huntress slowly fell forward into his arms.

"T'mara!" Arros lightly slapped her face to wake her. "Don't sleep, it will only make it worse."

He continued to hold her in his arms while considering their situation. It occurred to Arros that he might be able to walk the dome out of the area, yet that didn't prevent the creatures from simply following him for leagues. They had already begun to dig at the base of the dome in an effort to find a weakness. Due to the constant hissing of the creatures, Arros had failed to notice an unusual ringing beginning to emit from the emergency shelter. It had been designed to protect the occupants from harsh weather and hostile wildlife by drawing upon the ambient energy within the ground. However, the dome had never been tested in a place like Kohr, the nexus of all the Realms of Power.

Arros turned toward the staff to get a closer look. The buildup of energy was continuing to increase at an alarming rate. As the high-pitched tone rose in intensity, so did his fear of what would happen. At best, the shield emitter would eventually burn out and allow the swarm to set upon them. He searched through his pack to take inventory of what he still had, while the ringing continued rising to a deafening pitch. Arros abandoned his search and dropped his pack, then quickly covered T'mara with his body. The ringing abruptly stopped. Then, only a half-breath passed before the staff exploded in a deafening concussive blast that could be heard from leagues away.

Draxian's heart was racing. He managed to catch the reins of T'mara's taark when the worms began to slither toward them. Cam looked on the verge of panic as he tried to find the Huntress among the raging horde of creatures. Even he realized that there was no hope of fighting their way through an ocean of shadow beasts.

"We need to ride," Draxian commanded. "Arros will look after her!"

"T'mara!"

Ropes to the supply gekka were already attached to his and Nerris' mounts. They were all too happy to begin running from the encroaching swarm. "Cam! We're leaving!"

Finally, the Hunter turned his fearful taark and started after them at a run. "Dammit!"

They continued riding, easily outdistancing the slithering worms within moments. The group began to angle around to one side in the hopes of drawing as many of the beasts away from Arros as possible. Draxian knew the prince had brought along an emergency shelter but was unsure how long it would last against the constant barrage of attacks from the creatures, or if it would even work as expected on Kohr.

He glanced over to see Nerris digging through his belt pouch when a violent explosion erupted behind them. A concussive wave of force hit the group, knocking their mounts to the ground and sending Draxian tumbling a good distance away. Supplies scattered in every direction as a cloud of dry dirt covered the region, making it difficult to see more than a few paces in front of him.

As he pushed up to his hands and knees, a sharp pain in his ribs caused the young lord to wince in agony. Draxian spat out the coppery taste of blood in his mouth, then did his best to shield his eyes from the stinging dust. Tearing a strip of material from his cloak, the large man wrapped it into a cowl about his head to keep him from breathing the thick cloud while he waited for it to settle.

"Draxian?!"

"I'm here," he called back to Nerris.

Within moments, the middle-aged man appeared over him and knelt down. "Are you well?"

"Not as good as you, it would seem."

"What happened?"

He shook his head. "Arros' fault, I'd imagine." Draxian glanced around for his taark. "Did the mounts run off?"

"Nay. They're sitting right where they fell." He pointed toward his ear. "Loud sounds like that will cause them to become disoriented for a time."

Draxian tilted his head. "Apologies, I couldn't hear you."

Nerris chuckled at his jest, then gave the young lord a friendly slap on the arm. "Let's find our friends."

It did not take them long to locate Cam, face-down in the dirt. He had been knocked unconscious by the blast and took a moment to wake. As for the mounts, it was just as Nerris had predicted; they had remained where they fell, glancing around at the sky in a daze.

When Cam finally sat up, he glanced around at the settling debris. "Are we dead?"

Nerris slapped him on the back, causing a new cloud of dust to appear around the Hunter. "I assure you we'll not be sent to the same level of the Abyss." He laughed heartily, then helped Draxian lift Cam back to his feet.

"Where's T'mara?"

Draxian motioned for him to follow. "We're going to check on them now."

Without another word, the three men hobbled back toward the top of the hill. When they reached the summit, they all froze in place and Cam gasped. "What happened here?"

Where the field of mounds had once been, the ground had sunk into a large crater that was a good fifteen paces deep. Thousands of shattered worm parts and black gore were splattered about in a mass grave of epic proportions. In the center, a small, untouched circular platform of ground could be seen. Atop it, Arros cradled T'mara in his arms and spoke softly to her. Cam dropped to his knees and let in a breath upon seeing them still alive.

Nerris turned a haunted gaze back to Draxian. "Who in the blood-soaked Abyss *are* you?"

FLEETING HOPE

Kyreena remained quiet for the next few days of travel, as she didn't want to burden her new friends with problems they had no control over. It was becoming clear that she needed to escape her captors at the first hint of civilization. To make matters worse, the young woman had caught the attention of a depraved, gap-toothed caravan guard named Berus. He had been assigned to watch Kyreena ever since Ogrod had confessed to wrongfully capturing her. The slavers were smart enough to realize she had little motivation to behave.

"Lorisa?"

The woman turned to face her. "What is it?"

"When you first met me, how did you know my name was Kyreena?"

She considered the question for a time. "That's what the guards were calling you. When you responded to it, I just assumed the name was correct. Is it not?"

"I don't know anymore. Sifting through my memories before this cage is a lot like trying to see through murky water. I can feel the answers are there, just hidden somewhere beneath the surface."

"You still remember nothing at all?"

Kyreena frowned. "Glimpses of faces mostly – not anything of substance."

"You must have been someone of importance at one time."

"How so?"

Lorisa shrugged a single shoulder. "The way you speak and hold yourself. Not many people can read, and most that can only know enough to do business. Perhaps you were a scholar from Annis, searching for hidden treasures throughout the land."

"Why was I alone?"

"Maybe it was a secret mission from the Sect of the Green Flame."

At the mention of it, something flashed inside her mind. "The Green Flame is the last known elemental mage school in existence."

Lorisa grinned in victory. "You see? It's all starting to come back."

"Possibly." Kyreena glanced around at the faces of the women in turn. "If I could find a way to free myself, would any of you join me?" Most of them quickly looked away, or simply dropped their eyes to the ground in shame. It was just as she thought – they were afraid of what would happen to their families if caught.

"Kyreena," her friend gently began, "you have every right to want your freedom. However, it's unthinkable for the rest of us."

"I'll go." Illara leaned forward and placed a hand on Kyreena's knee. "If you can find a way to free us, I'm with you."

"Are you certain? It could be dangerous."

She pressed her lips tightly together. "I refuse to spend the next five years being punished for something I didn't do."

Kyreena bowed her head to Illara. "Your courage is appreciated."

Lorisa nudged her. "Just remember, there's a wide chasm between courage and desperation. Don't do anything foolish because you think there's no other choice."

"You've been a wonderful friend to me," Kyreena stated, as she turned to Lorisa. "As such, I say this with as much respect as possible: There is something important that must be remembered – some task I need to complete, and nobody will keep me from finding out what that is."

"I believe you." Lorisa leaned over and rested her head on Kyreena's shoulder.

Just ahead of the caravan, someone called back and forth in friendly greetings. The wagon continued for a little longer before rolling to a stop. From what Kyreena could see through the small gaps in the canvas, they were next to the stone wall of a small keep. It was not long before the sound of a key jingling on its ring could be heard, followed by the clicking of the padlock.

Berus threw back the canvas and gave Kyreena a dark grin before addressing the others. "Pleasant evening, slaves. We will be staying here for the night. Ogrod wants everyone out and lined up next to the wagon." He pulled open the iron bars. "If anyone misbehaves, all will be punished."

Kyreena noticed a few worried eyes darting toward her. She ignored them and unloaded from the cage with the rest. After filing up next to the wagon, she finally could see that the keep was near a small town. The ancient stone buildings sat hunkered together for protection from unseen foes outside the barriers. An additional palisade consisting of sharpened wooden stakes surrounded the village, providing a bit of extra defense against roaming beasts or raiders. Turret towers at every corner of the town wall and keep were manned by heavy ballistae to prevent attacks from the air.

A short time passed before Ogrod exited the reinforced gate of the fortress with an older man walking in step beside him. The noble was short and thin with a bald head and a long, drooping mustache. Three deep scars could be seen on his left cheek, as if a wild animal had raked his face with sharp claws. His eyes continually swept up and down the line of women with eager anticipation.

Ogrod stood before them and folded his arms. "Baron Clavius has generously offered to pay off one season of your contracts for any willing to… entertain his men for the night. It's more than most of you little dung-rats deserve, but still must be voluntary." He waited expectantly. "Well? Step forward."

When none moved, the baron folded his hands together and smiled, displaying several missing teeth. "We'll be preparing a banquet for those who attend: Hot meat pies with succulent brown gravy, served with boiled carrots glazed with honey. And, of course, all the wine you can drink from my own vintage stock." He gestured behind him to the keep. "Doesn't that sound divine?"

At the baron's vivid description of dinner, eight of the slaves stepped forward. Lorisa and Illara wisely stayed in line. Kyreena was very much aware of what was expected of any who accepted the invitation, and Ogrod's previous warning about Baron Clavius was still ringing in her ears. For whatever vile reason, the man was banned for a good number of years from purchasing slaves. A private deal would need to be made of mutual consent, or Ogrod's brother, Ullag, could lose his credentials to trade in slaves.

"Splendid," Clavius exclaimed. "Are there any others?" His gaze met with Kyreena's. "Well, now – you have some fire behind those eyes."

"Not interested."

Ogrod gestured toward her. "This little beauty is Kyreena. Careful, milord, this one may bite."

"Truly?" The baron placed a trembling hand on his chest and sucked in a breath of excitement. "Oh, my." Clavius grasped at Ogrod's arm. "I simply *must* have her."

"Apologies, milord – you know the law."

Much to Kyreena's displeasure, the baron was not easily dissuaded. "How much is her contract?"

"Thirty silver for seven seasons."

He licked his lips. "I'll give you sixty for her."

"Not possible."

"Eighty!"

Ogrod watched Kyreena with an unreadable expression. "Even if I wanted to, this one would need to agree to the new contract terms."

"Perhaps the three of us could speak in private?"

The repugnant slaver gave Kyreena a slight smirk of victory. "That would be just fine."

Not wishing to cause any problems for the other women, Kyreena was reluctantly escorted from the caravan by Berus and followed the two men into the keep. She fought down the fear that bubbled in her stomach, focusing instead on studying her surroundings for ways to escape.

They passed through a small dining hall, morbidly decorated with animal skulls and tapestries depicting hunts. Continuing down a corridor, the group entered an old study that smelled of musty books and burnt wood from the hearth. Berus shoved Kyreena down in a heavy oak chair, then clasped a steel manacle around her right wrist.

"So that you'll remember your place," he sneered. After twisting the holding screw in place, Berus withdrew the key and handed it to Clavius.

Ogrod dismissed the lowly guard, then waited until he had left the room before speaking. "Now then, let's talk some business."

"Indeed," Clavius agreed.

Kyreena narrowed her eyes. "I'm not for sale, and you know it." She held out her left wrist. "You see – no slave brand."

The baron ignored her outburst to speak with Ogrod. "Eighty silver, I believe was the price?"

"Correct."

"And what about the paperwork?"

The slaver gave Kyreena a cruel smile. "Won't be a problem. As far as my brother is concerned, Kyreena Davaros took her own life."

"Excellent." The baron turned his eyes to her and exhaled a long, shaky breath. "Oh yes, my dear, we are going to have such fun together."

Draxian sat next to T'mara's bedroll and watched her sleep. They had continued onward toward the Ebon Waste to get as much distance from the mass grave of the subterranean creatures as possible. Cam was especially quiet, offering to keep T'mara with him during the ride. The Huntress still lay unconscious since falling from her taark and failed to witness Arros' uncanny luck with the emergency shelter overload. Draxian was just beginning to appreciate T'mara's company and was terrified that he had lost her. Even worse, if Arros had been killed, the young lord was unsure if he had the will to continue searching for their fathers on his own.

"Any change?"

Draxian glanced up to Cam. "Nothing yet. She received a good knock to the head – all we can do is wait and see."

"I've known quite a few men who never woke from such injuries."

"That's a real possibility. However, the swelling appears to be receding and her heartbeat is strong. These are good indicators for a recovery. It just may take a bit more time."

Cam squatted next to T'mara and gently brushed the hair from her face. "She's always been reckless with her life, although this is the first instance I've ever seen where she risked everything for another." His eyes darted toward Arros, who was standing with Nerris at the edge of the Ebon Waste more than a dozen man-lengths from their camp. "With my own eyes, I saw your companion release powerful magic from his hands to battle those demons – and yet that cannot be true." Draxian didn't respond, but was content to let Cam speak. "I'm a Chosen Hunter. We are supposed to be able to sense when a mage is near."

"Arros isn't a mage."

"That's what I once believed as well. It's true that there are some types of rare magic that are undetectable to our sigil. However, this is my first encounter with one such as him."

Draxian had to be careful. He had no intention of revealing the magic Cam believed the prince wielded was nothing more than advanced metallurgy and technology from Ellandor. "Arros is certainly unique, I'll give him that."

"Whatever the explanation, I'm grateful he had the power to protect T'mara." He shook his head at the absurdity of it. "That was the most powerful spell I have ever seen – and I've tracked quite a few dangerous mages in my youth."

"You don't anymore?"

"No. I've found other ways to use my skills that don't require dragging innocent children from their homes to be tested for magic."

Draxian clapped Cam on the shoulder as he stood. "Perhaps there's hope for this land after all."

Without another word, Draxian made his way toward Arros and Nerris. The two men were standing motionless and staring at the ground before them. It was certainly a strange sight. On one side of the divide, life flourished as well as could be expected. Yet on the other side, Draxian only saw a powdery black sand, mixed with something akin to ash.

When he arrived, the prince pointed toward his hunting knife that had been thrust into the ground. "Drax – look at this."

"Yeah, amazing job stabbing the sand," the young lord chided. "What's your next great conquest – dirt?"

"Hilarious. You see how the blade is just inside the dividing line between live grass and ash?"

He leaned down to get a better look. "Just barely."

"I placed my knife just outside the Waste when we first arrived."

"It's actually growing?"

Arros glanced over with raised eyebrows. "At an alarming rate."

Nerris folded his arms. "I'd heard about this happening yet was never bold enough to get close and see for myself."

"I now understand exactly why our fathers came here. If this is allowed to continue, Kohr will eventually be lost, and far more, when all the Realms of Power are thrown out of balance. It would lead to the destruction of life on an immeasurable level."

"Please, Arros," Draxian shot wryly. "Don't dip your words in honey – tell us how bad it truly is."

Nerris somehow missed the young lord's ironic tone. "I don't know – that already sounded awfully terrifying to me."

The prince crossed beyond the line and into the Ebon Waste. "This is strange."

"How so?" Drax stepped forward and immediately felt a prickling starting in his toes, then moving quickly up to his face, as if his circulation were just coming back from being cut off for a time. "That can't be healthy."

"You can visibly see what it's doing to the land. Imagine what would happen to live flesh over an extended period."

Nerris backed away from the line. "You're either the bravest men I've ever met, or completely mad."

"Perhaps a bit of both, backed with a large helping of desperation," Arros answered with all honesty. He returned to the other side of the line and gave Nerris a friendly slap on the arm. "Don't worry, my friend – we're not that easy to kill."

"Like I said before, just bring back a few artifacts and I'll be a happy man."

"It's a two-day journey on foot to the ruins of Orakh," the prince began. "We'll need at least a day to find this hidden library and search through it for… whatever. Then, another two days back here. Think you can hold down the camp for us?"

The older mercenary glanced toward the canvas tents where Cam was tending to T'mara. "We'll have plenty of supplies to last that long. How about yourself? The gekka and taark won't go anywhere near the Waste."

Draxian considered the problem. "We'll take as much as we can carry. Water will be the most pressing concern."

"Truly," Nerris retorted. "I would think strolling into a desert cursed by death would be foremost on your list."

Arros huffed a laugh. "You're not wrong."

FORSAKEN

Immediately after a bargain was struck for Kyreena, Baron Clavius had three guards restrain her with ropes and a gag. She was then taken to an outbuilding where a set of stairs descended into a deep cellar – likely used at one time to avoid the red storms. Clavius had converted it into a dungeon where he kept tables holding oddly shaped tools and racks with chains for torturing his victims. Until that moment, Kyreena had been hopeful of an escape. There were only a handful of guards on rotation at any time, and the walls were designed to keep creatures out, not to prevent someone from leaving. The underground chamber, however, was designed for exactly that purpose.

Kyreena remained chained to a ring in the wall for the remainder of the night, and in total darkness. As she felt around for anything to help her escape the manacles, gloomy thoughts began to roll around in her head. It was likely that Lorisa and Illara might never learn what truly happened to her, and she would quickly fade from their minds. It would be as if Kyreena never existed. She was starting to greatly regret not taking the offer of the lady in white to learn from her. If what Aressa spoke of was true, Kyreena had a gift for magic she had never realized. Or it had fled her mind along with all her other memories.

Most magic came from the Elemental Realms to affect stone, fire, air, and water. However, there were some who touched the more peripheral and dangerous Realms, such as Spirit, Shadow, and Demon. As Kyreena pondered this, it occurred to her that she had no recollection of how she acquired that knowledge. Perhaps there was substance to what Lorisa had theorized, and that before her capture Kyreena had been a scholar from one of the mage sects. She wished it was true yet rebuked herself for such a desperate grasp at hope. If Kyreena was ever to escape, it could only happen from patience and careful planning.

After an unknown amount of time had passed there was the sound of the cellar door opening. The small amount of light that seeped inside was enough to allow her a view of the chamber. While the chain gave her a little movement, there was still nothing within reach to use as a weapon. Three sets of footsteps could be heard, one of them softer than the rest. The chamber door squealed open and two of Clavius' guards entered. Torches in hand, they were leading a bound woman in a torn red dress by her arms and kept a sack over her head. Without a glance of acknowledgement, the soldiers placed the girl in leg shackles across from Kyreena, then made their way back toward the door. Before they left, one of the men placed a torch in the sconce next to the exit.

Kyreena waited for the men to leave before speaking. "Who are you?" The woman reached up and jerked the sack from her head. Unruly blonde locks fell about her face, yet Kyreena recognized her right away. "Illara?"

"Kyreena?!"

Even in the dim lighting, she could make out the bloodied lip and swollen left eye. "What happened? Why are you here?"

The battered woman shook her head. "We were told that you happily came to an arrangement that would release you within two seasons. I thought my best chance to be free would only come from staying near you." Illara shook her head in sorrow. "I asked if it were possible to have the same arrangement."

"And they agreed?"

"Not at first. However, Ogrod told him that I was a risky contract because mine was a sentence from the magistrate, and not a debt. Upon hearing this, Baron Clavius agreed to reduce my servitude to half, if I stayed."

Kyreena's heart broke into pieces. "The only reason he agreed was that no one would come looking for you for at least another five years."

Illara nodded her agreement. "That's what the baron said as well."

"Why did he hurt you?"

"It wasn't him. Ogrod did this." She dropped her head, and her shoulders shook from crying. "The baron let him have me for the night as part of the arrangement."

Kyreena could feel the rage building within her. "When we are free from this cellar, I promise you will see him suffer far worse than what you endured."

"How?"

"I don't know yet. Just remain strong and survive."

Illara glanced around. "What is this place?"

"I would think it would be obvious."

"But why would he hold us here? Indentured servants are still to be treated with respect."

"Perhaps that's true of slaves, but not prisoners." Kyreena

stretched the chain as close to Illara as it would allow. "We *will* find a way free. I promise."

Nerris poked at the small campfire he had made to heat the pot of stew. There was certainly enough dried bushes and dead grass about the area to sufficiently feed the flames. Being so close to the Ebon Waste had a few positive aspects. First, the beasts of the Shadow Realm tended to avoid it. And second, the red storms appeared to lose their intensity when coming anywhere near the desolate region.

Arros and Draxian had left the camp at the first hint of dawn. Cam decided to stay with T'mara, but Nerris followed to the edge and was curious to watch them enter the Waste. The two men did not even hesitate at the border, they simply crossed into the land of death without a look back. It was little wonder the Lord of Shadows took such an interest in the mysterious outsiders. Nerris was not told anything of value, only that he was to stay near them and report their movements. However, even his master did not expect Nerris to enter the Ebon Wastes. For anyone not invited, the lost city of Orakh was a sentence of death.

"Cam?"

The Hunter turned at the sound of T'mara's voice. "You're awake!" He scooted in closer. "Take it slow."

T'mara pushed herself up to her elbows, then squinted. "Where are we?" The Shadiere woman's head swiveled around until she spotted the Ebon Waste. "Arros," she gasped. Panic became evident in her eyes. "We were surrounded!"

"Easy," Cam soothed. "Arros and Draxian are well. They left early this morning in search of the library."

"They left?" The Huntress reached up and pressed a hand to the back of her head. "You did not wake me?"

Nerris could see Cam struggling with his words, so he decided to help the Hunter out of the cage. "Drax wanted to bid you farewell, but Arros believed it would be dangerous to wake you before they knew you were fully healed. Every moment they delayed would place us all in further danger."

T'mara slowly stood on unsteady legs, then stared out toward the Ebon Waste. "I can see nothing of them."

"I was standing at the edge and I lost sight of those two after only a short time. It was as if they faded into the mist – there's no other way to explain it." Nerris lifted the lid from the pot and stirred at the broth. "Arros said you need to eat some food and drink plenty of water the moment you wake."

Cam grabbed one of the water skins and held it out to her. "He's right. Take it."

Without objection, the Huntress reached over and snatched the leather container, then removed the cork stopper with her teeth. She drank deeply before handing it back. "Now, would someone like to explain how I find myself still among the living? I remember Arros holding me and being surrounded by the shadow beasts."

The two men exchanged a wide-eyed stare. "Perhaps you should sit and get comfortable," Nerris started carefully. "It may take a bit to find the correct words."

Kyreena did her best to keep Illara's spirits from continuing to decline. Every few hours one of two guards would come down to check on the women, bringing small portions of food or water, and to refresh the torch on the wall. The captives each had a chamber bucket and wooden plate, yet nothing that would help with an escape.

It wasn't until late that night that Baron Clavius made his first appearance since Kyreena had been imprisoned. Even before the vile little man arrived, she knew he was accompanying his soldiers. The baron was humming a merry tune as he descended the stairwell to the cellar. When he entered the chamber, Clavius stopped near the door and placed his hands on his hips. He studied both women without a word, then pointed to Illara. "That one."

Kyreena shot to her feet. "What do you want with us?"

"Don't worry my lovely songbird, you'll have your turn."

At his command, Illara was taken from her corner and dragged over to a heavy wooden table. Kyreena could do nothing as the young woman whimpered to herself in terror while being bound. Once the baron was satisfied Illara was secure, he dismissed the two guards.

"Now then, shall we begin?" Clavius placed a blacksmith's apron over his head, covering himself all the way down to his knees. He pointed to a small iron pipe sticking out from the ceiling. "I had the most wonderful time listening to you speak this morning."

Kyreena's eyes widened slightly. That would mean the baron knew of her desires to escape. "What are you going to do?"

"As you desire to leave this place more than anything else, I will need to make certain you understand there will be dire consequences for such rebellious thoughts." Clavius retrieved a leather strap and cloth from a nearby box, then shoved the material into Illara's mouth. He then placed the harness over her head to keep his captive from spitting out the rag. "While I do enjoy the screams of my guests, the wailing will make it difficult to listen to your protests to my mistreatment of your friend."

Kyreena was quickly beginning to understand the deranged nature of their captor. "Why would you spend so much wealth only to damage your property?"

"If you wish to keep your songbird from flying away, the wings must be clipped." The baron began to pull at Illara's boots, gently removing them one at a time. "Lovely," he proclaimed, while tracing his fingers lightly over her toes. "Such a shame that I will need to break them." Clavius moved over to the wooden chest and began to sort through the various items. "Now where did I place that mallet?"

Tears fell freely from Illara's eyes and Kyreena's heart was pounding in rage. "Let us go, or I swear by the One Power of Darkness, you won't live to regret it." She was uncertain from what dark corner of her mind the curse originated, yet it was enough to give Clavius pause.

"And just what would you do to me if given the chance? Please, tell me."

"I would strangle you with my own hands, watching as the life faded from your eyes."

He stepped forward with the mallet in hand, then grinned. "What else?"

"Is dying not enough?"

"Oh, no. You must do something artistic with the body. Perhaps you might consider making a trophy of my skin or serve my flesh in a delicious meat pie to your companion. The possibilities are only limited to the imagination of the artist."

The man was not just debased, he was completely unbalanced. Her threats only fueled his perversion. "If you harm her, the only ending you can expect for your corpse is food for the carrion eaters. No ceremonious farewell, and no place of honor for your rotting skull – simply forgotten."

His lips drew back in a sadistic grin. "Ogrod was correct, you do bite. And while I'm certain you intend every word you say, I just don't envision it happening." Clavius moved back to Illara and lifted his mallet. "Too bad for this lovely creature."

"Don't!"

He slammed down the mallet striking Illara in the ankle. The woman's muffled scream could be heard beneath the harness.

"Now, for the other."

Kyreena's promise to protect the young girl echoed in her ears. A burning wrath seethed beneath the surface, causing her vision to go white and her muscles to flex. In one quick jerk, the chain holding her shackles was torn from the wall. Kyreena flung it around like a whip to wrap around Clavius' neck. A quick tug sent the degenerate into the air, only to land at her feet with a solid *thud*. As the baron struggled frantically to free himself, Kyreena dropped to a knee and grasped his throat with one hand while the other pulled the chain taught.

"This world will be a better place without you in it," she hissed.

Kyreena watched as his face turned blue and the thrashing of his legs began to slow. Despite her threat, she had no stomach for watching the life drain from Baron Clavius' face. Instead, Kyreena searched through his pockets until she located the key to her shackles. She wasn't certain where the temporary strength had come from, although Kyreena was smart enough not to rely on such an occurrence happening again. After the iron manacles had clattered to the floor, she quickly moved over to the table to free Illara.

"Hold still," she comforted. "I'll have you free in a moment."

As Kyreena began to work at the straps, the sound of footsteps coming down the stairwell was heard. She quickly abandoned the effort and glanced into the chest of tools. Inside, Kyreena discovered rusted cutting instruments of various types. After settling on a long, thin spike protruding from a wooden handle, and a thin knife in the other hand, she ran over to the exit and stood to one side of the archway.

"Milord? Do you need assistance?"

The door burst inward and the two soldiers rushed through with swords drawn. Not wasting an instant, Kyreena leapt forward and slammed the spike into the ear of the first man, killing him at once. Before the second soldier could turn, her knife was already slashing for his neck. The blade cut deeply, severing his arteries and vocal cords. Blood fountained from between the guards' fingers as he clutched at his ruined throat. Kyreena felt no pity for them. They had watched as Baron Clavius tortured his victims and done nothing to stop it.

As the blood pooled on the cellar floor, she continued freeing Illara. "Are you well?"

Her new friend sat up quickly and hugged Kyreena. "You saved me!"

"How bad is your ankle?"

"It hurts."

Kyreena reached down and lightly ran her fingers over the swollen bones. "It might be cracked. We'll need to wrap it tightly."

"What if more of his men come down here?"

She knelt low and shook her head while tearing strips of cloth from the uniform of one of the soldiers. "We would have heard a warning bell by now. It's after dark, so we'll have the cover of night to escape."

"I don't think I can walk on this."

"You'll need to try."

Kyreena continued to work on Illara's ankle until she was satisfied the wrapping was thick enough to keep it secure. She then used a larger boot from a guard to fit over the wrap. It would look odd to the casual observer, yet they didn't plan to go anywhere near people until far away from the keep.

"Should we take their swords?"

Kyreena helped Illara stand, then supported her as she hobbled toward the exit. "Do you know how to use one?"

"No."

"Then the added weight will only slow us down." Kyreena pulled another knife from the chest of tools and handed it to her friend. "Take this instead."

Illara slid the blade into her waist band then hugged into her from the side. "Where will we go?"

"They'll be expecting us to walk along the road or hide in the keep until morning. We'll need to steal some supplies, then head into the badlands."

"Won't that be dangerous? We can't see in the dark."

Kyreena gave her a tight-lipped smile. "Don't worry, I'll be your eyes."

THE VERGE

Arros and Draxian had been trudging through the desolate Ebon Waste for more than a day without seeing any sign of the city. Neither of the men spoke much, as they wanted to conserve as much energy as possible. The young lord could feel the prickling in his limbs getting stronger and more painful with each hour that passed. Beyond the obvious discomfort, he didn't notice anything physical to cause him worry.

Draxian leaned over and excitedly nudged Arros. "Do you see that?!" He pointed ahead of them. "More black ash!"

The prince rolled his eyes. "It ceased being humorous after the fourteenth time you said it."

"Are you certain we're going in the right direction?" Draxian threw his arms wide. "This mist is getting thicker, and considering how far we've walked, it wouldn't take much to miss an entire town."

"Are you afraid we're going in circles?" Arros withdrew his waterskin and took several gulps.

"I've heard of it happening."

The prince shook his head. "We're still heading in a straight line."

"How? Just because the fog is thicker, doesn't mean we're near Orakh."

Arros pointed toward the horizon. "I'm using the stars."

Draxian stopped in place and his shoulders dropped in dismay. "Is the desert drying out your brain? We haven't even seen the sun since coming to Kohr, much less stars."

The prince halted, then turned back to face him. "You don't trust me?"

"Do you truly wish me to answer that?"

"Very well." Arros brought his pack around and pulled back the flap. He withdrew the vision enhancer and held it up. "This is how I know."

Draxian folded his arms and narrowed his eyes. "It doesn't work that way."

"Says you." The prince turned the visor over and pressed the activation glyph three times in succession. "Here."

The young lord hesitated for a moment, then snatched it from Arros' hand. He placed it over his head and glanced around. "Well… this is new." The world around him was shown in reverse shades of grey. Above, three dark spheres were swimming within a milky sea of black dots.

"Do you see the smaller moon?" Arros asked from the side.

"The one with the stripes?"

"Correct. Just below it is a cluster of stars that looks like an arrowhead."

Draxian immediately spotted the constellation. "It could also be a fish."

"Anyhow, that's what I've been following during the day. Not much else to orient from."

The young lord huffed to himself. "I didn't even realize we had enhancers like this."

"Me neither. I discovered this setting by accident."

"Let me guess… the Twilight Protocol." He removed the visor and handed it back to Arros.

"This kind of technology has little use for our general population."

Draxian looked past Arros, then pointed. "Did you just see that?"

"Nope… not even going to give that credence," the prince grumbled.

"It looked like something moved in the sand." Draxian squinted. "Maybe it was the wind."

Arros' gave him a dubious expression, then shot his eyes to something behind Drax. "Wait. I just saw it too." He motioned them forward. "Let's keep moving."

The young lord glanced behind him yet didn't see anything but an endless sea of ash. As they continued onward, the swirling wisps of sand began to grow more frequent. It was almost as if the ground was softly reaching its fingers toward the clouds. The effect was quickly giving the region a haunted feel.

Neither man spoke of it, but continually darted their eyes back and forth. The small puffs of dust began to appear more and more like arms formed from ash, quickly losing cohesion and falling back to the ground. Some fingers of ash brushed their legs as though attempting to grab hold.

"How much further do you think?" Draxian asked.

Arros placed the vision enhancer to his eyes, then made several adjustments. "I see it."

"I know I've been a toad on this leg of the journey, but please just tell me the truth."

The prince withdrew the visor. "It's not a jest." He indicated directly ahead of them. "There're ruins of a city wall about a half-league from here."

As soon as his words left his mouth, a mound of black ash began to rise from the ground. They watched in horror as it attempted to take the form of a man, just before falling back into the desert. "We should hurry."

Arros pulled back his sleeve to reveal the black bracer, preparing for the worst. "Agreed."

Both men took off at a run. They continued heading through the thick morass of green fog. All about them, shapes began to take substance. The closer they came to the ruins, the more the ash creatures gained strength. Draxian glanced back for only a moment, then felt something catch his leg. He tripped, nearly sliding face-first into the ground.

"Drax!"

He quickly recovered and started running once again. "I'm fine! Keep going!" Just ahead, a wall twenty paces high appeared before them. "How do we get over it?"

"From what I saw, there were quite a few sections that had crumbled." Arros began guiding them to the left. "Let's just follow it until we come to an opening."

Moments later, a dark, man-sized statue of ash appeared in front of them and charged forward. Arros lifted his arm and released a blazing sphere of energy from his bracer. Upon impact, the ash wraith exploded into a spray of molten glass.

They both glanced at each other, then Arros chuckled to himself. "That works."

Just as Draxian spotted a broken section ahead of them, another wraith surged from the ground. Arros attempted to dodge aside – but the creature's hand reached out and caught his leg, pulling him down. Two more emerged from the ash as the prince wrestled to get in a position to fire upon the wraith. Draxian slid to a halt and drew his blade. He launched forward and slashed at the arm of the first ash beast. The edge easily passed through, causing the arm to lose its form and drop back to the ground in a burst of dust. To his dismay, the wraith kept going at him, seemingly unaffected by the loss of its limb.

A blast from Arros' mollifier caused the ash wraith holding him to explode backwards. Drax grunted in pain when a stray glob of fiery glass brushed his skin. The young lord shook his arm to alleviate the stinging, then dove back into the melee. "Watch your aim!"

"Apologies," Arros hollered back. "I don't have any other weapons that can hurt them."

Draxian gripped his handle with both hands and swung at the wraith, using the flat of his blade. The effect was devastating. Instantly, the creature burst into a shower of black sand, causing his sword to shimmer with greenish flecks of light. In all his time owning the weapon, he had never seen it react in such a manner.

Arros fired two more spheres of energy. "Why are you just standing there like a dullard?!"

Draxian glanced up to see six more wraiths beginning to take form. "Let's keep moving!" The Lord Prince took aim. Instead of a blast of energy erupting forth, the mollifier blew a shower of sparks in every direction. Arros cried out in pain. He jerked the smoking bracer from his arm and tossed it to the side. "Are you well?" Drax called out.

The prince cradled his injured arm, then nodded for Draxian to keep moving. "At least it didn't explode."

"I suppose we should just be grateful for that."

Without another word, both men rushed through the opening in the thick wall, leaving the ash creatures to the Ebon Waste. When they arrived on the other side, Arros motioned for them to halt. The glowing green mist was still above them, yet the city was shrouded in darkness. Draxian couldn't see through the grey haze more than a dozen paces in any direction.

"Now what?"

Arros rubbed at his arm, then pointed. "This way."

"Are you guessing?"

"Of course, I'm guessing," he shot back. "You have a better idea?"

Draxian pushed out his lower lip, then shook his head. "No. Just wanted to make that clear."

The prince huffed indignantly, then started forward. "At one time, the library was this civilization's most revered structure. If we follow the largest of these ancient roads, it should eventually lead us to the important areas."

"Assuming something doesn't find us first."

Arros scowled back at him. "Don't hex us. We're in the Verge."

"And?"

"*And* you can't get any closer to actually stepping into the Spirit Realm than right here. We have no idea what our thoughts or desires could summon."

"Such as?"

A small, female voice spoke from behind him, nearly causing Draxian to jump out of his boots. "Do you want to play with me?"

"Bloody Abyss!" The startled lord spun around and peered down at the child.

The girl was wearing a tattered dress and had heavy tangles in her shoulder-length hair. She lifted her chin to reveal hollow eye sockets and gaunt, leathery skin. Draxian felt a chill of dread shoot up his spine when she spoke again. "You have big muscles. Will you stay with me?"

He glanced back to check Arros' reaction but found him more than a dozen paces away and pointing a hunting knife. Draxian grimaced, then held up a hand to the lost soul. "I'm certain there are some other… spirits in the area to keep you company."

"I'm all alone." Her mouth barely moved when she spoke.

"Drax," Arros called over to him. "What are you doing?"

The large man waved the prince back, then knelt down before the lost soul. "Can you tell me which direction to the library?"

She pointed in the opposite direction of Arros. "That way. Past the ones who are always hungry."

"You have my gratitude. Perhaps later we can play with you."

The spirit shook her head. "You won't come back. They'll eat your heart and make you watch."

"That's disturbing."

Arros finally made his way over. "Stop speaking with the creepy child. It's just an echo of a little girl that died when the breach was created."

Draxian stood, then rounded on the prince. "Do you think I don't know that?"

"Just making sure that was clear," he mocked

The young lord turned back and found she had disappeared. "Nicely done, Arros. Don't ever have children."

"If we stand here arguing much longer, I doubt that will be an option for either of us."

Draxian glanced around, then started walking in the direction the spirit had indicated. "This is the way to the library – the girl said so."

"Seriously?" Arros threw up his hands, then began following. "Why not? What could possibly go wrong."

"I think we're lost." Draxian studied the broken tower remnants, then turned to speak with Arros. The prince was staring at a broken home that had been destroyed by the collapse of the tall structure. "What's wrong?"

Arros squatted down and then scooped up a handful of dirt. "There was a terrible battle here."

"What was your first indication?" Draxian chided. He stepped up next to the prince when Arros did not respond. "Forgive me. I'm trying to disguise my deep-rooted fear with poor attempts at humor."

"I know." Arros continued to feel the soil between his fingers. "I can't shed the feeling that I've been here before."

Draxian knelt to join his friend. "This is the Verge. Everywhere will feel both foreign and familiar at the same time. I know this because I feel it as well."

"It's more than that." Arros pointed toward the ground. "Look at the tread marks of these boot prints. They're Ellandorian."

The young lord studied them closer. "How do you know?"

"The people of Kohr use flat soles. There are no other tracks around, and the wind and weather cannot reach the Verge. These could have been made yesterday, or five-hundred years ago. Either way, two living people walked here."

"Our fathers?"

"That's my guess." Arros stood. "It appears that your disconcerting little friend spoke true."

Draxian also came to his feet, then nodded to himself. "Which means she also wasn't lying about the hungry ones."

"Hedge ghouls."

"How do you know?" Arros pointed ahead of them just as something darted between the buildings. It moved so quickly, Draxian couldn't make out anything of its form beyond a blur. "Perfect," he breathed. "Exactly where we need to go."

Arros started forward. "Just ignore them and they may lose interest."

"And what happens if they don't lose interest?"

"We'll soon find out."

The two men continued forward. Draxian kept his hand on the hilt of his sword for reassurance, even knowing the creatures were too fast to battle. A blur shot past him, then another. Arros was attempting to remain calm, yet even he flinched when the ghouls became more numerous and ventured ever closer. Twice, a hedge entity swiped at his arm, leaving a painful scratch. "Arros…" Draxian warned.

"I know." He continued walking as several lines of blood instantly appeared on the prince as well. "Keep moving. They're testing us."

"And what form of test would that be? Our tolerance to pain?"

"No. I feel something different – more instinctual."

They continued to endure the incessant pokes and swipes until finally arriving at a small, white building made from seamless stone. The moment Draxian's foot touched the first of the white stairs leading to the door, the attacks from the hedge ghouls ceased. "They don't like this place."

Arros turned, then glanced around. "Because this structure is outside the Verge." He grinned. "We've made it."

"Are you certain?" Draxian glanced over the small building. "This is not quite what I expected for a great library."

Stepping forward, the Crown Prince of Ellandor placed his hands on the door and pushed. The heavy door swung inward, allowing Arros and Draxian to enter. The young lord sucked in a long draw of air upon crossing the threshold. Rows of stone shelves reached to the ceiling and were arranged into a maze of tens of thousands of books and scrolls – far more than there should be based on the exterior dimensions of the building.

"This is definitely the library."

Draxian could only shake his head in wonder. He had never even imagined there were that many books in existence. Most of them appeared to be written in languages that were unknown to him. Arros continued walking around the corners to the next row in the maze, only to find more shelves waiting beyond. He reached out and dragged his fingers lightly over the spines of the books until stopping.

"What is it?"

The prince pulled a small tome from the shelf and grinned. "I read this one when I was young. It's a story about a stag that searches for its family after a forest fire."

"Why is it here?"

Arros replaced the book on the shelf. "I was researching everything available about Kohr before you arrived in Braethus – even went into the private vaults beneath the palace."

"What did you learn?"

He continued walking as he spoke. "This is the place where our ancient ancestors learned of the First Ones. All the knowledge of the ages is contained here."

Draxian glanced around. "You realize we didn't bring enough supplies for an extended stay? We could read for hundreds of years and never find what we're looking for."

"I don't think we were sent here to find a book," Arros spoke cryptically. The prince pointed behind the next row of shelves.

The young lord stepped around the corner and found a tiny building within the maze. It was elaborately decorated with an embossed relief of stone vines and wildflowers. Arros led them through the open door and into a short hallway. Beyond, a vast garden of trees and flowers was displayed before them. A dirt path continued to a bridge that spanned a small babbling brook of clean water. A black book sat nearby upon a wooden bench. Arros reached over and lifted the thick, ancient tome. He began thumbing through the contents. "Interesting."

"Can you read it?"

"I think so. The language appears to be a mix of ancient and Ellandorian."

Draxian drew in his eyebrows. "And what makes it interesting?"

He spun the book around to display the open pages. Inside were diagrams on how to properly step and swing two swords at the same time. "These moves look complicated."

"Even more so without being able to translate the notes on the sides." Arros snapped it closed, then started to place it back on the bench.

"Keep it, if you'd like." A familiar voice caused both men to quickly turn. An old man with a long white beard and balding head crossed the bridge. "My apologies for startling you, Lord Prince."

Arros tilted his head to one side. "Garran?"

"Wait," Draxian began. "How did your master archivist get here?"

The old man hobbled forward and seated himself on the bench. "You may as well tell him, Lord Prince."

"Tell me what?"

Arros slowly turned his head back to Draxian. "He's the Oracle of Orakh."

The old man cackled to himself in amusement. "You are correct."

Draxian took a step back as he attempted to understand what had transpired, content to let Arros speak for them. "Then you came to Ellandor to find us?"

"Correct again."

The prince brought a hand to his head, then began pacing back and forth. "If you were able to cross over to another Realm, why did you need us to open a portal?"

"Ah," the Oracle exclaimed, "that is a bit more complicated."

"How so? A lot of good people were hurt when the console was destroyed."

"I came there to teach you how to find your fathers, not to act as a carriage service. There are rules that must be obeyed – even by me."

Arros ceased his pacing then turned back to Garran. "It's been said that the Oracle of Orakh can see the past, present, and future."

"The past is not some grand secret, and the present is simply history in the making. The future is always evolving, and every choice opens the possibilities to an infinite number of outcomes."

"That's circular."

The old man stood and then stepped forward. "Perhaps, yet it wasn't always so. I used to know exactly how the ages would unfold, and every life that stepped through my door had a history and destiny that was as simple to read as plucking a book from the shelf."

"And now?"

Garran gestured toward the exit. "The tear within the boundaries of the Spirit Realm has distorted my vision and keeps me from seeing the paths going forward."

"To find our fathers?"

"If that's the path you choose to follow."

Draxian finally stepped forward. "Then you're saying our fathers did come here to speak with you?"

"Indeed, Lord Kalenthos. Five years ago, by your understanding."

"What was their purpose?"

The Oracle smiled warmly. "You already know the answer to this."

Arros nodded absently. "They came to find a way to seal the veil between our worlds."

"You must understand, at the time when they came here there was no solution available."

"And now?"

Garran pressed his lips tightly together. "There is a new opportunity to complete their primary mission if someone is brave enough to take up the challenge. It will not be easy, and success may come at a terrible price. However, if you can do this, I will be able to guide you not only to the fate of your fathers but prepare you for a much greater battle that is to come."

The prince glanced back to Draxian, then lifted his chin skeptically. "What would need to be done?"

"The Sword of Melkarick has been found."

Arros blinked several times, then folded his arms. "You say it like I would have any idea what that means."

Garran furrowed his brow. "Melkarick is the terrible weapon that was used to tear a hole into the Spirit Realm during the War of the Shadow Lords. It was also used to darken the skies and give perpetual life to the Undying abominations. Only that particular artifact can hope to repair the breach."

"And you know where we can find it?"

"It is currently in the possession of Regent Xaadier of Phondari."

The prince scrunched his face. "You expect us to steal this weapon from a high city official? Will it not be guarded?"

"Quite." He lifted a finger to emphasize his next words. "By thirteen Mellari."

"Again, I have no idea what that means." Arros shook his head. "We just arrived on this world – you can't possibly expect us to agree to this ludicrous heist. Can you not get it yourself?"

"I am the keeper of history, not its creator." The Oracle of Orakh reached inside his robe and withdrew two sealed documents. "Before either of you make any decisions, your fathers wrote these messages for you, and bid me deliver them if you should make it this far."

Arros carefully lifted the folded paper from the Oracle's hand, then handed the appropriate one to Draxian. The young lord's stomach twisted into a knot. He had spent years trying to move beyond the death of his father, only to have the old scars torn open with a simple whisper of hope. With no more debate, Lord Draxian Kalenthos broke the wax seal and unfolded the letter. It was written in his father's hand.

Draxian, my beloved son,

If you are reading this, then we have failed to return home from this oppressive land of nightmare beasts and veiled wickedness. As such, we could not educate you for this eventuality, and for that, I am filled with deep regret. Harden your resolve, but do not lose yourself to indifference. Whatever our fate, know that King Nemendes and I came here of our own volition to keep a great evil from seeping into our beautiful home of Ellandor. We have spent many years preparing an arduous path for you to follow. The journey will not be easy, and the trials you must endure will test you beyond comprehension. Trust no one who is not of our land. In this realm, this nexus of power, you will find yourself tempted to embrace the follies of our ancestors. Rise above it, and you will succeed where we have failed. One Power guide and protect you always.

Your father,
Lord Protector Borus Kalenthos

Upon finishing the letter, Draxian nearly wept for joy. His father had not died in a senseless explosion as the High Council had reported. They had been trapped in a forsaken Realm with no assistance given from the very leaders that were sworn to protect them. Draxian vowed to one day return and make certain all those involved faced justice under the Edicts of Accountability – but first, he had a magical sword to locate.

Draxian looked toward Arros to gauge his reaction to the letter from King Nemendes. When he finished, the Crown Prince's eyes turned darkly toward Garran, who waited patiently for his response. "If you are prepared, Lord Prince, I have the power to grant your father's request."

Arros watched him for a long moment, then angrily crumpled the letter in his fist. He held the note up for the Oracle to see. A white flash erupted from beneath Arros' fingers, and the ashes of the scorched paper fell to the dirt at his feet. "Both you, and my father, can drop straight into the icy Abyss."

Without another word, Arros stormed through the exit, still carrying the black book beneath the crook of his arm. It took a moment for Draxian to realize that his own jaw was hanging open. Never in his life had he seen the Crown Prince filled with such blatant contempt. And the bright burst of energy had certainly not been caused by any technology Arros had brought with him.

When the young lord turned toward the Oracle in confusion, the old man's warm and genuine smile returned. "Does this mean you've agreed to recover Melkarick?"

FLIGHT

With Kyreena's keen eyesight, she could easily navigate the rocky terrain of the badlands – even at night. It was Illara who held up their progress. The woman had underestimated her own injury and needed to make frequent stops to rest. Twice, Kyreena avoided encounters with strange creatures that hunted under the shelter of the darkest hours. Fortunately, she had recovered supplies, along with a bow and quiver. For whatever reason, that felt more natural in her hands than a sword.

By morning, the small keep was far behind them and the baron's body surely had long-since been found. Without their leader, it was unlikely the soldiers would pursue. According to the Treaty of the Seven Empires, indentured slaves had the right to defend themselves from being murdered by their masters. It was an extremely difficult defense to prove yet was taken seriously. From what Kyreena learned of this law, it was an added condition the Empress of Dragons had placed upon the Undying before agreeing to uphold the treaty. The problem being, deranged masters such as Clavius had ways of mistreating his servants and hiding the truth from the authorities. It was only when families came looking for their loved ones after an end to the contracts, that unexplained disappearances were reported and investigated. Few cases were ever solved.

Illara rubbed at her swollen ankle. "Have you figured out where we are?"

"Just north of the main road, nearly halfway between Breck and Phondari." Kyreena had found maps in the baron's private study and knew exactly where they were.

"Where should we go?"

"I'm not certain. Both cities might have your description sent ahead."

"And yours?"

Kyreena huffed a laugh. "I'm already dead, remember? Also, I don't have a slaver's mark."

Illara peered down at the diamond-shaped brand on her wrist. "I wish mine could be removed. It takes a Soul Singer to get rid of it without leaving a horrible scar." The former slave-girl reached over and touched Kyreena's arm. "I could have sworn you had a fresh burn when they first captured you."

Kyreena's attention snapped toward her friend. "Wait. You were there when it happened?"

"I didn't see you get captured. We had stopped for the night, and I think you may have wandered near our camp." Illara shook her head. "I only remember them tossing you into the cage without a word of explanation. You were unconscious at the time. In the morning, I noticed a fresh, black slaver's mark on your wrist – residue from the soot of a branding iron. They must not have got it hot enough to leave a scar."

"Or," Kyreena offered, "I used a magic spell to protect me." When her new traveling companion's eyes widened at the thought, she burst out laughing. "You should see your face right now."

Illara's shoulders dropped in dismay. "Magic is nothing to jest over. It was because of its misuse we lost our sun and moons to this bloodied veil in the sky."

"No. There is no magic that can accomplish such an epic feat. This was the touch of the One Power of Darkness."

"You mean, the Fallen One?"

Kyreena was not certain how she knew it, but there was far more to the history of the War of the Shadow Lords than what the Undying Emperors had allowed to be recorded. "The Fallen One was just an evil being who used the One Power of Darkness to further his own selfish ambitions."

Illara was immediately interested. "But why steal the sun from us? Was this a punishment?"

"It was a desperate ploy to obscure Kohr from the eyes of the gods and bring this land closer to the Void – the primary source of his magic."

"And this One Power is somehow different?"

Kyreena shrugged a shoulder. "It's difficult to explain, but yes. Magical energy is summoned from the Realms of Power, and yet there is something even greater than this – the True Source. No human could ever touch its raw energy without instant death. You might think of the One Power as a gatekeeper, who will occasionally call it forth at the bidding of special beings that are deemed worthy of its notice."

Illara puckered her face dubiously. "You're making that up."

"Am I?" Kyreena leaned over and playfully nudged her with a shoulder. "We should get moving. It's not safe to remain in one place for long."

Just as Kyreena started to rise, Illara reached over and caught her wrist. "Wait."

"I know it will be difficult…"

"No," the young woman interrupted. "I need you to promise me something."

Kyreena furrowed her brow. "What is it?"

"If we're ever found by those guards, swear that you won't let them take me again."

"I can assure you that I'll not ever surrender to an enemy without a fight." Kyreena lightly patted the bow slung over her shoulder.

Illara pressed her lips tightly together. "I already know this. But what I'm truly asking is, if there comes a time when there are too many for you to fight, please promise me you'll not let them take me alive." Her eyes began to well with tears. "I can't go through that again."

Kyreena reached down and wiped the tears from her face. "I may not remember who I was, but I do know that I could never leave a friend to such an awful fate."

Her companion nodded in gratitude. "I'm ready to continue."

The two women hobbled along through the arid wasteland. They took frequent breaks to rest or drink from their shared waterskin. Kyreena could not help but notice that Illara was imbibing an excessive amount of water. She surmised it would only be a couple more stops before their waterskin was completely dry. It would only be a matter of time before they would both die of thirst if another source were not located soon. Returning to the main road toward Breck was not even an option. Every caravan that passed near Clavius' keep would have been alerted to watch for two blonde assassins traveling on foot. Their only hope was to continue traveling a league north, and parallel to the route. That decision would prove lethal if caught in a red storm without a ward, although it felt better than the alternative.

It was not much longer before Kyreena smelled something in the soft breeze that caught her attention. She stopped, then pulled away from Illara to sniff at the faint scent.

"What is it?"

Kyreena glanced back, then held up a hand to calm her injured companion. "I believe there is a well nearby."

Illara wrinkled her nose as she tested the air. "You can smell water?"

"Not the water itself, only the damp clay. It's very distinctive."

"I'll just need to trust you on that."

Without another word, Kyreena began to follow the scent while Illara sat on a smooth rock to rest her ankle. It did not take her long to come upon a small, dug out pit about eight paces in diameter. Not far below, a shallow pool of fresh water rested, beckoning Kyreena to drink her fill. A sudden sense of dread prompted her to glance back toward Illara, just ten paces away, then scan the immediate area. Kyreena felt as though there were eyes upon her. Trusting her instincts, the pale-eyed woman brought her bow around and nocked an arrow. She continued watching the horizon as she began to slowly circle the waterhole. Such a place would be frequented by both predators and prey alike. A loud crunching noise beneath her feet caused Kyreena to glance down. Bones were scattered all about. This would not have been unusual on its own, save for their bleached white color and obvious fragile nature. The rib bone she had stepped upon crushed into powder under her weight.

"What is it?" Illara called over to her.

Kyreena turned and shook her head to get her companion to stop speaking. It was right in that moment when something large burst from the well and leapt into the air. Without thinking, she dove to one side, rolling on impact with the ground. Her attacker landed in the exact place where she had just been standing, allowing

Kyreena to see it for the first time when launching back to her feet. With a bulbous body in the shape of an egg and two over-sized, slender legs, the shadow beast stood twice her height. It was covered in sleek, dark brown scales, and had two small arms protruding from its front for grasping food. A large slit near the top of the body gave the beast a permanent smirk which opened to form a wide mouth, just below the six tiny black orbs for its eyes.

"Kyreena! Run!"

Illara's words echoed in her ears, yet she knew such a beast could easily overtake her in moments. She drew back the string to her cheek, then fired the first arrow. The tip sunk a short way into the scaly flesh, then fell to the dirt upon the beast flinching from the strike. Kyreena immediately realized that the broad-tipped arrows she stole from the baron were likely designed for shooting at men wearing cloth armor, not piercing the dense hide of a shadow beast.

As she continued to back away, the creature made a quick hop toward Kyreena to keep her in close proximity. Time appeared to slow as the nightmare beast opened its great maw to reveal rows of tiny teeth. A cylindrical protrusion bulged from the back of its throat, and a jet of clear fluid shot forth. Kyreena had no time to think. She dove forward and shot beneath the shadow beast's legs, spilling her arrows upon rolling to a stop. As she had hoped, the frog-like creature was not adept at quickly turning around to face an opponent. This allowed her valuable moments to gather a few arrows and run back to the safety of some of the neck-high boulders.

Kyreena slid to a halt upon reaching the rocky outcropping, nearly bumping headlong into a group of four men with spears. The first of the savage-looking warriors, a young adult with red hair braided down his back and in his thick beard, held a spear ready to throw. "Down!"

Kyreena did not wait for a second command. She ducked low as he made the first cast over her head. The shadow beast hissed in rage as the tip penetrating its bulbous body. In nearly the same instant, another light-haired man in dirty lizard skins stepped forward and hurled his spear. With the creature's mouth stretched wide in outrage, the point shot through the back of its throat and protruded from the other side. The frog-like beast slumped to the ground from the clean strike to its brain. It continued to shudder and twitch for several moments before going completely still.

The red-headed man placed his hands on his hips as he scrutinized Kyreena. "It is not safe to be alone in the wasteland."

She slung the bow back over her shoulder. "You have my sincere gratitude for the assistance."

"We have no need of such words. We are Shadiere." The man spoke the words as if that name alone explained everything.

"My name is Kyreena." She pointed toward her companion. "That's Illara."

He tapped his chest. "MorLaro." The Shadiere warrior nodded to the others, as they strolled over to survey their recent kill. "Legath, ValGan, Dari."

Kyreena tilted her head as something occurred to her. "Your name means, 'battle song,' does it not?"

A hint of amusement touched MorLaro's eyes. "You can speak the ancient tongue. Not many outsiders know this."

"Just a little."

He gestured toward the well, now much deeper without the creature hiding within. "You move like a Huntress yet know nothing of the shadow beasts." MorLaro motioned for Kyreena to follow. "The buldroc poison the waters with their vile spit, then wait for prey to drink and become injured. After it has turned your flesh into muck, it drinks in your body and leave nothing but white bones. They have grown bolder recently."

She swallowed hard at the thought. "Then, we are truly fortunate you were nearby."

"It was not fortune. We have been watching you for most of the day."

It was strange that Kyreena hadn't noticed them. She was just beginning to pride herself on being keen and observant. His declaration made her rethink her assumptions. "Why would you care?"

"We are Shadiere."

"I still don't know what that means."

MorLaro expertly caught his spear when one of his men tossed it back to him after retrieving it from the beast. "We are sworn to hunt the shadow beasts until the time the sun is returned to us, as promised by the Great Lord."

"The Great Lord?"

"He will soon return to us and lead the Shadiere in the last great hunt. If our people have not fulfilled our vow and destroyed enough shadow beasts in this land, the Great Lord will reject us, and the red skies will never end."

For whatever reason, Kyreena believed him. She gestured toward the dead creature. "The Shadiere have nothing to worry about. The land is safer because of your peoples' vigilance."

MorLaro appeared pleased by her words. "We think this as well." He turned in the direction of Illara. "Your sister is injured. We know of a safe place where she can rest for as long as it takes to heal."

Kyreena bowed her head to him. "We would be in your debt."

Arros began making his way back through the maze of infinite shelves within the library. It had been a long time since tears had touched his cheeks, and yet he couldn't withhold a few from escaping his eyes. The crown prince had sacrificed so much to find his father, only to read a letter by his own hand that tipped his entire world to one side. It was all too much.

After backtracking from several wrong turns, Arros finally reached the exit to the ancient library. He didn't need to wait long before Draxian's heavy footsteps could be heard shuffling around the corner.

"Arros?"

The prince shook his head. "I don't want to discuss it."

Draxian watched him from the side in silence, concern furrowing his brow. Finally, he took a deep breath. "I'm going after this Sword of Melkarick. I don't think I can do it without your help."

"Of course, you can't." Arros softened his rage, then gave Draxian a slight smirk. "You'd be lost without me."

The lord folded his arms. "Not certain I would go that far, but you're the one who studied the literature about this world before coming here. That makes you the expert of the two of us."

"In all fairness, you weren't meant to find yourself stuck here with me." Arros sighed heavily. "At least, that's what I understood before arriving. Now, I'm starting to believe that us coming here was no accident." He held up the black tome that he had recovered from the gardens. "Even this book."

"You'll receive no arguments from me."

Arros placed the tome in his pack, then turned toward the heavy door. "Let's just leave this place while we still have that choice."

"What do you mean?" Draxian glanced back toward the endless shelves.

"Garran is the Oracle of Orakh, and the master of the Infinite Library." When Draxian gave him a confused look, Arros continued. "This building exists outside of time. That's how he can see past and future events. If he wished it, we could become trapped in this place forever."

Draxian unfolded his arms and then stepped forward. "I think I'm ready to face those hedge ghouls now."

The prince huffed a slight laugh. "Agreed."

Just as Arros reached for the door, the handle disappeared, and he nearly fell forward into the black sand and ash. It only took a moment to realize they were no longer anywhere near the lost city of Orakh. Somehow, the Oracle had transported both men to the edge of the Ebon Waste. Arros spotted T'mara near their camp practicing her staff fighting with Cam, while Nerris silently watched them from the side. When Nerris caught sight of Arros and Draxian, the mercenary called out excitedly to the Hunters, bringing them to a sudden stop.

"Drax, Arros," T'mara called exuberantly. She dashed toward them, just as the young lord stepped up next to the prince.

"How did we get here?"

Arros turned and lightly shook his head. "Let's just keep that to ourselves for now."

"Probably best."

The Huntress jumped into Draxian's arms the instant he crossed over the boundary and onto the grassy field. Being outside the Ebon Wastes, he felt as if a heavy weight had been lifted from his soul, and he could finally breathe easy. T'mara affectionately clung to him like a second skin, refusing to let go.

"I missed you so much! The others were worried you might never return!"

Draxian rubbed her back comfortingly. "We were only gone a few days. I told the others it would take at least five."

T'mara released her grip, then stepped back. "It's been nearly six days since you left."

Arros' stomach twisted into a knot at the news, but he chose not to show it. He cleared his throat. "True," he quickly corrected for Draxian. "It just felt like much less time had passed while in the Verge. The days and nights all looked the same."

T'mara placed her hands on her hips. "Where is my new spear?"

The prince drew his eyebrows together in thought. "Oh. About that…"

"You found Orakh, did you not?"

"We did."

"And?"

Arros glanced over to Draxian for assistance. "Drax? Tell her."

The young lord took a deep breath just as Cam and Nerris reached them. "There was nothing left of that place but hedge ghouls and ash wraiths. As for the library, it was an endless maze of books. Most of them were in languages I doubt you would understand."

T'mara shook her head. "I don't know how to read. My training was solely for hunting, not as a keeper of lore."

"Oh." Draxian shrugged offhandedly. "It's never too late to learn."

She placed a gentle hand on his chest. "Will you teach me?"

"It would be my great pleasure."

Cam scowled at their display, then turned to Arros. "I can read a bit. Did you bring back some books touched by the Spirit Realm? They would be worth a fortune."

Arros pulled his pack around to the front, then reached inside and recovered the black tome. "I brought back *a* book. It's some kind of instruction manual on how to fight effectively with two swords."

The color visibly drained from Nerris' face. "Say that again?"

Rather than attempt to explain, the prince held out the book for him. "See for yourself."

They watched as it took an uncomfortably long time for Nerris to reach for the tome. The old mercenary held the ancient book as if he expected it to bite him at any moment. Ever so slowly, he opened the cover and studied the first few pages. An expression of distress was evident in his face. "One Power protect me," he beseeched in a whisper. "It's real."

Cam glanced over his shoulder, then scowled. "This isn't in any language I've ever seen."

"Because it was never meant for our eyes," Nerris shot back. He snapped the tome closed, then shoved it back into Arros' hands. "I take it all back – I want nothing from that cursed place."

Arros glanced over to Drax, then back to the mercenary. "It's just a book."

"It's not just a book," Nerris began heatedly. "That contains some of the most dangerous knowledge to ever touch the hands of mortals!"

"You know what it says?"

"Of course, not!" Nerris took a step back. "I only know what I've heard in legends."

Arros replaced the tome in his pack. "Then how can you be certain they're one and the same?"

"Because I spent the last ten years training in the original technique of the ancient Blade Masters. It was a similar style to what the Fallen One taught his dark minions. That very book was written by the vile Shadow Lord himself."

T'mara and Cam turned their eyes to Arros in horror, then took several steps back. "We should not possess a relic of the Great Master. It might call his servants to us," the Huntress warned.

"I wouldn't believe that for even a moment," Nerris argued. "But this is certainly not a good omen that you happened to find this one particular book amongst an untold number."

Arros stepped forward and stared hard at him. "No more games, Nerris. Why are you truly here?"

The Blade Master stood resolute, until Draxian stepped up

next to Arros and scowled down at him. "The Lord Prince asked you a question, soldier!"

Nerris took a deep breath as he looked between the two of them, carefully choosing his words. "Forgive me, my Lord, I meant no disrespect…"

"Do you see that black desert?" The prince motioned back toward the Ebon Wastes. "We know how to fix it. Will you help us?"

He nodded. "I've followed you this far. I'll see it through to the end."

"I'll take that as a yes." Arros glanced at the others. "How about you?"

T'mara stepped forward immediately. "A Shadiere always stands ready for the next great hunt."

Cam also joined her and lifted his chin. "This Chosen Hunter will answer your call, Lord Prince."

"Excellent." Arros turned his attention back to Nerris. "Now, tell me who sent you?"

The old mercenary looked behind him, as if expecting someone to overhear his words in the middle of nowhere. "I'm a member of a group that has been preparing for the downfall of the Undying for an untold number of years."

Cam folded his arms. "The Resistance? You must be jesting."

"Our network is far vaster than anyone truly realizes. If you require something specific to help fix this land, they can help you find it."

Arros smiled back toward Drax in approval. "Perfect. What we're looking for is in the palace of Phondari."

Nerris nodded thoughtfully. "Difficult, but not impossible. Can you give me a bit more information?"

"It's called the Sword of Melkarick."

"A sword shouldn't be…" The Blade Master's eyes shot wide. "Wait, the what?!"

THE RESISTANCE

Newly promoted to Guardsman First Class, Merrick had been transferred from pacing the gatehouse to a rotation as a palace sentry. The surprising jump in rank was issued by the Watch Commander for outstanding dedication to the welfare of the empire. It would have been considered an honor, if not for the fact that Merrick knew he had failed the loyalty test and would likely have been put to death if not for Captain Tollas' warning.

After being given a day-pass to get fitted for a new uniform, Merrick started settling into the royal barracks. Each room had eight beds with an iron lockbox at the foot for his possessions. The guardsman had been warned that any personal items he could not fit inside, did not belong in the palace. That was just as well, since the only item he had from his old life was a crude carving of a wolfhound.

"So, you're the dusty-foot who turned in the captain as a traitor." The snide remark came from one of the two guardsmen who entered the chamber. Both looked tired and worn from standing all day, mostly waiting to salute officers who passed.

"I'm Merrick."

The sentry tossed his helmet on his bed. "No one here gives a shite what you call yourself, dusty-foot. Just get to your shifts on time and stay out of my way. You do that, we won't have a problem."

The second guardsman smirked at Merrick. "I'm Jhonras." He nodded toward the other. "And the cranky toad there is Eralath."

"Piss off, Jhonras," Eralath countered. "You didn't just come off a double shift."

"True," the other chuckled.

Merrick stood, then nodded to them both. "I was just about to find the guards' mess hall, if either of you would like to join me. I hear they're serving a spiced stew and hot bread with honey butter."

Eralath began removing his boots as he spoke. "Would you like to know where you can shove your hot bread with honey butter?"

"I'd like to know," came a gruff voice from the door. All three men jumped to attention, then saluted. Captain Tollas was leaning on the doorframe and watching them with great interest. "Well, Guardsman? Where can I shove it?"

"Uh… In your mouth, of course, Captain. They're quite tasty," Eralath quickly amended.

Tollas continued to stare at the guardsman for an uncomfortably long time. "I prefer sticky bread, myself. Wouldn't you agree?"

"Yes, Captain," Eralath barked immediately.

The officer's eyes wandered back to Merrick's. "You're with me, Guardsman."

He saluted once more. "Yes, Captain."

As Merrick passed near Jhonras, the soldier whispered encouragement to him. "Stay strong."

Following on Captain Tollas' heels, they silently made their way around several corridors, then up two flights of stairs. Merrick had never been that deep into the white castle, and he attempted to memorize his surroundings as well as possible. One of the first rules of being in the Imperial Guard, was to pay attention to details.

They finally reached an iron-bound door. Tollas withdrew a ring of keys from his pocket and inserted the correct one into the lock. With a quick twist, the door swung inward. Captain Tollas entered, then closed the door behind Merrick. They had emerged into a small sitting room with a large, blue curtain on the far wall. The bench was ornately carved from a single piece of wood and preserved with a dark stain. Tollas bid Merrick to sit while he stepped over to the curtain and peeked through.

Once satisfied, the officer turned back to Merrick. "My friends have made several inquiries into the destruction of your town, and the whereabouts of the ones captured into slavery."

His eyebrows drew inward. "I don't understand, Captain. Wasn't that just some kind of test?"

"Yes, and no." Tollas folded his arms and gave Merrick a slight grin. "You weren't the only soldier who failed miserably, but you were the first to give the sausages to the starving children. That's why I strongly suggested you be promoted."

"You mean to say…"

Tollas dipped his head. "Welcome to the Resistance, Merrick."

It immediately fell upon him what the Captain had done. "You're using the loyalty test as an excuse to keep all suspicion away from you? If anyone were to call your actions into question, you would simply claim that it was part of the exercise."

"I knew there was a bright candle burning in there somewhere," Tollas praised him. "Being in the Resistance is not about loyalties to any single empire – it's about doing what's right for the people. Do you honestly believe Emperor Deathskull cares about such a petty concept?"

Merrick shook his head. "I wouldn't know."

"The answer is 'no.' The Undying only want their subjects to obey every command without question. Fear, is their most powerful weapon."

"Then why are we actively looking for the Resistance?"

The captain unfolded his arms, then stepped in closer. "Regent Xaadier is the one who feels threatened by us, not Thartalagor Deathskull. That's why he's been gathering Soul Singers to his command. With their constant protection, it makes the Regent nearly impossible to assassinate."

Merrick had yet to personally meet the Regent of Phondari, yet his reputation would suggest that such an encounter usually did not go well for young guardsmen who got in his way. "What if I don't want to be in the Resistance?"

"No one is asking you to take an oath, nor attend secret meetings in dark cellars. The Resistance is a conscious choice to place the welfare of others above your own." He pressed his lips together and smiled warmly. "It's about feeding hungry children when you have a little bit extra. Leaving supplies out for the less fortunate to find. Or perhaps, it's about helping a stranger find his wrongfully enslaved friend." Captain Tollas crooked his finger. "Follow me."

Merrick walked quietly over to the curtain with the captain. When Tollas pulled back the heavy fabric for him, the guardsman could see a balcony overlooking the Great Hall. It was not his first visit to the grand throne room, yet each time it took his breath away. Hundreds of statues were housed inside deep shelves built into the walls, each having a different story to tell or a historical figure to represent. Lattice scrollwork lined the balconies, with embossed ivy vines and exotic flowers. Atop the white marble dais, a large throne of polished silver shone as the central focus for all distinguished visitors.

A small group of five noblemen had gathered near the dais and spoke quietly among themselves. It was not long until Merrick noticed several women entering the Great Hall from a doorway near the dais, then taking close positions around the throne. Each wore a polished silver breastplate with a thick, white leather skirt, and a sword strapped to their backs. Merrick had been warned when he first became a guardsman to never make eye-contact with any of the Regent's women, or overtly stare in their direction. Sentries had been beaten for less.

Regent Xaadier finally appeared in black leather armor with his hand lightly caressing a wicked dagger at his belt. The Regent stood in front of the women to address the nobles. "I understand you have some concerns about the new taxes?"

As the first of the nobles began to speak for the group, Captain Tollas pointed toward the throne and whispered in Merrick's ear. "The girl in the back with the brown hair. Does she look familiar?"

Merrick narrowed his eyes as his neck stretched to get a closer view. "Wait..." A gasp escaped his throat. "That's her," he whispered. "That's Caela!"

Captain Tollas pulled him back from the balcony and drew the curtain closed. "Are you certain?"

"We grew up together. Why is she with the Regent?"

The captain motioned for Merrick to return to the wooden bench. "It appears that your friend was discovered possessing an untrained ability as a Soul Singer."

He shook his head in confusion. "That can't be right. She never showed me anything with magic – and we've been close most of our lives."

"I've known a few Singers in my time. They're quite easy to hide in plain sight with the taint of the Spirit Realm so prominent through this land. Only through intense magical scrutiny can they be revealed – and with mages outlawed within most of the empires, can you truly blame her for not telling anyone?"

Merrick stroked his chin in thought. "Now that you know she was stolen from my town; won't they allow her to go free?"

"With your personal testimony – normally, yes. However, she has been labelled as a specialty mage, and with that, her every breath is considered a gift from the Regent."

"But she didn't do anything wrong." Merrick shook his head. "They're condemning her because she was born different?"

The captain pointed a sharp finger at the guardsman's nose. "*You* are as much to blame for that girl being here as any."

Merrick was taken aback by his words. "How so? I came here to find her and the others."

"But you've joined the very monarchy who holds her prisoner. And now, it would be within your oath to the Emperor to execute Caela upon command. Is that not so?"

Merrick could feel the cage of his own making falling down around him. "Yes, Captain."

"Although that doesn't require you to like it." Tollas squatted down in front of him to better see his eyes. "It's too bad there isn't someone out there who would be willing to risk everything to free her." When Merrick did not speak, the captain continued. "Someone who saw there was a corrupt system and decided to change it from within by infiltrating the ranks of his enemies."

"I'll do anything you ask – swear whatever oaths. Just please help me get Caela away from here."

Tollas patted his knee. "Oaths can be easily broken. I've seen it happen more times than I care to say. What makes the Resistance powerful is hope. Walk down the streets of Phondari tomorrow. Every person you pass might be with the Resistance – or none of them. Not even *I* know how many will truly answer the call when the time is right."

"Are you its leader?"

Tollas' throat rumbled in amusement. "The Resistance hasn't had leaders for a very long time. If I were exposed as a member, another would immediately take my place without a single misstep. Why? Because ideas can never be contained."

"It would appear those with magic can," Merrick grumbled.

"Then you would be wrong, boy." Captain Tollas came to his feet, drawing himself even taller than he already was. For the first time, Merrick felt a deep-rooted sensation of fear when viewing the officer. "There are powerful forces in this world who have waited centuries for the call of the righteous. The Undying Emperors were never searching for mages who use magic. They're trying desperately to find the ones who were born of it."

The warriors of the Shadiere were far more gracious than Kyreena expected from a race with such a savage appearance. Using the extra spears and skins they packed, the Hunters created a litter for Illara to be carried. They continued heading west for the remainder of the day before coming to a stone dwelling, well-hidden among the low mesas and valleys. If Kyreena had strayed even a dozen steps from the path, she was certain to never have noticed it.

MorLaro motioned for them to halt, then called toward the dwelling. "Hunters returning!"

"Approach," came a man's voice from beyond a shuttered window.

ValGan and Legath waited in place, still holding the litter with Illara, while Kyreena stepped forward with MorLaro and Dari.

When they reached the narrow doorway, a darker-skinned man stepped into the threshold. Kyreena placed his age at around forty summers, with brown eyes and dark hair, cropped short. He wore baggy grey pants and a leather jerkin of thick hide. The man's smile was pleasant and welcoming.

MorLaro placed his hands on the upper arms of the man and nodded. "We have found two wanderers in need of help, hunt brother. We were hoping you would give them shelter."

The man returned the gesture. "I'm ever at the service of the Shadiere, my friend. You don't even need to ask." He released MorLaro's arms, then turned to Kyreena. "My name is Khazdus."

"Kyreena," she returned quickly. "My friend, Illara, was attacked and injured her ankle. These noble warriors were kind enough to help us."

Dari motioned with his spear. "She moves like a Hunter. Do not think her weak."

Khazdus' smile returned. "The fact that she lasted a single night in the wasteland speaks highly of her survival skills." He stepped closer to Kyreena and studied her face. "Your eyes tell a story of hardship and loneliness. I try to speak your name, but it somehow feels wrong."

"It's the only name I remember."

"No matter. Let us get your companion inside." He turned back to MorLaro. "I was just about to prepare supper. You're all welcome to stay for the evening."

The Shadiere Hunter shook his head. "I am grateful for this offer, but we must continue our hunt for the shadow beasts. Our chief believes the time of the Great Lord is nearly here. We must prove ourselves worthy of him, or all the sacrifices of our ancestors will have meant nothing, and their souls will never be at peace."

"Well, then," Khazdus exclaimed, "I should let you get to it."

After Illara had been settled inside the stone dwelling, Kyreena had a chance to look around. Khazdus had few possessions of note, and only a moderate amount of furniture chiseled from petrified wood, lashed together with leather cords. Multiple baskets, woven from dried reeds, held roots and salted animal meats, while large, fire-treated clay pots were being used for storing water. Khazdus was chopping vegetables on a table next to an iron cauldron. The large pot was hanging from a cooking tripod above glowing red coals. Kyreena mused how a person could survive for so long in isolation without a constant source of fresh supplies.

"Dear one," he called over. "Would you mind giving the coals a few blasts with the bellows?"

Kyreena stepped over to the pot and located the small, leather apparatus with two handles. She pointed the end toward the flames and squeezed out a few quick blasts of air. The coals responded by glowing much brighter. "We greatly appreciate you taking us in for the night."

"The night?" Khazdus chuckled to himself. "Illara's ankle is most certainly broken. She needs many days of rest before venturing back into the wastes." He gave Kyreena a sidelong glance. "And a bit of training in survival as well."

"I can hear you," Illara called from across the room. She was resting comfortably in a braided hammock that was stretched between two steel hooks embedded in the natural mesa walls.

"We don't wish to inconvenience you any more than necessary."

Khazdus scooped the last of the fire-root into his hands and dumped it into the steaming pot. "It's not about what might be convenient or troublesome – it's about doing my part in the upcoming conflict."

"Conflict?"

He gave Kyreena a bewildered expression. "Of course – the final war before the Great Awakening."

Illara asked the question for her. "What is the Great Awakening?"

"I'm not a Prophet of Avarron, so I can't speak to its exact meaning. However, there are those who believe that the endless nightmare is coming into its final days. It will be a time of healing and rejoicing – an end to the tyranny of the Undying Emperors, and a rise of a new era of peace."

Kyreena folded her arms and smirked. "You have been speaking with the Children of Dawn, I assume?"

Khazdus furrowed his brow. "What did you say?"

"They've brought a large army to battle the Undying. Your words are similar to theirs."

"I was referring to the Resistance. Are you not familiar with us?"

"Of course," Illara spoke quickly. "My mother was saved by the Resistance in Breck when she was a little girl."

He turned back to her and smiled warmly. "I'm not surprised to hear this. Our members are growing by the day. We only wait for the ones who will arise and lead us in the coming battles."

"You're a soldier?"

"Every man, woman, and child are soldiers whether they like it or not. Anyone may choose to avoid the fight when the time is upon them, yet no one will be free of its violent touch."

Kyreena's eyebrow lifted in amusement. "Can we expect you to be this cheery all evening?"

Khazdus placed a hand over his heart and bowed. "Forgive me – I'm being a rude host. You did not come here to listen to my touting." He turned, then stirred the pot with a large wooden spoon. "It's been a long time since I've had anyone visit but the Shadiere."

"There's no harm done." Kyreena reached over and touched Khazdus on the shoulder. He flinched, causing her to quickly retract her hand. "Apologies. I didn't mean to startle you."

He forced a smile. "It's not you, dear one. I just need to prepare myself before having contact with another." Khazdus waved her off. "Nothing to worry yourself over."

Kyreena narrowed her eyes in curiosity. "You're a Dream Rider."

"A Dream Rider," Illara said, confused. "What's that mean?"

"I'm not certain how I know this – only that I do."

Khazdus watched her for a time before speaking. "You are correct. I find it fascinating that you could even recognize one."

Kyreena huffed a laugh. "That makes two of us."

"Did you study the arts in Annis? I can't imagine there are many places that have existing lore on specialty magic."

"That's why you live out here, is it not?" Kyreena glanced around. "You're not hiding from Mage Hunters – you just can't remain too close to groups of people."

Illara scrunched her face. "Why is that?"

The mage turned to Illara and pressed his lips together. "My magic is born of the Astral Realm. It's extremely rare but allows me to enter the mind of another who is sleeping. I can see their dreams and help guide them through."

"That must be exceedingly difficult. My dreams are always frightening or filled with nonsense."

"Dreams are just the mind's way of sorting through our thoughts and experiences. Without them, we'd quickly go mad."

Kyreena shook her head. "I don't remember my dreams."

"That doesn't mean you don't have them." Khazdus leaned back against the table and folded his arms. "The Shadiere come to me for interpreting dreams or help to remember a loved one that was lost. In return, they protect me from the horrors of the Shadow Realm, and occasionally bring meat for the cauldron." Kyreena's eyes widened, causing the Dream Rider to burst out laughing. "Not that kind of meat, be comforted. I'd be a poor host indeed, if I ate everyone who came to my home." He chuckled to himself in amusement.

Kyreena grinned back. "I wasn't worried."

"Wait," Illara called over with exuberance. "Maybe you can help Kyreena get her memories back?"

"Oh?" Khazdus swiveled his head back around. "Were you injured?"

"I'm not certain *what* happened."

The mage furrowed his brow. "If the brain is damaged enough, the memories are simply lost. No amount of magic can restore them."

Illara wasn't so easily swayed. "But she's starting to remember little bits. How else did she know you were a Dream Reader?"

"Dream Rider," he corrected. Khazdus turned to Kyreena. "It's your choice. Just be warned that sharing your dreams is a highly personal experience. I cannot harm you, nor manipulate what you see – only walk beside you through the journey of your unconscious mind."

Kyreena took a deep breath as she considered his offer. She had been waiting for a long time to learn who she truly was. Her hope had faded over time. It would be foolhardy to turn his gift away. "Very well. How does this work?"

DREAMSCAPE

It was well into the evening before Kyreena was tired enough to attempt to sleep. She watched the soft embers from the fading coals as she lay in her hammock. Khazdus sat in a chair nearby, reading silently to himself from a worn book. An oil lantern rested on a hook and gave him just enough light to see the pages.

"What are you reading?" she whispered.

Khazdus peered up, then smiled. "This tells a story about a great sorceress from long ago, and how she became one of the five main heroes in the War of the Shadow Lords. I've read it so many times, it's practically memorized."

"Tell me," Kyreena urged. "It might help me sleep."

He gently closed the book, then reached up and handed it to her. "Would it not be better if you read it yourself? I am not good with regaling stories. My brother used to tell me that I always ruin the endings by not explaining them properly."

"I don't believe you."

Khazdus only smiled. He turned his eyes toward Illara, who slept soundly. "Her dreams are dark, filled with images of a cruel man wielding a hammer, and other brutish figures who have harmed her even deeper still. She bears the weight of these atrocities atop a crumbling foundation."

"Can you help her?"

"You've already started her down that path. Always, she calls out in her dreams, and you appear from the darkness to battle her greatest fears." Khazdus turned his eyes back to Kyreena's. "It seems you've already joined the Resistance."

Kyreena huffed to herself. "I can't even tell you my real name. How can I be of help to anyone?"

"Let's find out." Khazdus leaned in closer. "Close your eyes and listen to my voice." She did as requested, then tried to relax. "Think back to your earliest memories. Don't speak, just focus on those."

Kyreena remembered waking up in the covered wagon next to Lorisa, yet nothing before. She recalled their conversation, and the feelings of companionship that her friend offered. It made her sad to think that Lorisa was still with the slavers, and on her way to Phondari to be sold.

"Don't focus on negative experiences. I want you to remember something pleasant. Think of the sweet scent of wildflowers. Study one in your mind. Look at the petals… the colors. Feel the texture between your fingers."

It was strange how she could see the image so clearly in her mind. Kyreena peered up and found herself in a valley of purple and white flowers. Towering, snow-capped mountains were all around her, and a cool breeze gently brushed her cheek.

Khazdus was standing next to her, staring around in wonder.

"This is beautiful. Such stark colors and detail."

"Am I dreaming?"

He shook his head. "I don't believe so. This appears to be a memory projection."

"What does that mean?"

"I've only read about them from books, never experienced one for myself."

Kyreena leaned over and picked up a silver key lying in the grass. "What do you think this opens?"

Khazdus finally tore his eyes away from the valley, then stared at the key in her palm. "In dreams, objects can have symbolic meanings."

"Perhaps it's a key to unlocking my memories?"

He breathed an uneasy laugh. "Not here, I'm afraid."

"What do you mean?"

"That is quite literally a key." Khazdus could see that she did not understand. "Hold out your other hand." She did as instructed. "Now envision a padlock that the key would open."

Almost instantly one appeared in her hand. Kyreena gasped. She could feel its weight and texture as if it were real. "How did I do that?"

"Here, anything is possible. This isn't a journey of your mind – you've drawn us both to the edge of the Astral Realm."

"How is that possible?"

Khazdus' eyes widened, and he shook his head. "I have no idea."

"Are we in danger?"

"Only if you wish it so." He swallowed hard. "What happens here can manifest itself physically in our bodies."

Kyreena glanced down at the key. "This must be how we get out."

"That would be my guess as well. You're the one binding our souls to this place."

"We should probably leave."

"No." Khazdus held up a hand to stop her from inserting the key into the lock. "You wanted answers to your lost memories, correct?"

"Only if it's safe."

He waved his arm around in a grand gesture. "The Astral Realm is the space between all the Realms of Power. I believe you can navigate us safely through this."

"How do you know?"

"You're obviously a mage of significant strength. We just need to explore a bit longer, and I should be able to tell you more."

Kyreena somehow felt safe in her new world, and Khazdus didn't have any dark intentions that she could sense. He genuinely wished to help her. "What should I do?"

"I want you to show me what's on the other side of this valley."

"But I don't even know…" Kyreena stop speaking the moment the land shifted beneath their feet, and the scenery shot forward. They abruptly found themselves at the edge of a lush forest of needle trees. A large stream was nearby, gurgling from the sound of the water splashing against the rocks. "What in the Abyss?"

"No, dear one, this is definitely not the Abyss." He shook his head in wonder. "If I had to guess, I would say you've brought us somewhere past Kartal's Belt."

"I don't remember ever traveling there."

Khazdus spread his arms wide. "Obviously you have at some point in your life."

"How does this help me?"

"I'm still learning the rules you've set for us in this projection of reality. Although if I'm correct, all of your lost memories are accessible here. We just need to determine where to search, and what will allow you to access them freely."

Kyreena glanced around once more, then lifted her chin. "Show me my parents." Nothing happened.

The Dream Rider shook his head. "It doesn't work like that. You're not asking questions of an oracle; this is the landscape of your mind. Show me a place you once called home."

Instantly, the land shifted again, and they found themselves in a small chamber made of smooth stone. There was a soft bed in the center made of goose feathers, and a heavy table and chairs with various writing utensils. The smells were familiar, but the room still felt hollow.

"What do you think this means?"

"There are many places underground where people have learned to live and thrive. Annis has a network of tunnels behind the palace that go deep into the mountain." He shrugged. "Can you open the door and walk out?"

Kyreena stepped over to the latch, then hesitated. "I don't think I should."

"Then we'll trust in that." Khazdus stroked his chin. "Let me attempt something else. Try taking us outside the gates of Phondari."

Again, the vision changed. Before them, the great city of Phondari floated high above the Aldrinn River. A long causeway stretched from the cliffs, all the way to the front gatehouse. A palace of white stone rested on the far side atop a large hill. Just as with the rest of her visions, no one was around.

"It's amazing. I don't remember any of this."

She glanced over to see the Dream Rider scowling in thought. "What's wrong?"

"I've been to Phondari many times in my youth, and this isn't right."

"Perhaps my memory isn't as good as you thought."

He huffed a laugh. "The castle is perfect. It's just that the city is still missing many of the details. Perhaps you've only seen part of it." Khazdus pointed toward the entrance. "Take us inside Phondari."

At first, nothing happened. She focused harder. The land felt to Kyreena as if it was starting to shift, only everything around her began to vibrate and blur – everything except for Khazdus. "What's happening!?"

"I'm not certain. Perhaps you just need to focus harder on the details."

Many of the homes within the city began to break apart, as if the strain of the land shaking was truly having an effect. The towers of the white castle toppled one by one, and the great halls fell in upon themselves. Finally, thousands of buildings crumbled to rubble, and the walls surrounding the city and the causeway dropped to the river far below it. Ever so slowly, the entire city began to sink, as if the ancient magic had at last failed.

"Kyreena? We need to leave here... now!" Khazdus urgently called to her again. "Kyreena!?"

Her eyes shot to his, causing Khazdus to gasp in fright. "That's not my name!"

Kyreena abruptly awoke, then looked around. She found herself lying in the middle of the floor in the stone cabin with no memory of how she got there. Illara was still sleeping in her hammock – but Khazdus was nowhere to be seen. Without waking her companion, Kyreena crawled to her feet, then walked over to the door. It was partially open. Taking a step outside, her bare feet touched the cool, rocky ground. Kyreena immediately spotted Khazdus sitting on a small boulder staring silently into the night.

His head turned slightly at her approach. "Forgive me for not helping you back to your bed. I didn't feel it was appropriate to touch you without permission."

"What happened?"

"Can you tell me the last thing you remember?"

Kyreena stepped up next to him, then folded her arms. "We were in the dreamscape. The city of Phondari was shaking apart. I tried to stop it, but it only made things worse."

"I see."

"Do you remember how we got back?"

Instead of answering, Khazdus slid from the rock and turned around to face her. "Illara is a fragile girl, constantly running from the monsters she believes will overlook her if she just ignores them. I think it would be best if she remains here until fully healed – but *you* must leave in the morning."

When Kyreena moved forward, Khazdus immediately took a cautious step back. "I won't hurt you."

"That's not what you threatened earlier."

She was immediately confused. "Did we speak after the city broke apart?" Khazdus appeared reluctant to discuss it, so she tried a different approach. "Supposing that I did leave. Where do you think I should go from here?"

"You already have the answer to that question."

Kyreena nodded absently. "Phondari."

"Why do you think that is?"

"I'm not certain. I feel like something is waiting for me."

Khazdus shrugged his shoulders. "I've never met anyone like you, so I have no words of council."

"Did you learn anything about my background? Even if it's just my name?"

He took a long, shaky breath. "I dare not speak it."

"It can't be that bad… can it?"

"You must allow your memories to return in their own time. Forcing them to the surface will only cause terrible consequences to everyone you know." Khazdus shook his head in regret. "I can never leave this place with what I have learned, as it would mean the end of the Resistance if I'm captured. The darkness would endure for all time."

Kyreena knew within her heart that he meant every word. She retreated several steps. "Now you're truly starting to worry me. I must know *something* if you expect me to trust that my friend, Illara, will remain safe in your care. That's my only concern."

The Dream Rider shifted uncomfortably, then finally nodded. "It was said that long ago the ancient gods hid various weapons of tremendous power to one-day be called forth and used to destroy the Undying Emperors. The gods could not remain, but it was their promise that those weapons would someday end the Thousand Years of Darkness. The Shadiere have passed this legend down for centuries. I have seen it. If our enemies were to discover these places first, nothing would be able to stop them." Khazdus took a deep breath. "There are supposedly three people in this world who each were passed down this terrible knowledge and know exactly where to find these scattered gifts to the people of Kohr: The Empress of Dragons is believed to be one. The Lord of Shadows is another." His eyes locked to Kyreena's. "You, it appears, are the guardian of the third."

26

GRAZLAK'S BRIGADE

Draxian noticed a visible change in the way the others regarded both of them. Arros took the lead on his old gek after the tragic loss of the taark. Nerris was next, silently watching the horizon as they rode. He had spoken little since they confronted him about his intentions. It was a calculated risk to reveal his royal heritage, yet one that Draxian felt was necessary for their loyalty. T'mara stayed beside him as usual, occasionally offering a tight-lipped smile of support. Drax needed that more than ever. The young lord's outlook had been flipped on end with a single letter from his father – just as it was for Arros.

They had been traveling for two days before Draxian felt it was time to speak with the Lord Prince about recent events. Just as Arros had given him space to understand his own feelings, Drax needed to do the same. He waited until the group had settled in, just before the veil of night obscured the skyline. T'mara and

Cam had wandered off to scout the immediate area, and Nerris was busy cooking the evening meal.

"We should speak."

Arros set his pack beside him, then lifted his chin toward the young lord. "Is this going to be one of *those* talks?"

"It is," Drax began carefully. "You've spent your entire life worrying about how others will judge your every decision. I know from experience that this is a heavy burden for anyone to carry – and even worse for a child. It has left you guarded and unable to trust. Well, look around you. Those people aren't here – I am."

"How observant of you."

Draxian withdrew the folded paper from his pocket and handed it to the prince. "Read it."

"I already know what he wrote."

"Oh," he chided dubiously. "I had no idea what my father would say."

Arros stood up, then gestured with the letter as he mocked in a deep voice. "Lord Kalenthos likely apologized for not being able to speak with you in person and bragged at how proud he was that you made it as far as you did. And again, he was deeply sorry to place another burden on your shoulders, but he just *knows* you will rise to the occasion and be the great man that you always are." The prince stepped forward and slapped the letter against Draxian's chest. "Stop me at any time."

He took the letter and placed it back in his pocket. "It was something to that effect, yes. What did yours say?"

The prince folded his arms and watched Draxian for a long while. "My father told me that all this madness happening on Kohr is much bigger than me – that *you* were always meant to be here, not me. Apparently, my brash nature is not what Kohr needs for the trials ahead. He believed that I would only make matters worse, and that I shouldn't abandon my responsibilities to the people of Ellandor." Arros sniffed loudly. "My father claims that a bargain had been made at great cost to safely return me back home – alone."

Draxian was immediately baffled by this new information. "That doesn't sound at all like King Nemendes. He was essentially commanding you to abandon me to face all the evils of this world myself?"

"That's certainly how it would appear." Arros smirked. "I've been thinking about it a lot. My father was hailed throughout his life as a king of the people. But the truth is, he was just masterful at getting someone to go along with his arguments. He manipulated High Councilors into believing they had come up with an idea all on their own."

"Arros…"

"No," he interrupted. "You didn't know him like I do. This is likely his backwards way of pushing me into accepting this ludicrous quest." The Lord Prince stepped in closer and rubbed his first finger and thumb together. A soft light appeared, then faded just as quickly. "I'm starting to think we need to learn how to defend ourselves. Do you not agree?"

"In principle, yes. Although you seem to forget that this world doesn't appreciate those who use magic."

Arros sighed heavily. "Are we truly calling it that?"

"That's just how these people relate to the concept of energy manipulation. I should tell you that it makes you sound conceited when you speak down to T'mara about it."

The prince's eyebrows shot high and he grinned in triumph. "I knew it!"

"Whatever," Draxian allowed. It was only a matter of time before the young lord admitted he was quickly growing fond of the woman. "For now, let's just stay focused on finding Melkarick."

Arros slowly lost his grin and held up a hand to halt Drax from speaking. "Do you feel that?" It was only moments afterwards that T'mara's taark stomped at the ground and thrashed its head wildly.

At once, Nerris leapt toward his long, leather satchel and quickly withdrew two blades, while Draxian unsheathed his own sword and readied himself for whatever danger was beyond their view. Arros had begun to gather his bow and arrows when the first of the attackers appeared nearly two-hundred paces from them: Raiders. It was a horde of grimy men with makeshift armor and crude weapons carved from bones.

"Stay behind me, Lord Prince," Nerris called as he rushed past, swords twirling between his fingers. "And please don't do… whatever it was you did the last time. I doubt my luck could survive another explosion."

Draxian knew that wouldn't even be possible, regardless of Arros' wants. The emergency shelter had been damaged beyond repair from the overload of energy, and that was the only one the prince had brought with him. With his heart pounding in anticipation of the first attacker, Drax lifted his blade and started forward, when a knife whirled through the air past him and struck the bandit in the head. The man died immediately upon impact, falling to the ground just in front of the young lord. A second and third dagger shot past and hit with just as deadly accuracy. Draxian didn't know whether to cheer or be horrified.

T'mara abruptly appeared next to him with spears in hand. "Stay back and let the Hunters do their work."

"I'm not certain how to take that."

She grinned back at him while readying to hurl a spear. "It is meant with love." With a single cast, the spear skewered the closest raider, then passed halfway through his body and pierced a second in the side. Both ruffians fell to the ground, clutching at the shaft.

Arros climbed to the top of a waist-high rock to get a little more elevation. In one swift motion, he drew an arrow and fired. It hit a charging bandit in the leg, causing him to drop to the ground, screaming in anguish. The next shot skipped off the hard-packed dirt. He shot again, and again. Each successful hit striking in similar places.

T'mara called up to him. "Are you not using that correctly? Try aiming higher."

"Think so?"

Draxian already knew the prince would not intentionally kill a man unless there was no other choice. They had grown up in a world that viewed killing as a terrible crime, and the absolute last resort in a fight. The bandits apparently believed their group had something valuable enough to be willing to risk their lives for it. He could only imagine what that might be.

Arros started to aim for another, when he slowly lowered his bow and looked into the distance. "That's... frightening."

Unable to stifle his curiosity, Draxian climbed up to join the Lord Prince on the rock. He instantly spotted the source of Arros' distraction. Nerris was darting between oncoming attackers, slashing and thrusting with deadly precision. Each swing of his blade found a target, then was brought up to defend as the second sought out another victim. He alternated this movement, never attacking in the same manner twice, and always shifting his feet to keep a strong stance. It was the most graceful, and violent, dance he had ever seen.

"Let me see," T'mara called up, as she caught Arros' wrist and pulled him back down to the ground.

"Hey, now! I need to be up higher to shoot effectively."

"You do not know how to use that anyhow," the Huntress shot back. She quickly hopped up in Arros' place and leaned on her second spear. T'mara whistled to herself in amazement. "That is most definitely a Blade Master."

"How can you be certain?" Draxian teased.

T'mara must have missed his ironic tone. "He did not even allow us to look at his weapons until it was necessary to use them. I find that the more one brags about their skills, the less their confidence. Your new friend was trained for fighting groups of many men. Hunters are best used against a single foe, or large beast."

"Where's Cam?"

The Huntress stretched her neck high to search around the area. "There."

Draxian tried to look where she indicated. "What?"

"Do you see the large man near the back?"

"The one with the silly hat made of bones?"

She wrinkled her nose and giggled at him. "That is the one. Watch close."

Draxian only needed to wait a few moments longer before a spear struck the unsuspecting leader in the head from somewhere off to his flank. Almost immediately, a war horn sounded, calling the remaining thirty men to flee.

"You Hunters don't hold anything back."

Without answering, T'mara slipped from the rock and began marching toward the three men Arros had wounded, while they attempted to crawl away from them in retreat. Arros called to her back. "Leave them be. We'll be long gone by the time their wounds heal."

"They would not be so generous, I assure you." The Huntress tossed her spear to one side, then caught the first man by his hair. She jerked his head back with one hand, then drew another knife from her baldric.

"I command you to stand down!" Arros' words finally reached her.

"Very well." T'mara released the vile man with a shove, then watched him continue to scramble away. "He will likely die from sickness anyhow."

"They're retreating. I thought the Shadiere would have more honor."

"It is not about honor, Lord Prince. This is just about protecting those I care about."

As the three men nearly made it to safety, Nerris came jogging back into view. Without even breaking his stride, the Blade Master cleanly took the heads of the fleeing men. His clothing was coated with blood, and he wore a smug grin from ear to ear – until seeing the outrage on Arros' face. The Blade Master slowed to a halt, then glanced around behind him. "What's wrong?"

"You see, Lord Prince," T'mara remarked snidely. "When someone has come to kill those you love, *that* is all the mercy you give."

Nerris withdrew a clean rag from his pocket, then began wiping the gore from his swords. "She's not wrong."

Merrick tried as best he could to keep from appearing nervous as he strolled down the corridor toward the west towers. He was dressed in his best uniform and had polished his boots with tallow and oil. It had taken several days to arrange it, and Captain Tollas had assured Merrick that it would all go well if he did as instructed. It was his first time visiting the private sections of the palace, and he was greatly relieved to learn that Emperor Deathskull was not present. The Undying could change into titanic dragons at will, giving them the ability to travel quickly from city to city. None truly knew where the Emperor went, and none ever questioned it for obvious reasons. The daily operations of the palace had always been left to the Regent.

As Merrick approached the sentry at the bottom of the stairwell, the royal guardsman held up a hand. "Guardsman. What's your purpose?"

"Just a nice night for a walk."

The soldier gave Merrick a slight nod, then covertly held up three fingers on one hand, and two on the other. "Just stay out of the gardens tonight. It might rain."

Merrick saluted, then walked past him. "I'll bring a cloak." He continued beyond the archway, then climbed three flights of stairs. After going through the door, he stopped and looked up and down the twisting corridor. He couldn't remember if it was the second door to *his* left, or the sentry's. After a moment of indecision, Merrick chose a door and stepped in close. Lightly knocking on the wood, his stomach twisted with a mix of fear and excitement.

It took only a few moments for him to hear a latch being pulled back, then the door creaked open. A woman stood before him, head and eyes down, wearing a thin robe of silvery material that allowed Merrick to see the faint outline of her body. "How may I serve?"

"I wouldn't mind a cup of your spiced cider."

Caela's eyes shot up to his. "Merrick?" She stuck her head out the door, then quickly looked from side to side. Once she was satisfied nobody was nearby, the girl caught his sleeve and pulled him into the room and quietly closed the door. "What are you doing here?" Caela shook her head. "Wait… how did you find me?"

Merrick placed his hands on his hips. "That's truly the greeting I get?"

She immediately relaxed her stance, then quickly moved forward to embrace him tightly. "Forgive me. I'm so happy you're here – but I'm also afraid for you. If they catch you wearing a guard's uniform, they won't hesitate to have you executed."

He pulled back from her and smiled. "Relax, Caela. This is *my* uniform. I joined the palace guard to find out what happened to you and the others."

"Truly?" The young slave watched him with astonishment.

"You came all this way for me?"

"Of course. You still owe me a silver piece for fixing your privy door back in Turan's Run."

Caela broke into a fit of laughter. "As I recall, you were the one who broke it."

"Is that what happened?" Merrick reached out and took her hand, then squeezed.

"I've missed everyone so much."

He glanced back toward the door, then lowered his voice. "They say you're a Soul Singer."

Caela released his hand, then slowly walked over to her small wooden bed and sat on the edge. There was very little furniture in the room, as it appeared to be intended for temporary usage, and not an extended stay by any one person.

"I knew there was something wrong with me, just not what it was until after I was captured by those slavers."

"Now that you know, can't you use some magic to help you escape?"

She barked a fake laugh, then held out her right arm to display an ornate silver bracelet. "You see this?"

"What about it?"

"This has been enchanted to keep me connected to Regent Xaadier." Caela dropped her hands in her lap. "If I try to escape, he can find and punish me with it. There's no way to remove it without killing me in the process."

"Or maybe that's just what they want you to believe."

The Singer shook her head. "Others have tried. Xaadier uses our Singer powers to keep him safe and heal any injuries he might receive from assassins."

"That's why he keeps you here?"

Caela threw up a hand. "It was either this or death. You know that specialty mages are forbidden to exist."

"Not in Annis." Merrick seated himself next to her. "I've made some new friends that might be able to help. How did you think I was able to get in here to see you?"

For the first time, Caela peered up at him with genuine hope in her eyes. "Do you mean that?"

"You didn't actually think I came all this way for a cup of cider, did you?"

She gave him a tight-lipped grin, then leaned her head against Merrick's shoulder. "At first, I was so angry that you went to Breck to trade when the town was attacked and wasn't there to help defend us." He didn't respond. "But later, I was just glad you weren't killed with the others. They used Mage Hunters to murder anyone who got in their way. It was absolutely awful. Your father tried to hide me…"

"I'm here now. If there's a way to get you free, I promise we'll find it."

Caela snuggled into his side. "Knowing you, I have no doubt this is true."

He reached into his belt pouch, then withdrew the small carving of a wolfhound. "I have something of yours."

"Barkley?" The Soul Singer giggled as she took the figure from his open palm. "Where did you find him?"

"It was under your bed, in what remained of your home. Do you remember when I carved that for you?"

Caela lightly stroked her fingers over its head, as if petting a real dog. "It was my seventh summer, and I was sick with fever. You said that Barkley would watch over me until I felt better. He sat next to my bed every day after that." She handed it back to Merrick. "Keep him."

"I brought it here for you."

"No. I'm not allowed any possessions, and I don't want Regent Xaadier's vile fingers to ever touch it."

Merrick gently took the carving from her, then replaced it in his pouch. "I'm just keeping it safe for now. When I get you free, you can have it back. Agreed?"

Caela hugged into his side and smiled beneath streams of tears. "Agreed."

27

CARAVAN

Kyreena wasn't surprised to learn that the Dream Rider had a hidden door that led into the side of the mesa. There was a clean well for gathering water, and a large cache of weapons and dried provisions the Shadiere had helped him gather for emergencies. After being loaded down with plenty of supplies, Kyreena bid Illara farewell, then started heading south to the main road between Breck and Phondari. Her newest companion was sad to see her go yet understood that she needed to find her own path.

Without Illara clinging to her shoulder, Kyreena found it much easier to navigate through the rocky terrain. Despite this, it still took another two days on foot to find her way to the road. Without a pack animal to assist, and another set of eyes to spot dangers, the lone woman needed to be careful of her surroundings. As the previous encounter with a shadow beast had taught her, not all predators could be easily spotted – or defeated.

Kyreena still had the silver pieces that the lady in white had given to her back at the slave camp, plus more that Khazdus, the Dream Rider, had generously given. She decided it would be unwise to be seen traveling alone, so she hid among the large boulders and scoped out patrols of guards and caravans that passed on their way to Breck. Kyreena had estimated she was nearly halfway between both cities and would need to sneak by the recently deceased Baron Clavius' home. It was unlikely any of the guards would recognize her among a group of merchants, but traveling alone would most certainly invite questions.

As it was nearing midday, a small group of wagons pulled by gekka appeared in the road heading in the correct direction. It was being guarded by four lightly armored men with crossbows. On the lead wagon an older man with a grey beard halfway down his chest urged the gekka forward with a thin bamboo stick.

Not wishing to appear as if she was skulking in the shadows, Kyreena started walking in the same direction they traveled. It didn't take long for the caravan to overtake her. As expected, when she stepped aside and smiled warmly at the wagon master, he pulled alongside her and called the three wagons to a halt.

"Evening youngster." He glanced around at the barren lands, as two of the guards rode in closer to observe their exchange. "You traveling alone?"

"Not by choice, my lord."

The concern was evident in his eyes. "Where abouts you headed?"

"Phondari. My gek was killed by a shadow beast while I was camping for the night."

"Aye. They tend to get bold when spotting a lone traveler." He nodded toward a large storm obelisk in the distance. "Better to camp near the black wards. The beasts don't like them for some reason."

"I'll remember that. You have my gratitude." Kyreena started to walk away when he cleared his throat to get her attention.

"If you don't mind listening to the ramblings of an old man, I wouldn't mind the company."

"You're heading to Phondari?"

He shook his head. "This load is going to the market at Fidonn. It's a little over a day from Phondari, but you'd at least be a lot closer."

"That would be lovely."

"Elgran Lannis. My friends call me Ell." He reached down to her.

She accepted Ell's hand, allowing herself to be pulled up to the seat next to him. "I'm Kyreena."

"You be as light as a feather, Kyreena." The older man leaned over and retrieved several sticks of salted meat from a bag near his feet. He handed one to her, then bit down on another. "Try it. My wife makes them for me to snack on while traveling."

Kyreena nodded her appreciation, then tore a chuck off with her teeth. The meat was smoked thoroughly and wonderfully spiced. "It's delicious! Please tell your wife that she's an amazing cook."

"I'll do that." Ell grinned back at her with an adorable gap between his front teeth. "Shall we go?"

The city of Breck couldn't arrive any sooner. Nerris was just relieved the ferry ride across the river was without incident. They had one less mount to worry about, and far less supplies than when they left for Orakh. He noticed that T'mara had been getting cozy with Draxian in the early hours of the night when her watch shift was over. Arros had tried to take a turn at watch, but Nerris had insisted he and Draxian get their rest. This gave the Blade Master plenty of opportunities in the night to report the progress of their group. The Lord General was still as cryptic as ever about who the men were, and why they were important to the Resistance. However, they were attempting to seal the breach of the Spirit Realm, and he had given Nerris the authority to assist them in any way possible.

Nerris had told the Lord General that they sought the Sword of Melkarick. From what he had been told, the weapon was supposed to have been buried under a mountain of rubble after the destruction of the Black Citadel in the War of the Shadow Lords. If the user was a mage, it was said to grant them tremendous power by greatly amplifying their magical abilities. Nerris also knew that it was one of the items the Fallen One had used to draw the world partway into the Shadow Realm. If there was a way to close the rift to the Spirit Realm, it surely would come from the Sword of Melkarick. And the thought of Regent Xaadier possessing such a weapon made Nerris' skin crawl.

What the middle-aged Blade Master failed to tell the Lord General was that a book had been found which Nerris believed was written by the Fallen One himself. He certainly didn't want to be an alarmist if wrong – nor did the Master wish to test the Lord General's patience by speaking of it. The Fallen One was a forbidden subject, and the Lord of Shadows was not known for his tolerance of those who disobeyed orders.

"Nerris?"

The Blade Master glanced over to Arros as they approached the main gateway into Breck. "Yes, Lord Prince?"

He gave Nerris a glare of annoyance. "First – don't call me that in public."

"Apologies."

"And second – I'd like your help with something."

"I'm at your command, Lord… Arros."

The prince patted the exquisite leather pack slung over his shoulder. "Can you assist me with finding two swords, exactly like the ones in the book?"

"They're a specific type of single-edged curved blade. A shamshir would be closest," Norris suggested.

"I don't want close. They need to be exactly like what he described in the beginning."

Nerris could feel his eyebrows drawing inward. "You can read that language?"

"It's a mix between two. One of them I already knew, and the other is not too difficult. I've already transcribed a few pages without any problem."

"You actually wrote in the cursed tome?" He shook his head. "Won't that devalue it?"

Arros narrowed his eyes and soured his face. "I'm not selling the book. I want to learn this style. You said it's the original Blade Master techniques, correct?"

"Are you certain I can't just show you some moves from how I was taught?"

"Can I not learn both?"

He shook his head. "From what I saw of the pictures, it has some similarities, I'll grant you. However, the curved, single-edge swords require a certain… agility to the footwork and wrist movements. My instructor discussed this with us during a session of our training."

"You're saying there's actually a type of school to study this?"

Nerris chuckled to himself, then cleared his throat. "Not exactly. There are currently less than thirty true Blade Masters in existence. You're looking at one of them."

"If I hadn't seen you fight, I might not have believed you. Although I can say with all sincerity, I've never seen your equal."

The Blade Master leaned toward the Lord Prince and lowered his voice. "If you think my skills are impressive, you should meet the one who trained me."

"I think I'd like that." Arros gave him a sidelong glance. "Is he also the one who sent you?"

Nerris gave the prince a sly grin. "You already know the answer to that."

"Indeed."

He nodded to Arros as the prince rode ahead to declare their intentions and goods to the gate sentries. Draxian and Cam joined him, while T'mara hung back and watched Nerris with a curious gaze.

"Was there something you wanted to ask me?"

The Huntress dismounted from her taark, then stepped in closer. "What were you and the Lord Prince discussing?"

"He wants to learn a bit of swordplay."

"From you?"

Nerris turned to face her. "Are you just upset that he didn't ask to be taught by a Shadiere?"

"No." T'mara stepped close enough that Nerris could feel the heat from her body. "He could not learn this without at least some skills in *banth sen shar*."

"Shadow magic."

"Which is how I know he cannot learn from you either."

Nerris narrowed his eyes. "Careful, little one."

"You are no Blade Master." Her lips moved in close to his ear. "You... are a *shar'dehr*."

He matched T'mara's harsh whisper. "They're a myth."

"Most myths are based on a seed of truth." The Huntress took a step back from him. "We are not so different."

"Think so?"

"We both are willing to die to see an end to the darkness."

Nerris gave her a wisp of a smile. "Perhaps. Except we serve different masters."

The Huntress tilted her head to one side. "Are you certain?"

She turned away, then strolled up to Draxian and looped her arm around his. Nerris placed his hands on his hips and sighed. *That girl is far too clever for her own good*, he thought to himself.

Draxian placed several silver coins into T'mara's outstretched palm. "That should cover the boarding expenses for the mounts."

"Can I keep what is left if I can get a better price?"

"Whatever suits you."

The Huntress leaned up and kissed Draxian on the cheek, then headed toward the stables. He smiled softly while watching her hips sway with each step. The woman certainly knew how to catch his attention, and the young lord had promised T'mara that he would make a genuine effort to reciprocate her affections. It wasn't easy for him to open up to someone from another world. As much as he wanted to be with her, there were just some relationships that could only progress so far. Arros knew this as well, yet his reasons for pushing Draxian toward T'mara were mostly out of regret for getting him trapped on Kohr. However, the truth was, Arros had nothing to do with it at all. The prince was a victim of their fathers' intrigues, just as much as Draxian.

With Arros and Nerris off to the blacksmiths' district to buy two swords, Cam decided to join the young lord as he purchased new supplies for their trip to Phondari. He had mostly kept his distance throughout the journey, and finally appeared to accept that T'mara was taken with Draxian, and it would do him no good to brood over the subject.

"We should buy some jumeba fruit for the first couple days on the road. They go bad quickly but are quite satisfying."

Draxian nodded as he looked over the oddly segmented produce. "Should they be this color?"

"The yellowish skin means that it's ripe. Greener ones tend to be a bit tart for my liking."

"Ah." He began picking through the cart as the merchant watched him with a silly grin. "How many do you think we need?" When the Hunter failed to answer, Draxian turned and nudged him.

Cam was staring toward a crowd of people who had gathered further down the cobbled road. "What is that about?"

"You don't have street performers here?"

"We do. I've just never seen so many people gather to watch a single person."

Draxian selected fifteen jumeba fruit, then counted the coins to the vendor. "We can go watch if you'd like?"

"It's not important."

He shrugged a shoulder. "Actually, I'd love to view some of the culture of your land."

Cam turned his head and his face held a dubious expression. "Truly?"

"Have you ever known me to do anything I didn't want to?"

"No, my Lord, I haven't."

As they made their way closer to the crowds, Draxian could see a pale man in white robes calling out and gesturing toward the crowd. He was standing on something unseen to allow him some height. It was then he noticed several women in color-shifting armor watching the speaker suspiciously from the side. They wore the same attire as the ones T'mara had told Arros were sent from the Dragon Empress. It seemed a bit odd that they would take the time to listen to a performer, until the young lord realized the nature of the man in white. He was not acting out a story.

"… and I say again to all who hear the sound of my voice: The prophesy of the glorious dawn is nearly upon us! It is an end to the suffering! It is an end to the tyranny you have endured for too long! Embrace this new beginning for your children! Join with the Lady of Dawn and find your salvation through her!"

As the people cheered at his speech, Cam nudged Draxian. "This kind of discourse is forbidden in Breck. We should move on before the guards come."

Draxian nodded toward a group of men. "They're already here." The city patrol was leaning on their spears and watching the newcomer with interest. It didn't appear to him that they had any intention of censuring the public from the man's words of hope.

"Perhaps they've been properly bribed?"

"Or," Draxian began, "they might actually be using proper discretion, as intelligent, free thinking guards should."

The man in white continued. "Do not fear this change! A vision has been granted to the people! I know you have heard the rumors on the lips of many from the Guardian's Keep! For only a precious few moments, the sky was torn asunder, and the light of the sun spilled through upon the land! This was a gift from our Lady! A promise of things to come if you would only place your faith in her! Join us! Join the Children of Dawn! Together we can snuff the fires of evil, and finally greet the new day with the radiant sun upon our faces!"

Draxian scowled as his jaw flexed from grinding his teeth. "I take it all back. We're done here."

Cam shook his head in disbelief. "Agreed."

DISSONANCE

"You're favoring your right arm, Lord Prince," Nerris called from the side.

"That's because I was trained with only one blade. It'll just take some practice."

Draxian and T'mara sat on a large stone and watched in amusement while Arros attempted to mimic the movements of a technique within the book. They had been on the road for two days, heading toward the city of Phondari.

"I spent the first season learning how to draw and sheathe my swords. You're not going to learn anything of worth before we reach the city."

Arros whirled his curved blades around in a circle, then made several quick steps and slashes. "I think you'd be surprised at how fast I can adapt."

Nerris chuckled to himself, then nodded. "Of that, I'm quite certain."

T'mara leaned over and nudged Draxian. "Is he always this way?"

"Yes." The young lord quieted his voice even further. "But there's a reason for it. Watch."

"I'm ready to try this," Arros proclaimed.

Nerris stepped forward and drew a single blade. "Shall I come at you slow, or with a typical clumsy strike from an undertrained guardsman?"

Arros narrowed his eyes. "Just swing the damn sword."

"As you wish." The Blade Master abruptly jumped forward and stopped just shy of the point of his blade piercing the prince's throat. Arros had yet to even move. "Like this?"

"Just like that," he returned.

Nerris stepped back, then reset himself for an attack. There was a tense moment when neither of them appeared to blink. Then, the Blade Master lunged in once again. That time, Arros blocked the blade with his right, and thrust with the left. Before it had come close to Nerris' gut, the Master darted aside and brought his blade back down to parry the attack. Arros was anticipating the move. With a second slash of his right sword, he forced Nerris to flinch back, giving the prince a moment to kick him with the toe of his boot, just above the Master's knee and into his inner thigh.

Nerris grunted in pain and fell backwards to the ground. "Hold!"

Arros sheathed his blades, then squatted down in front of him. "I guess it worked."

"Indeed," he managed through clenched teeth. "You kicked the meridian point on my leg just right."

T'mara gave Draxian a sidelong glance. "It appears I have misjudged him."

The prince held out his hand and pulled Nerris back to his feet. The Blade Master still limped a little but was recovering quickly. "You might have warned me. I thought you were practicing a sword technique?"

"Then it wouldn't have been as effective. This book doesn't just teach swordplay, it trains on how to use your entire body as a weapon." Arros shrugged. "And in all fairness, you're only using one sword and going easy on me."

Nerris' eyes widened. "Actually, I was planning on smacking you smartly on the arse for being too confident." He huffed a laugh. "When you change the rules on a new recruit during practice, they always overcompensate, or freeze in place while they decide what to do. Expect the unexpected is the second rule for being a Blade Master."

"What's the first?"

He winked at the prince. "Always obey your instructor."

"And the third?"

"Don't ever make your instructor look like a fool, because he'll always find ways to revisit that tenfold."

Arros chuckled to himself. "You just made that up."

"Are you certain?"

The prince slowly lost his grin, then backed away from him. "I think I'll just practice by myself for a bit."

Draxian was about to comment, when T'mara abruptly jumped to her feet. Cam came jogging back into their camp with a look of concern. The Hunter gestured behind him. "We may have a problem."

"What's wrong?" Draxian said, while resting a comforting hand upon his hilt.

"I spotted several dragons descending from the east."

The Lord Prince abandoned his practicing to rush over to his pack. He withdrew his vision enhancer. "Show me."

Cam wrinkled his forehead. "What do you plan to do with that?"

"Just point where you last saw them," Arros argued. Slipping the enhancer over his head, the prince stepped into the center of the well-traveled road and activated it.

The Hunter gestured with his spear. "You can see me through that metal?"

Arros continued to ignore his questions while he made several adjustments. "Dammit."

"Let me see!" T'mara ran over to him and snatched the enhancer from Arros' head, then placed it over her own. "How do you make it work?"

The prince cleared his throat. "As I was going to say before you took it from me, the power ran out just as I was trying to focus it."

"How do we get more?"

"More what?"

T'mara pulled the enhancer off as she looked back at him. "More magic to make this show me the land."

"It doesn't use..." Arros stopped himself upon catching Draxian's hardened gaze. "We don't have the proper type of... magic...to replenish the supply."

Nerris stroked his unshaven chin. "I'll bet it'll still fetch a good price to the right buyer."

"This is true," Cam agreed. "I know a few collectors in Phondari."

"Arros..." Draxian warned.

The Lord Prince swiped the enhancer back from T'mara. "No one is selling anything." He held it between his hands and concentrated. An abrupt burst of light caused everyone to turn away and shield their eyes. When he looked back, Draxian saw that the enhancer was blackened and cracked in several places.

T'mara recoiled with a gasp, nursing her wrist. When Draxian quickly approached, he saw her Hunter's mark glowing a deep crimson. "What's wrong?"

She gritted her teeth. "I do not know. It burns."

He looked over and saw Cam studying his mark as well. It too was glowing – yet not as brightly. "I've never seen this happen before."

"Arros!" Draxian caught the prince's arm and spun him around. "Stop whatever you're doing!"

"I'm not doing anything." Arros reached over and lifted T'mara's wrist. He placed his hand over the Huntress' scar and watched her eyes. She stiffened in response, and then gasped in surprise. "How does that feel?"

She slowly relaxed her stance, then watched him with wonder. "Who *are* you?" Arros lifted his hand, revealing that T'mara's scar was completely gone. Her wrist appeared as if it had never been branded with the Hunter's mark.

Cam stepped forward and also studied her arm. "That's impossible. The mark is permanent."

Draxian folded his arms and watched Arros intensely. "Do you even know what you're doing, or are you guessing?"

"I can't explain it. It just felt right."

He shook his head angrily. "This is exactly what your father was worried about. You're acting on instinct, instead of thinking your way through the problem and all its possible consequences."

"Careful."

"Drax," T'mara said, trying to comfort him. "He did not harm me."

"This time." The young lord pointed toward the charred vision enhancer. "I know you've been wanting to find your purpose here, but at least *try* to show a little restraint."

Arros lifted his chin. "Perhaps you're right. Next time someone is injured, I'll follow your example and choose apathy over action."

"That's not what I meant, and you know it."

Nerris held up a restraining hand. "Forgive me for interrupting this stimulating discussion – but what's that?" Everyone turned to look where the Blade Master was pointing. Far to the East, large plumes of black smoke were stretching to the sky.

Cam placed his hands on his hips. "I think that's coming from

Fidonn, the trading outpost."

It was late in the day when Kyreena arrived at the small town of Fidonn. Elgran had entertained her the entire way with tales of his youth and the problems they faced with the beasts from the Shadow Realm. It was amazing the man was still alive after so many dreadful encounters.

Her own experiences with survival were nothing short of miraculous. Whatever secret hid within the fog of her memory, Kyreena believed she must have been trained to defend herself to some degree. She could not imagine being trusted with the welfare of so many and not at least have some magical aptitude. It was just as the Dream Rider said, Kyreena needed to be patient and let the memories return on their own.

The town was located near a larger storm ward and surrounded by walls at least three times her height. Like the baron's keep, they had two ballistae perched high for repelling larger shadow creatures; they liked to follow and spawn from the red storms. Just inside the large gates, merchants of every kind had set up temporary carts and stands to peddle and trade wares with others of their kind. While there were no shortages of residents in the town, most of the buildings were set up for boarding visitors or entertaining the masses with food and spirits.

Kyreena assisted Elgran with setting up his wagons to trade his goods. She had learned he was an artisan who worked with rare wood to carve the most beautiful bed frames and tables. The stock he had brought with him was the culmination of an entire season of work. Kyreena had even remembered seeing one of his tables at Baron Clavius' keep.

"Again, you have my gratitude for the ride here."

Elgran cackled to himself. "In truth, I enjoyed the company.

Although I'm fairly certain I did most of the talking. Hope you didn't think me rude."

Kyreena reached out and gently touched his arm. "Not at all. I'm certain the tales of my life would be trite compared to what you've told me."

"Well, I may have exaggerated a few of the details to keep them entertaining." He leaned in and winked. "Don't tell anyone."

"You have my word."

"Perhaps a bit of fatherly advice?"

She nodded. "Of course."

"I know you can likely take care of yourself, but it seems to me that a lovely young woman shouldn't be wandering about the Blood Plains without someone to help keep her safe. These are dangerous times."

"I'll remember that."

She started to turn when he called over to her. "Whatever you be looking for, I truly hope you find it."

"My gratitude. I do as well."

Kyreena had enjoyed the company of the old craftsman and knew she would miss him, but her spirit never felt so alive. She was finally free of the slavers, and able to follow her own destiny. And to find it she would need to start in Phondari, according to the Dream Rider.

Her first stop took her to one of the inns where she rented a small room for the night. No one would be leaving until morning, so she took the opportunity to meet some of the merchants. Kyreena received lustful looks from many of the caravan guards as she entered the common room but was able to divert their gaze with a steady gaze of her own, causing many to blush. It was somehow satisfying. Through speaking with Elgran, she had learned that being a lone woman armed with a bow tended to mark her out as a Hunter. With the leather archery bracer that she had received from the Dream Rider, along with Kyreena's steadfast confidence in herself, it was difficult for the ogling men to determine her true nature. Instead, they simply left her be, in favor of visiting the town brothel.

By the time she found a vendor who agreed to let her ride to Phondari, a pale Annisian eager to get back to his home, it was getting close to dusk. Kyreena purchased a small bag of roasted nuts and climbed the ladder to sit on one of the back walls. She did not wish to be around the loud crowds any more than necessary, and it gave her comfort to sit up high and dangle her legs over the edge.

"Evening, Master Hunter," came a voice from nearby. Kyreena looked back to see a younger guardsman approaching from the side. "I see you found the best view in town."

"I didn't think anyone would mind me being here." She decided it was best to keep them believing she was dangerous. It served no purpose to say otherwise.

"Not at all. We could always use fresh eyes on the wall." He leaned against a parapet and looked out. "What brings you to our exciting little outpost?"

Kyreena smirked at the young man's attempt to be subtle. "Just passing through to Phondari."

"Ah, yes. There's quite a bit of that. Some of the other soldiers believe this is the worst assignment, but I actually like seeing different people every day." He shrugged. "We have our regulars, like everywhere else. Though it's great to see all the crafts and wares that come through here to be inspected and sold on their way to the city."

"I'm not certain I would be happy remaining in one place for long."

He huffed a laugh. "I figured that about you."

Kyreena frowned as an odd feeling swept down her spine. "Do you have problems with the shadow beasts?"

"Not here. They added some form of repelling ward to the obelisk to make them stay far away from this place. Why?"

"I'm not certain. It's just that…" Kyreena stopped speaking when she spotted something flying overhead.

"What's wrong?" The guardsman looked up, then sucked in a sharp breath. "Shite. It's that damn dragon again."

She continued to watch it circle, as if looking for something. "I didn't think they attacked people."

"Not people, but we have a lot of animal stock over on the far side of town. They're getting bolder all the time. Some of the juveniles are wild, and out of the Empress' control. This one has been eyeing us for some time now."

No sooner had he spoken the words, than the young dragon dove toward the town. The guardsman began calling out to warn the other sentries. The mighty beast landed just beyond the far wall to the screams of townsfolk and visitors. Kyreena had trouble seeing exactly what it was doing, but it was apparent the whelp had found easy prey when it snatched something from the ground before it and swallowed it whole like a great serpent, the muscles of its neck rippling as it pushed the thing down into its stomach.

"Bring the ballistae about," the guardsman called out frantically. In response, several sentries armed the war machines and brought them to bear.

"Don't shoot," Kyreena screamed. She jumped to her feet and clutched at the guardsman's arm. "Just let it have whatever it killed."

"We can't! If we don't act now, it will just keep coming back here every time it gets hungry." She knew he was making the wrong decision, but Kyreena feared being taken into custody again if she pressed too hard.

The first bolt whistled as it cut through the air, piercing the dragon through its left wing. It hissed in rage, then abandoned its dinner to seek out the new threat. A second siege weapon fired, hitting it in the side. That time, the juvenile shrieked in pain. The frightened juvenile cried out to the skies over and over as the guards loaded the jagged spears.

"You shouldn't have done that," Kyreena spoke softly, as tears blurred her vision.

Two more spears were launched with deadly accuracy. The young drake wailed one final time, before falling to the ground and lying motionless. Below, the multitudes of people cheered toward the guards on the wall. They believed them to be heroes. Kyreena knew otherwise.

"You see," the young guard called to her with pride. "That's the only way a beast like that will ever understand."

As though in response, a distant roar echoed from high in the clouds. The people quickly fell silent as they listened for more sounds. Meanwhile, the guards began loading their ballistae once again.

Kyreena caught the guardsman's arm. "We should take shelter."

"The adults don't attack. It's probably just calling out to find it, like wolves do."

"Dragons don't communicate by sound. They hear the thoughts of those nearby."

Again, the roar sounded, only much closer.

"The juvenile you just killed told every dragon within range you were murdering it."

His face paled. "Oh, shite."

They both looked up to see a massive drake descending from the clouds. It was easily ten times the size of the one they had killed – and it was not alone. Three more appeared just behind it, all diving straight for the town. Their scales quickly began to shift color, blending into the dark reddish hue of their background. Kyreena could still make out the faint outline of the dragons, but no real detail. They fully intended to attack.

"Run!" She pushed the guard toward the ladder.

Not stopping to argue, the young man quickly climbed halfway down before jumping the rest of the way. Kyreena had already leapt from the top of the wall and landed safely on the ground. She grabbed the guard's arm just as a blazing inferno erupted from above, sending flaming cinders of ruined buildings through the air. People screamed in horror as the scaled titans swooped low and opened their maws. Liquid fire spewed into the streets and along the walls, just as a ballista managed to get off a single shot. Kyreena watched as the spear shattered upon the thick hide of the ancient beast, causing it no more distress than if they had hurled a toothpick.

Most of the town was destroyed or set on fire in moments. Blackened bodies were strewn about in horrific repose, and citizens wailed in anguish at the fiery wounds that scorched their flesh and continued to burn without end. Kyreena renewed her efforts to run with the guard amongst the choking smoke and searing heat. They had nearly made it to the front gate when the ancient dragon landed just outside and snarled in rage.

She withdrew her bow and readied an arrow.

"What in the Abyss are you doing?" the guard cried over the roar of the flames.

"If you hit them in the eye, just right…"

Without warning, the drake spun to one side, flinging its massive, spiked tail at the gates. The stone walls exploded into a shower of flying debris. In desperation, the guardsman grabbed her by the waist and dove under a wagon that Kyreena recognized as belonging to Elgran. The raining stone was far too much for the rickety timbers and wooden wheels, crushing it around them and pinning Kyreena to the ground.

FIERY CONSEQUENCES

Arros carefully approached the smoldering ruins of what he assumed had been the front gates. They had ridden all night to reach the town and arrived just as the dawn ignited the crimson Veil above. With the Hunters guiding their mounts, the prince was confident they would arrive safely through the darkness. However, they were far too late to save the town from destruction.

"There's nothing we can do," Cam called over to him. "No one could have survived this."

The Lord Prince continued toward the broken wall. "Someone might have. Probably hiding in a cellar or underground shelter."

T'mara remained on her mount, surveying the damage. "Why would the dragons attack a town? Does that not break the truce with Dellahara?"

"I don't even know what that means," Draxian returned.

"The Empress of Dragons made a vow that none of her dragons

would attack humans so long as they do not hunt them in return."

Nerris pointed further down the way. "Looks like someone broke the truce." There, just outside the walls, a small dragon lay with large spears protruding from its belly and neck.

Arros started making his way into the wreckage. "I'm still going."

"Leave him be," Draxian told the others. He continued after the Prince had moved some distance away. "Arros needs time to reflect. We'll search elsewhere."

He had heard every word but chose to ignore Draxian's comment, a barb meant to show his displeasure at Arros' use of magic earlier. The prince moved away from the group and climbed over piles of stone to reach the first building, well out of view of the road. His heart sank upon finding nothing but burnt shells and the charred bodies of men and women of every age. Not all had died from the fiery breath of the drakes – some had suffocated in the thick smoke. The smell was revolting.

He finally came upon several broken wagons. From what he could see, they had once been filled with carved furniture to be sold at the market. Arros finally understood why the Undying were fearful of the Dragon Empress. With an army of fire-breathing drakes, she could annihilate a large city and all its occupants from the air without losing a single soldier.

As the prince started to move further down what remained of the street, he heard a cough from somewhere nearby. Arros rushed around to the other side of the broken wagons then halted. A woman laid among the broken and charred furniture, covered in dirt and soot. Her clothing had large burn holes in some places, the material stretched and torn from her attempt to free herself from the wreckage. Despite the ruined state of her attire, she was still breathing. The burnt remains of the person who lay next to her told a more tragic story.

Arros cleared a broken wagon axle from the woman's legs, then knelt down to her. Carefully, the prince rolled her over to check for any serious wounds. The woman's eyes immediately burst open and she flinched away from him.

"Easy," Arros soothed. "I'm here to help." She held completely still and watched him with an unreadable expression. "Can you understand me?" The woman slowly nodded. "That's a good start. My name is Arros Nemendes. Will you allow me to check you for injuries?" Instead of responding, the woman slowly reached up and caressed his cheek with her fingertips. The prince smiled warmly at the pitiful figure covered in soot, then took her hand. "You're very lucky to be alive. It appears the wagon shielded you from the stone and flames. It's a miracle your legs aren't broken. Do you have a name?"

"Sel…" the woman began, then shook her head as if trying to clear her thoughts. "Kyreena. My friends call me Kyreena."

"I'm greatly relieved to find you, Kyreena." Arros pulled a waterskin from his pack, then handed it to her. "Drink as much as you can."

She nodded her appreciation, then drank deeply of the fresh water. Kyreena handed it back while looking around to survey the destruction. "Did anyone else make it out of the town?"

"If they did, it was late last night. You're the only survivor I could find."

Kyreena took a deep breath, then coughed several more times. "I told them not to attack that young chromatic dragon. They didn't listen to me."

"We assumed that's what happened. I'm deeply sorry for what you endured. Is there anything I can do for you?"

"Take me with you."

Arros tilted his head to one side. "Do you have family somewhere close?" His eyes took in a nearby building with charred supports poking out from the sides. "Hopefully not from this area."

"Family?"

He continued to watch her as she stared off in the distance. "Are you well?"

She once again reached over and lightly pressed her hand to his chest, as if trying to feel his heartbeat. "Oh my." Recognition came to Kyreena's eyes, and they filled with tears while she laughed to herself. "I know you."

"While I'll admit it's difficult to tell with all the ash covering your skin, I'm fairly certain we haven't met before." Arros grinned back, then retrieved a cloth from the pack sitting at his side. The prince soaked it with water to begin cleaning her face.

"We may not have seen each other before today, but you're the one I've been searching for my entire life – I'm sure of it."

He continued to clean her cheeks and neck. "Well then, I'm glad one of us is certain about their destiny. I'm still trying to find my purpose in this abysmal world."

Kyreena lifted his hand with both of hers. "I'll help you find it."

"My destiny?"

"The weapon – it was meant for you."

Arros drew his neck back in surprise. "How do you know about that?"

"They entrusted this knowledge to me." The woman shook her head again. "I just need more time to remember where it was hidden."

"Are we discussing the same thing?"

Kyreena shrugged a single shoulder. "Not sure. My memory is still finding its way back to me."

The prince continued cleaning the soot from her skin. "I'd like to believe you, truly, but if you can't remember much about yourself, then how can you possibly know if I'm the person you seek?"

"That's a fair question." Kyreena considered it for a moment, then looked up. "Does the name 'Ellandor' mean anything to you?"

Arros' body tensed, and his eyes shot wide.

After scouring much of the western side of the ruined town, Draxian had decided to take a break from their search for survivors. He located the last of his jumeba fruit among their supplies, when Nerris approached him. They had decided to remain near the ruined town for a bit while Arros and Cam finished searching the area for more survivors.

"My Lord? T'mara is with the Lord Prince and the girl, helping to get her cleaned up and into some new clothing."

Drax shook his head in disbelief. "Leave it to Arros to find the only half-naked woman within leagues of any hint of civilization."

"Aye. It's a wonder how she stayed alive through all this." Nerris pointed toward the jumeba. "You going to eat all of that?"

"Want half?"

"Please."

Draxian broke off a large section and then handed it to the Blade Master. "What did he say was her name?"

"Koronna... No... Kyreena?"

"That was it." The large man bit into the over-ripened fruit, then chewed. "Tell me about the Resistance. Will they help us steal this sword?"

Nerris finished his own mouthful, then nodded. "You can be certain of it."

"But can we trust them?"

"No. I would take care not to trust anyone fully. Tell them only what they need to know, and nothing more." He gestured with his jumeba. "A bit like you're doing now."

Draxian narrowed his eyes. "You can't actually expect me to reveal everything about us."

"I'm not judging. As I said, trust is a liability."

"And yet you seem awfully eager to assist us without even knowing who we are."

The Blade Master popped the last segment into his mouth, then winked. "I know enough. Anymore, and I become the liability." He wiped the juice from his fingers onto his trousers. "Bad things happen to those who know too much. It's a historical fact."

"You're a dangerous man, Nerris."

He smirked, then turned to walk away. "Not so much as you, I think."

It was not much longer before T'mara and Arros exited the ruins with a shorter woman walking between them. She was wearing one of T'mara's sleeveless tunics and leather pants. They looked a bit long for her, yet it was better than the alternative. As they came closer, Draxian could make out Kyreena's ashy-blonde hair and soft grey eyes. Looking at her, the young lord would not have guessed she had just survived an apocalypse.

"Kyreena," Arros introduced. "This is Draxian Kalenthos. You can trust him the same as me."

Draxian nodded to her. "You don't look any worse for the dragon attack. I suppose I owe you an apology. Arros was the only one of us who believed someone could have survived in that place."

Instead of answering, Kyreena watched him with a distant look. He met her gaze with eyebrows drawn inward in consternation. She stepped forward and lightly touched his chest. "He's a Traveler... like you."

When Draxian glared at Arros, he shook his head. "Not a word, I swear."

"Uh, yes," the lord began, as he took a step back from her. "We'd rather not discuss that subject."

Kyreena retreated back to Arros' side and dipped her head

apologetically. "Forgive me, my Lord. I didn't mean to insult you."

"Startled, maybe, but not insulted." Draxian took a deep breath. "If we leave now, we can expect to arrive in Phondari by midday tomorrow."

Arros nodded thoughtfully. "Good. Kyreena is coming with us."

"As you wish." Draxian decided it was best not to argue further with the prince. The last few days had placed a strain on their friendship, more than any other time in their lives. And the fact that Kyreena knew more about them than anyone else, save for the Oracle of Orakh, told him the woman was somehow important. He no longer believed in chance encounters.

The Empress of Dragons sat on the couch in her private study, reading over the stack of reports from the short table in front of her. There were far more than usual. It was as if the arrival of the Travelers had heralded an awakening of activity with all the various factions and players. Even the Undying had ceased their hostilities and began to meet in secret locations to discuss the end of the prophesied Thousand Years of Darkness.

She was just reading over an interesting report for the second time when Commander Rellan appeared at the doorway. "Mistress? You have an unexpected visitor."

"I know. See him inside."

"Yes, Mistress."

Rellan disappeared into the corridor, only to be replaced by another. His tall, lean frame nearly took up the entire doorway. "Adreana, you wished to speak with me?"

"Yes, Lord General. Care for some wine?"

He remained still. "What's this about?"

"Can we not be civil?" The Empress pointed toward the pitcher and silver cups on the table. "Indulge me."

The cloaked figure in black moved toward the side couch, then seated himself. Almost of their own accord, the pitcher and a cup slid over to him. The Lord General reached out and poured himself some wine. "Satisfied?"

"Tell me, Lord of Shadows, did we not broach the issue of interference with the Travelers?"

"I've mostly kept my distance."

Adreana's head swiveled toward him. "It's the 'mostly' part that has me concerned."

"Noted. Now, what's this truly about?"

"What do you know of this new cult? The Children of Dawn. They're prophesying the end of the darkness and gathering many to their side. Are they truly rising to battle the Undying? Or is this just another group of charlatans trying to bleed coins from the people?"

He went quiet for a time. "Don't trust them."

"I'll need more to go on than that, Lord General."

"I can't give you details I don't have. This warning came to me long ago by the Dragon King."

Adreana felt as if a dagger had been plunged into her heart. She sat up straight and gritted her teeth. "If you have any honor left within you – do not ever speak his name again."

His eyes showed genuine sorrow. "Forgive me, Empress. I only mention it to relay the magnitude of this foretelling."

"Noted," she mocked.

"My inside man tells me that the Travelers are seeking the Sword of Melkarick."

The Empress of Dragons lifted the report she had previously been reviewing, then handed it over to the Shadow Lord. "I've come by the same information."

His eyes turned to the document and he silently read to himself. "This intelligence is days old."

"Do you have something further to add?"

"I do." The Lord General set the page on the table, then looked up. "The Travelers will arrive in Phondari tomorrow. They believe the Sword of Melkarick is with Regent Xaadier, although I can't confirm this. It's been ages since anyone has laid eyes upon that terrible weapon."

"My spies tell me the Regent has become more and more paranoid in the last few seasons. He often speaks to himself and remains in seclusion with his gaggle of Soul Singer protectors."

The Lord of Shadows exhaled a deep breath and nodded. "Your information is accurate. We must assume the sword is in his possession. I've seen this kind of madness before in others who tried to harness its power. The city of Orakh is the perfect example of why it must never fall into the hands of men."

"In that, we are in complete agreement." Adreana scooted herself closer to the Lord General. "Do you truly think the Travelers can seal the rift?"

"Do you?"

"I need to believe it. My pets are becoming increasingly more difficult to control." She shook her head in regret. "Last night, soldiers from the town of Fidonn were forced to kill a young drake that was feeding on their livestock. I could feel her pain as she was penetrated with spears from ballistae."

"One Power!" the Shadow Lord breathed. "What happened?"

"Her cries of despair did not go unanswered. As I feared, her mother heard and descended upon the town with other *drakara who were* nearby. Nothing would have survived."

"Could you not stop them?"

"A part of me wanted to… and yet another didn't care if they burned. I believe this inner conflict was the reason my command failed to reach them. With the distortion of the Spirit Realm, magic has been increasingly difficult to manage. If the Travelers don't recover Melkarick and seal the breach, my control will eventually be lost, and the drakara will be free to pillage at will."

"Then we'll do whatever it takes to make certain they find this blade."

The Empress of Dragons lifted her chin. "Agreed."

THE FLOATING CITY

With Cam and Nerris taking the lead, Arros rode with Kyreena clutching his waist and leaning her head against his back. The woman had barely spoken since the town of Fidonn. She would simply smile and nod or shake her head when the prince asked her various questions. It was difficult to say what was going on behind those silvery eyes, yet Arros was just relieved Kyreena had found some inner peace. Her knowledge of their place of origin began to make the Lord Prince wonder if she had encountered his father at some point in her journey. Arros believed that theory would make the most sense of any explanation they could formulate. Furthermore, it would likely be within King Nemendes' power to dampen her memories of their meeting as well.

"It's just over this rise," Nerris called back to them.

Arros' first hints of the city of Phondari was from the distant towers of a palace made of bleached stone. As he continued to climb the hill, the lower keeps and curtain walls could be seen. By the time he reached the summit, his breath caught in his throat. The entire city was hovering over a deep ravine with only a single causeway extending up to the main gatehouse. And just before the bridge, a second city had been built nearby to accommodate the growing population. From Arros' view, it's primary purpose seemed to be for quick trading without the need to climb the causeway to the floating city.

Draxian appeared next to him riding a taark. He grunted in dismay. "And the sword is located way on the other side, in that tall castle?"

"That's what they're saying."

"Did you happen to bring any climbing gear from home?"

Arros huffed a laugh. "Didn't expect to have a use for it."

Nerris called over to them. "Don't worry – we'll be able to get inside without a problem. It's the getting out that currently has me concerned."

"Is there anything we need to know before attempting to enter the city?"

"Actually," Cam began carefully, "we should discuss what happened the other day with our Hunter's marks. Phondari has similar warning glyphs at the main gates to identify people with dangerous magic." He pulled his sleeve back to display the deep scar on his wrist. "It never once gave me any indication, until you summoned that flash of light to destroy your metal hat."

Arros glanced around. "Then, you're telling me that I only need to refrain from doing anything like that again?"

"Possibly."

"Go on."

Cam stroked his short beard in thought. "They're designed to alert us with a pulse of magic when someone is nearby, and always it glows a brighter blue the closer we get. I've never even heard of it turning red – much less causing pain to the one with the mark." He shrugged. "Then again, it doesn't identify every kind of mage. Only elemental and spirit magic."

"And if you had to guess?"

It was Kyreena who spoke. "The mark of the Mage Hunters was originally created to identify the Travelers – should they ever return to this land. It was later adapted to allow the Undying to hunt those with elemental magic as well."

T'mara glared at Cam. "You need to tell them."

Draxian glanced back and forth between the Hunters. "Tell us what?"

Cam exhaled noisily, then shook his head. "When we received our mark from the guild, we were all told to report any unusual changes to the magic or coloring when performing our duties. They weren't even certain what to look for, only that it would be much different."

Arros turned back toward T'mara. "Why didn't you tell us this after it first happened at the Guardian's Keep?"

Cam narrowed his eyes. "It's happened before?"

"She probably didn't know what it meant," Draxian defended.

"T'mara can speak for herself." Arros refocused his attention back on her. "Well?"

The Huntress shifted uncomfortably in her saddle. "At first, I was a little frightened by this. But then, I found it made me feel special to know something none other did. My people have a legend, that the Lord of Destruction would one day return to us if we honored our promise to him."

Kyreena placed a hand on Arros' shoulder and whispered to him. "She speaks the truth."

"And you believe Drax might be a rebirth of this myth?" The prince shook his head. "I'll admit that he's quite clumsy at times – but the title of Lord of Destruction is a bit harsh."

"Easy now," Draxian warned. "Nobody is insinuating anything."

T'mara patted her taark reassuringly. "I am not a child. The Shadiere do not place trust in myths or stories passed by mouth. We have writings that go back to the first of our tribe to return from the Realm of Shadows, when the Lord of Destruction appeared and carried my people to this land. He walked among us – protected my people as would a father his children. And when the Fallen One chased us to this land and stole the sun from the sky, the Great Lord joined with the Dragon King and went on a final hunt to end him forever. He never returned, but we promised him before he left that we would always keep this land safe from the shadow beasts that follow the red storms." She pointed a sharp finger toward the white palace. "Because of the laws of the Undying, the Shadiere have been unable to hunt many of the creatures that still hide within their borders. They keep us from fulfilling our sacred oath."

Cam folded his arms. "Is that why you wanted to join the Chosen Hunters? To give you unrestricted access to all the Empires?"

"In part, yes. I also wished to look inside the great cities and experience the stories you and so many others had spoken."

Draxian held up a hand to halt the conversation. "Enough. T'mara isn't on trial. We all are here for the same reason: that we must do whatever it takes to protect the ones we care about." He sniffed loudly. "Arros and I started this journey to find our fathers. Nothing else mattered. Then, I met all of you, and we learned that the corruption here could spread to our land as well – potentially destroying all life if left unchecked. Arros and I have a duty to fix whatever damage was caused by the careless use of magic. Do we understand this powerful energy? Yes – to a certain degree. Although you must consider that our culture believes magic was the foundation of every problem our ancestors faced. We don't hate it – we just fear it's influence." He gave Arros a sidelong glance. "This is why our people have chosen to live further from its reach. You can't abuse what you don't have."

Nerris cleared his throat. "What if you have no choice?"

"There are always choices." Drax sighed to himself. "But if it comes down to ignoring the call of magic, or embracing it to defend the ones you love, I'm with Arros. We can't allow pride or arrogance to keep us from reaching our goal. That's not the path of wisdom, it's the deep chasm of self-deceit."

Arros grinned back at his old friend. "It's about damn time."

Draxian was amazed at how easy it was for Cam to get the group through the gatehouse and into the floating city. The Hunter only needed to pull back his sleeve as he walked past, and the sentries went back to questioning others who pled for entry. They were forced to leave their mounts in the lower district, but he knew that making a hasty exit would be the least of their problems if the group was caught trying to steal the sword.

Arros decided to splurge on more expensive lodgings in the noble district. Draxian could not blame him after they had spent most of the previous twenty-three days sleeping on the hard ground with buzzing insects all around them. Perhaps the prince was trying to impress the new girl. He had to admit he was curious about Kyreena. Such as why she refused to leave his side, and how she had survived the destruction of a town. He could not even imagine what that must have been like for her.

Cam had set off to secure provisions and check on the caravan he had sent on to Phondari when joining the group. As for Nerris, he immediately left to contact the Resistance and seek their aid. This placed him in the perfect position to betray them, and after learning that each of their new companions had an ulterior motivation for traveling with them, Draxian was in short supply of trust. Because of this, he insisted they sit near the window of the inn after they had a chance to clean up in their rooms. Arros had only purchased three for the night. Kyreena had insisted on staying with the prince, and one glare from T'mara told the young lord that any objections to the Huntress sharing his bed would likely be met with violence.

"Do you think they serve spiced tarlagon soup here?"

Arros scratched at a piece of dried food on the table, then looked up at T'mara. "I should probably tell you that I hated it."

T'mara giggled to herself. "I knew this. It was fun to see your face as you tried to remain polite. We are not accustomed to such manners here."

"Is that why you later ordered the fire-root ale?"

"Precisely. I wanted to see how far that extended."

Arros rolled his eyes, then waved for the barmaid to approach.

"My lords and ladies, welcome to the King's Chambers." The older woman was decorated in gaudy jewelry and wore a strong-scented perfume that tickled Draxian's nose.

"Honey wine for everyone. And what's that delicious aroma?"

"Ah," she began with pride. "That's the inn's special recipe – a hot vegetable and meat broth, baked into a flakey pie shell. It's served with barley rolls and melted butter."

Draxian felt his stomach rumble with anticipation. "How big are they?"

She turned toward the large man, then held up her hands about a pace apart. "They will serve four easy enough."

"I'll take one for myself."

The woman blinked in confusion. "An entire meat pie?"

Arros shook his head. "Just give it to him. Back home, Draxian won the sausage eating contest three summers in a row. It was impressive, if not horrifying."

"Very well."

"The rest of us will share one."

"Excellent." The woman darted off to tell the kitchen of their request, leaving them alone to speak once again.

It wasn't long before their bellies were full and the wine was running low. Nerris finally returned and seated himself between Draxian and Kyreena. He reached over and lifted the empty pitcher, then frowned. "I've spoken with my contacts here and they've agreed to assist us."

Arros narrowed his eyes suspiciously. "That was easy."

"As I said before, they've been in place for a long time just waiting for someone to stand tall and give them a true purpose."

"What did you tell them?"

The Blade Master leaned in closer. "This isn't the place to discuss such things. I've arranged for you and Draxian to meet with their palace representatives in one turn of the glass." He wobbled his head from side to side. "Actually, it's more like a half-turn now. We should probably get moving."

T'mara caught Nerris' arm before he could stand. "And what about us?"

"Apologies. I don't know you, and neither do they. Arros and Draxian only."

Arros nodded to him. "We accept their terms."

"Then, shall we?"

It did not take long for the three men to reach the boarding home in the residential district. Arros had to assure Kyreena that he would not be gone long, and her presence might keep the Resistance from agreeing to assist. T'mara was especially helpful in that regard, promising their newest member to an evening browsing through the merchant shops and stands. Arros had given them enough coins to purchase an entire wardrobe, which

Draxian felt was uncharacteristically generous of him. They had brought a finite amount of gold with them, and there was no telling how long it would take to find their fathers.

Upon entering, Draxian glanced around at the interior of the ancient stone building. An old woman was working away at a crude loom, tediously piecing together a blanket, string by string. The furniture was worn and rickety, and most of the chairs appeared barely capable of supporting the large man's weight. Nerris ignored the woman to knock on a door that was covered with nicks and dents from throwing knives.

"Come on, Veklass," Nerris called out. "I know you're standing right there."

The door cracked open and an older man with a grey beard poked his head out. "How do you do that?"

"I can smell you – open up."

Veklass pushed the door wide, then stood back. "Did you bring me some wine?"

"You whine enough as it is."

The old man cackled to himself, then nodded. "True enough." He smiled pleasantly to Arros and Draxian as they passed the threshold. The entire room was nearly filled with stacked crates with a royal seal painted on the sides. "They're waiting for you."

"My gratitude." Nerris motioned for the two men to follow. He moved around the high stacks until coming to a closet. "Watch this."

The Blade Master opened the door to display a small, empty space with only a few ragged garments hanging from a stretched rope. Nerris closed it once more, then reached to one side and twisted an iron sconce set in the wall. Draxian heard a clicking noise, followed by the scraping of wood on wood. When the Master reopened the closet door, they found a stairwell descending into darkness.

"Clever," Arros admired.

"It sticks at times if not oiled properly. Allegedly, the previous owner sold illegal magical items out of his home." Nerris motioned for them to follow. "Veklass once got trapped down here for two days."

"I heard that," the old man called from above.

Once Draxian had squeezed his way down the narrow staircase, the door above him slid back into place, then a metal bar latched it tight. They entered a short tunnel that extended for only a dozen paces before it terminated inside a chamber with heavy support beams. A round table sat in the middle with six chairs. To one side, several iron-bound chests were stacked next to a shelf with various scrolls and books.

Two men were waiting patiently at the table, both in guard's uniforms. The first was around Draxian's age, with dark hair and pale skin, and the other was middle-aged, his hair greying at the sides, wearing emblems that marked him as an officer. For a brief moment, Draxian wondered if Nerris had led them into a trap.

Both soldiers stood at their approach. The officer was tall and lean, with a look in his eyes that made Draxian want to grasp his sword handle for comfort. "I'm Captain Tollas of the Phondari palace guard. This is Guardsman First Class, Merrick Whiteforge." He reached out a hand to Arros. "We're deeply honored to meet you."

The prince clasped wrists with the man and watched his expression. "I'm Arros. This is Draxian."

"Well met," Draxian said, greeting the man forearm to forearm in kind. "We understand you can assist us with procuring a rare item?"

Tollas gestured for everyone to sit. "We've listened to what Nerris had to say on the subject, but I'd like to hear this in your own words."

Arros sat back in his chair. "Why?"

"Call it my lack of trust and leave it there."

The prince exchanged a look with Draxian, then turned back to the captain. "Someone in the palace has an item we need, which is paramount to sealing the breach in the Ebon Waste."

"The Sword of Melkarick."

"Correct."

Merrick had a look on his face that said he had no idea what that meant, a stark contrast to the captain's confident gaze.

"If the Regent truly has the blade, I've not seen it on him."

"How would you even know what it looks like? I heard this artifact has been lost for an untold number of years."

Captain Tollas gave him a wisp of a smile, then leaned back in his chair. "We know what it looks like."

Merrick turned toward the officer. "Forgive me, Captain. What about the dagger he carries with him? Can the sword be disguised with magic?"

Arros raised an eyebrow. "Can it?"

"Possibly." The captain considered the question. "I once saw a powerful weapon that could do that. It would alter its form to match the individual's preference."

"We don't know anything about it – that's why we're here. Can you help us recover it?"

Tollas laced his fingers in front of him and looked at both men in turn. "I don't think you truly understand what that entails, so I won't dip this in honey. If Regent Xaadier has the Sword of Melkarick on him, it will be impossible to steal. You'll need to kill him."

Arros sat up straight, then held up a hand. "I assure you, that's not going to happen. We didn't come here to assassinate your leaders. This is about saving the land from the taint of the Spirit Realm before it engulfs all of Kohr."

"That's right," Draxian added. "No one needs to die. There must be a way to separate him from the weapon. I doubt he sleeps with it under his pillow."

"Do you know what a Soul Singer is?" When neither man responded, Tollas continued. "They're women with a unique connection to the Spirit Realm. They use their magic to draw from an opponent's strength or turn the energy back around to be used against the attacker. Also, they can heal others with their power. A lone, fully trained Singer is terrifying at best. Xaadier has gathered thirteen to his command. All of them are connected directly to his life essence. If he's wounded, they can quickly heal the Regent without ever touching him."

Arros leaned in closer. "So, you're saying it's possible."

Tollas watched him for a time. "Every suit of armor has a weakness." He nodded to the young guardsman.

Merrick cleared his throat. "One of the Soul Singers is a good friend of mine. Before she was captured and enslaved by the Regent, we were even talking about the possibility of getting married someday."

"How does that help us?"

Tollas tapped his finger on the table. "I believe she might be able to temporarily poison the supply of healing energy to the Regent – or at least keep the others from helping him."

"Are we still on this assassination plot?"

"Don't pity him, Lord Prince," Captain Tollas sneered. "The man deserves death a thousand times over for his war crimes and unspeakable cruelties." Draxian couldn't help but notice that he already knew Arros' title. Nerris apparently talked too much.

The prince narrowed his eyes. "That's not for me to judge… or convict."

"Why are you here?"

"Nerris told us you could help me get into the palace. Can you do this or not?"

Tollas shook his head. "No. Why are *you* here?"

"There are far more lives in the balance than those you know."

"Don't patronize me, boy. I'd wager you know far less about this situation than you would have us believe." Captain Tollas matched Arros glare for glare. "You think this stance of pacifism will earn you value in the eyes of your father? So far, you're a complete disappointment."

Arros lifted his clenched fist, causing it to burst to life with a radiant light. "Choose your next words carefully."

Merrick flinched away from the light, but Tollas leaned forward. "Or what? You'll kill me? Not very civil for an Ellandorian."

The light faded from Arros' hand. "How do you know all this?"

"Your fathers once came to us for assistance. At the time, we didn't have the knowledge or opportunity that we do now."

"Where are they?"

"Haven't seen them in years." Tollas tilted his head in amusement. "I make it my business to know people. With enough motivation, I found that a man will do just about anything to protect the ones he loves."

Arros' gaze turned dark. "Is that some kind of threat?"

"A great man once told me to never threaten if it can be helped. It places you in a position to either act on it, and appear cruel – or not, and prove yourself a coward."

"That sounds exactly like my father."

Tollas finally let slip a grin, placing the entire table at ease. "I considered him a close friend for the time we knew each other. You look a bit like your father – but you lack his convictions." He gestured toward both men. "Have either of you killed a man?"

"I don't see that having any bearing on our conversation."

He ignored Arros' comment. "The first man I ever killed, was in defense of someone I cared about. Murder leaves a deep scar on your soul. It didn't matter if he deserved it or not, only that it was necessary at the time. We're not asking you to enjoy it, just be ready to do whatever is necessary to save the people you love, and so many countless others, as you put it."

The prince turned to the young guardsman. "And what are your thoughts?"

"Me?" Merrick glanced over to the captain to make certain it was appropriate to speak. "I came here and joined the Phondari guard to find a way to free Caela from being a slave to the Regent. At the time, I didn't know exactly where she was, or that she was a Soul Singer. I only had been told that she was sold to the palace. Caela won't confirm this, but I've heard whispers of what Xaadier does to these women to amuse himself." The guardsman balled his fist, then hammered on the table. "He cuts them. He cuts them with that cursed knife whenever it suits his perverse desires. Regent Xaadier knows that another Singer will heal them and remove all traces of the wound."

Draxian leaned forward. "And you believe this is true?"

"I'm certain of it." He shook his head. "When I asked her, Caela didn't deny it – only got real quiet, then asked me not to speak of such things." Merrick clasped his hands together. "I'm begging you, if you have the means to stop this monster, please do so. You don't know what it's like to watch someone you love suffer every day at the hands of another and feel so powerless to do anything about it."

Tollas lifted a hand to accentuate his point. "If you're seeking a justification, Lord Prince, you now have it."

Arros huffed a soft laugh. "Well fought, Captain. I've clearly misjudged you." He glanced around the underground chamber. "When do we leave?"

SOUL SINGER

Merrick was trembling with excitement as he walked to the upper gardens to meet with Caela. Captain Tollas had gotten word to her that the Soul Singer was needed to heal a minor training injury. Regent Xaadier was not always accommodating of such things, but he was also being detained in the Great Hall by a lengthy discussion about a recent dragon attack that razed an entire trading outpost, leaving no survivors.

"Well, if it isn't our good friend Dusty-Foot," one of the two sentries called out upon his approach to the stairs. "This area is currently off limits. Go away."

He nodded to Jhonras and Eralath. "Just wanting to stretch my legs in the gardens."

The sentries exchanged confused expressions, then Eralath narrowed his eyes. "You're the one we're supposed to let by?" When Merrick didn't answer, the guardsman rolled his eyes.

"Don't stay long," he spoke with overt sarcasm. "It looks like it might rain."

Merrick forced a smile. "I'll be quick."

As the young guardsman climbed the central spire to the roof gardens, he couldn't help but chuckle to himself. Captain Tollas had cleverly used his false loyalty test to replace many, if not all, of the palace guard with Resistance sympathizers. If Regent Xaadier were ever forced to call for aid, he would likely find none waiting for him.

When he emerged on the roof of the palace, Merrick halted and took a moment to admire the large planters containing a wide variety of colorful flowers. He had seen them from a distance many times, but the garden was far more beautiful up close. Emperor Deathskull had insisted that it be maintained by a sizable staff, and most believed he was trying to emulate the Empress of Dragons' garden in Dellahara. It was rumored that she had her own private orchard that bloomed no matter what the season.

Merrick continued toward the center and to a large circle of ancient stone columns standing on a marble platform. It was a serene view, where one could sit on stone benches, chiseled with beautifully embossed patterns. He imagined thousands of years of rulers and nobles visiting that very spot to discuss matters of importance.

It wasn't much longer before the sound of female voices came from the stairs. Merrick had assumed Caela would be alone. He quickly drew his hunting knife and made a painful slice to his leg that cut into his uniform. Blood immediately began to pool around the wound as Caela and another Singer appeared at the edge of the garden.

He sat on a nearby bench and pressed his palm over the wound. "I'm over here."

Caela's eyes shot wide as they approached, but it was the other Singer who spoke. "We understand you were injured?" The woman glanced around. "In a training accident?"

"Apologies. Me and some of the other guards were fooling around in the night air. They left on the chance we might get punished."

The woman shrugged. "It's not up to me to decide such matters." She turned to Caela. "This will be your first opportunity to heal another outside our group. It's a bit more difficult without the collective."

Caela forced a quick smile. "I'll do my best." She knelt down to examine the wound by the light of a nearby torch. Merrick flinched at her touch. "Apologies. It's not too deep." Shortly after placing her hands over the cut, a soft ringing began to fill the air. The haunting tones echoed around him as if originating from somewhere beyond his senses.

"Excellent," the woman coached from the side. "Now, redirect his life energies to focus on the wound."

Almost immediately, Merrick felt the pain dissipate, and his head began to swim with a strange euphoria. "Am I supposed to be dizzy?"

"Caela," the other Singer scolded. "You're pushing too hard. It's a slow and gentle process. His life-force needs to be persuaded, not stolen."

"Apologies, Efayne."

"You don't need my forgiveness – ask for his."

Caela bowed her head to him. "Forgive me, Merrick."

"Not to worry. I appreciate you taking the time to come here."

The other woman frowned. "You know him?"

"I've been trying to learn the names of all the palace guards," Caela quickly lied.

Merrick wasn't certain how to get Caela alone without raising suspicion. As such, he tried a different approach. "I'm certain the Regent feels safer with you around."

"I have no doubt," Efayne sneered.

"Why do you think he needs so many of you?"

She narrowed her eyes. "You ask a lot of questions."

Caela ignored her comment and spoke for them. "As you can see, healing even a minor wound will take some time. With a collective of Singers at his command, the Regent can tap into our life-energies as well, healing even the most devastating wound much faster."

"And what happens if his head falls off? He grows a new one?"

Caela giggled at his jest, causing her spirit tones to waver for a moment. "No. That would kill him and sever the link."

"And then we would die as well," Efayne added.

Merrick's stomach turned. "Why would that happen?"

"Probably to keep any Singer from ending Regent Xaadier's life to escape from the palace." Caela shrugged. "The Regent thought of everything."

Efayne leaned in closer. "We should not discuss such matters – especially with a palace guard."

He held up a hand in defense. "I report to Captain Tollas, not Regent Xaadier. You can say whatever you wish about him. It wouldn't surprise me at all if someone decided it was time for a change in leadership."

Caela's eyes shot up for a moment, then back to the wound. "Well, they would be foolish for trying. We always have at least six Singers nearby – unless he's requested fewer."

"Why would he ever do that?" Merrick could tell she was beginning to understand his intentions.

"If he wishes to be alone in his chambers with only one of us, that's not uncommon."

"Although," Efayne added in a stern tone. "There are always others in the next room to assist him when summoned."

Merrick smiled up to her. "He's truly fortunate to have you."

"You have no idea."

It was about that time, Captain Tollas appeared at the edge of the garden. "Efayne?"

"Yes, Captain?" The Singer moved away from the group to join him.

"I wanted to speak with you in private about some training exercises we'll be initiating over the next few days." Captain Tollas began leading her down the stairs.

Efayne called over her shoulder to Caela. "I'll see you back in the tower when you're finished." It didn't take long for them to disappear beyond his sight.

"Finally," Merrick breathed.

"You take too many risks." Caela ceased her work, causing the spirit tones to fade.

"Did you heal the wound already?" He fingered at his torn pants. "That's incredible."

"I was just stalling. It doesn't take that long, normally."

Merrick stood and glanced around to make certain nobody was listening. "We have a plan to get you free."

Caela involuntarily gripped at the silver bracelet. "You can remove it?"

"I'm not sure, but others have come to help." He leaned in closer and lowered his voice to a whisper. "Do you know if Xaadier has a sword he keeps hidden?"

"A sword?"

"It's extremely important."

She thought for a time. "I've only seen him with that dreadful knife."

"Is it magical?"

"For certain. The older Singers claim that he was once an enchanter of little significance, then everything changed when he acquired the knife. That's how he made the bracelets that bind us to him."

"If he was attacked, and we managed to get the blade from him, do you think it could be used to free you?"

Caela shrugged. "I don't know anything about magic, other than how to be a Singer."

"Captain Tollas believes you might be able to stop the others from using their power to heal him. If so, we only need to keep him down long enough to get the dagger away from him." Merrick reached out and took Caela's hands. "Do you think it's possible?"

"I don't know. A lot of things could go wrong, and Soul Singers can be dangerous." She considered it for a time. "Unless…"

"What?"

"If I pulled at their essence before any could use their magic, it might keep them from accessing it for a short time. The only other option would be to feed harmful energies into the collective. The problem with that, is it would not just hurt the other Singers, it would damage me as well."

"We don't have any good choices here. This needs to happen soon."

Caela folded her arms and hugged herself. "If you fail, they'll kill you for certain."

"I'm not the one who will be going after Xaadier. The Resistance has brought in some powerful people to do this. These men claim to be able to seal the breach if they can get the dagger from the Regent. Captain Tollas believes them, and so do I."

"You've met these men?"

"Aye. There is something about them that I can't put into words. They refused to do it at first, because they don't believe in killing."

"That's certainly rare."

Merrick chuckled at her. "Agreed."

Caela stood quiet for a long moment as she stared at the red flowers nearby. "I'll do it."

"Are you certain?"

"We need to try something. I'd rather die than be a slave to him for even one more day. You don't understand what he does to us." Tears began to well in Caela's eyes. "They won't openly say it, but I'm certain most of the others agree."

Merrick hugged her tightly. "You might be right. Just don't speak to them about it. If even one decides to betray us, everyone will pay with their lives."

"I understand. Do what you must."

"We strike tomorrow, so stay close to the Regent if you can. You'll know its time when you see my face."

Kyreena silently watched from the bed as Arros stood next to the window and pondered their situation. He had been there most of the night, searching through the darkness for answers. She desperately wished to give them, but her memories were only returning in minor bursts of information. It was strange that Kyreena somehow knew the name of his homeland yet could not even imagine what it looked like. There was something greatly familiar about his essence, as if she had found a part of herself that had been missing for an untold number of years. There were vague images flashing through her mind of traveling through the countryside, yet none with any people. Until recently, she had instinctively spent most of her life avoiding civilization.

"You should try to rest your eyes," Kyreena coaxed. "I won't bite."

Arros focused his gaze upon her. "I'm not trying to be distant. There's just a great deal of questions that have been circling my head since we arrived."

"Perhaps just talking about them will assist me in remembering something that could help. I'll never lie to you, Arros."

He smiled warmly. "I know this about you. It's the only reason you're here with me."

Kyreena smirked at the prince. "The only reason?"

Arros' expression switched to one that was far more serious. "I won't lie to you either, but just know that there are subjects I can't discuss. Is that fair?"

"I sense the same from you. I have always had a sense when someone lies, like a cold wind blowing toward my heart. I can't explain it."

The Lord Prince crossed the room and sat on the edge of the bed. "What else have you noticed?"

"I am much stronger than others."

"Truly?"

To demonstrate, Kyreena reached over and caught Arros beneath his arms. She abruptly lifted and twisted her hips, flipping him around to the middle of the bed. In an instant, Kyreena found herself straddled atop him, with her lips nearly touching his. Arros watched her with a boyish grin.

"As I said," Kyreena began in a breathy voice. "I won't ever lie to you."

Arros continued to smile at her. "The demonstration was unnecessary – but appreciated."

"Do you sense anything from me?"

"Absolutely."

She moved her lips close enough to lightly brush with his. "What do you feel?"

He gently reached up and combed several strands of hair from her face. "Loneliness."

"I'm here now. You don't need to be this way."

"You asked me what I felt from you."

Kyreena pulled back, then studied his face. "From me?"

"I know a lost soul when I see one. You're trying desperately to find a place where you belong – a purpose. I'm not certain if you're clinging to me out of this great longing, or if we truly have a connection."

Kyreena slowly traced her fingers where his tunic opened to expose his chest. "Can it not be both?"

"It can." His hands found their way to her hips. "Where I come from, we consider pleasures with another to be natural and beautiful. There's rarely any commitment beyond that, just a desire for shared company." Arros slowly reached up and held her fingers to his chest. "But here, I found most men to be wretched and cruel, and many of the women are distrustful and conniving."

"We are of the same belief." Kyreena leaned in closer. "I can't even remember being with another, and yet my body longs to feel you. Do you understand what I mean?"

"It's possible I've heard this speech a few times before."

Kyreena burst out laughing, then pressed her lips to his. Arros cradled her cheeks, pulling her to him even harder. Without objection, she allowed the prince to remove her tunic and toss it to one side. There was a burning hunger within her. Upon tearing open his shirt, Kyreena pressed herself against his body to feel the warmth of his skin, while placing hot kisses on his neck. The Lord Prince's life essence was powerful – unlike anyone she had encountered before. It was following this thought that an image passed abruptly through her mind. Kyreena gasped, and quickly sat up.

"Are you well?" Arros watched her with genuine concern. "Did you remember something?"

"I believe so." Kyreena lowered herself back down and laid her head upon his bare chest. "I saw a boy of perhaps eighteen summers. I think I may have loved him."

"That's good. You're starting to associate current experiences with older memories." Arros gently kissed the top of her head, causing Kyreena to close her eyes and smile. "Was he a past lover?"

"I don't believe so." She snuggled into him, taking in Arros' warmth. "I feel protective of him."

"Like a brother?"

"Perhaps." Kyreena fought to hold tightly to the image in her mind. "He was taken from me suddenly, leaving a hollow place in my soul." She shook her head. "I don't want to discuss this further."

Arros wrapped his arms around her affectionately. "Forgive me. I didn't mean to cause you any grief."

"There's nothing to forgive." Kyreena sat back up, then smiled down at him. "I only meant that I wish to feel something different than sadness when I'm with you."

The prince studied her face in wonder. "There's something about your essence I find intoxicating."

She nodded her agreement. "It's as if we are in balance."

"Yes. That's the word I was searching for." Arros huffed a laugh. "Such strange happenstances to bring us together."

"It was the will of the One Power."

Arros pressed his lips together and stared into her eyes. Then, quickly as it had come, he lost his grin. "Wait. What do you mean by that?"

"I somehow believe we were guided together for a purpose. No matter what trials come to you, I'll always be at your side." The Lord Prince continued to watch her with concern in his eyes. He abruptly pushed Kyreena to one side, then moved away from the bed. Arros donned a new shirt from his pack while she watched. "Are you upset with me?"

He gave her a quick glance. "No – I just need to speak with Draxian. If I'm right, we're both in terrible danger."

T'mara ran her thumb over the carved face of the wooden necklace that hung on Draxian's neck. He had just woken and was enjoying the quiet of the morning. It was the most relaxed he had felt since arriving on Kohr. Turning his head, he admired the beauty of her eyes, framed perfectly by strands of messy blond hair.

"I've seen this pattern before."

"Seriously?" Draxian blurted in surprise.

The Huntress shrugged. "I believe so. My father had a scroll that had a pattern drawn on it like this one. He never would tell us what it meant." She paused a moment to look at him. "Where did you find this?"

"At a ruin back home."

A knock at the door interrupted them. The young lord estimated it was close to dawn, and he had barely slept more than an hour. T'mara's affections had done well to keep his mind from wandering to what they might need to do to get the Sword of Melkarick. Nothing about their plan was simple, and all of it rested on the young guardsman convincing a specialty mage to betray her friends.

"I would like to know more about this ruin," T'mara pressed.

Slipping out from under the blanket he made his way to the door. "We'll talk more later."

The moment he opened the door, Arros pushed his way inside, then headed straight for his travel pack. "Enter," Draxian exclaimed dryly.

"Where did you put it?"

"I didn't take your gold, if that's what you're asking."

The prince grunted in annoyance. "No. The letter from your father."

Draxian walked back over to the bed and retrieved his trousers. Just where he had left it, the folded paper was in a pocket. "It's right here."

T'mara sat up in bed and watched them curiously. "Is everything well?"

Arros abandoned his search, then turned back to the young lord. He quickly averted his eyes. "Do you both mind?"

Draxian chuckled to himself while stepping into his pants. "You're awfully serious this morning."

Seeing an opportunity to twist the knife, T'mara crawled out from the bed and stood in front of Arros without a stitch of clothing, completely unashamed. "Would you like me to leave so you may speak?"

"Careful, T'mara," Draxian warned. "Arros may invite you to join him and Kyreena in their room after we're done here."

Arros met her gaze without blinking. "It's true, I might."

She reached up and patted his cheek. "Perhaps later. She is quite beautiful." T'mara snatched up her clothing, then walked outside the door and closed it behind her.

"Now, what's this about?"

Without answering, Arros unfolded the letter from Draxian's father and began reading it to himself. His hand swept through his dark locks as he appeared to be studying it for a second time. "This can't be happening."

"Arros? Seriously – I'm about to pound you over the head if you don't speak with me."

He looked up, attempting to find the right words. "I've been trying to understand why everyone has been flocking to us, without revealing their true purpose. If these people had dark intentions, you would think they would try to maneuver and push us to make certain choices to follow their agenda."

"Exactly why we should probably trust them."

Arros shook his head. "You don't understand – we're being observed from afar."

"Why?"

"I told you that I did extensive research into Kohr before ever considering coming here to find our fathers, correct?"

"And?"

He stepped over to the window and looked out. "This place has long been the battlegrounds for some of the most terrible wars ever conceived. What happens on Kohr can easily offset the careful balance in a thousand worlds beyond. And don't forget, this was also the home of the First Ones. It's where our ancient ancestors uncovered their secrets to traveling among the stars through the portals."

"That's common knowledge on Ellandor."

"Correct. But what everyone seems to have forgotten is that this Realm is where the Trials of the True Bloods are conducted."

Draxian could feel his blood turning to ice. "As in…"

"Exactly." Arros lifted the letter and pointed to the writing. "Your father specifically mentions the word 'trials' in here, and so did mine."

Draxian glanced around the room in thought. "This is just speculation. You don't know anything for certain."

"True. Everything that happened could all be chance: Garran, the Master Archivist; the dragon that forced us here; the Guardians' Keep; finding the book in Orakh; Cam being a Chosen Hunter, and T'mara, a Shadiere; the Blade Master, Nerris, and now, Kyreena, the only survivor of a holocaust that should have killed her. Do all those encounters, when viewed as a whole, match your definition of a coincidence?"

The young lord brought a hand up to his head and began pacing back and forth. "No. They would never do that to us."

"If it meant saving our people, I think King Nemendes is capable of far worse."

Draxian ceased pacing, then turned back to face him. "But if that's true, it would mean our fathers brought us both here to die."

TRIALS

After a long debate with Arros on what they should or should not do, Draxian agreed they needed to proceed with the current plan to seal the rift in Orakh. If they did nothing else, it would at least help maintain a careful balance within all the Realms of Power. After they succeeded, there would need to be another discussion on whether they would abandon their search for their fathers in order to find a way to return home. They knew the Oracle had the power, just not if he was willing to use it.

From their previous conversation, it seemed as if the Oracle expected them to dive headlong into Kohr's brewing civil war. That went against everything the Ellandorians believed. Their fathers would have known this as well – which is why Arros' theory about the Trials of the True Bloods made sense. It was an ancient right to be used only in the direst of circumstances. If the Trials were somehow initiated on their behalf, it meant all laws would be set aside, and the two men would be judged by their intentions, not their actions. Their deeds would be above reproach, giving absolute authority to act in the best interests of the trials. No matter what the outcome, neither participant survived it. This was the sacrifice that needed to be made to harness the power they would require. There were always two chosen – never more, never less. They both succeeded, or they both failed.

Draxian had just finished changing into a palace guard's uniform when T'mara came up behind him. "They did well to find that in your size."

"Think so?" He smoothed the wrinkles from the tunic, then studied himself in the polished looking glass the inn had provided for them. Draxian glanced back to find T'mara wearing a work dress that was used by the palace staff. "You don't have to come along if you don't wish it. I certainly wouldn't blame you."

She took a dangerous step forward. "Say that to me again, and I'll break my spear over your head."

"Easy. I just don't know what to expect. If anything were to happen to you…"

"I have seen the way you swing that weapon. You need a Hunter at your side to tell you which end to use."

Draxian reached out and pulled her to him. "Is that explanation truly what you're going with?"

T'mara watched him with sad eyes. "I need to be your weapon against this man. Killing another comes much easier for a Hunter. You should know that I would trade my life to save you from this burden."

"We're still holding out hope that it won't be necessary. If he dies, it may also kill the thirteen women he bound to his life-energy."

"And how many more will die if he is allowed to continue breathing?" The Huntress moved away from him, then seated herself on the bed. "There is something I must tell you about this weapon you seek."

Draxian folded his arms. "Oh?"

"I do not know if it is the same one, but I believe so. There is a story from our lore keepers that tells of a sword that was cursed in its creation by a sorceress with the blood of many magi. The Lord of Destruction was entrusted by the Dragon King to keep if from the hands of mortals. But the Great Lord was betrayed by the one closest to him, a Singer of Souls. The essence of the magi within the sword began to call to her. In this madness, she believed she had found her purpose and stole the weapon and ran away from the Black Citadel. The Great Lord was heartbroken. He sent the first Great Hunter to find and bring her back to him. It took many days and dark magics to tear the madness from her mind."

"Why are you telling me this?"

"If you do not kill this man, he will risk no end to find his stolen sword and make those who did it suffer greatly." T'mara stood, then glared darkly at the young lord. "I will do what I must to protect the ones I love – even if you will not."

Draxian's shoulders dropped in defeat. "There's simply no scenario available where everyone walks away, is there?"

"You already knew this."

"Indeed, we did," Arros called from the door, with Kyreena close behind him wearing a dress like T'mara's. Draxian was uncertain how long the prince had been quietly standing there in his new uniform. "It's time."

"We're ready." Draxian retrieved the large pack from the bed and slung it over his shoulder. Together, they exited the room and moved down the hallway toward the stairs.

Arros glanced back at them as they descended. "Nerris is checking in with our allies and will be waiting for us near the gatehouse."

"And Cam?"

"He's just outside with…" Arros slid to a halt upon reaching the ground floor, just beneath the large archway to the dining hall.

Draxian cleared the remaining three steps in a single leap, and his hand went to grip his sword upon learning what had caused the prince to hesitate. The inn had been completely cleared of all patrons and staff. Tables still displayed half-eaten plates of food and cups of wine remained full. A single woman wearing ornate, color-shifting armor, exited the kitchen. She was chewing on a thin stick of bread and watching the two men with interest.

Arros folded his arms. "Commander Rellan. Why am I not surprised to find you here?"

Cam stepped into the room just behind her and nodded to them. "I told her where you could be found."

In an instant, T'mara dashed forward and snatched Draxian's dagger from his belt. He nearly missed catching her arm as she drew it back to throw. "Wait," Drax coaxed.

"Traitor!" The Huntress was in tears as she tried desperately to free her arm from the muscular lord's grip.

Cam held up both hands in an attempt to calm her. "Just listen to what they have to say. There's no amount of payment I could receive that would ever justify causing you harm. You should know this about me."

As Draxian held T'mara tightly and whispered words of comfort in her ears, Arros stepped forward to meet the commander. "You have my undivided attention."

Rellan swallowed the bread, then casually strolled up to meet the prince in the middle of the dining hall. She bowed formally to him, then lifted her chin. "The Empress of Dragons is aware of your plans to seal the breach to the Spirit Realm and offers her assistance in this delicate matter."

"You're going to help us get the Sword of Melkarick?"

"No."

Arros glanced back toward Draxian. "How typical of her kind. Always meddling in the affairs of others, without the appearance of doing so."

Commander Rellan gave him a knowing smirk. "She has every confidence in your success. No. What we offer is safe passage out of the city and back to the Ebon Waste."

"There is no way in the Abyss we're going anywhere near her… pets."

"I don't blame you. The *drakara* have become quite unmanageable with the Verge extending so far into our land, yet we have other means of swift travel." Rellan spread her arms wide. "How do you think I was able to get here so quickly?"

Arros glanced over to Cam. "Perhaps someone told you where we were going."

"That too." Rellan smiled. "The Empress has been waiting for your arrival for some time now."

"Of that, I have no doubt."

"Do not mistake her intensions. She needs you to succeed as much as any and has authorized me to give you access to our network of information."

Draxian wrenched the dagger from T'mara's grip, then pulled her behind him. "What does that mean, exactly?"

"Just as I stated. Dellahara is the information capital of the world. Nothing escapes the eyes of the Empress of Dragons. If you need assistance understanding anything you might encounter, we will be at your disposal."

Arros narrowed his eyes. "Nothing comes without a price, and we already have friends helping us."

"The Resistance?"

"That's right."

Commander Rellan gave him a chiding grin. "We *are* the Resistance. Perhaps a different faction of it, if you will. But every alliance, every historical group that has arisen in the last thousand years, was started from a common single leader, before expanding."

"Empress Dellahara?"

"No," T'mara called from behind Draxian. "It was the Dragon King."

Rellan nodded. "Your friend is correct. Even the Hunters know this to be true. The Lord of Destruction stepped up later as their leader, then commanded the Shadiere to assist the Resistance by ridding the land of the monstrosities from the Shadow Realm."

"And we have kept our word! Have you done the same?"

Arros glanced back. "T'mara. That's not helpful."

Commander Rellan's gaze was unreadable. "The Empress has kept the peace for as long as she could. If not for her, there would have been far more wars over territory than this land has already seen."

"If we are so important to her," Arros began, "why has she not come here to speak with us in person?"

"She's no longer safe outside the halls of the Blessed Mother Dragon. If anything were to happen to her, we would all be lost. Every last one of us."

Draxian huffed a laugh. "That's a bit dramatic."

"She speaks the truth," Kyreena called from his side. "The Empress has knowledge of a weapon to defeat the Undying."

Rellan narrowed her eyes. "Do I know you?"

Arros snapped his fingers in front of the commander's face to gain her attention. "If the Empress wants our assistance, she knows where we can be found. Until she agrees to meet, we have nothing more to say."

"Why are you so insistent upon this meeting? Is it not enough that I'm here to answer your questions?"

Arros moved in closer to her. "Who am I?"

"Lord Prince Arros Nemendes."

"Of where?"

Commander Rellan lifted her chin. "I'm not privileged enough to have that information."

"Why do you think that is?"

"Some knowledge is far too dangerous to possess. Just knowing you're here is enough that I've been commanded to sacrifice my own life before allowing you to be captured by the Undying."

Arros tilted his head to one side. "Truly?"

"If I'm lost, another will take my place. There's only one Arros, and only one Draxian. We don't get a second chance at this. The Order has made this fact perfectly clear."

"The Order?"

Commander Rellan stepped to one side. "I shouldn't keep you from your duties."

The Lord Prince turned to Draxian, then motioned for him to follow. "Let's go."

"Behave," Draxian whispered to T'mara, as he started toward the exit.

When Cam started to follow, the Huntress shot an accusing finger at him. "Not you."

"You need me to help with the Singers."

Arros held a hand up to the Hunter. "We'll speak afterwards. I need T'mara focused, or people will get hurt."

"I'm truly sorry," Cam called after them. "It was just a job."

When the four companions reached the exterior of the building, Draxian saw more than thirty Chromatic Warriors out in the streets, staring hard at anyone curious enough to brave their gaze. That number could easily be counted on one hand. As with the Guardian's Keep, the people wanted nothing to do with the soldiers from Dellahara.

The walk to the main gate took nearly a half turn of the glass. Arros and Draxian were given the rank of lieutenant to keep questions from other guards to a minimum. No sentry would believe someone foolish enough to impersonate an officer, and if they were wrong in their accusations, it would mean severe punishment. Yet, just to be on the side of caution, Arros was also given transfer papers by Captain Tollas in the event another officer got involved.

As the group neared the lower gatehouse, Nerris abruptly appeared in step with Draxian, seemingly from nowhere. "What kept you?"

"Nothing."

Nerris glanced at the others. "Where is Cam?"

Arros called back to him. "He'll join us when it's done."

"Makes no difference to me."

The Blade Master hurried ahead of them to meet with the six gate guards that had gathered into a small group to speak quietly among themselves. One of the sentries stepped away, then lifted a hand. "State your business."

Nerris handed the man a long, sealed tube. "We have an urgent message for Captain Tollas."

The guard looked at the decorated seal. "What am I supposed to do with this?"

"Open the gate and allow us to deliver it. Can you not see the Watch Commander's stamp?" He started to object when Arros stepped forward. "What's your name, soldier?"

The man slapped his fist to his heart. "A thousand pardons, Lieutenant. We'll open the gate for you immediately." He quickly called up to the men controlling the large portcullis. Within moments, the large gate began to draw upwards, allowing the group to proceed.

"I could've handled that," Nerris protested.

"The other guards were trying to memorize our faces. When you create a scenario where someone might get punished, no one will want anything to do with it."

The winding cobblestone road to the palace took longer to ascend than Draxian would have thought. He had suggested finding an alternate route through the trees, but Nerris believed it would take longer to pass through the thick foliage and rocky terrain than simply going around.

When they reached the front gate to the palace, Guardsman Merrick was already waiting. Without a word, he motioned for them to follow. Draxian was immediately impressed with the size of the main structure. There was certainly an element of magic that had gone into its creation. When he asked Nerris about it, the man muttered something about stone shapers, then changed the subject.

Merrick led them down a series of back corridors until they came to a storage room filled with barrels of wine. After they had all gone inside, the guardsman closed the door and turned to them. "The captain took all the guardsmen not loyal to the Resistance on a training exercise in the lower city. We already cleared this area of all sentries. The back, center spire is where Regent Xaadier is staying."

Draxian placed the large pack on a nearby barrel, allowing T'mara and Kyreena to arm themselves. The Huntress looped a baldric over her head containing six daggers, and then attached bracers, each with three small throwing knives. "I wish we could have brought my spear."

Arros pulled a black rod from the side of his high boot that was a pace long. He tossed it to T'mara. "Press the circular glyph on the side – the one near your thumb."

T'mara wrinkled her brow while she did as instructed. In an instant, the shaft extended to the size of a staff with a wicked spike mounted on the top. "This is for me?"

"I did promise to bring you back something."

Draxian tilted his head. "Was that the emergency shelter?"

Arros shrugged. "It was broken beyond repair, so I modified it when we stopped in Breck. The new tip is just hardened steel, but the shaft is etherium. It's virtually unbreakable."

T'mara crossed the room and hugged him tightly. "I will treasure this always."

"Don't lose that. Draxian will never let me hear the end of it."

"I think we're long past any of those concerns," the young lord defended. "We need all the advantages we can get."

Kyreena finished tightening the arrow quiver around her chest, then began to string the bow. "I'm nearly ready."

Merrick pointed at it. "That's an awfully heavy wood. Perhaps I could find..." He stopped speaking when Kyreena quickly bent the bow down and looped the twine over the end. She then lifted it in front of her and easily drew the string back to her cheek to test the weight. "Damn. You're really strong," the guardsman marveled.

Those were exactly Draxian's thoughts. "May I?"

"Certainly." Kyreena handed over her weapon with a slight grin.

He placed three fingers on the thick twine, then pulled back until they touched the side of his face. It took a good deal more effort than he would have guessed, and his strength had always been exceptional. The arrows would easily penetrate armor, although it would take him longer to draw and shoot such a sturdy weapon. "Damn," Draxian mirrored the guardsman's remark. He shook his head in disbelief, then returned the bow to Kyreena. The young lord finally brought his attention back to Arros. "Now what?"

Merrick took a deep breath. "At the end of this hall is a door leading to the back towers. We recommend waiting until Xaadier crosses over toward the archway leading to the Great Hall. The door will be locked from the other side. If he flees back to the tower, the Regent will be able to summon more Singers to help him fight and escape. So, whatever you're going to do, move quickly."

Arros nodded in agreement. "How many will be with him?"

"We have no way of predicting that, but most likely only three or four."

Nerris drew his blades, then whirled them around. "Not a problem."

"And if the Singers decide to mimic your skills with their magic?" the Lord Prince queried.

T'mara answered for him. "It takes more than skills with swords to be a Shadow Master."

Draxian frowned in confusion. "Is that somehow different than a Blade Master?"

"It is," Nerris replied with confidence. "You'll see soon enough."

Merrick bowed to their small group in respect. "If all goes as planned, the Soul Singers won't be able to use their powers to help Xaadier. I'm leaving to inform Caela that we're about to begin and get the Regent out of his tower. Remember, she'll be the brown-haired Singer not attacking you."

Arros clapped Merrick on the shoulder. "We'll do our best to quickly get the dagger away from Xaadier, then force him to remove the binding magic from the other Singers. That's the best outcome we can hope for."

"I know what a risk you're all taking to save her. The Resistance is in your debt. *I'm* in your debt."

THE SWORD OF MELKARICK

Caela paced back and forth across her chamber floor. She had donned her silver breastplate and white leather skirt in preparation for what was to come. The morning had gone by agonizingly slowly, and she had barely slept the previous night. A part of her prayed that Merrick would abandon whatever he had planned, and just leave the palace forever. Although a larger portion wanted to see Xaadier suffer for every cut he had made into her flesh since she had been sold to the Regent. Twice, Caela had nearly died from blood loss, only to be saved by her sister Singers. There were many days she wished they had not gotten to her in time. Caela could scarcely close her eyes without worrying she would find Regent Xaadier standing over her bed with that cursed knife in hand.

Finally, a soft knock came on her door. She took a deep breath, then opened it. Merrick nodded to her. "Are you ready?"

"What do you need me to do?"

"Captain Tollas has taken most of the palace guard on a training exercise. Here, take this." He handed her a folded piece of paper with the wax seal of High General Gredlass.

"Where did you get this?"

"Don't ask." Merrick stepped forward and kissed Caela on the cheek. "When you see our team come through the south corridor, don't hesitate."

"How will I know it's them?"

Merrick chuckled uneasily. "You'll know it, I guarantee."

"And where will you be?"

"I need to lock the back entrance to the Great Hall and make certain no one comes around and opens it."

Caela pursed her lips and exhaled slowly to help calm her stomach. "I can do this."

"Just hand that note to Xaadier. I promise he'll not have time to punish you for it." Merrick pressed his lips tightly together, then nodded to her. "I'll meet up with you afterwards."

Without another word, Caela's lifelong friend departed through the archway and down the stairwell. She wanted to tell him how much he meant to her, that Caela had dreamed of being his wife for most of their lives. If all went well, she promised herself to do so afterwards. Yet, should she be killed in the attempt, Caela didn't want to make Merrick's grief any worse with thoughts of what might have been.

The Singer exited her room and began to ascend the stairs toward the fourth level. It was the only section that didn't have windows and this made it harder to hear the screams of the Singers he tortured. Emperor Deathskull had forbidden him from harming any of the cleaning staff. If word had gotten around of the Regent's perversions, it would reflect poorly on the monarchy.

Even before she reached the door, Caela could hear the muffled cries of one of the Singers on the other side. It turned her stomach to think of what was happening, and yet she was also grateful it wasn't her being mutilated.

In response to her knock, the door flew open to reveal Xaadier in a blood-splattered shirt and his ever-present knife in hand. Behind him, one of the Singers was sitting on her knees with her robe pulled down to her waist, and shallow lacerations covering her back in a strange pattern. She wept softly to herself. "Caela, my little brown sparrow. Have you come to join the fun?"

The Soul Singer held out the folded note. "An urgent message for you, Master."

"Oh?" Xaadier snatched the letter from her, then broke the seal with the edge of his bloodied blade. He stopped, then glared at her. "You didn't peek, did you?"

She kept her head low. "No, Master."

"Why not? What if there's poison inside? Better you than me." He burst out laughing, then unfolded the paper. "I thought General Gredlass was out investigating the dragon attack on our outpost?"

"A soldier delivered it, Master."

He continued to read over the script, then drew his neck back in surprise. "Wait… How long ago was this delivered?"

"Only recently, Master. I came as soon as it was handed to me."

"Shite!" The Regent tore off his shirt as he ran over to the nearby wardrobe. He grabbed a clean tunic, then quickly began to don it. "Efayne!"

The Soul Singer came out of the adjacent room with three other Singers at her side. "Yes, Master?"

"General Gredlass' wife has been kept waiting in the Great Hall to present me with a token of her gratitude for promoting her husband." He rushed over to a vanity and began furiously scrubbing at the blood on his hands in a ceramic bowl of water. "Someone is going to pay dearly for not informing me sooner!"

"Would you like me to go keep her entertained until you arrive?"

He finished up, then snatched a clean towel from next to the bowl. "You will do no such thing! She came here to speak with me!" The Regent dropped his voice down to a normal tone. "Such arrogance from these foolish girls. I don't know why I bother with them." He glanced up as if listening to someone. "What's that?… Yes, I'm aware that I need the Singers for protection. My enemies could be hiding around any corner." He started toward the door. "Caela? You may heal Jessalyn while we're gone. I'm no longer amused with her."

"Of course, Master." She moved aside, then watched as the Regent and four Soul Singers descended the stairs. Caela knew there wasn't any time to waste healing Jessalyn. Instead, she walked over and knelt next to her. "Forgive me, sister. Remain here, and I'll return in a bit to help you."

On her way out the door, Caela grabbed the key hanging on the wall. She closed the door behind her, then locked it tight. The Regent was only one level below. Keeping her distance, Caela hurriedly began dropping the metal door bars in place to each level. It would help keep any Singers from coming to Xaadier's aid when they felt his distress through the magic. Everything was set, and there was no turning back. Caela reached the bottom level of the tower, just as the Regent crossed toward the door with his Singers. Efayne grabbed for the door ring, then pulled.

"What's the matter?"

She tried again. "I'm not certain, Master. It's stuck."

Caela spotted three men in guard's uniforms walking toward the group. Behind them, were two armed women in cleaning-staff dresses. They must certainly be the ones Merrick spoke of, she thought. Caela concentrated, pulling at the pool of collective Soul Singer energy. Her spirit tones filled the air. It took a lot more effort than she realized to hold the magic away from the other Singers. If someone didn't strike soon, Caela was certain it would be over before it began.

Arros stood next to the archway leading to a waiting area just before the Great Hall. Merrick had only recently crossed the chamber and disappeared beyond the heavy door. It would not be long before they would finally face the man holding the key to saving everyone he knew. The prince turned back to the others. "Take a deep breath and relax. Remove any dark intentions you might harbor, and just think of sitting at a table, eating meat pies and drinking honey wine. Nothing else."

Kyreena smiled warmly at Arros, while T'mara leaned her head against Draxian's shoulder. Nerris had taken the prince's advice to heart and had closed his eyes. He was mimicking chewing food in his mouth.

The Blade Master swallowed hard, then opened his eyes and looked at Arros. "What?"

"Nothing at all."

"It's hard to picture supper last night, since none of you thought to save me any."

Draxian chuckled at Nerris. "It was certainly tasty."

"Wait," Arros called to the others. "I hear footsteps."

Kyreena tilted her ear toward the door. "Five of them. One man, and four women."

"This is it. When we sense Caela's magic activate, everyone knows what to do. Correct?" Arros waited for the others to nod their heads. "One Power guide and protect us." He turned back toward the chamber and waited for the group to emerge. The women wore polished, decorative breastplates and thick hide skirts that dropped halfway down their thighs. Each was armed with a thin sword strapped to their backs to give them quick movements.

Upon them reaching the other side, Arros stepped into the open and started walking at a steady pace to not alarm the Singers. Draxian was to his left, and Nerris moved to his right. T'mara and Kyreena followed just behind them, shielding their weapons from sight. They had crossed half the distance before a strange sound erupted into the air. Arros felt the power of the Spirit Realm being accessed as the shimmering tones continued to escalate. He recognized Caela standing at the base of the stairway, concentrating hard. It was immediately evident she was struggling to maintain her hold over that much power.

Not waiting for a command, Kyreena swiftly drew back her bow string and released. The arrow struck the Regent in the right shoulder, piercing all the way through his leather armor to stick partially out the other side. The force of the hit spun him around, and Xaadier dropped to the stone floor hollering in pain. "Assassins!"

The four women quickly drew their blades just as the group reached them. Fear was evident in their eyes, as they attempted to access their power to no avail. Nerris quickly disarmed the first of them by knocking her weapon away, then slapping the flat of his other blade against the Singer's hand.

Draxian didn't even bother drawing his sword. Instead, he dodged to one side when she came in for a strike, then caught her wrist in one hand, and her throat in the other. The Singer's eyes went wide as he gripped her tightly.

T'mara simply spun her spear around, striking her opponent in the leg. The effect sent her Singer backwards to land straight on her back. From there, the Huntress simply held the point to the woman's throat, daring her to make a threatening move.

As for Kyreena, she only needed to draw back her arrow and point it directly at the remaining Soul Singer's eye. Without so much as a word of contempt, the mage dropped her sword and held up her hands in surrender.

"Damn your hides to the Abyss! Fight them!"

None of the Singers moved as Arros launched forward and caught the Regent's left hand, as it scrambled to reach across his waist for the knife on his other side. The Lord Prince jerked the dagger free of the scabbard, then pointed it toward the Regent's throat. "Enough!"

Xaadier narrowed his eyes menacingly. "How dare you attack the Regent of Phondari! I'll see your skin flayed from your bodies for this!"

"You have two choices: Remove the magic binding the Soul Singers to you, and we let you live. Or, do nothing and I use this to gut you like a fish." Arros stood, then watched the Regent. "Choose quickly."

He sneered at Arros as he considered his dwindling options. "Very well." The Regent snapped the arrow shaft from his shoulder, then reached behind his back and jerked the bloodied tip free. It was troubling that Xaadier seemed almost impervious to the pain. "I'll need to be healed before I can use my magic."

"He lies," Kyreena called from the side. "Kill him quickly."

"Wait!" Xaadier lifted his arms up in surrender. "Perhaps we can come to another arrangement?"

Arros shook his head as he tapped the dagger blade in his opposing hand. "I don't think you quite understand how this…" The prince glanced down at the weapon and furrowed his brow. "Something's not right."

Kyreena lowered her bow then reached over and took the dagger from Arros' hand. She lifted the weapon into the air to study it closely. "This has been magically enhanced to keep a sharp edge but is most certainly not the blade we seek."

Xaadier tilted his head. "Ah, yes – now I understand. You seek the Sword of Melkarick?"

Arros leaned over and caught the Regent by the neck of his armor and pulled him close. "Where is it?!"

"Well, my dear assassin, it's been right here the entire time." Faster than Arros could react, Xaadier reached behind his back with his right hand and gripped the gilded handle of a sword that materialized from nowhere. He jerked it free of the scabbard, striking Arros in the cheek with the pommel. The Prince jumped backwards against the explosion of pain in his head, then fell to the ground. At once, a pulse of energy blasted forth, knocking everyone in the room to the ground. Caela was also caught within the attack, forcing her to release her hold on the Spirit Realm.

Xaadier climbed to his feet and pointed the blade at Arros. "Didn't see that coming, did you, fool!" He turned to the Singers. "Kill them!"

A cacophony of sound rang out as the Soul Singers went on the offensive, renewing the women with enhanced vigor. They jumped up as one and refocused their efforts. Kyreena was the first to recover and sprang to her feet. In one swift motion, she drew and fired an arrow at Xaadier. The bolt shattered on an invisible barrier, just shy of striking the Regent in the forehead. The Singer darted at her, forcing Kyreena to block the attack with her bow.

Draxian reached for his blade while coming to his feet. The woman he once held by the throat launched forward and caught his arm before he was able to draw it. "You're strong," the woman taunted. With a quick movement, she kicked his leg, all while swinging him to one side. The effect hurled the young lord a dozen paces to hit a nearby wall.

T'mara jerked a dagger free of her baldric and immediately sent it toward the nearest Singer. The woman brought up a blade to deflect it, then launched at the Shadiere Huntress. With as much dexterity as she could summon, T'mara kicked her legs up and back, jumping off the floor and landing back on her feet. She brought up her spear in time to block an attack that was aimed at her heart.

It was Nerris who fared the best. He leapt to his feet just after Kyreena and was already spinning his blades in deadly arcs. The Singer had drawn upon Nerris' skills to enhance her own, giving new life to her weapon, but it wasn't nearly enough. As she desperately tried to block his furious onslaught of attacks, the Singer continued to back toward the Regent. With a quick parry, then a feint, Nerris managed to pierce the woman in the abdomen. She shrieked in pain, then fell to the ground with blood seeping from beneath her fingers.

While all this happened, Arros slowly sat up to gain his bearings. A cold sensation shot up his spine, warning him of imminent danger. The Regent stepped forward with Melkarick raised high. "You should have stayed in bed this morning, assassin." Just as Xaadier sliced downward, Arros brought up his fist. A white-hot burst of light blinded everyone in the room for an instant, giving the prince a precious moment to roll out of the way of the sweeping razor-sharp blade.

It was right then Arros felt something shift in the eerie melody of the Singers' magic. The Singers were redirecting their power. He feared they were healing those who had been taken out of play.

As Nerris attacked the woman facing Draxian, the first Singer the Blade Master had injured removed her hand to reveal the wound quickly fading. The Master thrust his blade at the second, striking her in the arm. This left him exposed from behind to the first. Slashing from a low angle, the Singer caught Nerris with a deep laceration in his calf. He immediately spun around in retaliation to slice cleanly across her throat. The tones of her spirit ended abruptly, as she clutched the fountaining spray of crimson gore. Nerris dropped one of his blades to nurse his own gushing leg injury.

Draxian took advantage of the second woman's surprise wound to the arm to jump to his feet. With both hands, he brought down his blade upon her. The Singer tried to parry with her sword, but Lord Kalenthos' weapon was forged of etherium. A metallic crashing filled the air as her blade snapped in half. Unable to halt his swing in time, Draxian's sword cleaved the Singer's head down to her nose. She froze in place, mouth gaping wide, eyes staring in astonishment. The young lord released the grip on his blade in horror, allowing the woman to fall to the ground, convulsing.

T'mara had been fighting the third blow for blow, neither one gaining much advantage over the other. Their battle consisted of traded strikes and desperate dodging, with each blow aimed to kill. The Singer she faced possessed all of her own reflexes, yet not her connection to the Shadow Realm. T'mara retreated for an instant, gaining a moment to tear away the storm ward bracer. The moment the Singer struck her staff, the connection was completed. A surge of dark energy traveled in an instant, through their weapons and into the woman before her. The Singer shrieked in surprise from the life-draining effect, causing her to momentarily lose her power. T'mara didn't hesitate. She struck the woman across the side of her head, sending a spray of blood across the nearby wall. The Singer stumbled backwards to hit Kyreena, who was darting aside from the fourth woman's blade. Both fell to the ground, giving the last woman a clear strike at Kyreena.

Without hesitating, T'mara hurled her spear with all her might. The tip impaled the fourth Singer in the neck, sending her backwards to the opposite wall. "No," Regent Xaadier shouted angrily. "Assassin bitch!" With a quick flip of his wrist, T'mara's daggers jerked from her baldric and hovered in the air. Kyreena was already on her feet, firing arrow after arrow at the Regent, to no effect.

Arros drew his new blades and rushed Xaadier. With his focus divided, the prince was able to get in a slash to the Regent's forearm. A focused blast of power shot forth from Melkarick and hit Arros directly in the chest. He felt himself soaring through the air and back to the tower stairwell, where Caela cowered away from the battle.

The Lord Prince coughed out bloody foam as he tried desperately to catch his breath. Caela reached over and placed her hands on his back as he sat up to view what was happening with the battle. That's when he saw Draxian was no longer frozen in despair at what he'd done, but instead was squatting on the ground with Kyreena. Between them, T'mara lay on her back with four of her own daggers sticking up from her chest.

Xaadier laughed cruelly. "Was she the best you had?"

As Arros fought to stay conscious, Caela continued to heal him. "Hold still," she whispered.

Draxian cradled T'mara's head, then stroked her hair. Kyreena sneered in rage, then started to stand when the young lord caught her wrist. Carefully, Draxian set T'mara's head back down with his free hand, then rose to his feet. He turned and faced the Regent, head lowered and eyes darkening to a deep onyx. A dangerous feel of magic swept through the air as Arros continued to gasp for air. The ground began to softly quake, and cracks formed in the walls of the tower. The Lord Prince tried to call out a warning, but his voice still wouldn't come.

Draxian charged.

FALL OF HEROES

Merrick waited impatiently on the other side of the door. The plan had gone terribly wrong; he just knew it. There were raised voices and the sound of Caela's magic. Then, something struck the door with a thunderous impact. It startled Merrick enough that he cried out in fear. In that moment, his hopes for a peaceful resolution were shattered. The sounds of battle erupted amongst a cacophony of the chorus of Soul Singers. Caela had failed to hold back the other Singers' magic. He wanted badly to open the door and find out what was happening, but that meant giving Regent Xaadier a path to escape.

The clashing steel and strange feel of magic in the air caused Merrick's arm hairs to stand on end. He knew it would take quite a long while for any guards loyal to Xaadier to return to the palace – although the remaining ones were still unaware of what was truly happening. They were simply told training exercises were being performed, and they needed to remain at their posts no matter what they might believe was happening.

Merrick's darkest fears of what transpired beyond the door escalated to near insanity. There was a sudden halt in all the noise of battle and the song of the Soul Singers, causing the guardsman to wonder if someone had emerged victorious. It was then the door began to splinter, and large chips of rock burst from the nearby walls, as if struck with a thousand mallets at once.

What in the bloody Abyss is happening back there? he thought to himself.

Then everything went immediately quiet. He hoped that it all was over, and the new Resistance heroes would finally force the Regent to free Caela, but it was evident the battle was going poorly. Without any warning, a deafening blast shook the very ground beneath him. Merrick fell to his knees at what sounded like the palace crumbling in upon itself.

Kyreena's heart was aching from what had happened to T'mara. The poor woman didn't have a chance when the four daggers were hurled at her through the Regent's magic. The Huntress had used her only other weapon to save Kyreena, and it left T'mara defenseless. Draxian had rushed to her in an instant, but she quickly died in his arms with little more than a soft smile of encouragement for him. One of the knives had pierced her heart, and another had hit a lung. There was nothing anyone could have done to save her.

It was Arros that had Kyreena concerned. She could feel his great distress. As the Soul Singer, Caela, attempted to heal the ruptured blood vessels throughout his chest. Draxian had reached the end of his sanity. Tapping deep within the powers he had so carefully pushed to the side, a burst of pure Void energy was unleashed. The air was crushed from Kyreena's lungs with the sudden expulsion of magic. All around her, the walls cracked from the stress of the Void. While Kyreena attempted to recover her own wind, Draxian charged toward the Regent. Even with the Sword of Melkarick in his hand, Xaadier's wall of force was dissipated under the awesome fury that Lord Kalenthos called forth. He barreled into the Regent, sending him flying to the ground. The Sword of Melkarick spun from his hands and skittered close to where Kyreena sat. She quickly crawled over to it, then grasped the handle. Almost immediately, Kyreena felt a surge of energy throughout her body. It was dark and evil, whispering promises of greatness should she submit to its influence.

When she looked up, Draxian had lifted the Regent by his neck and thrown him hard into the back wall. The large man lifted his hand, drawing the darkness to him. Nerris limped over to Kyreena and placed a hand on her shoulder to steady himself. "What's he doing?"

"Drawing on his birthright."

"But that isn't shadow magic."

Kyreena crawled to her feet. "No. He's summoning the Void itself."

"That's impossible…"

With a cry of wrath, Draxian released the power into a single beam of darkness. To Kyreena, it appeared as if the world had been torn open for an instant to a place where no light existed – only the purest darkness. The Regent imploded from the touch of the Void, and with him, a sizeable portion of the wall burst into powder – sending a massive wave of force up the back tower. Caela's spirit tones immediately ceased, and she fell forward against Arros. The light in her eyes was gone, just as they had feared would happen with the death of Regent Xaadier. All about them, the walls began to crumble, and support beams splintered.

Draxian glanced around quickly, immediately made aware of the devastation he had wrought. Without hesitation, he ran to the base of the tower stairs and lifted Arros to his feet, while stones began to fall around them. Kyreena screamed a warning, just as a large chunk of stairway broke loose from above, plummeting toward the unsuspecting men. Draxian shoved Arros out of the way an instant before it dropped over the young lord, pinning him to the ground.

"Arros!" Kyreena launched forward and caught the Lord Prince before he stumbled to the floor. She immediately pressed the blade into his palm. "Help him!"

The instant the Sword of Melkarick touched his hand, Arros' eyes lit with blazing white fire. He spun around and lifted his fist, just as the entire back tower fell in upon itself. Kyreena winced from the flying debris and cloud of dust, yet none of it hit them. The Lord Prince was surrounded in an aura of pure Radiance.

Nerris shook his head in disbelieve. "One Power wake me."

With a strained effort, Arros guided the power of the Radiant Realm to hold back the massive weight of the collapsed tower from crushing Draxian. "Hurry! I can't hold this for long!"

Kyreena ducked into the swiftly closing ceiling of rubble. Calling upon her tremendous strength, she lifted the section of stairs from atop Draxian. After shoving it aside, she caught his arm to pull him clear of the debris. Arros released his hold on the power, allowing the remaining immense pile of stone to collapse to the ground. Soft light from the late afternoon spilled through the gaping hole in the wall and touched their faces.

"Arros! He's not breathing," Nerris cried in alarm.

Arros could scarcely believe what was happening to them. In Draxian's moment of rage, he had executed the Regent of Phondari, therefore killing all the Soul Singers with him. The prince couldn't begrudge his friend this action, as Arros was already resolved to finish the degenerate himself, if given the chance. It was the unexpected destruction of the tower that had caused so much trouble for him. Arros was certain the falling stairs had broken more than a few of Draxian's bones, and he wasn't responding in the slightest. With the Sword of Melkarick in his hands, he felt as if all the magic of the world was immediately at his command. He was enlightened enough to realize this wasn't the truth, that it only enhanced what was already there. This was the only reason the Regent didn't have a great deal more magic to use against them. It was likely Xaadier had little to begin with, and the greater the natural talent, the more power could be amplified through it. Arros could somehow feel the blood essence of the hundred magi used to create the cursed sword. It was a vile weapon he was eager to be rid of – but first, they had to see to their injuries.

"Arros! He's not breathing!"

The prince nodded to the Blade Master, then knelt down and placed his hand on Draxian's chest. His body was growing as cold as the icy Abyss. Arros recoiled his arm. "Something isn't right."

Kyreena touched her palm to his head, then stared off to one side. "I can't explain this. He's not dead, but neither is he alive. He's lost somewhere between."

Arros sat back in defeat, then slowly shook his head. "There's nothing more anyone can do for him. We failed."

"No," Kyreena protested. "You still have the Sword of Melkarick. We need to get it far from this place."

A pitiful voice spoke to them from the door to the Great Hall.

"Where is she?"

Arros turned to see the young guardsman standing nearby, staring over the bloodied corpses of the four Soul Singers. "Merrick."

"Where is she?" he repeated more forcefully.

Nerris nodded toward the massive pile of rubble. "She couldn't be saved. Our plan always had only an outside chance of success."

Tears flooded his eyes, and the guardsman dropped to his knees. "I promised Caela you would free her."

Arros reached over and touched Nerris' leg. He concentrated, causing the Blade Master to gasp from the unexpected flood of power. "What in the…?" When the Lord Prince lifted his hand, the wound in his leg was gone. Nerris climbed to his feet, then danced back and forth to prove he could support his full weight. "How did you do that?"

"I don't fully understand it myself. I just can."

The sound of marching footsteps caught their attention. Arros and Kyreena quickly stood to learn the identity of those who approached. Almost immediately, he recognized the Chromatic Guard crossing the Great Hall. Commander Rellan was in the lead, making a straight line for them. They finally came to a halt at the archway.

She stepped forward and clucked her tongue at the mess. "If Emperor Thartalagor wasn't already obsessed with the Travelers before, he undoubtedly will place an extra effort into hunting you now."

"We need to leave immediately."

The commander looked back toward her soldiers, then nodded. Six women came forward and surrounded Lord Draxian Kalenthos. They bent down and lifted his body, then carried him back to the remaining soldiers. "We have a temple here in Phondari. It's considered a part of the Dellaharan Empire and cannot be entered without permission of the Empress of Dragons."

Arros passed the Sword of Melkarick to Kyreena before stepping over to T'mara's corpse. He slowly knelt to one knee, then removed the knives sticking from her chest. After tossing them to the side, the Lord Prince lifted T'mara into his arms and hugged the Shadiere Huntress to his chest. "Nerris? Grab Draxian's sword. T'mara's coming with us."

"Of course, she is," Commander Rellan acknowledged. "We never leave our fallen soldiers to feed the crows."

None made a move to halt the Chromatic Guard from exiting the palace. They had extra horses waiting for them just outside. Draxian was tied over a large black mare to keep him from falling, but T'mara stayed with Arros on his own mount. None spoke a word. As they began riding toward the lower gatehouse, the Lord Prince looked back and saw Merrick standing just inside the palace. The expression on his face held a mix of grief and hopelessness. Nothing had gone right, and Arros' determination to find a peaceful resolution had ended with the death of so many innocents. Kyreena could have slain the Regent in an instant with a single shot of her bow. Arros and Draxian had failed the trials before they even began.

The temple of the Chromatic Guard came into view not long after they exited the lower gate. It was a large stone building with beautifully sculpted statues of women near the gated entrance, and fluted columns that held up a marble awning leading to the front door. The architecture was reminiscent of what he knew from Ellandor yet had a regal elegance that came from the embossed carvings of dragons and fallen Chromatic Warriors adorning the walls.

Once all were through the black iron gate, it was closed and sealed behind them. Cam was waiting patiently at the entrance to the building. When he spotted T'mara in Arros' arms, he rushed out to meet him.

"T'mara!" He held out his arms, beckoning Arros to release her. "Please, Lord Prince."

Arros carefully lowered the body of the Huntress into his care. "She fought bravely. We couldn't have succeeded without her." Cam didn't respond. He simply wept openly, rocking T'mara back and forth with his head pressed to hers.

When the prince dismounted, Kyreena crossed over to him and hugged him. "What will we do now?"

"We need to get Melkarick out of the city. It's far too dangerous to be out in the open."

Nerris stepped over to join them. "I'll see to Lord Kalenthos. Are there any special rituals or preparations that your customs require?"

"No," Commander Rellan called over to them. "His body will remain under our care until the Lord Prince returns from the Ebon Waste. That is the command of the Empress of Dragons."

Arros released Kyreena and then stepped forward. "How does she even know what happened?"

"I've already informed her." Rellan withdrew a clear gemstone the size of her fist from a pouch on her belt. She tossed it to Arros. "Keep this with you."

He caught it with one hand, then held it up to the light. "What's this?"

"Look closely."

Kyreena stared intently at the elegantly cut crystal. "It's a vision stone."

Commander Rellan drew in her eyebrows. "Correct."

"Is this a Heart Crystal?" Arros asked with genuine interest.

"Straight from the crystal cave behind the fallen city of Avarron."

The Lord Prince shrugged that he had no idea what she meant, then placed the crystal in his pocket. "Nerris?"

"Yes, Lord Prince?"

"I need you to recover all our possessions from the King's Chamber Inn."

Commander Rellan snapped her fingers. "No need." Within moments, a dark-haired woman in red robes stepped out from the temple, carrying Arros' pack. "We anticipated you might be forced to make a hasty exit. Nothing inside has been touched."

Kyreena nodded to him. "She's speaks the truth."

Again, Rellan glanced at Kyreena and narrowed her eyes suspiciously. "If you'll follow me, I'll show you to the portal."

"Portal?" Arros immediately started forward.

He followed the commander into the temple with Kyreena close behind. They went down a narrow hallway to a granite staircase. It descended to a series of sub-levels, giving the temple far more living space than he had expected. They arrived in a chamber with a stone frame standing in the middle of the floor. Ancient glyphs were carved into the surface, along with writing that Arros recognized as coming from the First Ones.

"Can this gateway cross worlds?"

Rellan gave him a look that made him feel suddenly foolish. "That's preposterous. This is a portal we use to move back and forth from Dellahara."

"They were stolen from sanctuaries," Kyreena commented to the side.

"Their origin predates my life by hundreds of years." Rellan pointed to the glyphs. "We believe one of the ancient 'sanctuaries' still exists in some ruins within the Ebon Waste."

Arros watched as Kyreena stepped up to the archway and studied it closely. "Do you know the sequence?"

"We do." Commander Rellan stepped forward and handed over a small piece of paper to Kyreena, then turned to Arros. "Portals from here to Dellahara, don't require an outside source of magic. However, the journey from this place to the Ebon Waste will require you to activate it with Radiant energy."

The Lord Prince approached the stone gate. He placed his hand on the surface, then concentrated. Almost immediately, the symbols lit, starting from the bottom left, then traveling all the way up and then back down the other side. "Like that?"

Rellan lightly shook her head. "You're truly dangerous."

Kyreena immediately began touching the sequence in order, until a shimmering in the air announced the activation of the archway. A wall of green haze appeared from within, confirming that they had indeed opened a portal somewhere deep inside the Ebon Waste, a lot closer to the lost city of Orakh.

"It worked," Kyreena called back.

She started to walk through when Arros caught her arm. "You can't go in there."

"Why not?"

"It'll kill you to be near the Verge."

Rellan nodded her agreement. "I wouldn't last more than a few hours at best. He's like our Empress – a being born of magic."

Arros shook his head in annoyance. "It's nothing that miraculous, but she's correct. I'm not that easy to kill."

"Neither am I," Kyreena spoke resolutely. "I'm going." She jerked her arm free, then stepped through to the other side.

The Lord Prince shrugged toward Commander Rellan, then followed Kyreena into the haze. The Chromatic Warrior called at his back. "One Power guide and protect you, Lord Prince."

Within moments, with a soft vibrating sound, the portal had vanished.

Arros' skin crawled with the touch of the Spirit Realm. The portal had brought them to another archway located within a small cave.

Kyreena was squatting next to a pile of human bones, studying them with interest. "I wonder how long these have been here?"

"Hundreds of years by the look of them." Arros started toward an incline that appeared to lead to the surface. "How are you feeling?"

She stood, then looked around uneasily. "I'm doing well for now. Although I won't be able to follow you into the Verge." Kyreena held out the Sword of Melkarick. "You'll need this."

Arros reached over and took the cursed blade from her fingers, immediately feeling the rush of power. "I have no idea what to do."

"There is an Oracle said to be in the city. If he would be willing to speak with you…"

"No," the prince interrupted. "I want nothing to do with him."

Kyreena came forward and touched her hand to his chest. Her eyes began to well with tears. "I'm afraid for you."

Arros dropped his pack from his shoulder to the ground, then pulled Kyreena into a tight embrace. "If nothing changes within a few hours, take my pack and leave the Ebon Waste. Will you do this?"

"I will."

"There's enough gold in there to feed you for a lifetime."

She shook her head against his shoulder. "I don't want your coins. I just need you to return to me." Kyreena squeezed harder, nearly taking the breath from his lungs. "Promise me."

"You know I can't do that." Arros pulled back, then pressed his lips to hers. They stayed that way for several long moments. Finally, the Lord Prince released her, then smiled. "Live well, Kyreena… Live free."

As he started toward the slope, she called to his back. "Selvenarra."

Arros stopped, then turned. "What?"

"I just remembered my name." Selvenarra giggled as tears fell down her face. "I *will* see you again, Lord Prince. We're bound together."

He gave her a chiding smirk. "Farewell, Selvenarra."

SOULFORGE

Arros emerged from the cave and glanced around at the large boulders that obscured his view. After crawling up to the top of one of the rocky outcroppings, the prince was high enough to see further into the Waste. He lifted the Sword of Melkarick in front of him and concentrated. The blade began to tingle within his hand. The more he turned to his left, the stronger the sensation became, until he finally felt a pulse. That was the direction of the Verge.

The prince began walking among the ash and black sand for a good distance. All about him, the green haze pressed on his skin like thousands of tiny needles. Arros had never felt so alone in his life. He was trudging along, teetering somewhere between two opposing Realms of Power: Life and Death. It felt as if his father's judgmental eyes followed his footsteps, mocking him from on high over his failures. He began to wonder if the letter the King left for him was true, and Draxian would still be alive if he had only taken the offer the Oracle had given him to return home.

The familiar hands of the ash wraiths began once again reaching for him through the ground. With ever-strengthening resolve, they began to hold their forms for several moments, before falling back to lifeless sand. Several times, one of the wraiths managed to maintain their essence long enough to grip Arros' heel. On a third attempt, he stumbled forward, then angrily turned to face it. Holding Melkarick high, the prince slammed the tip of the blade into the ground, releasing a violent pulse of Radiant energy. The black sand rippled outward in a great, circular wave, scattering the green mist. Inhuman screams erupted from the wraiths in a chorus of hundreds of echoing voices. The haunted cries ceased as suddenly as they began.

Arros continued forward. Not a single ash wraith followed him the rest of the way to the walls of the lost city. The prince had arrived from a different direction than last time, and it took a while before finding a hole in the stone that was large enough for him to crawl through.

When he emerged on the other side, someone was already waiting. "You must be Arros."

The prince jumped upright at the sound of his name. A woman in flowing white robes was standing before him. Her long, dark hair was elegantly braided on the sides to meet behind her head, then fell in thick, wavy curls down her back. Golden paint adorned her eyelids, lined with thin black coal dust. She watched him with an amused grin.

"Who are you?"

"My name is Elleri Talanar. I heard your call through Soulforge."

He followed the specter's gaze to the sword in his hand. "You're the sorceress who created Melkarick?"

"Correct."

"You can't have it back."

Her laugh was delightful. "I couldn't touch it, even if I had the desire." Elleri lifted her hand and waved it through the air, as if she were made of smoke.

"How are you…?"

"Sentient?"

Arros shrugged. "Exactly."

"Long ago, before the War of the Shadow Lords, I lived in the mystic city of Avarron. It was home to the greatest magi, scholars, and prophets the world has ever known. You must understand, a sorceress is a rare and powerful birthright. It was once believed that we were descendants of the old gods – a reemergence of their powerful bloodline."

"Go on."

She gestured into the air, causing the mist around them to form into vague images of a city. "I created the sword to assist in my revenge against the ones who betrayed me. The people who killed my unborn child." The fog changed to show crowds throwing stones at a lone, pregnant woman. She fell to the ground, broken and near death. "Years later, I returned to Avarron with my armies of devout acolytes. In a fit of rage, I used Melkarick to slaughter every man, woman, and child within the city. None survived." Elleri turned back to Arros. "For my terrible crimes, the Lady of the Order cursed my soul to never find peace. She denied me entrance to the Spirit Realm, locking my life essence within my bones. After my death, it was many hundreds of years before the Lord of Destruction found the tomb where my acolytes hid my body. In his benevolence, he used his great power to free my soul to reunite with my child."

Arros watched her with interest. "And because you were touched by his power, it allows your spirit to endure beyond death?"

"In a manner of speaking, yes."

"Why are you here now?"

She smiled warmly. "I've been waiting for you. The souls of a hundred mages are bound to the sword you wield. It was named Melkarick, the sword of vengeance, and served its purpose well. But the days of vengeance have passed. Now it is simply Soulforge, and it is time to put them to rest." Elleri motioned for him to follow her. "This is the way to the breach."

The prince walked a few paces behind her, always looking over his shoulder for enemies. It was bad enough that he endured the pain of being on the edge of death, but everything about the Verge made his skin crawl. "How much further?"

"We're nearly there."

Arros rounded a broken building, then stopped in place. Hundreds of swirling forms, like deadly black vortexes, stood in place – watching him with menacing eyes. Just ahead, a bright green line of energy hovered in the air, wiggling and rotating like a viper searching for prey.

"Is that it?"

"Walk to the rift. The hedge ghouls will not attempt to harm you – not while holding Soulforge."

Ever so carefully, the Lord Prince made his way around the disembodied creatures, whose eyes followed his every movement. When he got within six paces, Arros stopped to study the tear into the Spirit Realm. "What now?"

"This won't be easy." Elleri floated up next to him and pointed. "The blade must be extended partially into the Spirit Realm. From there, focus all your will into drawing the Verge back through the sword, and into the rift."

"Sounds easy enough to me."

"You must understand, that if the breach had been sealed after it was first created by Arch Mage Belcron, it would have been a simple matter, just as you say. However, you'll need to maintain this funneling of the Verge far beyond what any natural mage could endure. Furthermore, once the process is started, you can't end it until the rift is fully sealed. To do so, would rupture the breach far worse than what you see now."

Arros frowned wryly at the spirit of Elleri Talanar. "You're coming dangerously close to talking me out of this."

"The choice must be yours, but only Soulforge can seal this breach. And you are the only one strong enough to wield my sword to its fullest potential."

He shook his head and stepped forward. "Guilting me is not making this any easier." Arros took a deep breath, then shoved the blade halfway into the rift. He cried out from the shocking pain of the spirit energy surging through his body.

"Fight against the magic attacking your essence!"

Arros summoned the Radiant power within him, sending it back down the length of the sword. He instantly felt relief from the intense agony. All about him, the wind began to rise. Streams of sand and ash began stretching tendrils into the rift. Slowly they flooded back into the Spirit Realm, then swiftly gained in momentum. Soon after, the hedge ghouls were pulled inside, and the sand whipped past him, grinding at his skin in a powerful torrent. Still, he held strong.

"Keep going," Elleri urged from the side. "It's working!"

Specks of blood began to form in patches on his arms where the skin was wearing away. As he gritted his teeth in concentration, a high-pitched ringing met his ears – then another. Arros stared at the Sword of Melkarick. Tiny cracks were beginning to form in the surface of the blade. "Something's wrong!"

"The enchantment within my blade is failing," Elleri called to him. "Use your own life essence to grant it strength, just as you did when healing the Shadow Master, Nerris."

Small fissures continued to appear across Melkarick's surface. "I'll try!"

Arros was not only holding onto the power of the Radiant Realm, he was also trying to force his own life-energy into the blade. The effect was making his head swim, and his stomach felt as if he were about to vomit. Melkarick lit with a blinding white light. Arros could feel his strength waning, and the grip on his power slipping. The green mist quickly faded as the last of the ash retreated into the Spirit Realm. He only needed to hold on for a few more moments.

"Well done, Arros." Elleri spoke, just before she too was pulled into the breach.

The last of the ash and sand disappeared, and the green rift winked out of existence. For just an instant, Arros could feel a warm presence surrounding him – like a parent smiling down upon their child. Then, the last drop of life-essence faded from Lord Prince Arros Nemendes, and the Sword of Melkarick shattered into hundreds of white-hot shards.

Selvenarra stood at the mouth of the cave, waiting for any sign of success from Arros. There had been a pit in her stomach ever since he left. It had been several turns of the glass by her estimate, and she began to wonder if something had gone wrong. Everything just felt in balance when he was around – even her memories began to return quicker. Most of her life had been spent avoiding cities and living off the land. Just as the Dream Rider had spoken, Selvenarra had a mission that was given to her alone. No one else on Kohr would know what knowledge she possessed, and it was burning her that she couldn't remember exactly what that was.

Ever so slowly, Selvenarra began to notice the wind rising. It started as a whisper and built to a roar. Faster and faster it rushed past, picking up large quantities of sand and ash with it. It was Arros. He had begun the process of closing the rift to the Spirit Realm. Selvenarra placed her back against a rock to shelter from the maelstrom of sand that swept by with deadly velocity. Something inside her was changing. It was as if the haze of the Spirit Realm had been withholding power deep within her. When the last of the ash blew past, Selvenarra could finally see exactly where it was headed. Only a league away, the city walls of Orakh could be seen, as the cloud of dark fog was sucked into its center. Then it was gone. With the lifting of the ash and sand, a new terrain was revealed. The grass was brown and dried, but she knew it would begin to recover in the days to come.

With tears of joy filling her eyes, Selvenarra burst out laughing. Arros had accomplished what every mage in the last thousand years had said was impossible. However, it was right then that Selvenarra doubled over from a pain in her gut. It was the same hollow sensation she had felt one time before. Selvenarra could no longer feel the tiny portion of the prince's essence within her.

Summoning the magic that she felt deep inside, the last Guardian of Kohr took off at a run toward the city. Selvenarra's muscles filled with boundless energy, giving her legs everything they required to maintain her top speed.

It took less than a quarter-turn of the glass for her to reach the edge of the city. In a burst of power, Selvenarra leapt high, diving over the top of the wall. She spun midair, then landed softly on her feet. The ruined city was large, and it would likely take her a good deal of time to search for Arros. Despite the thousand years that had passed since being destroyed, Orakh did not look as if more than a dozen had gone by. With a bit of work, most of the stone structures could be salvaged.

As Selvenarra continued to search up and down the main roads, she passed a white building that appeared familiar to her. She took only a moment to study the untouched architecture, before turning away and heading down another street.

"That's the wrong way," someone called out. Selvenarra spun to see an elderly man hobbling toward her. He wore a dirty grey robe and had a long white beard and balding head. His smile was genuine. "I can show you, if you'd like?"

She studied his face for a time. "Do I know you?"

"I'm afraid we've never had the pleasure."

Selvenarra stepped forward. "You're the Oracle of Orakh."

"That's what they call me." The old man approached her, then sighed heavily. "Such a long journey to reach this place in history, was it not?"

"I can't remember much of it."

His brow wrinkled in confusion. "How is this possible?" The Oracle stared off to the side for a moment, then looked back. "Ah. Now I understand what happened to you. My vision has been distorted for ages. As such, I couldn't even predict your coming until after you already arrived in the city."

"I'd love to speak with you further, but I have someone I need to find."

She started to walk away when the Oracle reached out and caught her arm. "You have my deepest sympathies, Selvenarra. Some events just don't proceed as we would have them. Duty and sacrifice must always come first for those like you and the Lord Prince. One day, you'll understand this cumbersome truth." He pointed down a side alley. "Through there, then turn left. Go three more streets, then turn to your right."

Selvenarra bowed to the elderly man. "You have my gratitude."

Without looking back, the Guardian followed the directions she was given that led between the buildings, then down a smaller road. She continued across three more intersections before finding the correct one. As she turned the corner, Selvenarra slid to a halt. Arros lay unmoving, face down in the dirt. All about him, tiny shards of broken metal were scattered. As she approached, her stomach churned.

"Lord Prince?" Selvenarra knelt before him. "Arros?" She started to reach for him, then stopped. His skin was pale, and the prince was not breathing. Even without touching his body, Selvenarra could sense there was no life within him, only a shell. The Guardian sat mute in disbelief for several long moments. Her hands went to her face, and she burst into tears. Selvenarra had found a part of herself within him, then lost it in a glance. It was not fair. She lifted her head skyward, then screamed in rage and anguish. The sound of her powerful wail pierced the air and echoed throughout the city. Backed by her magic, it caused the ground to tremble and dust to fall from buildings.

It was moments later that a dark shadow passed over her head. Selvenarra looked up through glassy eyes and saw a chromatic dragon circling nearby. It flapped its mighty wings, then softly landed on the city wall.

Selvenarra reached down and drew one of Arros' blades. She came to her feet, then held it before her. "You can't have him!" The massive flyer simply watched her with interest, then turned its gaze down to Arros. It sniffed in his direction, then let out a mournful bellow from its throat. "What do you want from us?"

The dragon continued to watch them. Selvenarra was not certain how she knew, but it had no intention of harming her or Arros. Instead, it appeared to be standing guard over them, but the reason escaped her.

Selvenarra slowly dropped back to her knees, then placed the sword next to the fallen prince. As she reached over to take his hand, Arros' eyes burst open, and he gasped for breath.

Draxian awoke suddenly with images of the tower falling around him still fresh in his mind. The last thing he had seen was the prince in great peril from the destruction he had wrought. "Arros!" Sitting up quickly, Draxian found he was in a small chamber resting on an altar, lined with red pillows. There was only one heavy door to and from the room, and it was closed. Two softly glowing yellow orbs sat in sconces, giving a soft and warm ambience. Draxian's confusion only lasted a few moments. His hands went to cover his face, and the young lord gritted his teeth against the pain of his heart shattering over the loss of T'mara. It was his fault she was gone.

"You're awake," came a lovely female voice from nearby.

Draxian slowly turned his head to see a lady wearing an elegant blue gown with hundreds of glittering gemstones affixed to the material in swirling patterns. She was tall and impossibly beautiful, with thick, dark brown curls that flowed to the middle of her back. Her eyes were hazel green, holding a gaze of deep concern. The woman could not have been more than twenty-eight summers, yet there was something uniquely timeless about her that Draxian immediately recognized.

"Where am I?"

"You're in my home of Dellahara." She stepped forward. "My name is Adreana."

He breathed a long sigh of resignation. "The Dragon Empress."

"You have nothing to fear from me, Lord Kalenthos."

Draxian swung his legs around and placed his feet on the floor. "Arros?"

She shook her head, allowing her soft curls to spill from her shoulders. "He's not here. Prince Nemendes went to the Ebon Waste to seal the rift."

"Alone?"

"He did it," Adreana said, smiling. "Arros closed the rift."

Draxian glanced around cautiously. "How long have I been asleep?"

"You weren't asleep, my Lord. The collapsing tower ended your life."

"But…"

She smiled warmly. "How are you alive?" He could only nod his head at her. "Through the will of the One Power."

His heart sank. "The Trial of the True Bloods."

"This is my belief, as well. Fortunately, someone has initiated it on your behalf."

"How can I see that as anything but a curse?"

The Empress of Dragons placed a hand on his leg. "You live. Is that not blessing enough?"

"That would greatly depend on your definition of living."

"Make no mistake, you only get one return from death. If you fail again, it will be your last."

Draxian climbed to his feet. "There was a woman with me before the tower fell."

"The Shadiere Huntress. Yes, I had her brought here as well. My agent, Camoranthus, is preparing her body for transport back to her people."

"She died because of me." The young lord dropped his chin to his chest. "They all died because of me."

Adreana gave him a soft smile of reassurance. "I wasn't there, but I'm quite sure you didn't kill that woman. Failing to protect her is not the same thing. *That* is your crime – and one you must find a way to live with, no matter how abysmal that might sound."

"I didn't ask for this!"

The Empress of Dragons shoved Draxian back down to the pillows with more force than he would have believed her capable of wielding. He suddenly found her staring down at him with rage in her eyes. "No one would ever be foolish enough to ask to undergo the Trials! But you were chosen to do this, and until you die for a second time, no others can be born to take your place. Arros completed the first Trial for the both of you. I felt it the moment the Spirit Realm was sealed, and his life left his body." Adreana held up a hand to keep him from asking. "And yes, he thankfully came back to us, just as you did."

Draxian narrowed his eyes. "You're an Ictharian."

"And you're Ellandorian. What of it?"

"I thought your kind were long gone from this world."

Adreana softened, then retreated a step. "I'm the last of my bloodline."

He shook his head. "But that would make you…"

"Well over a thousand years old," she finished. "A long time to wait for an end to the darkness, I assure you." The Empress of Dragons stepped to the side. "I'm certain you'll wish to get cleaned up so that you can rejoin the Lord Prince."

"No."

"Believe me, you need a bath." She tapped the side of her nose.

Draxian fingered the wooden amulet hanging at his chest, his finger tracing the intricate patterns carved within it. He had lost control of his destiny long before he arrived on Kohr. It was time to take it back and create his own. "There's something I must do. Alone. I'm going to return T'mara's body to her family. I owe her that."

ᛘ·↑·ᛗ

EPILOGUE

THE BEGINNING OF THE END

Nerris trudged along the back alleys of Phondari. After his last report to the Lord of Shadows, he knew his time in the city was nearly finished. He had never known what it was like to live without the Spirit Realm distorting the shadow magic he used to enhance his abilities. It was like living with a foul smell around him for his entire life, and then suddenly it was gone. The people were just so used to it – they had no concept of a world without the taint. Whatever Arros had done with the Sword of Melkarick to seal the breach, it had worked perfectly.

Draxian's and T'mara's bodies were spirited off to Dellahara with Cam, but Nerris was not allowed to join them. He needed to return and assist in guarding the Twelve Gateways. There was a valid reason the world believed the Shadow Masters were a myth. None could leave their mountain fortress for fear its secrets would fall into the hands of their enemies. Nerris was the first allowed on a mission, due to his knowledge of the land from time spent commanding the Free Companies. After the Shadow Master saw for himself the raw power Arros and Draxian commanded, it was little wonder the Lord General took such a close interest in them.

The night was beginning to fall when Nerris made his way to one of the higher end brothels for a last night of release. As the Shadow Master approached the building, he spotted a familiar face in the dwindling crowds. The young guardsman, Merrick, was following him from a distance. It was likely he wanted to speak more about what had happened to the lovely Soul Singer, Caela, but Merrick was in no mood to discuss such a depressing topic. He had other thoughts in mind.

"Welcome to the Maiden's Passion, my lord," an older woman greeted at the entrance. "Fancy a bit of company for the night?"

Nerris glanced around at the red curtained walls and smelled the delightful flowery incense burning from a nearby lamp. "That's exactly why I'm here."

"Excellent. If you have the coins, we have the women, unless there's something else you desire?"

The Shadow Master opened his palm to reveal a handful of silver coins. "I'm certain this will cover all the entertainment, and a good bottle of honey wine."

The brothel mistress stepped forward and looped her arm around his. "Right this way, my lord." She brought him to a back room where seven scantily clad women of various ages were lounging about the padded furniture. "Form a line, ladies," the mistress called to them.

They immediately stood and gathered into a half circle. Nerris huffed a laugh as he looked each woman up and down with his heart racing in anticipation. It was likely the Lord General would not approve. However, his mission was successful, and the Shadow

Master believed he deserved a reward for his efforts.

After selecting a thin redhead with pale skin, Nerris followed her back to the front to find a room for the evening. He had taken only a few steps before his young companion halted, then backed away from Nerris in alarm.

"Well now, what have we here?" The Shadow Master spun around to see a tall woman in white robes. Her blonde hair was braided back; she had eyes as blue as the sea. With a voice like a beautiful song, she spoke, "A handsome man like yourself shouldn't have need for such a loathsome place."

"Who are you?"

"They call me the Lady of Dawn."

Nerris pulled the long pack from his shoulder that contained his blades, bringing the handles within reach. "Not interested."

"You haven't even heard my offer." Her words came out as if they were a warm breeze blowing across his cheek.

Nerris was finding it hard to concentrate on anything but her lips. There was dangerous magic within her, and he was losing himself to the woman's spell. He shook his head. "You have nothing I could want."

She took a step forward, then lifted her palm. A sphere of light appeared within, illuminating the entire chamber. Its radiance seeped into every corner, eliminating all traces of shadow. "But you have something I need... Shadow Master."

Nerris immediately realized what she was doing. Without the darkness, he had no way of escaping through magic. It was fortunate that only a few of his abilities were dampened. The woman would obviously need to die.

The Master jerked his blades free from within his pack, then charged forward. Before he had taken a second step, an invisible force struck him in the chest. Nerris fell to his back and slid into a table, breaking the legs and flipping it sideways. By the time he crawled back to his feet, a large man was standing next to the Lady of Dawn.

"Pathetic," he called to Nerris. "I expected better from one of the Lord General's men." His new opponent was as tall as Draxian and built with thick cords of muscle that made him look impossibly strong. However, it was not just the dangerous glint within his opponent's eyes that caused Nerris the most alarm, it was the two blades he held at his sides.

"I know what you are," the Shadow Master called to him. Nerris' heart was threatening to pound from his chest. He already knew that he had lost the battle. "If you believe I'll betray my friends, then you truly have underestimated us."

The towering man had the gall to smile, but it was the woman who spoke. "We don't wish to see you come to any harm. Will you not at least listen to my words? Like you, we're here to see the sun restored to its former radiant glory."

"Beware the Children of Dawn." He sneered at the woman in white. "That was the last warning passed down to the Lord of Shadows by the Dragon King."

Nerris reached under his leather bracer and withdrew a metal vial. Before it could touch his lips, the large man casually lifted a hand. The poison was jerked from the Shadow Master's grip and flew into the man's awaiting palm. "The Dragon King has been dead for a thousand years," the man spoke in a deep voice as he approached. "He can't save you... no one can."

ABOUT THE AUTHOR

Brian Zeeff is a photographer, martial artist, writer, and author of the new novel *Soulforge*, the first in the *Legends of Kohr* series. After years of inspiration and procrastination, Brian finally realized his dream of becoming an author with his debut novel. When he's not writing or coming up with new story ideas, Brian likes to spend time with his wife and son, camping in tents, and hiking or climbing mountains.

WWW.BRIANZEEFF.COM

@BRIANZEEFF1

Utani-Dannu Territory
Sea of Death
Forsaken Isle
Darmon
Bog of Terror
Suuk
Serpent's Breath Mountains
Deep Water River
Annis
Guardian's Keep
Blood Plains
Mist Valley
Wayfarer's Bay
Feldara
Breck
Feldaran Wilderness
Black Citadel Ruins
Sallendrow
Aldrinn River
Ebon Wastes
Dragon Tooth Lake
Boundless Jungles
Nyamla Tribal Grounds

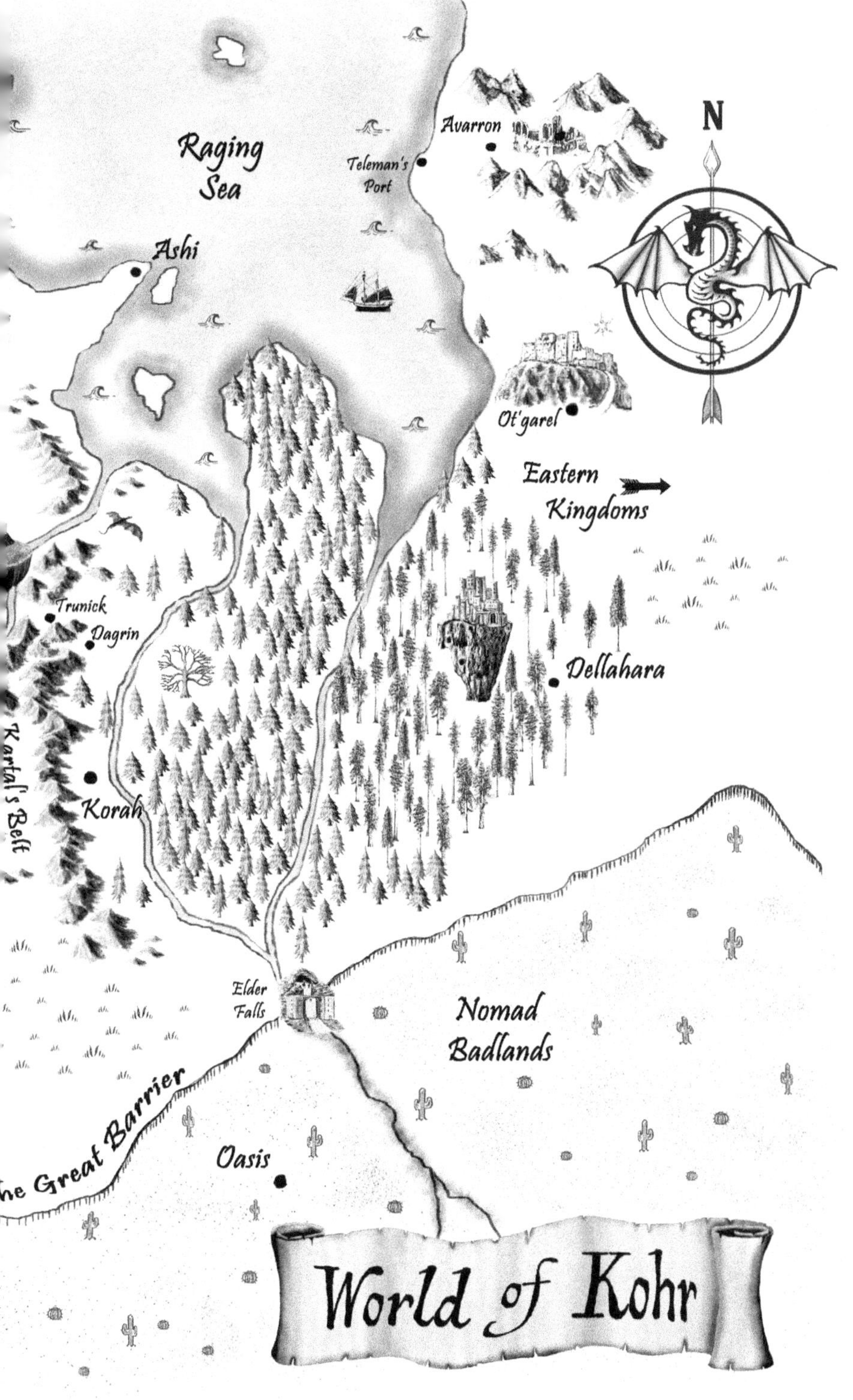

N
Raging Sea
Avarron
Teleman's Port
Ashi
Ot'garel
Eastern Kingdoms
Trunick
Dagrin
Dellahara
Kartal's Belt
Korah
Elder Falls
Nomad Badlands
The Great Barrier
Oasis
World of Kohr

446